taming it down

taming it down

a novel

Kim McLarin

William Morrow and Company, Inc. | New York

Library of Congress Cataloging-in-Publication Data
McLarin, Kim.
Taming it down : a novel / Kim McLarin.
p.   cm.
ISBN 0-688-15516-2
I. Title.
PS3563.C38357T36   1998   97-47035
813'.54—dc21   CIP

Printed in the United States of America

First Edition

1   2   3   4   5   6   7   8   9   10

BOOK DESIGN BY CHRIS WELCH

www.williammorrow.com

To my mother, who taught me to be strong.
And to Matthew, who showed me I didn't always have to
be that way.

acknowledgments

First things first: Thanks be to God for everything I have and everything I am. His generosity staggers me. Hallelujah.

My deepest gratitude to my amazing mother, Ethelene; to my sisters, Michelle, Benita, and Melinda; and to my brother, Benjamin, for a lifetime of love and support. I want to thank also Carol Dixon and the other talented members of the John Oliver Killens Writers Workshop in Brooklyn for making me one of their own, teaching me about craft, and shoring up a few of my weaknesses.

I'm grateful to my agent, Suzanne Gluck, and to my editor, Claire Wachtel, for believing in the work and in me. Thanks to my girls, Vanessa Williams, Charisse Jones, and Kimmerly Scott, and to my boys, Larry Copeland and Terence Samuel—especially Terence, who got excited about this thing even before I did. And thanks to Jennifer Doerr, Beverlee Bruce, Sue Rukeyser, Leslie Alderman, Mary Ann Schwalbe, Deborah Futter, Gerald Jordan, Marjorie Horvitz, and a hundred other unnamed folk.

Most of all, my love and thanks to Matthew, who said, "Follow your passion. The rest will come." And to Samantha Grace, my gift from God, for so much joy.

November 1990

I looked around the grungy marble lobby of the *Philadelphia Record* in a daze, wigging out, thinking: How interesting. This is what losing it feels like.

You wake up one day, a little cranky but otherwise normal. You skip breakfast because everything in your refrigerator smells like fish gone bad. You burn the back of your ear with the curling iron. You get in your car and go to work, and as soon as you get there you have to deal with some crazy jerk screaming at you for something that was in no way, shape, or form even your fault. This is not unusual, dealing with jerks, but for some reason on this day, maybe because you're tired and cranky and more than slightly hungover, dealing with jerks is more than you can handle, and you get mad, really mad, raging mad almost, in the true sense of that term, and you feel your head is about to rupture from all the pressure building up inside, and so for no reason at all except that you're mad and you really can't stand the sight of her dippy whitegirl face, you haul off and smack this woman. Smack her—*bam!*—right in the face, as hard as you can. And then she stands there gaping at you, and you stand there gaping back at her, realizing in your still befuddled mind that you've just joined the ranks of the certifiably insane.

I needed to use the lobby pay phone to call my health insurance company's referral line. I wanted them to find me a psychotherapist, and quick. Like this afternoon. But I couldn't find enough change in my purse, and I was worried that Stephanie, the woman I'd smacked, or David, her boyfriend, or somebody else was going to come charging off the elevator any minute, screaming at me for what I had just done. And I kept dropping the book with the phone numbers in it. When things start spinning out from the center, nothing can stand, apparently. Restraint, common sense, hand-eye coordination—everything goes.

The security guard, this thick-waisted Teutonic blonde, stared at me, apparently fearing I was going to do something criminal, like rip the phone from the wall and take off running down the street, dripping change. I knew most of the guards in the building, but this woman must have been new. She wore her dirty yellow hair pulled back tight into a ponytail, like some plumped-up cheerleader gone bad, and her battleship-gray polyester uniform was not working for her at all. The slacks stretched across her thighs like sausage casings. She was a doughy rent-a-cop from the Northeast, but she kept her eye pinned on me like she was the lead agent at the FBI and I was at the top of the most wanted list. Thank God they didn't give these morons guns. She was one of those types that shoot first and question later.

Normally I might have pulled out my reporter's notebook— one of those official-looking pads with a *Philadelphia Record* emblem on the front cover—and waved it in her face for her moronic edification. Normally I might have asked her what the hell she was staring at. Normally I might even have gotten on the phone and called—very loudly—the head of security, a good friend of mine, just to chat and to scare the piss out of her fat blond ass, but after the scene upstairs, I didn't need another confrontation. A calmer person might have just dug around in her bag for her employee ID, with her name in big black letters—in this case, HOPE ROBINSON—and helped the blonde relax. But screw it. Calming down white folks was not part of my job, despite what many people thought. I slammed the phone back into its snug black cradle and gave the blonde a smirk as I spun through the revolving door. Hope has left the building.

On the drive home, I tried to calm myself by mentally listing my qualifications for this therapist, this person who was going to sit there and help me figure why my life was so out of control. First, she'd have to be a black woman; no doubt about that. But what if I couldn't find one? How many black female psychotherapists were there in Philadelphia anyway? I had no idea. More important, how many were there on my health insurance plan?

Okay, so if I couldn't get a black woman, at least I'd get a woman. But maybe that was shortsighted. Maybe a black man would be better. Maybe I'd get lucky and find someone like Alvin Poussaint. I imagined Alvin, dressed in an impeccable blue silk suit, sitting in a deep burgundy armchair with his hands clasped beneath his chin as if in prayer. Behind him stands a bookcase filled with leather-bound books. He nods slowly as I speak. He knows exactly what I am saying. He gives me miraculous advice and I feel a million times better and at the end of the session Alvin stands and embraces me with a warm and fatherly hug, giving me strength.

At home in my apartment, I headed straight for the telephone. Some chipper, twentyish bimbo with a breathless voice answered the HMO mental health emergency referral line. Her joyful

"May I help you?" struck me as wildly inappropriate. If I were suicidal and I heard that voice, I'd hang up the phone and start swallowing pills. Instead I gave the cheerleader the short version: professional, stressed out, dangerously so. Lost it today, details unimportant. Need to talk to someone, and fast. I gave her my preferences. The chick clucked and cooed and promised to call right back with a list of potential therapists.

"Will you be at this number long, Ms. Robinson?" she chirped.

"Of course," I said. Idiot. Where else was I going to go?

My apartment exuded a sad shadiness in midafternoon. A towering maple blocked sunlight from the living room with the last of its brilliant red leaves. My bedroom looked out over a back alleyway. For some reason, the idea of living in an apartment had seemed glamorous when I moved to Philadelphia. Television, I guess. I'd envisioned myself dashing across a sky-blue hallway to borrow olive oil from my neighbor-and-best-girlfriend for the candlelight dinner I was preparing. But the hallway in my building was painted toast brown, and I never knocked on the door of the smelly old man across the way. Not unless one of his cats escaped.

I shoved a pile of clothes off the bed and sat down. The bedroom was a mess—clothes piled on the pine chest beneath the window, on the floor, on the dresser, flung across the door sill. My black pumps lay scuffing each other in the corner. I picked up a sweater from the nightstand and found a jelled cup of coffee hidden underneath. The place sagged with abandonment, as if I had been gone a long, long time. And the air felt weird. Something about being home in the middle of the day. The entire building was silent, sluggish; no barking dogs, no thumping kids upstairs. Even the next-door murmur of Mrs. Scott's television had ceased. At night the evidence of her insomnia was so constant I held it in my dreams.

I moved to the living room, pulling the telephone along with me, and turned on my TV. A familiar sculpted face loomed pale against the screen. Erica Kane. It was *All My Children,* my favorite soap opera in college days, although I hadn't seen it in years. I turned up the volume. Erica Kane, ten years older, pouted into the camera lens. Her ivory neck was looser now and lined like used aluminum foil. But still she held her face out like a prize, and still some man bent to kiss her lips as if they were sunshine and he had been too long in the rain. I didn't recognize the guy, but it was comforting to see Erica. Except for the neck, she looked remarkably unchanged.

The phone rang. I was still holding it.

"Ms. Robinson? I'm afraid I couldn't find a black psychologist."

She didn't sound afraid. She sounded just as chipper as she had the first time, stupid twit. I might have been sitting with a gun at my temple, but she was happy. She was going to get off work in a couple of hours and go out drinking and laughing about all the nuts she had spoken to today. She told me she had found a woman therapist, properly accredited and operating not far from where I lived. The shrink even had an opening that day, at 5 P.M., which worried me a little. How could anyone who was any good be so available? Any doctor worth his salt would take weeks to get in to see.

But maybe she was treating me as a special case. Maybe the receptionist had sensed a certain tone in my voice. Maybe she had called Dr. Whoever and said, "Listen, I think you'd better see this one right away, or tomorrow we could be reading about a woman who went to her job with an Uzi and an attitude."

I made the appointment. Erica Kane began to cry, and I followed her lead. Of course, Erica looked much prettier crying than I did.

I get nervous driving around strange all-white neighborhoods, as if I'm doing something wrong. I imagine I'm being watched, that pale eyes have spotted me and nervous lips are telegraphing the alert from house to house. So I sit upright in my car and turn down my stereo. I roll up my window, smooth my hair, try to look purposeful and nonthreatening. Prepare to smile if I am stopped.

Then I think: What the hell is this, South Africa? Did I need a pass to drive the public streets? I look at the sweeping lawns, the driveways as long as a freeway entrance ramp, the homes big enough to shelter an order of nuns. I turn up the volume on my radio, roll down the window and let the wind do a buckwheat on my hair. Let some pig cop hassle me! I imagine flashing my *Record* ID and threatening to call the newspaper's attorney and mentioning that I know the DA. I don't, really, but I met her once.

After ten minutes or so of driving the neighborhood, I found the shrink's house. Not one of the biggest in the area, but nice enough. Gray stone, two stories, set far back from the sidewalk under a canopy of graceful arching trees. Flagstone circles curved from the driveway to the front door. I rang the bell. Soft chimes drifted through the house. What kind of therapist would work out of her house? Who'd want crazy people knowing where you lived?

Standing on the doorstep, listening to the wind, I realized I felt much calmer now. Maybe I didn't really need to do this. Maybe all I needed was a vacation, a break from those idiots at work, and from David and Malcolm and everyone else. What I needed was an island, a white-sand sanctuary in the middle of some azure sea, where I could sit and read and be away for a while. How did people stand being around people all the time anyway? It was a wonder the whole world wasn't mad.

Inside the house, a dog barked. From the sound, it had to be a poodle or some other stupid little dog. I heard a voice call, "Just a second!" Then, more softly: "Come on, Sigmund. Get in there. That's a good boy."

Sigmund? I turned away, but the opening door caught me.

"Hi!" She gave the word two syllables, the last one sliding sympathetically downward. "I'm Cindy Shepherd. Come on in."

She directed me up a narrow stairway to a small office that must once have been a maid's room. The room was painted a pale blue, was carpeted in white shag, and had a picture window looking out over a rolling backyard. Diplomas and certificates lined the wall—the only one I could read without staring said University of Pennsylvania. Not bad.

She came up behind me and I turned to face her and my first thought was: I knew she was going to be white, but did she have to be blond too?

"Where should I sit?" The room had two stuffed armchairs covered in floral print, a rocking chair, and a couch. No way was I lying on the couch.

"Sit wherever you like," she said, and plopped into the arm-chair facing the window. Next to her stood a small side table, with a notepad, a box of tissues, and a cup full of pens. I sat in the other armchair.

"Have any trouble finding the place?"

"No, none at all. Good directions."

"Fine. Why don't we start with you telling me what it is that brings you here?"

So. One perfunctory sentence and she was right into it, no unnecessary chitchat. She waited, a half-smile of encouragement on her heart-shaped face. She was not quite beautiful, but pretty enough. From her coloring and her eyelashes, I could tell the blond hair was real. She was younger than I had expected: mid-thirties at the most, although it is always hard for me to tell with white women, because they age so badly. It occurred to me that I had expected a motherly shrink, someone plump and gray-haired, who would wrap me in her hefty arms and stroke my head.

"Do I call you Dr. Shepherd or Cindy or what?"

"Call me whatever you like."

Oh, yeah? How about Barbie?

"I hate it when doctors make you call them 'Doctor' and then call you by your first name without even asking, like you were a child. I find that incredibly rude."

"Then call me Cindy," she said with a smile. "Most of my patients call me Cindy."

Cindy. The only thing worse would have been Tiffany. Or Stephanie.

"Do you have a lot of patients?"

"Pretty many."

"I ask that because, to be frank, you don't look very old. How long have you been, ah, practicing?"

Again she smiled, a very tolerant smile.

"I'm thirty-one, probably not much older than you," she said. "I went to college early and was one of the youngest people ever admitted to Penn's clinical psych program. I'm fully licensed and certified. I've been practicing for nearly five years, I've seen hundreds of clients, and I've helped a lot of people."

"I didn't mean . . ."

She shook her head, still smiling. The light from the window glinted off the wire rims of her glasses. I wondered if she really needed them or just wore them to make herself look smart.

"No, no. I get that question all the time. It's important that you be comfortable with me, so ask anything you want."

We sat in silence for a second.

"However," she said finally, "I think we'd put our time to better use by talking about whatever it was that brought you here in such a hurry today."

I looked at her diplomas, at the bookcase filled with psychology books and journals. What the hell? I was here, I was paying her, or at least the insurance company was. I might as well see if this thing was going to work.

"I want you to know that I'm not interested in talking about my mother or my childhood. I just want to figure out what's going on with me right now."

"Did something happen today?"

As I tried to figure out where to begin, she just waited. Chick had the patience of Job.

"Well, okay. I guess so. I was at work. I'm a journalist, a reporter for the *Philadelphia Record.* . . ."

"Hmm. Interesting."

"Yeah, well, sometimes. More and more it's a big pain. So I was at work, and it's been a shitty day, a shitty week, really. I've been feeling so pissed off about everything. I woke up in a bad mood and then I burned my ear curling my hair and got to work late and had to deal with a correction on this obit they made me write yesterday even though I'm not an obit writer. This woman, the widow, was screaming in my ear because I put in the wrong medal that her husband had won in the war. She acted like I'd killed the man. It was a stupid mistake, and I hate it when I make stupid mistakes; I felt bad enough as it was, but this woman would not let it go. She just kept screaming and threatening to call my editor, and I finally hung up on her because I couldn't take it anymore."

I stopped, took a breath. I was rambling. This wasn't what I wanted to talk about, not at all. Cindy waited. She wore a big and silky man-tailored shirt and, underneath, thick black leggings made out of something soft like cashmere. Though she wasn't really beautiful and she wasn't very tall, she looked like a model.

"Anyway, that's not important," I said. "That's just the usual crap."

"Did you get in trouble with your editor?"

"Yeah, but who cares? He gets on my nerves. A lot of people at work get on my nerves. That's nothing new. They've been doing that for a while."

"What made things different today?"

It was the obvious question. But now that it was here, I felt myself reluctant to get into all that.

"Oh, probably some stuff that happened last night with this guy. But I don't want to talk about that. I just wasn't in the mood to deal with it. I was at the end of my rope, and I probably should have just gone home and called in sick. That's what I was going to do, in fact. I was leaving. But on the way out, this chick, this woman, got in my face."

"Got in your face?"

"Yeah, got in my face. I told her to go away. I told her to leave me alone, but no. She had to keep at it, had to keep pushing. One of those people who don't understand the meaning of the word no. One of those people who think they own the whole damn world, just because—"

"Because what?"

Because what? That was a good question. Because she looks like you? Because she's white? Part of me wanted to say it, but it sounded bad when you put it like that.

"Just because," I said, looking down at my lap. "Anyway. The bottom line is that I hit her. I smacked her across the face."

As soon as I said it I heard someone laugh, but I knew it wasn't Cindy because I was looking at her and her mouth stayed shut. So it must have been me, the person emitting this manic giggling noise. It scared me because I never giggle. And because I didn't feel like laughing. Not at all.

Cindy handed me a box of tissues, which seemed strange until I realized that the wetness on my face was my tears.

"I want you to know, I'm not the kind of person who goes around slapping people. I'm not violent. I wasn't raised that way. My mother stopped whipping us when we were ten. She said if we didn't have enough sense to do what's right by then, she couldn't beat it into us."

Cindy nodded.

"I don't hit people. I don't. I don't."

Silence.

"I'm scared."

Cindy was quiet. In the silence I heard her dog, far away in the house somewhere, whining to be back at his mistress's side.

"Afterwards I felt terrible. Really bad. I tried to apologize. But what was really scary was that at the moment that I struck her, in that split second when my hand slapped her face, I felt good. Shoot, I felt wonderful. Released. It felt like slipping into a hot bath, when you sit back against the cool porcelain and your shoulders go under the water and all the tension just leaks from your body into the tub. It felt really, really good.

"And that," I told Cindy, "is what really scares the piss out of me."

part 1

chapter one

April 1990

Life is hard. My mother used to say that all the time when we were growing up, back in Memphis. It was her one-size-fits-all answer to the complaints my two sisters and I lobbed at her over the years. Sick of eating canned mackerel and rice for dinner because the food stamps ran out? Too bad; life is hard. Humiliated because one of your friends saw you in the grocery store spending those candy-colored food stamps? Life is hard. Mad at something silly and throwing a fit and screaming that one of these days your daddy, Prince Daddy, was going to come back from the North and take you away from all this? Well, maybe. But I doubt it. He ran away and left you, and we haven't heard from him in years, and you're just going to have to accept that fact. Your daddy's gone. Life is hard.

My mother wasn't trying to be mean, although my sisters and I surely thought so at the time. She was trying to prepare us for what she saw as the rock-bottom truth: life *was* hard. Might as well deal with it. But when something really bad happened, when we came to her not with our mouths stuck out in childish anger but in tears, real tears, my mother would open her thin brown arms and pull us inside and tell us the other saying passed down from her mother that got her through the days. "I know it's hard," she would murmur. "But whatever doesn't kill you makes you stronger."

She was right, of course. My sisters Faith and Charity and I had all come out okay, more or less. Faith was still struggling, still trying to dig herself out from the hole she dug by getting pregnant as a kid, but she was making it. Children are supposed to grow up and go on, building upon their parents' foundations. I took my mother's philosophy to heart, refining it a bit to address my times. I believe that, yes, life is hard. But not for everybody, not equally, and that realization is not some minor disgruntlement. Life has been harder for my mother than it has been for me; 1960 was harder, in that way, than 1990 is. And life has been harder for me than for a lot of the people I find myself surrounded by day after day. Some people, you just see them and know—by the tilt of their heads, the easy set of their faces, the way they hold themselves out to the world, unafraid— you just know that life has been a dance for them. I see this a lot in people. I've learned to recognize it instantly, and usually it makes me angry, but I try just to let it pass, duly noted.

That might help explain why I became a journalist. I remember clearly the moment, freshman year in college, when the idea first occurred to me. I had gone to hear this guy from the *Washington Post* give a lecture about First Amendment rights and freedom of the press. It was an assignment for my political science class; I figured I'd go, listen, take a few notes, and sneak outta there if the guy droned on and on. But he turned out to be fascinating. He talked about the Vietnam War, how he had fought to print stories about disastrous battles while the government was crying national security. He talked about covering the student protests and the civil rights movement and a lot of other amazing stuff. During the question period someone stood and asked if he had a personal philosophy of journalism. I thought it was a stupid question, one intended more to give the asker something to say than to elicit a response. But the guy took it seriously. He thought for a second, then stroked his chin and opened his mouth.

"We-l-l," he drawled. He was a southerner, a white southerner. "I guess if I had to sum it up, I'd say my underlying principle has always been that a good reporter should comfort the afflicted and afflict the comfortable."

He grinned, and everyone in the lecture hall laughed. I did too, but I could tell he was serious. He was serious and he was speaking right to me. "Here is your future." For the rest of that week I walked around campus with his words ringing in my head. Comfort the afflicted and afflict the comfortable. It sounded like fabulous work.

Every newsroom I've ever been in was a dump. People say the *Washington Post* is nice—clean, well lit, rodent-free, the kind of office where normal people might enjoy spending ten or twelve hours a day. If so, it's an aberration. Most newsrooms look like prison rec rooms. Or maybe homeless shelters. The walls are grimy, the floors are grimier and snaked by enough electrical wires to give a fire marshal a heart attack. People work at desks packed so tightly together you could scratch your neighbor's nose without leaving your seat. There are stacks of yellow newspapers, and bookcases filled with ancient reports, and the only decoration, aside from awards, is usually some faded city map taped to the wall. Now, this casual clutter may seem unplanned, but don't believe it. This decor has been carefully nur-tured over the years. Journalists feel uncomfortable around too much glamour.

The newsroom of the *Philadelphia Record*, my new home, was bigger than the one I'd left behind in Greenville, North Carolina, and twice as dingy. But Betty Ann Simmons acted as if it was the Metropolitan Museum of Art. She couldn't wait to show me around.

"As soon as you get through with orientation, come back here," she bubbled. "I've got so many people I want you to meet."

Betty was the *Record*'s recruiting editor, the woman who had rescued me from an increasingly miserable life in Greenville and shepherded me across the Mason-Dixon to the promised land. She was the highest-ranking woman at the newspaper and the only woman on the masthead. A woman among boys, standing firm for the good of all the helpless sheep below.

"Sometimes I need an ax to cut through all the testosterone," she liked to say. Betty had started out not as a reporter but as a copy editor for what was then the women's pages. She had gone on to stints as assistant city editor, copy desk chief, and features editor, before finding her niche as unofficial mom to the news-room neurotics. She was the mother confessor for most of the staff, especially women and blacks and Latinos. She told me that when things got rough, I should come to her for advice. She would run interference for me with the big boys, whom I didn't want to tackle alone.

"Everybody comes to me," she said, and sighed a weary sigh.

So after my tour of the building, I searched Betty out as in-structed. Her office was stuck back at the end of the newsroom, in a windowless space barely larger than a closet. All the (male) assistant managing editors had offices at the front of the news-room, near the elevators, with nameplates and guard-dog secre-taries who all but frisked you before you were allowed to enter their masters' domains. Betty had a part-time clerk who refused to answer the telephone. She was afraid her nails might break.

When I poked my head into her office, Betty smiled and waved me in. She was reading the *New York Times*, her telephone receiver cradled between her head and the padded shoulder of her kelly-green jacket. Betty was one of those women who co-ordinate their outfits by wearing the same color from head to toe. Today she wore a green suit over a pale-green silk shell and pea-colored shoes. A clip-on earring the size, color, and shape of a tiny lime lay on her desk.

Betty was telling some eager beaver out in the heartland to forget his dreams of working for the *Record*, and in no uncertain terms. Her jackhammer voice bounced against the walls.

"Listen," she said, "I'm very busy. I've already spent fifteen minutes trying to explain it to you, but you don't seem to be getting it. So here's the bottom line: You're just not what we're looking for right now. You need more experience and you need to get to a bigger paper before you can think about making the leap to us, and anyway, you're too . . . de-ethnicized. Keep writing, do some investigative stuff. Send me some more clips if you want, although I doubt it will help."

She banged down the phone.

"Everybody thinks he's the next Carl Bernstein. So, Hope, how was orientation? Meet everyone?"

I rambled off a list of the names I could remember.

"Good, good. Come on, let's go. I want to introduce you around."

We stepped out of her office, into the newsroom. It was about 11 A.M., still the crack of dawn as far as most journalists were concerned, and the newsroom was fairly quiet. A few people sat at their desks reading various newspapers, a few more spoke softly into their phones.

Betty grabbed my arm with her red-tipped claw and dragged

me through the desks toward the front of the newsroom, where a row of dirty windows looked out onto Broad Street. As she led me around the room, I realized again how tiny she was. Probably a foot shorter than I was. Her short black hair curled tightly around her face, giving her the appearance of a poodle. Which I guess made me a lumbering black Lab.

Betty seemed to be zeroing in on a young blond woman who sat near the window, glowing in the sun. The woman was dressed in a long-sleeved silk shirt the color of ripe peaches, and as we got closer I saw that her pants matched her shirt. Well cut. Very stylish. The outfit probably cost three hundred dollars if a dime. Nobody in any newsroom I knew dressed that well. Print reporters in general were a nonstylish bunch; again, deliberately so. Most of the guys stuck to the standard uniform of wrinkled khaki pants and blue oxford shirts, with a navy blazer and a shapeless blue knit tie thrown in on special occasions. The women, well, the women were all over the map. The few black women journalists I knew dressed decently enough, but the white women wore bulky A-line skirts, or corduroy pants that stretched across their flat butts, and sweaters they seemed to have salvaged from their grandfathers' closets. It was like they were trying to be as unsexy as possible. Usually they succeeded.

Me, I favored clothes that disguised the hips I had inherited from my grandmother. She and my mother used to tell me all the time how much men liked big women, and maybe that was true, but I could tell you who didn't like big women. Clothing manufacturers. I had to be very, very careful about clothes so as not to look like the Pillsbury Doughboy being pinched at the waist. I liked big shirts over skinny pants; long straight skirts that drew the attention downward, away from my hips; jackets that fell to the thigh; things like that. When it came to clothes, I also preferred gray and brown and black to bright colors. My mother hated that about me. She was always sending me fluffy pink dresses and delicate yellow blouses. I gave them away.

This woman, though, had a great body, which her clothes let you know without making her look like a tramp. She had that kind of polished American attractiveness available to anyone with enough money in her purse. Her hair shone like a shampoo commercial and fell about her delicate face in a perfect blunt cut. She wore pearl stud earrings and a thin gold watch that slid beneath her shirt cuff as she reached across her desk for a pen. She had flawless skin and long, dramatic lashes; she reminded me of my old prep school roommate, a girl I'd disliked intensely.

"Got a minute, Stephanie? I'd like to introduce you to Hope Robinson. She's just joined the staff."

Stephanie swiveled in her chair and stood up, shaking her hair from her face in that horsey way whitegirls have. She stuck out a manicured hand and smiled, all ivory teeth.

"Stephanie Woodbridge," she said. "Nice to meet you, Hope. Welcome!"

"Thank you."

"Stephanie's fairly new too," Betty said.

"Really?"

"Yeah. I've been here, let's see, about six months now."

"She was in Asia before that, stringing for the *Boston Globe* and AP, and she was in China when Tiananmen Square happened!" Betty was breathless with excitement, as if she had personally arranged the trip that put Stephanie at the right place at the right time.

"How exciting," I said.

"Where are you coming from, Hope?"

"Greenville, North Carolina. The *Morning News.*"

"Oh, I've heard of that. It's a pretty good paper. What are you going to be covering?"

"Just GA for now." General assignment.

"Oh, GA." She wrinkled her nose and laughed, a high, girlish sound. "Well, a nasty necessity, I suppose. Good way to learn the city, but get off it as soon as you can, or they'll run you ragged covering street fairs and broken water mains."

I smiled although I did not feel like it. Stephanie was clearly my age or a bit younger, and she was giving me unsolicited advice about how to manage my career. As though I were some kid straight out of college.

"And what do you cover?"

"Right now I'm helping out with the elections." Her phone began ringing. "I'd better get this," she said. "Let's have lunch sometime, Hope."

Did she have to keep repeating my name like that? It sounded silly in her mouth; Hope the dope. I'd always wished my mother had named me Monica or something like that.

Betty beamed as we walked on. "You should get to know her," she said. "That girl is going places."

Next Betty marched me over to two white guys. One sat with his feet propped on a desk. The other was standing. He had been talking and gesturing with his hands.

"Michael Brown, Richard Goldin, this is Hope Robinson. She just joined the staff."

I said hello and smiled like an idiot; the men murmured their hellos. The one who had been talking, Richard, was tall and thin and pale, with large, sallow eyes and a mouth that turned down at the corners and a jaw that barely moved as he talked. He looked like a grouper.

"Well," Richard said, crossing his arms. "Where do you come from?"

I told him and he smiled. Or rather, his lips slid across his ocher teeth. He seemed surprised. "Oh," he said. "That's a fine paper. How long were you there?"

"A couple of years."

"That's not very long." He raised his eyebrows at his friend, who looked away. Richard turned back to me. "And you're so young. You've moved up quite fast, haven't you?"

Richard was still smiling, but it was clear he didn't mean this as a compliment. He kept pivoting toward the other guy, trying to catch his eye, but the other guy was studying something on his desk. Richard swiveled from his feet as though his waist didn't work. Or as though someone had shoved a piece of pipe up his butt and he was hoping to minimize the pain. Asshole waves shimmered off him like moonlight. I smiled at his comment but didn't say anything. My mother taught me when dealing with sharks it was best to stay still.

I turned to Betty, hoping she was ready to move on. But she wasn't.

"Hope," she said, drawing out my name, "graduated from Dray University." She paused to let that sink in. "And before that, from Astor Academy." I expected her to add that I was five feet ten, brown-eyed and black-haired, and weighed about fifteen pounds more than a twenty-seven-year-old should according to the in- surance charts, though it was justified by my big bones. I won- dered if she would pull back my lips to display my teeth.

"You've heard of Astor, haven't you, Richard?"

"Indeed."

"It's a very good school."

"Indeed," he said again.

"I'm sure you guys have lots of work to do," I said. "Nice meeting you."

We moved away. Betty took me around and introduced me to a few other people in the newsroom: a copy editor, a nice older white woman named Margaret, the all-important clerks. But I noticed that she avoided a black woman who sat in a corner near the back of the newsroom. I tried heading toward her, but just as I did, the woman picked up the phone and began to dial.

"Who's that?"

"Who?" Betty turned to look. "Oh. That's just Melvia Wallace. You can meet her later. Come on."

We headed back to Betty's office.

"Betty, is there something going on around here?"

"What do you mean?"

"I got funny vibes from those guys you introduced me to."

"Well . . ." Betty ducked her neck into the collar of her green suit. She looked like a turtle retreating into its shell. "Things have been a little tense."

"Tense."

"It's not a reflection on you." She patted my arm.

"Why would it be a reflection on me?"

"It's not."

"Well, I didn't think it was. But why would you even say that?"

"Look, it doesn't matter. Whenever there's change, people resist it. It's not important. The important thing for you right now is to settle in and get to work and do the job the way we know you can."

"Right," I said. Clearly there was more to it than that, but I decided not to push. I was tired of dealing with it anyway, all this stuff. All this emphasis. Maybe I *could* just settle in and do my work.

chapter two

The metro desk started me off with the usual stuff. My first story was a stirring feature about the unusually hot spring Philadelphia was experiencing. Eighty-five degrees in April. I don't understand why we do weather stories, stories that say, essentially, "It was hot yesterday" or "Boy, did it snow." Like everybody doesn't know by the time the paper comes out.

But I drove over to Kelly Drive, a road that winds along the bank of the silvery Schuylkill River, figuring I'd find some people there. It was a great place to hang out, one of the really nice things I'd discovered about Philadelphia. The whole area was really one big park, and to the right of Kelly Drive were these big black boulders and steep hills leading up to an old cemetery and another part of the park. And to the left lay the wide, grassy river banks, flung with trees—all of them now blooming pink and white like crazy—and picnic tables and a jogging path and some sculpture here and there. There were always people jogging or biking or just sunbathing by the river, but it never seemed too crowded. It seemed peaceful and elegant, with rowers skimming silently along the water like something in a painting. I interviewed a couple of people about the weather, including a skinny guy with a ponytail who was practicing tai chi near the sculpture of three angels.

"The weather is just as it should be," he said slowly, not breaking his graceful dance. "Right now, this moment is perfect. The rain is as necessary as the sun, the snow as good as the wind."

I wrote down everything he said and put it high in my story. Eccentric people can make a reporter's day.

My next assignment was covering an Italian Day parade on Sunday afternoon. Philadelphia was big on ethnicity. Italian, Irish, Swedish, Armenian, whatever: everybody was something and clearly marked. During weekends in the spring and summer, the groups gathered for festivals with lots of music and smelly foods, and ended up parading down Broad Street to display their ethnic pride.

So I hauled my butt over to South Broad, waited until the first band blared past and then pushed my way into the crowd, looking for someone with kids. Ahead of me stood a man with a small girl perched on his shoulders and his left hand on the head of a boy of about six.

"Hi." I brandished my notebook so he wouldn't think I was some nut. "I'm Hope Robinson from the *Record*, doing a story on the parade. What do you think of it?"

"It's nice," he said. A stirring quote. I wrote that down.

"Um, are you Italian?"

"Yeah, on my mother's side."

"And you brought your kids out today so they'd learn something about being Italian?"

The man reached down to grab his son's collar to keep the kid from squirming away into the crowd.

"My wife kicked us outta the house," he said. "She wanted to do something. I don't know what."

Not prize-winning stuff, but at least I was learning my way around the city and figuring it out. Philly likes to call itself a city of neighborhoods, which sounds pleasant enough until you realize that what people really mean is that there are certain neighborhoods where certain people are allowed and certain other people are not. South Philadelphia, for example, was the city's Little Italy. North Philadelphia was largely for blacks, with certain parts reserved for Puerto Ricans. Chinatown was for the Chinese, Korean, Thai, and Vietnamese but not the Japanese. The Japanese lived out in the burbs.

The Great Northeast, as they called the flap of land at the city's top, was reserved for hard-core whites of various ethnic stripes, the ones still unwilling to let their children sit next to black kids in school. The Northeast was one of the safest places in Philadelphia, because all the white cops lived there, along with white schoolteachers and other city workers who needed to meet the residency requirement. *In* the city but not *of* the city, that was the Great Northeast.

Chestnut Hill, in northwest Philadelphia, was for old-money liberal types. Mount Airy was the place of choice for middle-class blacks and really liberal whites, the ones still willing to march on Washington. Living in Mount Airy was like walking around with a T-shirt that read, "Some of my best friends are black. Really, they are."

But maybe that's too harsh. Actually, I liked Mount Airy. I decided to live there. I had to put a lot of thought into it, too, because the truth was that where I chose to live would be a political statement, whether I liked it or not. I learned that the hard way in college, when some of the black students ostracized me because I didn't want to live in the Central Campus apartments.

They called it Central Campus, but that was a joke. There was no campus there, no dining hall or classroom buildings or grassy quad where people played football into the twilight. The apartment complex sat in a kind of no-man's-land between West Campus—home to the administration buildings, most class-rooms, and various dorms and white fraternity houses—and East Campus, where all the theater and arty types lived.

The Central Campus buildings were squat, two-story, brown-brick affairs, and the apartments were just as squat and just as ugly and just as bad. The front door opened onto this boxy living room, then to a dining area and tiny kitchen, then to a dingy concrete terrace, barely wide enough to stand on. Standard features included beige carpet as soft and plush as drought-stricken grass and plaster walls that cracked and crumbled when you tried to drive in a nail. And no windows, to save heating costs. The only natural light you got came from the sliding door to the terrace. The campus buses, which ran between East and West every ten minutes, ran to Central at twenty-five-minute intervals and stopped two hours earlier. To sum up, I thought the apart-ments were ugly, inconvenient, and isolated. When my friend Tanya suggested we share one of them sophomore year, I balked.

"I don't really want to live in Central," I told her.

"You'd rather stay out here with *them?*"

"It's not about that. I just don't like Central. Why do you want to live there?"

Despite its flaws, Central was the residence of choice among black upperclassmen. It was *the* black community on campus: it had all the football players and the best parties on Saturday night and the best cookouts on Sunday afternoon. People referred to it, affectionately, as the ghetto. The only other people who lived there were graduate students with families and kids.

"You'd rather stay in a dorm?" Tanya was incredulous. "Girl, I'm sick of that noise. I'm sick of stepping out my door Saturday morning and having my feet stick to the floor because of all the beer. I'm sick of their music and their parties and their nasty ways."

"Okay. Then let's get an apartment off campus. They have some nice places over there off East."

Tanya rolled her eyes, as if I had suggested moving to the moon.

"That's just as bad! You ever been over there? It's like one big fraternity row. You'd still have to listen to that crap they call music." She cocked her head suspiciously. "But then you like that stuff, don't you?"

Tanya always teased me about my music collection. I still liked Earth, Wind and Fire and the Sugar Hill Gang. But I also had tapes of Billy Joel and the Police and other white bands. It was the music I'd listened to at Astor.

"I don't understand why you don't want to live in Central," Tanya said.

"I just don't like it." I felt helpless. "I'm sorry, but I don't."

Tanya was one of the few black-black friends I had. Black-black meaning she grew up in Newark and talked black and belonged to the Black Student Union and had pledged Delta and pretty much associated with white people only in class. There were other blacks like me at Dray, blacks who walked around dipping our fingers in both worlds, and I was friends with some of them. But I treasured Tanya. She was like my guide back to a place I couldn't quite find on my own anymore. After three years at Astor, I couldn't always find the direction, and sometimes I wanted to go home.

"Well, I'm gonna live in Central," she said, finally. "You can come or not."

I chose not. I tried hanging on to Tanya after she moved to Central, but it was useless. She moved off into her world and I moved off into mine. We would pass each other along some campus walk and sometimes stop and chat for a few minutes if both of us were alone, but that was it. I didn't really see her again until near the end of the year. She turned out to be one of a group of people who came to my off-campus apartment to confront me about a piece I had written for the student newspaper.

Nobody told me they were coming. It was a Tuesday evening. I lay on my bed, which was actually just a mattress on the floor of my room, trying to decipher a statistics problem. My roommate Sylvia knocked on the door and said, "There are people here to see you," in a strange little voice. Sylvia was the daughter of a wealthy Greek shipping tycoon, trying to broaden her isolated life by living with a black girl and a guy. We'd been introduced by a friend who knew I was looking for roommates. When her parents moved her into the apartment, her father installed a lock on the inside of her bedroom door.

I walked out to the living room. Sitting on the sagging brown couch we had bought from Goodwill for twenty dollars was a senior I recognized as president of the Black Student Union and two other girls I knew by face but not by name. Tanya sat off to the side, in an orange overstuffed chair that belonged to Robert, my other roommate. Robert was a friend of Sylvia's. He was rarely home, and when he was he stayed in his room smoking dope and listening to the Grateful Dead, and although he said he was a senior I didn't believe it. I never saw him crack a book. Robert was a pothead, totally useless, but Sylvia liked him. She said she felt safer with a man in the house.

"Tanya! Hi!"

Tanya smiled weakly at me, then glanced toward the Black Student Union president, as if protocol called for allowing her to speak first. The girl stood up and held out her hand. She was tall and skinny, fair-skinned and very attractive. It was hard to tell in the dingy light from the one lamp we had in the living room, but her eyes seemed to be the color of spring grass.

"I'm Lola Stone," she said. I shook her hand. She had one of those women's limp handshakes.

"We've come to talk to you about this."

From behind her back she whipped out a copy of the paper with my story in it and waved it accusingly before me. Besides being president of the BSU, Lola was an actress. When she stood there flourishing the paper like a bloody knife, I didn't know whether to cringe or to applaud.

"Can I get you guys some soda?"

"We'd prefer to get right to the issue," Lola said prissily. She was actually too tall to be prissy, but that didn't stop her. "Why did you write this?"

The story was about a sophomore named Randy Jones, who dropped out of school after pledging one of the black fraternities. He was a small, skinny kid who had been picked on all his life, and he figured that if he could pledge the toughest black fraternity—and all black fraternities are pretty tough—and survive, no one would ever mess with him again. He'd have his brothers. But the strain was too much for him. He couldn't take it. He had to wear the same clothes every day and march around campus single file with his pledge brothers. He had to shave his head, eat crap, and be harassed every night of the eight-week initiation. They beat him once. Then one night, a week before the pledge class was about to "go over," one of the brothers blindfolded Randy, took him down into a basement somewhere, and whispered that he wasn't going to make it. He was too pitiful, too weak, an embarrassment to the brotherhood. The next day a janitor found Randy floating in the East Campus pool. They pulled him out in time and fixed him up at the university hospital. Then they sent him home.

This was back before I really understood how serious it was to be a journalist, how the stories I wrote could be used or misused, how my words could affect people's lives and also mine.

So I answered Lola by saying, "Because it was a good story," and I meant it. Even though it was also the standard excuse.

"It's racist propaganda," Lola said. "Don't you see these white folks are using you? They put you up to it because they think we can't protest if a black reporter wrote it. But we're going to protest anyway. You need to join us."

The two girls standing behind Lola like twin pillars of support murmured assent. Tanya kept quiet.

"I can't protest my own story unless I think it's wrong. And it's not wrong. It's true and you know it."

Lola flung the paper to the floor. "Yeah, it's true. Their version of the truth. Did you even talk to Howard?"

Howard was the head of the fraternity.

"I tried. I called him twice. He wouldn't talk to me."

Lola scowled in exasperation. "He wouldn't talk to you because he thought you were white! You should have gone to his apartment. Then he would have told you that we don't need to be airing our dirty laundry in front of them. It just gives them an excuse to say how barbaric we are. They want to make us look like animals, and you helped them! How could you do that?"

Lola was in my face now, breathing hard, and my own breath tightened in my chest—from anger or from fear or from fear she was right. One of the other girls spoke up. She was like a dark-skinned version of Lola, tall and skinny and pretty. Pretty girls often run in packs.

"You know what some of those white fraternities do? They make their boys eat vomit and crawl around in garbage cans and run across campus naked. Last year a boy got hit by a car because they made him so drunk. How come you didn't put none of that in there?"

"I mentioned it," I said. My voice sounded weak even to me. There had been a whole section about all the atrocities committed by campus fraternities over the years, most of them white.

But the editor cut it down to just a few sentences. "Don't want to dilute the impact of this story," he'd said.

"Are you going to join our protest?" Lola demanded. "You going to quit that paper?"

"I can't."

In the silence that followed, I heard music start up in Sylvia's room, and from the first guitar screech, I knew it would be some head-banging noise. She had a nice stereo in there, very nice. At first she'd set it up in the living room, so we all could use it. But when her parents came to visit they made her move it into her room.

"Listen," Lola said. She glanced around the living room, her mouth twisted in disgust as she took in the sofa, the milk crates we used as bookshelves, the piece of tie-dye fabric Robert had stapled to the wall. "No matter how many whitefolks you live with, you're still black. You need to remember who your people are."

"I do! How could I not remember?!"

I looked at Tanya, desperate for her to speak up and tell these girls that I had wanted to room with her, that we were friends and that I knew exactly who I was. But Tanya was moving toward the door.

"Let's go, guys," she said. "We did what we came for."

I spent the rest of the night facedown on my bed, crying, trying to figure out what to do. I couldn't quit the student newspaper, even if I wanted to. If I wanted to be a journalist, I'd need experience and clips and connections to find a job. I couldn't throw away my future for some people I wouldn't know in five years, could I?

When Sylvia knocked at my door, I screamed at her to go away.

.   .   .

That episode pretty much set the tone for the rest of my college days. I went on working for the paper. After a few days, the protests stopped and people went back to the business of trying to get through school, and I prayed it had been forgotten. But it was like I'd been sprayed with some kind of staining ink. Every black-black student I met walking across campus turned away or refused to smile.

By senior year I was going on campus for class only and to work at the newspaper. The rest of my time I spent in Durham, mostly working as a waitress in this funky restaurant where the staff included gays, lesbians, communists, drag queens, coke-heads, and an Italian who said he was on the run from the mob. One guy called it the land of misfit toys. I felt right at home.

After college I landed a job at the newspaper in Greenville, and almost as soon as I got there, I flubbed things up again. I kept to myself my first few weeks, and by the time I was ready to trust people and make friends, the blacks at the paper—who had all gone to local black colleges and were already suspicious because I'd gone to Dray—had decided that I was a wannabe. By the time I realized they didn't like me, it was too late. It was as if there was some strange vibe I was putting out into the air.

Part of me was exhausted by the whole damn thing, trying to make sure people didn't get the wrong idea about this or that. I wished everybody would just leave me alone. But part of me wanted to break the cycle in Philadelphia. Maybe I could just start off right, right from the start, signaling that I was one of the black-blacks, a true member of the race.

Which is why I kept trying to talk to Melvia Wallace, who always seemed to be on the telephone or on deadline or gone. Most reporters spend much of their time sitting around the newsroom, feet propped up on their desks, jawing to one another. But not Melvia. I could never catch her. I managed to introduce myself one day, and she shook my hand, but her eyes were cold. Then her telephone rang, and ten minutes later she was gone. We didn't speak much after that.

"What's up with her?" I asked Georgia. Besides me and Melvia, Georgia Stanton was the only other black reporter on the city desk. There were a few people in other departments, like features and photo and sports, and apparently a few other folks out in the suburbs that I hadn't met yet, but only three of us reporters in the main newsroom. I called us the Three Musketeers—like the candy bar, not the book.

"Melvia? She's just . . . a little standoffish," Georgia said.

Georgia sat on my bed, waiting for me to get dressed so we could go to a cookout at the metro editor's house. I didn't particularly want to go; I would rather have spent the time fixing up my apartment. I still had unopened cartons of books in my living room, reproaching me every time I walked in the door. But Georgia insisted I come with her. Skipping the metro editor's party would be a political faux pas, she said. Especially for someone new.

"You have to go," she said. "Besides, it'll be fun!"

She seemed to believe it. Georgia was from Texas, which surprised me. It had never occurred to me that they had black folks in the land of cowboys and big hats and big boots. But Georgia was living proof, not particularly big but certainly wide open. You could read this woman like the back of a matchbook.

"Melvia is actually very sweet once you get to know her," Georgia said. She bounced over to my closet and started pawing through the clothes. She was the kind of woman who liked swapping things.

"Your clothes are all so . . . dark," she said, holding a skirt against her waist. "Why do you wear so much black?"

"I'm in mourning for my life. I'm unhappy." It was a joke, but Georgia didn't get it. She threw me a worried look, then smoothed her face with a smile.

"Melvia is very nice," she emphasized.

"Hmm."

I had a sinking feeling about Melvia, that she had somehow gotten that old bad vibe about me even though I'd made it my business to talk to every black person I met in the building, from Georgia to the security guards downstairs. It was possible that Melvia just didn't feel the need to come and befriend me simply because I was black. There are people who choose to make their way in the world that way, and it's fine. But Melvia didn't strike me as one of those people. For folks like her, being black in a predominantly white business was like being a foreigner somewhere, living among strangers for years and years until you speak the language perfectly and wear the local dress. But one day, as you are shopping in the marketplace, a sound comes to you. It takes a minute for it to sink in, because you haven't heard your own language, not even in your head, for many years. But then it clicks. You can't just ignore that voice, or its owner. You've got to seek him out, if only for a minute.

"Are you guys friends?" I asked Georgia.

"We're friendly." Which from Georgia could have meant anything. She wouldn't say a bad word about a snake who crawled up and bit her in the ass. Which I guess was a good thing.

"Do you think she'll be at the party?"

"I doubt it," Georgia said. "Melvia never comes to newsroom parties."

Jack, the metro editor, lived in Chestnut Hill, in a large stone three-story display of his wife's wealth. Georgia parked on the street and we hiked up the curving driveway, following handwritten signs that pointed toward the backyard. Most of the staff was there already, milling about on a flagstone patio shaded by trees or getting drinks from a bar on one side of the enormous lawn. From the patio, the yard stretched wide for a hundred feet or so, then sloped downward toward a pool.

"Hey!" I said, looking around. "How much money does this guy make anyway? I need a raise."

Georgia giggled and steered me toward tables piled high with food.

"Eat and mingle," she said, then disappeared into the crowd. I packed a plate full of ribs, shrimp, and little pieces of toast topped with smoked salmon, then got a glass of wine and wandered off to an empty table under a tree. As soon as I ate, I planned to find the editor, shake his hand and compliment his home, then get out of there.

"Hi. I'm David Carson."

I turned around to see this white guy standing over my table grinning at me. And he was cute. Now, a good-looking print journalist is like a smart TV blonde—it can happen, but it's rare. Print reporters tend to be unattractive. Most of the men are short, or doughy, or balding on top like Bozo the clown, or so effete that compared to them, Audrey Hepburn is a truckdriver scratching his balls. Most reporters were the dorks of their high schools; they joined the student newspaper in a desperate attempt to make friends, or to take revenge on the jocks and cool kids who beat them up. What was strange to me was how men didn't seem to learn humility from being unattractive, the way women do. The ugliest, dumpiest, goofiest guy in the newsroom was usually the biggest prick. The homeliest woman sat in a corner and kept her mouth shut.

But David was attractive. He was tall, with an angular face and wavy black hair and those round wire-rim glasses John Lennon used to wear. And there was something else about him, an intensity that made him seem even better-looking. Some people have that.

"Hope Robinson," I said, and wiped the rib juice from my fingers so that I could stick out my hand.

"I know," he said. "I've seen you around the newsroom from

time to time when I walk through. My office is upstairs on the eighth floor. I'm on the editorial board."

"I guess that means you know a lot," I said with mock earnestness. He didn't get it.

"Well. My area of specialty is politics, although of course we all pitch in on any topic. You do have to be something of a Renaissance person to work on the board." Like he was giving me his résumé and a lesson in journalism at the same time.

"Or a dilettante," I said.

David relaxed when he saw that I was smiling.

"Touché." He sat down in a chair across from me and grinned. "I am now firmly in my place. Thank you."

All around us, the party buzzed. Everyone seemed to be making a big effort to have a good time. People poured in with kids hanging off them, talking loud and laughing. The metro editor held court near the bar, and one by one people approached him with their heads suitably bowed. I glimpsed Georgia, standing across the lawn in a little knot of people, laughing. She seemed comfortable and happy.

A few tables away sat another cluster of people, among them Stephanie. She wore pleated walking shorts and, despite the heat, a crisp white long-sleeved shirt. Her hair was tucked behind her ears, emphasizing their delicateness. She felt me looking at her, turned toward me, and smiled. I turned back to David. Something about that girl bugged the shit out of me.

"So what's an editorial elite like you doing in a place like this?" I asked David. He sat with his long legs stretched out across the grass. "This is a gathering for metro slaves."

"Oh, I like to keep in touch with the little people," he said.

"The commoners will be so pleased."

I couldn't tell if this guy was a snot or not, but he interested me.

"You're not so common." David finished his drink and tilted

his glass back to catch an ice cube in his mouth. A faint shadow stained his chin. Hmm. A man who could grow a beard.

"I've been reading your stuff," he said. "You have a wonderful touch."

"Yeah. Did you read that rain story? I'm waiting to hear from the Pulitzer committee."

He laughed again. Apparently I was hilarious.

"Not that stuff. Nobody can do much with that. But that story you wrote about the bus driver was almost lyrical. Tightly written, beautiful lead. It deserved much better play than it got."

The air around my face grew warm, as though an oven door had been opened. I looked up expecting to see the sun, but instead I saw a canopy of palm-shaped leaves, still spring green but darkening nicely. We were sitting in the shade of a tree, its bark smooth and cream-colored, like melted ice cream. A white tree for white people. I giggled. Must be getting drunk. What was it, oak? Nah. My mother would have known just by looking at the leaves. It was a failure not to know the names of things.

I looked back down at David. Of all the stories I had written for the paper since I arrived, the one about the bus driver was the only one of which I was proud. It was good work. No one else had seemed to recognize it.

"Thanks," I said.

Stephanie walked over. She flopped into a chair next to David, who pulled in his legs and turned his whole body toward her.

"Hot out here, huh?" Stephanie said, fanning her face with her hand. She smiled at David and turned to me. "Good to see you, Hope."

"Stephanie. Having a good time?"

"As good as could be expected," she said with a grin.

She asked if I had been inside the house, and when I said no, she began describing the place. As she talked, I watched David inch his chair closer to hers. His fingers seemed drawn to her hair, which fell in a little waterfall of light. He started playing with it, like a child fascinated by a button. Stephanie babbled on.

"Almost ready to go?" David murmured to her when she paused.

"Oh, no." She pulled herself away. "I want to stick around a while longer. You can leave if you want."

"I don't want to leave without you."

"I'll meet you later."

"You said we'd only have to stay a little while. We've been here three hours."

"I'm not ready to go."

"Excuse me," I said, getting up from my chair.

"Oh, don't go, Hope," Stephanie said. "Please. We haven't really had a chance to talk since you began. How's it going?"

"Great. I'm going to refill my glass."

I left them in the midst of their lovers' quarrel, knowing Stephanie would win. That girl really did have everything, including the only decent-looking whiteboy in the building. And she probably didn't even have to work hard to get him. She probably walked into the newsroom one day and picked him up the way a dog picks up a tick in the woods.

I got another drink, then wandered over to make chitchat with the metro editor so he would know I had been there. After that I looked for Georgia but couldn't find her. I'd have to take the bus home. On my way out I passed Stephanie and David. She was talking to the managing editor, who lived in the neighborhood and had just stopped by, sending ripples of delight among the staff. David stood close to Stephanie, just behind her elbow, sucking on his drink. He smiled at me as I passed.

chapter three

I had lived up North before, when I was a teenager, at a prestigious New Hampshire boarding school called Astor Academy. My going there was all my mother's idea. There I was, in the eighth grade, busting my butt to prove to my mother that I wouldn't get pregnant like my older sister, Faith, and the next thing I knew I was getting letters from some prep school telling me my application had been accepted and I'd been granted a full scholarship.

"I sent it," my mother said. "I signed your name."

"You can't do that—that's forgery!" But my thirteen-year-old sense of outrage didn't faze my mother. I argued the rest of that school year and throughout the summer, and when fall came, she said, "You're going."

"But I don't want to go!"

"Lots of things in life I don't want to do," she said, packing my suitcase. "Makes no difference at all. I got to do them anyway."

I flew to Boston, then took the shuttle to a parking lot as I had been instructed. A big blue bus, the kind with a bathroom in the back, sat idling among a sea of cars. The destination sign said "Astor" in big white letters. I climbed on board, acutely aware of the ridiculous gray pleated skirt my mother had insisted that I wear. The seats were filled with pink-eared ferret boys in ties and girls in corduroy pants. My courage sank. New students all, we eyed each other warily, too frightened to say anything, too terrified not to smile.

The bus rolled out of Boston and up the highway toward New Hampshire, houses and buildings and cars thinning out along the way. We arrived in town about an hour later and drove straight to a campus of emerald lawns and crisscrossing paths and red-brick buildings that looked both arrogant and plain. The place seemed vast; the bus made three stops before it reached my dorm. A tall, skinny black guy helped me pull my trunk from the bus.

"My name is Kevin," he said. "Welcome to Oz."

I must have looked confused, because he laughed. "That's a joke. I'll carry this to your room."

As we walked Kevin told me about himself. He was from Chicago, on scholarship like me, a senior who'd been at Astor for three years. He seemed confident and relaxed, and the sight of him helped ease my fears a bit.

"Do you like it here?" I asked.

"It's not really about liking it. It's about using it."

"I'm scared."

We'd reached the third floor of the dorm. Kevin paused to catch his breath.

"Don't be," he said. "The thing to do is to not shut yourself up too much. These people are going to be powerful someday—make use of them. But don't lose yourself in the bargain."

I had no idea what he was talking about. Lose myself? I wanted to grab him, curl up in his arms and ask him to explain again and again until I understood, but he was already moving down the hall. As he reached the door to my room and set down my trunk I touched his arm.

"Is it worth it? Being here?"

He patted my shoulder. "I think this is the kind of place that's worth it in retrospect," he said, then turned to go. "I'll see you around."

Inside the room, a whitegirl about my age and a white woman, clearly the girl's mother, were making up the bed near the window. There was already a poster of the Boston Symphony Orchestra hanging on the wall.

"Oops, sorry! Is this my room?"

"It is if you're Hope!" the girl said. She dusted her hands against the narrow planes of her hips. "Come on in!"

She was shorter than I was, which made her about average height, with thick blond hair she wore pulled back from a heart-shaped face. She had on faded blue jeans and a white T-shirt, tucked in at the waist. I dropped my bags on the unmade bed and sat down.

"I'm Amy Stockton," the girl said. "This is my mother."

The woman had hair the same color as Amy's, but she wore it in an elegant bun. She smiled and stuck out her hand. It was as soft as baby skin.

"How do you do, Hope," she said. "You and Amy are beginning a wonderful adventure today."

Amy started right in, asking my age, where I was from, how I heard about Astor, what sports I intended to play. We had to choose a sport for each season, a requirement I had been dreading. Amy played field hockey in the fall, ice hockey in the winter, and lacrosse in the spring. She pointed to a nest of sticks and plastic masks propped in a corner by the door. Ice hockey I knew about, but lacrosse and field hockey were anybody's guess.

"I'll probably go out for track." Which was crap, because I hated running. But I couldn't think of anything else.

Amy's mother bustled about the room unpacking her daughter's things while I unpacked my own. When Amy's questions slowed down, her mother started in.

"What do your parents do, Hope?"

"My mother is kind of a practical nurse," I said. It was the answer I'd come up with; it sounded better than housekeeper. I knew lots of people would be asking me that question.

"And your father?"

"My parents are divorced."

"Of course." She gave me a smile.

After a while a man came in. He was tall and tanned and wore a blue sports shirt with a little alligator on it, the first I'd ever seen. He smiled briefly at me but addressed his wife.

"Well, I've set up her accounts at the bookstore and the bank. We'd better be going."

Smiling at his daughter, he held out his arms. Amy raced across the room into his embrace.

"You going to be all right here, pumpkin?" he asked, stroking her hair.

"Yes, Daddy. Don't worry. I'll be fine."

"I'll always worry," he said. "But I know you'll be fine. My little girl . . ." He leaned over and buried his face in her hair. I sat there for a second, feeling awkward but not knowing what to do, then I got up and left the room.

I fooled around in the bathroom. First I checked my hair in the mirror; it was a mass of wool, curly and glistening and heavy against my head. My mother had forced me to get a Jheri curl before leaving Memphis because she was worried I wouldn't be able to find any place to get my hair pressed or relaxed. I hated it. I turned away from the mirror and peeked into each one of the four dazzling white shower stalls. They had outer compartments where you could leave your clothes and inner compartments with the shower itself. Our house in Memphis didn't have a shower. We all took baths, and just before I left my mother had finally scraped up enough money to have the hot-water heater fixed. It had been out for nearly two years, during which time we heated our water on the stove.

I headed back toward my room to finish unpacking. In the hallway, I ran into Amy's father as he headed for the stairway. He'd been wiping his eyes with a handkerchief. His wife was nowhere in sight.

"Take good care of my daughter, now," the father said. He wagged his finger playfully at me. "She's the most important thing in the world to me."

"Oh. Sure," I said, grinning like a fool. Take care of his daughter? "Sure."

I planned to make it a point to join the Philadelphia chapter of the Association of Black Journalists. I hadn't joined in Greenville because I didn't know the damn thing existed. But ignorance of the law is no excuse.

The Philly chapter met once a month, in the evening, at the Afro-American Historical and Cultural Museum downtown. I drove over after work, rolling down my window to suck in the fragrant spring air. The museum was on the edge of center city, in a commercial area that didn't see a lot of foot traffic after dark. I parked as close as I could, then walked the two blocks back to the entrance. Inside the museum lobby, a guard sat at the front desk, watching a game show on a small black-and-white TV. When I asked for the ABJ meeting, he pointed upstairs without lifting his eyes from the screen.

"How do I get there?"

"Take the elevator," he said, yawning. "Take the ramp."

I walked up the ramp, which led from one open level to the next. The museum was featuring a show about the migration of black farmworkers into the city after World War I. There were paintings of people piling into trains and photographs that showed some of the overcrowded living conditions that resulted.

At the top level, the ramp spilled out into an open room with rows of chairs lined up neatly, facing a table. Behind the table, on the wall, hung a painting of an old black woman sitting before a fire. A young girl leaned against her leg. The woman was braiding the little girl's hair.

A handful of people were standing around in front of the chairs, talking. One of them was Melvia. I walked up to her and stuck out my hand.

"Hi. I'm Hope. I've been trying to meet you."

She shook my hand stiffly. "Yes. I saw Betty showing you off when you first came."

"Yeah. That was so embarrassing. I felt like I was a prize show horse or something. I kept expecting her to raise my lips and show off my teeth."

I didn't know if this was the right thing to say to Melvia; she was hard to read. But it seemed to be, because after a second she laughed.

"That's Betty."

"Listen, maybe we could have lunch sometime. You could give me the inside dope about the place."

"Girl, you should have gotten that before you came. But sure, let's have lunch sometime."

We didn't sit together during the meeting. Melvia was vice president or secretary or something; she sat up front with three others, at the long table facing the small crowd. I sat toward the back, trying to listen as the president talked about appointing new people to various committees. The truth is, I barely listened, so focused was I on the tide of relief rising up in my heart now that it appeared Melvia and I would be friends. Or at least friendly.

The next day I E-mailed Melvia to see if she was free for lunch. She was. Just before one o'clock she walked over to my desk.

"Let's go," she said, pulling on her jacket. "I'll drive."

Melvia was beautiful, although her features were too angular to be considered pleasant. She was like some rock formation erupting up from the desert, dangerous and gorgeous and sharp. We were more or less the same height, but Melvia seemed taller because she was thin, a sinewy kind of thinness. She wore her hair in a little Afro that shaped her narrow face, and she drove a silver Corvette. She drove it fast. We raced up Broad Street into North Philadelphia, rap music thumping on the radio.

"I never eat at Rachel's or the Blue Room or any of those places," she yelled over the music. "When I go to lunch, I like to get as far away from the paper as possible. Seeing those people eight hours a day is quite enough."

At Lehigh, Melvia swung left, then swung right at the next street and slammed the car to a stop. A sign over the door announced the storefront restaurant as Mamma's Ribs. We stepped inside. While my eyes adjusted to the dimness, I heard a cry. Out of nowhere, a short but quite significant woman rushed past me to where Melvia stood grinning from ear to ear.

"Girl, where you been hiding!?" she screamed, hugging Melvia. "Ain't seen you in forever!"

"Been working hard, Miss Ethel. You know how that is. But I promise I'll get by more often." Melvia had to bend down to keep the woman from hugging her around the waist. She straightened now and turned to me.

"This is Hope Robinson, Miss Ethel. She just joined the paper. I figured I'd show her where the best ribs in town were made."

Miss Ethel turned on me and went for my waist. I tried to cut her off, but even as I stuck out my right hand I knew it was fruitless; these big black women would not be deterred. Miss Ethel grabbed my shoulders and wrestled me toward her like a reluctant chicken. Her big body was as soft and warm as fresh-baked bread. She smelled of onions and boiled greens and, faintly, of Jean Naté.

"Well, Hope! What a pretty name! Where you from, gal?"

"Tennessee, ma'am." When was the last time I called anyone ma'am? She released me and I straightened up. "Memphis."

"Memphis!" She smiled approvingly. "We used to drive up to Memphis once a year. Had an aunt there who worked at the children's home. You know the children's home? Good job. Good money and they left her alone. But not as good as you children have. I'm so proud of Melvia. Sit down here and have some catfish. The catfish is good today."

We both ordered catfish with greens and corn bread. A young woman with a sour look on her face brought us glasses of sweetened tea and set them sweating on the orange plastic tablecloth. Every one of the restaurant's twelve or so tables was occupied. Men, mostly. Workingmen in oil-stained jumpsuits or uniforms that identified them as being with the phone company or the gas company. Three old men in button-up sweaters came, pulled off their hats, and stood scowling at two gas company guys who sat at a table near the window. After a while Miss Ethel came out of the kitchen and whispered something to the two men, who wiped their hands and left. The three old men descended on the table, still grousing about the nerve of someone else sitting in their seats. Miss Ethel brought them tea and told them to hush.

"You look mighty fine today, Miss Ethel," one man said.

Miss Ethel rolled her eyes. "Hush up and get some catfish before it's gone."

"Never be afraid of the truth."

I pulled a tiny bone from my mouth and wiped my lips on a paper napkin.

"Delicious," I said.

Melvia nodded. A halo of oil shone around her lips. Grease was the essential ingredient of southern cooking.

"So you going to join ABJ?"

"Of course."

"Good. I was glad to see you there last night."

Melvia was from South Carolina, had been at the paper for seven years and was over thirty-five, although how much over she refused to say. She was covering local politics, a good beat, one she had fought hard to get, but what she really wanted was to go on a national or foreign assignment. Every year she went in to make her case to Rob Tyler, the managing editor. Every year he told her how wonderful she was, so hardworking, and gave her a raise, then sent her back out to her desk.

"It's a boys' club, a whiteboys' club," she said, placing a piece of sun-yellow corn bread into her mouth. "All the glamour beats are reserved for the members. The only reason they finally gave me politics is because I bitched so loud and so long, and because it's really a lot of grunt work."

The waitress came out again and refilled our glasses with tea so sweet it made my teeth ache. That was the way we had always drunk it when I was growing up, but now the cloying sweetness was too much. I sipped my water.

"So," Melvia said, "you heard about the committee yet?"

"What committee?"

"Couple of months ago, some black reporters sued one of our sister papers, the *Jacksonville Times*. They charged racial discrimination. Corporate got really scared. They were worried it would start a domino effect. So they ordered all the rest of their papers to come up with affirmative action plans. That way they'd be covered. So that's what this committee is doing."

"Who's on it?"

"Oh, I don't know. I haven't paid that much attention. I think every department has its own committee. I know Georgia is on the news department's, but I don't know who else."

"So people think that's why they hired me?"

Melvia shrugged. "Some people think that's why they hired all of us. Don't matter. They hired you and three white people at the same time, two of them men. You deserve to be here as much as any of them. Don't let them make you think otherwise."

Melvia drained off her tea and patted her mouth with the paper napkin from her lap.

"You can't let people run you crazy. It ain't worth it. Is it, Miss Ethel?"

Miss Ethel had come over to inspect our plates for signs of leftovers. The neat little heap of bones on my plate earned a satisfied smile.

"Child, no." She let out a laugh and rubbed my shoulder. "You'll be laying up in some nuthouse while they out dancing in the street. When people act ugly, you got to look at them like they the crazy one, and then smile and just go on."

A few days later, I was out interviewing people on the street about the cost of parking tickets going up fifty percent. When I got back to the office, around four o'clock, I felt a tension in the air. People stood around in little clumps, talking intently.

I messaged Melvia.

"What's going on?"

"The affirmative action committee released a report," she wrote back. "Haven't seen it yet, but the whiteboys are pissed. Yee haw. The battle begins. We'll have to talk. But I'm on deadline now. Gotta run."

Georgia was nowhere to be seen. I grabbed a copy of the report from the clerk's desk and slipped out of the newsroom, headed up to the cafeteria for coffee.

The report meandered and generalized, like a small boy who

had something to say but was embarrassed to say it; it took me nearly twenty minutes to cut through the garbage and get to the meat, which was essentially this: The *Record* had done a dismal job of hiring and promoting blacks and other minorities. Colored folk of all kinds made up less than eight percent of the staff, which was triply embarrassing for a news operation in a city like Philadelphia, where fewer and fewer white people cared to live. The paper would have to do better, the report said. The same was true to a lesser extent with women. To make sure, every department should be required to set hiring goals. Fairly tame and predictable stuff, like fertilizer piled in a basement, waiting to be made into a bomb.

On my way back into the newsroom I passed Richard Goldin in the hallway. We hadn't spoken much since that first day, when we met as I was being paraded around by Betty, so it surprised me when he stopped.

"Hope. I see you've had a chance to read the report. Tell me, what do you think?"

"I just read it, Richard. I haven't formed an opinion yet."

Richard grinned, a movement that had the unfortunate effect of squeezing his eyes into little slits. He was an unpleasant man to look at. I wondered how he ever got people to talk to him on interviews.

"Oh, come on. I'm sure you have some thoughts on the matter," he said. "Everyone else in the newsroom does."

"I thought it was a reporter's job to remain objective." I pushed past him and continued down the hall, but Richard followed.

"Don't you think quotas are a terrible idea? They won't help the quality of the paper, and they won't help the people hired under them."

"I didn't see anything in there about quotas."

"No, they said goals. A pleasant little euphemism. But I'm sure a smart reporter like you knows how to cut through rhetoric like that."

"I have work to do."

I walked away, feeling Richard's eyes cool upon my back. I knew what he wanted. He wanted me to agree with him, to validate his position. Not that he had any doubts, but it would make him feel better about where he stood.

The problem was, part of me did agree with him. Not about lowering standards—that was crap. But I'd gone to Astor under a quota system, and probably college too—I wasn't sure—and although I always said screw off to people who suggested I didn't deserve to be where I was, sometimes I wondered. And I hated having to wonder. On the other hand, some people would say the same thing no matter what I accomplished. Just like Melvia said. And if somebody didn't set goals, if everybody just vaguely promised to do better, would things ever change?

Back at my desk I looked across the newsroom, and my glance fell on Stephanie. She wasn't taking part in any of the little discussion groups clustered around the newsroom. She sat at her desk, typing away at her computer, earphones used like a headband to hold her golden locks back off her face. She was working on a story for the front page; I'd seen it in the daily budget earlier. She could afford to be above it all. She didn't have to choose between being consumed and being a sellout. She got to just be.

David came through the doorway and into the newsroom. He was wearing a dark-green shirt and a golden-brown tie, which was interesting because almost none of the guys in the newsroom actually wore ties, except stiffs like Richard. David's tie was made out of silk the color of pinewood, and it made him look taller somehow, more mature than he had seemed at the party. He walked over to Stephanie and kind of perched on her desk, and he smiled and leaned toward her to say something. But Stephanie didn't look up from her computer screen. She said something quick, and David stopped smiling and stood up and moved away, slightly embarrassed. He seemed like a little boy who'd been pushed outside to play because his mother was busy. He ambled over to where the week's papers were kept in bindings and flipped through them, then stopped one of the clerks, who was scurrying to his desk to answer a ringing phone, and engaged him in conversation. I heard the clerk's annoyed "I don't know! It's not my department," before he escaped, and David was left standing in the middle of the bustling newsroom, appearing lost. I turned away. I could feel, rather than see, David find my back in the midst of all the backs bent over their desks. I felt him walk toward me, stop behind me, try to read the lines on my computer.

I swirled around in my chair. "Take a picture. It'll last longer," I said.

David stared at me, bewildered.

"It's something we used to say when we were kids. It means that it's impolite to stare."

"I'm sorry." He smiled. "I was just trying to figure out whether you were on deadline or not. Don't want to disturb you."

"Some people would say I'm already disturbed."

David chuckled, his lips pressed close but his whole face turning upward toward his eyes. He had very, very nice eyes, light brown, the color of sandalwood, or maybe what was nice was the way he used them. Usually I hate to be stared at, but David's look was not obtrusive at all. His eyes seemed to penetrate but it was a surprising and welcome penetration, like the heat of the sun on your shoulder during the first days of spring. David stood there looking at me, still chuckling. Either he was easily tickled or I was funnier than I thought or something was going on here between us. I couldn't tell. I didn't know him well enough, but he acted the way my mother always told me to act to get a man: laugh at everything he says, whether it's funny or not.

"I'm not on deadline. What's going on?"

"Not much. I've been out all day doing research for an editorial about the upcoming city council primaries. It's pretty much an exercise in futility. People don't vote in presidential elections, let alone off-year council primaries."

"Which makes your job all the more important, I guess."

"I used to think so."

"You can help me. I have no idea who to vote for."

"What district are you in?"

"Actually, I have no idea. I'm ashamed to admit it, but I'm not even registered to vote here yet."

"See? And you're one of the good guys."

"Am I?"

"I'd bet on it."

We stopped talking for a moment. The newsroom was buzzing now with people speaking loudly into their phones and clicking away at their computers. Up near the city desk, a clerk turned on the television to watch the five o'clock news and make sure they didn't have any stories we didn't know about.

"Well, I'd better get back to work," I said.

"Me too."

I saw him look at the affirmative action report on my desk.

"Now, that little document will get people talking." David pointed. "I'd like to hear your opinion on it."

"Oh, I don't know. Maybe I don't have an opinion."

My phone began ringing.

"Of course you do," David said.

"I have to get this."

"Let's talk tomorrow." He moved away.

I picked up the phone, but whoever was calling had hung up. Which was just as well. I was ready to go home. The report had really depressed me. For some absurd reason, I had thought that race relations might be easier up here in the North. Even though part of me knew better. It must have been some lingering southern belief, passed down in my genes.

I wondered if David really wanted to talk about the report or was using it as an excuse. One way or the other, race was always the starting point between black people and white people, and one way or the other, I'd be expected to come up with an opinion on this issue, even if I didn't have one. Even if I didn't care.

But of course I did care. I was just tired of thinking about it. The thing about race, or really about being black in America, was that it was a full-time job.

The next morning a memo began circulating in the newsroom, calling the "diversity" report a prescription for mediocrity. It called for a ban on using race or gender as a factor in any hiring or promotion decision. Without naming names the memo demanded restitution in two specific cases, where, it said, a black man and a black woman had been unfairly promoted over two white men. Everybody knew whom the memo referred to, but the two white guys in question expressed surprise and swore they had nothing to do with it. The memo was signed, "Concerned members of the staff."

chapter four

The memo hit the newsroom like a missile. Most of the (few) black reporters, editors, photographers, and copy editors were furious. The morning after the memo began circulating, Melvia marched in and wrote "Cowards!" on a copy posted on the bulletin board. Then she signed her name.

"I'm calling a meeting," she said.

Speculation about authorship ran rampant. A few people, such as Richard, kept stating loudly that the origin of the memo was unimportant; what mattered was that it had brought to the surface feelings a lot of people shared. Which of course led everyone to believe that he had written the thing, though he denied it. And I believed him; it didn't seem prissy enough. Plus, I would think that if Richard had written it, he would have wanted everyone to know.

One by one people chose sides, and every day for a week they convened in the aisles of the newsroom to do battle in words.

"I'm not saying I defend everything in the memo," said Donald, a white business reporter. "But race-based quotas are discriminatory. And destructive."

He was arguing with Nancy, an assistant editor in the features section, about forty or so, with shaggy brown hair, blue eyes, and a face that usually looked as though somebody had promised her a pleasant surprise somewhere down the road, if only she would wait a little while and be patient. But as she argued with Donald her face flushed.

"And the status quo is not discriminatory, I suppose?" she asked.

I sat at my desk, trying to ignore them and finish a story I was working on about a public school in North Philadelphia. Frustrated by the violence and low achievement of her students, the principal had created several all-male classes focusing on the special needs of black boys in the city. It was an interesting story. Parents loved the class, but the school was being sued by the ACLU. I kept hoping Donald and Nancy would take their argument out into the hallway, but I knew better. Donald was hoping to draw me in.

"I don't see any barriers here." He spread his hands, as if demonstrating the lack of brick walls in the newsroom. "I think we should be a society that guarantees equal opportunity, not equal results."

"You are either incredibly naive or incredibly disingenuous," Nancy said. "Institutions perpetuate themselves. It's the rule of nature. I could look around this country and name you ten white men in positions of power at various papers whose careers have been fostered by this place. Bet you can't name me two women. Or one black person."

They went on like that for a while. My phone rang; the principal was having second thoughts about the story, and while I soothed her fears I managed to tune out Donald and Nancy. But when I hung up the phone Donald was speaking. Loudly.

"Reverse discrimination is not what Martin Luther King would have wanted," he said. "That wasn't his dream."

Then he turned to leave and Nancy marched back to her desk, which was near mine, and flung herself into her chair.

"These men!" she said, exasperated. "They are so childish, so threatened by the rise of women. Chickenshits!"

I smiled at her but kept typing away at my computer.

Nancy was one of those women who rarely cursed, so that when she did, it sounded both shocking and funny. I could tell she was all worked up over this, in part because she was a serious feminist and in part because she was worried the memo had somehow hurt me. She had taken a special liking to me because she had worked at the Greenville paper five years before I did. It was a little connection for us.

"If they were as good as they think they are, they wouldn't have to worry about dealing with a level playing field. They're just mad because their advantage is being taken away."

I shrugged. "Nobody ever gave up power willingly, Nancy."

"No man anyway."

Melvia called a meeting of black staff members for that afternoon, somehow managing to alert all the people out in the suburban offices. There were only three black reporters on the city staff—me, Georgia, and Melvia—but there were black sports reporters and copy editors and a few black reporters out in the suburban region, as well as people with other jobs. By the time I made it upstairs to the fifth-floor conference room, there must have been fifty or sixty people crammed inside, some sitting around the long table, the rest leaning against walls. Georgia sat at the head of the conference table next to Melvia, calling out to people as they entered and trying to look stern.

"All right, let's go." Melvia raised her voice over the din. "Let's get started. Here's a copy for anybody who hasn't read the memo."

She held the papers by her fingertips and passed them down the table. A few people chuckled.

"Now, we're here to decide on a response," Melvia said, wiping her hand on her sleeve. "Suggestions?"

"File a complaint!"

"Demand an apology!"

"Slap somebody!"

"Yo, people! Quiet down!" Jonathan, a sports reporter, stood, hands raised. He was a great big high school football player of a guy, and his shoulders strained the fabric of his white dress shirt. He glared around the room until it was quiet. "One at a time, please.

"Now, I suggest we write our own memo, condemning that memo and announcing our support of the diversity report," he said.

People around the table murmured their approval.

"Wait a minute. I think the memo was right in condemning the idea of a quota system," said a stout woman. "It's insulting to us, really. It casts a bad light on whoever they hire. I know I wouldn't want to be brought in that way."

The room erupted in noise. Several people pshawed out loud, and one woman called out, "Oh, please, Ruth!"

"Well, I wouldn't!" Ruth stuck out her chin.

"Sister, you part of a quota whether you want to believe it or not," said a skinny man standing near me. I recognized him as a photographer; he wore one of those beige jackets with a hundred pockets for carrying film and other things. "They ain't going to let but so many of us in here anyway!"

That broke the crowd into shouts of agreement or disapproval and laughter.

Melvia raised her hand for order. "There are two issues here," she said. "One is that memo, which cannot go unanswered. If I have to write a response, calling whoever wrote it a coward and challenging that shit about people being mediocre, I will, and sign it myself. But I think we should all sign it."

Several people called out: "Yeah!" "I agree!"

"The report itself is really a separate issue," Melvia said. "We can give it a vote of confidence or not. That's up to you."

"I think the report is the main issue," Jonathan said. "You are not going to change some folks' minds, so there's no use even worrying about that memo. The important thing is to support the report, so that Rob knows it and the people down in corporate know it too."

He looked around the room meaningfully. "We can't afford to be divided on that issue."

"Disagreeing doesn't mean we're divided, Jonathan," said a youngish guy in glasses and suspenders. "We need to realize that all black people don't speak with one voice."

"Man, I realize that!" Jonathan said. "What you don't seem to realize is that we don't have the luxury of division. There aren't enough of us in the place. When we get something approaching the right numbers, then we can afford to get all fancy about this shit, but right now, if we don't present a united voice we're dead."

Some people applauded.

"Okay, okay, let's take a vote," Melvia said. "All those in favor of writing a memo in support of the report, to send to Rob and corporate, raise their hands."

Everyone but Ruth and a few others raised their hands. I put mine up.

"Okay, that passes. Jonathan, you can handle that."

"I think we should take our memo to Rob," Jonathan said. "I think we should meet with him face-to-face."

"Fine," Melvia said. "Set it up. Now, I plan to write a response to the memo this afternoon. Anybody who wants to come to my desk and sign it, feel free."

The meeting broke up and I wandered downstairs, back to my

desk, feeling discombobulated. In the newsroom, people glanced up from their desks as I passed, then looked away again, quickly.

Melvia strode back into the newsroom and sat at her desk. Banging away at her keyboard she was magnificent, her dark face giving off an angry glow. None of the white reporters glanced over at her; instead they spoke louder to one another, and feet tapped, laughter echoed, the general hum of the newsroom rose a notch, as if unconsciously the entire place was trying to muffle the psychic noise Melvia was pouring out. She amazed me, Melvia. She was one of those people who always seemed to know exactly where they stood and how they felt about things and what to do about those feelings. No doubts, no questions. She didn't waste precious time vacillating. She got angry when she had a cause and a target she could shoot for. And when she didn't have a target, she didn't squander energy getting angry. Like a scrap of leftover fabric, she saved it for another time.

Half an hour after she sat down Melvia stood and walked over to my desk, paper in hand.

"Here's the memo," she said. "Read it. Sign it if you want. Pass it on."

I read:

To the newsroom staff:

We, the undersigned, want to express the shock and dismay we felt upon reading the memo attacking the affirmative action report that appeared this week. By refusing to sign their names, the authors proved themselves cowards. By attacking the report, which is, after all, just a starting point, the authors proved themselves reactionary, inflexible, and fearful of change. By attacking two individuals with baseless accusations, the authors proved themselves to be indecent and without honor of any kind.

That the *Record* needs to make some effort to increase the

hiring, promotion, and retention of people of color seems clear to us. The numbers tell the story, clearly and without shading. That this effort would improve, not damage, the quality of the newspaper is also clear. To suggest otherwise is nearly as insulting to the editors as it is to us.

The argument that the low numbers of minorities at the *Record* and other newspapers somehow reflects a shortage of "qualified" minorities in the industry is specious at best and inherently insulting. Leaving aside the entire debate about the word "qualified" (it's not like we're performing brain surgery here), let us say, in plain English, there is no such shortage. Any black staff member here could name dozens of talented black journalists scattered across the country, and many more graduate from college every day. The failure of the *Record* to attract and retain these journalists is just that, a failure. And it must, and will, be addressed.

This is not an easy issue. It won't be easily decided, and whatever steps the paper makes, not everyone will agree. But taking potshots at individuals and writing anonymous missives will not serve whatever argument the writers of the memo wish to make. It only makes them look like sniveling, whining children. And drives wedges of suspicion between us all.

We will sign our names.

Below the last line, signed in bold, black strokes, was Melvia's name. I put my own name right below it, the *e* in Hope bumping up against the *J* of Melvia's middle initial. As if crowding my signature next to hers might make some of Melvia's certainty rub off.

As things turned out, I missed the big meeting with Rob, the managing editor, a week later. I was down in center city, tagging along with two city inspectors and making surprise inspections about Dumpster violations. Titillating stuff. But the inspectors were into it.

"Look!" one yelled as we rounded the corner into an alley. He broke into a sprint, charging toward a Dumpster, and as I followed him, walking, I saw what had excited him so: a rat as big as a cat, with beady white eyes, sat perched defiantly on top. The inspector whirled around, snapping photos.

"Rats don't come where they can't get food," the other one explained to me.

Sure enough, the Dumpster was not only unlatched, it was packed much too full, causing garbage to spill over into the alley. One of the inspectors lifted the top, releasing a smell like none I'd ever known. Water filled my eyes but the inspector didn't even wrinkle his nose.

"And look at what we have here! Glass," he said, gesturing me over to take a look.

"That's okay, I believe you."

He let the top clang shut. "Supposed to be recycling that." Shaking his head, the inspector made a note in his neat blue pad. I made a mental note: The next time my editor came to me with one of these can't-miss stories, I was going to pretend to be in the middle of something else.

I got back to the office at three, wrote the story, and turned it in. By the time I was finished, Melvia had gone home. But Georgia sat at her desk, chatting with another reporter. When he left, I walked over and asked her what had happened with Rob.

"Oh, it was great! He really listened to us, and he promised to implement the diversity report! He said he thought it was full of good ideas."

"Really?" For the first time, it occurred to me that Georgia's relentless optimism might be more than just annoying. Maybe it actually affected her work. She wrote about schools, and for the most part the schools in Philadelphia were pretty grim. It was frightening to think that things might be even worse than Georgia said in her stories; that when forced to write about some ugly situation, she just couldn't help niceing things up a bit.

"What about the first memo? He say anything about that?"

"He said he was appalled by it and that he'd considered calling a meeting of the staff but decided it would only make things worse. So he's going to ignore it."

"And hope that it just goes away?"

"Yes." Georgia paused. "I think that's probably the best thing, don't you?"

"I don't know," I said. And I didn't. The only thing the memo writers had done was express their opinions. You couldn't stop people from doing that, especially at a newspaper, and you couldn't browbeat them into feeling the way you thought they should. But if the writers were editors and not just reporters, they were in a position to sabotage the managing editor's plans for hiring and promotions. Rob could sit back in his office and spout platitudes about affirmative action all he wanted, but it was the people on the front lines who handed out assignments and promoted stories and influenced what was played where. It was those folks who would ultimately decide whether black folks succeeded at the *Record* or not. So maybe something more did need to be done.

"I believe most people will come around to the right thing eventually," Georgia said. "If you don't push them."

I had to smile at her.

Somebody, maybe Melvia, sent a copy of her letter to corporate headquarters. Within a week a fair-haired, blue-eyed, big-smiling man named Sam Johnson showed up at the paper and told Rob that he wanted to have a little talk with some of the staff. Johnson held some bogus title, like vice president of corporate personnel affairs, but word was his real power came from being the son-in-law of the chairman of the board. He was in training for a more important position, and this little national guard assignment was one of his tests. His job was to get in, quell the riots, and put down the insurgency quickly, before any more ugly publicity about the situation leaked out. Already the *Washington Post* had done a story about it, under the headline "Affirmative Action Wars at a Nation's Newspaper." As if they didn't have their own problems.

Johnson was a big guy, muscular, thick-necked, one of those Texas high school football types grown up. He wore tailored blue suits that emphasized the vast expanse of his back and had the additional effect of making the suits Rob wore look shabby by comparison. He joked a lot in his booming voice and smiled from the nose down. But his eyes were serious. "I'm here to fix this problem," they said. "And you'd better not fuck me up."

The first day he spent meeting with Rob and the other top editors. The second day he met individually with members of the staff. Melvia was first. When she came out, I E-mailed her.

"What happened?"

"We talked about my memo, about my career here, about racial relationships in the newsroom. He said corporate was very concerned and liked some of the diversity report recommendations and planned to implement them. He said maybe quota was a hot-wire word and shouldn't be used but that he supported efforts to step up the hiring of minorities. A lot of other stuff. He seemed sincere, but you never know. We'll see what happens."

All day long people trucked in and out of the office where Johnson had set himself up. At one point Betty summoned me.

"Don't you want to meet with Mr. Johnson?"

"I don't have anything to say."

"Of course you do! Tell him how much you like it here."

"What makes you think I like it here, Betty?" I said, then laughed. She took it as a joke.

"I'm afraid he's getting a skewed view of the place. I sent Georgia in, but I'd like you to talk to him too."

"If Georgia went in, she said enough nice things for all of us. I don't really have anything to add."

At the end of the week, Johnson called a staff meeting. We

all piled into the company auditorium, where he stood up on the stage, erasing a blackboard.

"Now, the first thing I want ya'll to remember is that we're all a family," he boomed. "The *Record* family. And like any family, we may have our differences, but we also share a common goal. That's to put out the best, most profitable newspaper we can. We all want that, right?"

Being reporters, we took it as a rhetorical question. But Johnson wanted feedback.

"Ya'll awake out there?" he said, pretending to shield his eyes from the stage lights and peer out into the audience. "I said we all want to put out the best, most profitable newspaper we can, right?"

A few people, mostly editors, yelled out "Right!" while the rest of us mumbled some kind of grudging assent.

"Right!" Johnson said. "And to do that we know that we need to have a trained, talented, and diversified staff with wide-ranging interests and backgrounds, and the kind of mutually respectful atmosphere that allows us all to thrive. Right? Right!"

He went on and on like that, prowling across the stage, slashing up diagrams on the chalkboard like a coach as he exhorted us to work together for the good of the team. No man was an island. No one man, or one group, had all the answers in this world. He had been very impressed with every one of the people he had spoken to over the past few days, and he'd come away with the belief that we were not divided on what we hoped to accomplish, only confused about the best way to get there. That's where he came in.

"Now, I've created a little report, incorporating many of your suggestions, including some of my own, and I'm going to leave it with Mr. Tyler here," he said, gesturing to Rob, who sat miserably in a corner of the stage, trying to smile.

"In a few months, I'll come back for another visit and see how you're doing on these goals. I have nothing but faith that this staff will get the job done."

chapter five

Among other things, Johnson suggested that the staff undergo a diversity sensitivity program. So Rob hired two consultants to come in and teach us how to get along better with one another. In the newsroom the idea went over like an IRS audit.

The consultants turned out to be two women, one white, one black, who finished each other's sentences and moved in concert like some yin-yang Bobbsey twins. They pranced around the conference room where the sessions were held, both wearing copious eye shadow and tailored suits with short skirts for that Don't-forget-I'm-a-woman-but-don't-try-anything-either-pal look that bewildered most men. You could tell they thought they were something, running their own business, telling corporate giants how to avoid getting their asses sued. I wondered if the white chick had gone out and recruited the sister to cement her qualifications as a diversity guru. If the sister had started the business, she wouldn't have needed the white chick. Black women are diversity personified.

So these two chicks herded us into a conference room in groups of twelve and showed videotaped scenes of problematic situations. In one scenario, a black woman strolled around her very proper corporate office wearing a boubou and an African headdress. Her boss didn't like it. He thought it gave the place a bad image, but he wasn't sure what he should do.

Black Bobbsey hit the pause button.

"Okay. Suggestions for handling this situation?" she asked.

Silence. We all stared at Black Bobbsey as if she had suddenly broken into Latin.

"Okay," White Bobbsey said. "He might confront her, demand that she wear something more quote-unquote professional." She hooked four fingers in the air to make her point.

"Or he might ask someone else to talk to her, a black manager if he had one," Black Bobbsey said. "Or a woman manager."

"Or he could dig up a copy of the dress code and post it on her computer screen while she was at lunch."

"Or he could just fire her and not tell her why."

"Let's see what he does," White Bobbsey said, turning the videotape back on.

Turned out the boss sought the advice of his good friend Jake, a black golfing buddy, who explained that African dress was important to the employee as an expression of her pride in her heritage but it had nothing to do with the quality of her work. The boss saw the light. He complimented the woman on the pretty colors of her clothes. She explained her garment's significance and offered to wear only the boubou or the headwrapping, not both on the same day. They smiled happily at each other as the music swelled and the credits rolled nimbly past.

"Any questions?" White Bobbsey asked.

"Can we go now?" said Dick Thompson under his breath, like some high school class clown. White Bobbsey squeezed out a perky, screw-you smile.

"You're perfectly free to leave. We're not your prison guards," she said. Then: "The company has required this training, not us. We have no reason to make you stay."

No one stirred.

We learned that Asians find direct eye contact disrespectful and Hispanic men have this machismo thing you have to step around, while Indians prefer to be criticized in private (as opposed to who?). Awkward scene after awkward scene rolled before our eyes, stilted and so badly acted we cringed for the poor souls stumbling through their lines. I felt like that guy in *A Clockwork Orange*, his eyelids propped open with toothpicks as he watches scene after scene of unimaginable violence. We were being conditioned not to hang up pictures of half-naked women or call people gooks or make fun of Martin Luther King. I kept waiting for something I didn't know.

But whoa, back in the newsroom! People grumbled furiously about the sessions, and they always seemed to want to grumble to me. As if I had something to do with it.

"But don't you see, as reporters we're supposed to focus on the truth, whether or not that hurts somebody's feelings," a guy named James said to me. "If we start tiptoeing around this group or that group, we're in trouble. Don't you see?"

I did see. And I saw the need for my approval in his eyes. This was a man I barely knew; he covered real estate and sat on the other side of the room, but here he was, searching me out, trying to get me to voice agreement. It would have been funny if it weren't so tiresome; there were a lot of white people to absolve and only a few of us. And they never went to Melvia. That left, on the metro desk in the main newsroom, pretty much Georgia and me.

.   .   .

One day in the middle of all this Rob called me into his office. I was nervous, because the managing editor didn't want to talk to you unless it was something important. Normally I dealt with one of the assistant metro editors or, at the most, Jack, the metro editor himself.

"Well, Hope!" Rob came grinning toward me as soon as I stepped in the door. "You're off to a great start."

He gestured toward the couch, and I took a seat. "All the editors are very pleased with your work," he said.

"Glad to hear it."

"In fact, we think it's time we took you off general assignment and gave you a beat, something you can sink your teeth into," he said. "How would you like to cover North Philadelphia?"

I was surprised. I'd been at the paper only a couple of months, and when I first began, everyone had warned me I'd probably be stuck on general assignment for at least a year.

"It's a great beat, lots of interesting stories," Rob was saying. "We haven't had anyone on it for a while, and we think you're just the right person to get us back on the ground up there."

"Why hasn't there been anyone on the beat?" I asked.

Rob relaxed into his seat and crossed his legs, staring up pensively at the watercolor of a rower behind my head. He was a pretty good-looking man for a whiteboy in his fifties, with blue eyes, black hair going gray at the sides. Word was that he could charm a pig out of a poke when he wanted. I wasn't sure if this was charm he was unleashing on me, and whether I should resist it if it was.

"We haven't found the right person," he said. "Not everyone can cover a neighborhood beat. It's not like City Hall or education, where the stories are obvious. You have to be more of a writer to do this job, to express the soul of a neighborhood, to explain how it works and why or why not. What do you think?"

I knew this probably had something to do with all the affirmative action going on, but still it sounded like a good beat. I couldn't think of any reason not to take it.

"Thanks, Rob," I said. "I'd love to."

I didn't know much about North Philadelphia yet, and that didn't make me unusual. It was possible to live an entire life in Philadelphia without once venturing north of Spring Garden Street. A lot of people did it, frightened off by the perception that North Philly was some kind of black Wild West, lawless and ruinous, streets out of control. That was exaggerated, but it was true that there was very little reason for an outsider to ever go to North Philadelphia. Very little reason at all.

There was Temple University, and the Temple hospital, and if you knew where to look, a handful of places like Miss Ethel's, greasy dives with good food and good people, where you could smack your lips and relax your command of standard English without fear. But even Miss Ethel's food couldn't offset the curtain of graffiti that covered every building. She couldn't offset the bombed-out houses and the dirty streets and the sheer deterioration of it all. That's what got me about North Philadelphia, how old and decrepit everything was. Used up and left to rot, like a car rusting at the dump.

But the beat got me up there, and that was good, because part of me felt like I needed to go, should go. Like it was my home, although of course it wasn't. Like ignoring it was turning my back on something central to myself. Guilt. And I recognized Memphis in North Philadelphia, in bits and pieces. The smell of fried chicken on the corner. The old women hobbling home in the summer heat. The plump church ladies in white and the old men in hats, always in hats, waiting for the bus. Most of all I recognized resignation when I saw it. And I saw it a lot in North Philly.

I spent a lot of my time at first trying to ingratiate myself with the regulars. One day someone told me about a man named Joe

Jackson, who kept turning vacant lots in his neighborhood into community gardens. He fought rats, crack addicts, and sometimes the city bureaucracy to do it, but he did it. I called him up.

"Mr. Jackson, my name is Hope Robinson. I'm going to be covering North Philadelphia for the *Record*, and I was wondering if I could come up and spend an afternoon with you to talk about your neighborhood and your gardens?"

He hesitated. Then: "I don't believe I care to do so. No."

"May I ask why not?"

"I used to take the *Record*, but I quit because it seemed that the only time you saw somebody black in the paper was when they done robbed somebody or shot somebody or done something wrong."

"I understand. But when did you quit taking the paper, sir?"

"That paper never had nothing good to say about black people," he went on, getting warmed up now. "And it sure never had nothing good to say about North Philadelphia. And even when we finally got us a black mayor, the paper was always picking on him, trying to pin this mess or that mess on him, trying to bring him down. Got so I couldn't stand reading it no more, so I quit."

"I understand, but—"

"I ain't got time to contribute to none of that mess," he said.

"But that's just what I'm trying to change, Mr. Jackson," I said. "I want to do stories that show the other side of North Philadelphia. Stories about people like you, trying to do something good."

Mr. Jackson chuckled. "Young lady, I'm seventy-three years old. I'm not saying nothing against you, because I don't know you. But I've lived in this city all my life, and I know the *Record*. They don't mean no good. Not to nobody black."

"I'm black, Mr. Jackson."

He chuckled again and I felt like a fool. "Darling, I know that. Why you think I'm trying to tell you the truth?"

I had a lot of those conversations. Distrust of the media was an article of faith among black people, no matter where they lived. Same thing back in Greenville. Folks hated the *Morning News*, complained that the paper portrayed all black people as criminals and thugs, while ignoring the positive aspects of the black community. Which of course meant that I, by being there, was somehow conspiring with the white man to sell out my people. I used to get that all the time in Greenville. At first it hurt. Really hurt. But you have to get over stuff like that. Get over it or let it drive you mad.

A lot of times, if I could get to people face-to-face, they'd give me a chance. Especially older people. Mr. Jackson notwithstanding, many older people seemed to give me credit for just being there.

"Honey, I worked up at Children's Hospital for forty-five years," one woman said to me. "I know how it is. It's still their business; you just work there."

We were standing outside a church, having both just come from a community meeting on starting up a basketball clinic for boys. Although it was Wednesday evening, the woman was dressed to the Sunday nines, in a red suit with matching pumps. Her face was powdered with makeup two shades lighter than her skin—I could tell because a spot near her earlobe had worn clean.

"You just do the best you can," she said, pulling me close for a hug. These black women, with their fleshy cinnamon arms, trying to encircle the world. She smelled of layers and layers of matching soap and skin lotion and cologne. "We're so proud of you!"

Proud. A strange and terrifying word.

Sometimes, walking the streets of North Philadelphia, I felt like a spy; only I wasn't a very good spy. I didn't really fit in, didn't speak the language. My black English was southern black English, softer, rounder, more liquid than the hard urban slang of the Northeast. And there wasn't much left of it anyway. What my mother had not drummed out, Astor had neatly excised with the scalpel of embarrassment. My only true cover was my skin. If I kept quiet most times, it worked. Finding myself along some broken block of row homes in the butter-yellow light of early summer, I'd affect a neighborhood casualness. I met eyes, but not for too long. I strolled with a purpose, but not with fear. I exuded comfort but vigilance and—surprise!—I blended in. I would park my car and walk invisible among the residents, a ghost creeping along the shattered sidewalks, silent and observant, while some braided little girl whirred down the street on her bicycle, shouting to her friends, "Hey! Hey! Hey!"

But sometimes my cover slipped, and most often it was women who found me out. Young boys were too busy thumping their chests; older men could be thrown off the scent with a smile or a flipped finger, if it came to that. Just some acknowledgment of the dick swinging between their legs, and the men were happy. But the women were much harder to fool. They sat on their porches, hopeless and hostile, and sniffed me out the way a dog sniffs out a rat.

One day I was scheduled to interview a pastor and some of his congregation for a story on how cutbacks in city funding were affecting their work with homeless families. It had rained all morning, then stopped; the air was moist and dense. I turned the corner onto a block of matchbox wooden row homes. The church, I believed, was at the end of the block. But before I could get there, I heard a woman yelling. At first I thought she had been hurt, and my heart pounded, but then I realized she wasn't in pain. She was mad.

"Get outta here before I come down there and kick your ass!"

I stopped, looking up toward the sound. A young woman, a

girl, really, no more than seventeen, glared down at me from a second-floor window. From what I could see, she was thin, the mean, stringy kind of thin, with little muscles bulging just beneath the skin of her upper arms. I could see her upper arms because she held a baby on her shoulder, like a sack of potatoes. Beneath her, the porch roof tilted crazily toward the right.

I scanned the block for antagonists. Nobody there but me.

Maybe she mistook me for someone else. "Are you talking to me?" The question seemed to infuriate her. She shifted the baby to her other shoulder and leaned so far out the window I was afraid she would drop it.

"I said, 'Move, bitch!'" she yelled, her voice increasing in volume with every word. "Get off my street before I come down there and whip your ass!"

Thoughts bounced around my head; I couldn't figure out what was going on. One minute I was walking down the street minding my own business, and the next minute some woman was leaning out a window, shrieking at me to get off her street! As if she owned it. I looked around again. There were good blocks and bad blocks in North Philadelphia: blocks where fresh paint covered every porch rail and impatiens bloomed in window boxes, and blocks where every other house sat shut-eyed and boarded, shrouded in graffiti. This was one of the good ones.

"What the hell is your problem!" I liked the harsh, dangerous tone of my voice. What instinctual animals we still were, we human beings! When attacked, we defended ourselves, fought back. My heart pounded, and I felt a trickle of sweat collect on my back. "I didn't do nothing to you!" I yelled, the voice and the language not my own.

"Bitch!" she shrieked, and disappeared from the window, presumably to come downstairs and kick my ass. Okay. Fine. She wanted it; I was ready. I stood there, trying to slow my heart, until someone drove up behind me. Then the thump of a closing car door spun me out of my daze, and suddenly I woke up. What was I doing? I was going to stand here and wait to get into a fight with some crazy girl? Over what? I saw these girls all over North Philadelphia, these tough, hardened children battling furiously against all the things they did not understand. Sometimes just looking at them scared me; it was easy to forget just how young they really were, hard to equate them with the way I was at their age. They fought each other on street corners after school, and not the rolling-in-the-dirt fights we used to have. Once, as I was walking back to my car, I saw a crowd of teenagers gathered outside a convenience store. The owner, who was Indian, ran out and pulled down his shutters as the crowd thickened. I walked over, trying to see what was going on. Inside the hot little circle two girls were slashing each other across the face with box cutters. My yells to stop were drowned out by the cheers of the crowd. And when two friends of one of the girls tried to stop the fight, they were held back by a knot of exhilarated onlookers, boys and girls.

And now this girl was on her way outside with a box cutter or a gun, and even if I was the wrong person, she was angry now, and I'd be dead on the sidewalk and she'd be rotting in some jail before she even began to understand what she was so mad about.

"You all right, sister?"

The man from the car stood before me, peering into my face. "You lost or something?"

"I'm fine, thanks." I turned to walk away. Behind me, a screen door slammed. The girl had made it to her porch.

"You better keep walking, bitch!" she screamed. All the anger in her young voice trailed me down the street.

At the church, nine smiling old people brushed aside my apologies for being late. Twenty minutes, half an hour . . . they'd been there all morning, and they would be there all afternoon. They were long past the time when rushing around seemed important, they said. They had all the time in the world.

A few weeks after that incident, I met Malcolm. Malcolm Blackwell. We met at a press conference, also in North Philly, called by this group of ministers who wanted to start a tough-love mentoring program for boys in trouble with the law. I wanted to meet the ministers for future reference, not because I expected to get an immediate story. People call press conferences for all sorts of things—to announce that their dogs won a ribbon, to tell the world that their company hung on for another year. This program wasn't in that category; it was just too young to write about yet. You have to weed things out.

I drove up Broad Street past the yellow check-cashing signs, past the towering, intricate hotel built by Father Divine. Near the university, a white woman and her daughter struggled to load a box into the back of a Volvo station wagon. Temple had a surprising number of white students, given its location.

Every few blocks or so, I passed a bus stop where a crowd waited in the heat. Only the poor took public transportation in Philadelphia. Anyone with enough money for a car, no matter how rusted, how ancient, how taped together, avoided the stinking subways and the lumbering buses, which doubled your transportation time anywhere. I drove past a dozen overpriced minimarkets and a hundred fast-food joints, past piles of rotting garbage as well as stoically tended blocks. Traffic crawled. At a light, I watched a man in neat blue sweats and a black baseball cap tilt back his head to receive the last drops of beer from a can. He walked toward a gated alleyway and slipped the can through the iron bars as if depositing it in a recycling bin. An old mattress stood silent sentry as he marched on.

The church sat right on Broad, just north of the hospital. I turned left onto Venango, searching for a parking spot, but the streets were lined with the cars of hospital workers and visitors. I found a spot three blocks away, parked, and headed back toward the church, guessing that the press conference would take place in the new building. The original church sat on the east side of Broad

Street, a graceful Gothic building with arched doorways and stained-glass windows and a bell tower reaching up into the sky. The new building was modern and angular, all slants and hard lines, as if even the church had to toughen up to deal with sinners in these times. Right in front stood a forty-foot gray steel cross.

A woman in white directed me along a hallway and into a large conference room, where biblical verses lined the walls. Two young women stood in the corner, whispering and giggling, one with a small video camera perched on her shoulder. Students from the Temple communications department.

At a table in the middle of the room sat Samuel Carver, a *Daily News* reporter, whom I had met before. He and his photographer were the only white people in sight, the only whites I had seen since crossing Spring Garden Street. Their skin seemed to glow in the dim light. They were snickering when I walked in; seeing me, they stopped.

"Hope. Hi," Sam said.

"Hi, Sam. How did they get you up here for this?"

"They wouldn't tell me what it was about. Do *you* know?"

I laughed. No way would Sam have wasted his time on the announcement of yet another social service program, no matter how well intended. Obviously the folks setting up the press conference knew it.

"I have no idea, but I think it's pretty important."

Sam grunted. He knew I was lying, and he suspected that whatever was up was not really important. But he was just mean enough and just scared enough of getting scooped to stick around.

A stout man in a dark suit approached the head of the table. Sam glanced at me, reached into his pocket, and pulled out a notebook and pen. But the man waved his hand and shook his head. Although it was cool in the room, his forehead glistened; he dabbed at it delicately with a folded white handkerchief.

"No, no. Only wanted to tell you the press conference would begin a little late. All of the ministers have not yet arrived." He nodded and left. Sam smacked his notebook onto the table and rolled his eyes.

"Oh, for goodness' sake! It's already four-fifteen, and he's saying it's going to start a little late! Tell me something I don't know."

Sam looked to me for confirmation, but I only smiled. I had grown up in a church just like that one, with a minister like the dignified man who had just left the room. As far as I was concerned, they still had forty-five minutes to kill.

I pulled the day's crossword puzzle out of my bag. Sam and his photographer were still griping and trying to decide whether to risk leaving or not, when a guy sauntered into the room carrying two large black tape recorders and a camera.

"Well, well," he said, grinning at Sam. "Representatives of the mighty media empire ascend into our neighborhood! We are honored."

The first thing I noticed about Malcolm was his eyes. They were hazel and so light they seemed almost transparent. He was short—any man under six feet is short, as far as I'm concerned—but cute, standing there in his black jeans, black T-shirt, and brown jacket, a kente-cloth stole around his neck. His skin was the color of butterscotch Jell-O.

"Go to hell, Blackwell." Sam seemed irritated by this guy's presence, which intrigued me.

"Samuel! This is a church!" I pretended to be shocked. In fact, I was, a little. No black person I knew would curse in a church. Not without ducking his head.

Malcolm turned to me and smiled.

"Guess his mama didn't raise him right," he said in his best outraged-black-mama accent, which sounded the same in North Philly as it did in the streets of Memphis. I dropped in there with him, slowing my words until my grandmother's voice came dripping out of my mouth.

"It's a shame before God!" I shook my head. "Boy ain't got no home training a-tall. You bets to be careful there, Samuel. God don't like ugly."

Malcolm and I laughed. Sam started to mutter something, but just then the dignified man came through the door followed by eight other black men, some in religious collars, most in dark suits, all of them as sober as rain.

It was a good idea, to set up a mentoring program for first offenders. Using volunteers from their churches and the neighborhood the men would take the boys out to a camp in the burbs weekends and summers and spend time with them, showing love and discipline, teaching them how to fish and chop wood and fix cars, and holding sessions about love and sex and responsibility and self-respect. They were going to try to get the family court to force kids to do it as a condition of their probation. I hoped it would materialize, but just as I had thought, the program was in too early a stage to write about. Dozens of well-intentioned programs were developed every day, but most of them had the life span of a butterfly.

After the press conference, I shook the ministers' hands and distributed my card and tried to slow my exit to match that of Malcolm. But he was absorbed in interviewing the head minister, and from his questions and the glowing look of pleasure on the minister's face as he thundered on, I could tell the whole thing would take some time. Malcolm, I learned from Sam, worked for two black radio stations as well as the *Philadelphia Herald*, the eternally struggling black newspaper. According to Sam, Malcolm was a black nationalist in thin disguise, an angry young man with an agenda and not even a pretense of objectivity in the stories he wrote.

"He's always showing up, asking stupid questions, and dragging things out," Sam groused. "He's a pest."

"I thought asking questions was our job." For some reason, toying with Sam gave me pleasure.

"He's no journalist! He's a loser." Sam dismissed Malcolm with a nod and a grunt. What he really wanted to talk about was a story about some irregularities in the Democratic ward leader's spending account. Sam was afraid I was going to scoop him.

"So what you got on the commissioner, eh? Heard you were digging around his office the other day." Sam tried to sound casual.

We stood on the church steps. I had pushed us outside when Sam dug into the pocket of his dirty slacks and fished out a crushed pack of cigarettes. It was after five, but still the sun sat buttery and warm in the sky.

"Who?"

"Aw, don't give me a hard time. You know what I mean."

"Why, Samuel, I have no idea," I said in my best Scarlett O'Hara voice. "Must run, darling."

I was headed down the steps when the door opened. There was Malcolm, punching through the door, tape recorders strapped like ammunition belts across his chest. He was grinning.

"Well, Master Sam," Malcolm said. "Attempting to collude with the competition. Not very energetic of you."

"Screw you, Blackwell." Sam dropped his cigarette onto the ground and headed off. Malcolm stepped on the stub, then picked it up and placed it in his pocket.

"Malcolm Blackwell," he said, sticking out his hand.

"Hope Robinson." Malcolm's hand was dry and warm.

"You doing a story?"

"On this? Nah. You?"

"Of course. You should too."

I looked at him to see if he was kidding. He wasn't. "You don't write stories about programs that haven't even begun yet."

"You do if you're trying to build up your community instead of tear it down."

"I'm trying to do my job. Maybe after the program is up and running."

"It might not get up if it doesn't get enough support. Publicity brings support."

"I'm not a publicist. I'm a journalist."

"A black journalist."

"Or a journalist who is black."

"Those aren't the same thing," he said, smiling slyly at me. "Not the same thing at all."

I hoped Malcolm would ask for my phone number, but he didn't. Obviously I wasn't his idea of what a black woman should be. We parted with a handshake, and I headed back to work, an image of Malcolm's smile stuck in my mind along with his words. Not the same thing at all.

chapter SIX

Sunday morning, lying in bed, too hot and sticky to get up. When I moved into my apartment back in April air-conditioning hadn't seemed like a major concern. A big mistake.

The phone rang. I reached over to the nightstand and picked up the receiver and something about the quality of the silence in the half second before she spoke told me who it was.

"Oh, no. Did I wake you?" my mother asked, her voice more disappointed than sorry.

I glanced at the clock: nearly ten. My mother would have been up for hours. She was probably getting dressed for church, which is what I should have been doing instead of lolling about in bed.

"No. I'm up. I was getting ready to go out," I lied.

"Well, I won't hold you."

"You just called, Mom. I'm not in a hurry. How are you?"

"I'm fine. Fine and blessed. The weather is beautiful here. What ya'll getting?"

My mother couldn't abide cold weather. If the temperature in Memphis dropped below forty degrees, she'd wrap a blanket around her shoulders and refuse to go out. She always worried that I was snowed in and starving to death in my apartment, way up North. If it was this warm in Philadelphia, I knew it would be sweltering in muggy Memphis, but the hotter the better as far as she was concerned.

"It's very nice. A beautiful day. Probably already eighty outside."

"That's good. I just called to check on you. Hadn't heard from you for a while."

That was true. I had gotten bad about calling my mother. At Astor I called her once a week, without fail, sometimes just to say "Hi! I'm fine!" and hang up quick, because I was calling collect and she couldn't afford exorbitant long-distance bills. And I went home whenever I could. But that stopped in college, and it never really got started again; I told myself it was because I was too busy getting my life set up. That's what my mother wanted. She knew how it was when you were young and still striving. She would understand.

"I'm fine. I've been busy, working hard."

"How's the new job?" My mother still couldn't understand why I had chosen to become a reporter. She liked newspapers; she always found money to subscribe to one. My mother thought that reading the paper made you smarter, proved that you were educated. But she certainly didn't mean for me to waste a college education, not to mention those years at Astor, being a reporter. I was supposed to have gone on to medical school or at least law school, and every time she asked about my job I felt the weight of disappointment in her voice.

"It's fine. It's a really good paper, very well respected. They gave me a beat already. Usually you have to wait a year or so before they give you a beat."

"Hmm?" she said, not listening. "And how are other things?"

By other things she meant men, as in: Haven't you met anyone to marry yet? That was my mother's big concern, that I was still single and not even seriously involved. She was so anxious about it that she'd started giving out my phone number at her church. Strangers would call me up long-distance and want to talk about their ex-wives. Instead of answering my mother, I started whistling, as if distracted.

"Hope!"

"Hmm? Oh, I'm sorry. What were we talking about?"

"Nothing," my mother said. She'd gotten the message. "You shouldn't do that, you know. Whistle. A whistling woman and a crowing hen will surely come to no good end." It was another one of her sayings.

"I know, I know. You used to say that all the time. I have no idea what it means."

"It means men are men and women are women. It means don't try to be what you're not."

"Right." Whatever. I changed the subject. "How's Faith?"

"Spoke to her last night. Harold's been staying out late at night and coming home drunk. She thinks he might be cheating on her."

"*Might* be?"

I had never met Harold, though he and my sister had been living together for a couple of years. Still, from the descriptions of him I got from my mother and from knowing the long line of losers that had preceded him in Faith's life, I could pretty much sum Harold up. He would be good looking, with the oily charm of a snake and enough sense to recognize that Faith thought little to nothing about herself. He'd be snaky enough to take advantage of her low self-esteem. He wouldn't work any more than was necessary, but he'd always have some game running, like selling home water purifiers, or be getting ready to open a black laundromat. He'd call himself a businessman, an entrepreneur, but what he'd really be was a hustler, a dog, and most certainly a cheat.

"I'm two thousand miles away and I can tell you he's cheating on her. Why doesn't Faith just kick him out? It's not like he contributes much to the household."

"It's not that easy, Hope."

"Why not?"

Even though Harold lived with Faith and her kids, Faith, as I understood it, was still pretty much living on welfare. She had done so for the past ten years or so, since she got tired of living with my aunt in Sacramento and ran off to Las Vegas with a pre-Harold. She'd been off, once, for nearly a year, while living with a blackjack dealer who had promised to marry her and adopt her kids. But the dealer ended up running away one Saturday morning, leaving Faith with a host of credit card bills.

"Faith can't live alone. She needs somebody. Some women do, you know."

"Everybody needs somebody," I said, sidestepping the personal jab. I was getting irritated now, because I could tell my mother was about to embark on one of her any-port-in-a-storm crusades.

"But this jerk is not somebody! He doesn't help her. He's nobody."

"He's something. Sometimes something is better than nothing."

"That's ridiculous! Why would you tell your daughter that?"

"She's running her own life."

"Yeah, but you're supporting it when you talk like that! She knows how you feel, and she never makes a move without calling you up."

"You're too young to understand."

"I hope I never get that old."

"Oh, don't say that!" My mother believed that if I lived long enough, my youthful follies—made worse by my being around white people too much—would fall away and I'd come to realize, in spite of her example, that a woman needed a man, if it could be managed. "Someday you'll figure out what's important in life, and it ain't what you think it is now, believe me. It'll happen when you have your own kids."

"What if I don't have kids?" I wasn't sure whether I ever wanted kids or not, but I couldn't help teasing her. "What if I don't want the little screaming brats?"

"You will," she said, then changed the subject. "When are you coming home?"

She asked the same question every time we spoke. My trips home were as infrequent as snow in Memphis. I thought back and realized that I'd last gone home nearly a year before.

"Maybe for Thanksgiving. Or Christmas."

"Charity's coming in August. The Prices are giving me a week off. Be nice if you could come too."

The Prices were the old white couple my mother had been employed by for twenty years. They seemed to believe giving her a week off now and then was an act of almost saintly generosity.

"We'll see," I said.

"Have you talked to Charity lately? You should call her. She's up there in Washington; ya'll could see each other sometimes."

"Washington is two hours away. It's not like she's down the street. Shouldn't you be getting to church?"

"Lord, yes. Look at the time. Okay then, Hope. Mama loves you."

"I love you too. Talk to you soon."

After I hung up, I thought about calling Faith, telling her not to listen to Mom, to kick Harold out and try to make it on her own. But it would be awkward, and why would she listen to me? We lived in two entirely different worlds. It amazed me that

Faith told my mother so much about her life—not only because I would never dream of doing so, but because I couldn't remember when they had become so close. It was sometime when I was away at prep school, caught up in my own life, because the next thing I knew, Faith was living in Las Vegas and calling my mother twice a week. But what surprised me most was that my mother stopped criticizing Faith and began defending her. Instead of "That girl ain't got the sense God gave a turkey," it was "Well, at least she's trying" or "She's doing the best job she can." I tried not to begrudge Faith this maternal pardon, but it seemed that the more compassion she got, the less flowed my way. I rarely spoke to my mother about my problems. Once, in Greenville, I phoned her, upset about some crap that was going on at work. It was the usual stuff, nothing special, but I was looking for comfort. My mother acted as if she didn't understand what I was complaining about.

"As long as they don't put their hands on you or on your paycheck, it don't matter what they say," she said. "People always gonna talk. The world don't have to love you. It just has to leave you alone."

Thanks, Mom.

I thought then about calling my baby sister, Charity—twenty-three and beautiful and in her first year at Howard Law. The distance between Washington and Philadelphia pretty much mirrored the distance between Charity and me. Not that far, but far enough if you wanted it to be.

Charity was very busy with law school, and even when we did find time to talk we had little to discuss beyond family matters. Charity, who somehow managed to resist my mother when I could not; who stayed in Memphis, did not get pregnant, went to public school, and kicked butt. Charity, who wore her hair in dreads long before they became fashionable. What spare time she had these days was devoted to some quasi-revolutionary group attempting to sue the federal government for slavery reparations. Charity was probably too radical for Howard, but she loved it and was determined to get her law degree so she could, as she said, do some real damage to the system from inside. We were sisters and we loved each other, but we had little in common. Thinking about it, I realized that Charity and Malcolm would be perfect together. A really good sister would bring them together and step aside.

Thinking about my sisters made me think about the city where we had grown up. Memphis, Tennessee, home of Elvis and the Mississippi and other things great and wide. It was hard to remember now, but I had liked the South. It wasn't a place or a region or an attitude then; it was just home. Old hot and muggy Memphis. We had a walnut tree in the backyard and a Sears Roebuck store, and the mighty Mississippi rolled silver through downtown.

We understood that northerners were weaker people, that shoveling snow and eating stingy meals and rubbing against one another in their garbage-strewn cities made them irritable and haggard and sick. The only good thing about the North was that somewhere up there, our father lived. We felt sorry for our father, as though he had been forced to leave us and return to such a place by dire circumstances beyond his control. We knew he loved us, although we never heard from him. He was just building his strength for the day he would return.

But the South seemed strange to me when I returned to Memphis for the summer after my graduation from Astor. Things had shifted. The city seemed sluggish and thick, the air wetter—it flopped against my skin like wet leaves and clung there while I tried to brush it off. I found a summer job making salads and sweeping floors at a restaurant in downtown Memphis, a section of the city slowly dying an early death. Until I showed him my class ring the restaurant manager did not believe I had graduated from a fancy New England prep school and was off to college in the fall.

"Well, good for you, gal!" he said. "Guess you won't be raising any trouble, then, will you? We don't have no trouble here. All my folks is loyal folks."

"Et tu Brute?" I said, taking a chance.

"What's that you say?"

"It means 'Whatever you say.' In Latin." He wouldn't know the truth.

"Oh," he said. "Here's an apron. Get in the kitchen and have Myrtle show you what to do."

Every morning I rode downtown, surrounded by old women in faded housedresses and young girls with yowling babies on their hips. We sat turned away from one another, swaying sleepily in our seats with the rhythm of the bus, which seemed powered by weary sighs. People in Memphis were always tired, as though the sticky delta air had taken any energy they might have had. The bus crawled along its route, groaning to a stop every few blocks so that some prematurely old woman in thicksoled shoes and stockings two shades too light and knotted at the knees could haul herself up the steps. As she shuffled to her seat, I saw her face, limp with resignation. She was already exhausted, and the day had not yet begun.

Of course, everyone riding the bus was black. White folks in the South had the final victory with that one. "You want to sit in the front of the bus? Fine. Take the whole damn thing. We'll all get cars, and we'll let public transportation rot like tomatoes left on the vine."

Everybody sweating inside the restaurant kitchen was black too. But the people who swarmed in at lunchtime to sit at the draped tables and dab their faces with soft handkerchiefs were all white. The restaurant was a favorite among city officials, located as it was just three blocks from City Hall. We always knew when somebody important had come in for lunch, because the manager would burst into the kitchen and hover around the sizzling stovetop, dripping sweat into the pans.

"Cut that bigger!" he screamed over the din of the kitchen. "Use more butter! Take it out—it's going to burn!"

After he careened back into the dining room, someone would take a peek and announce, "It's the mayor." Or the head of the council or the sheriff or some untitled businessman who quietly ran the town. I'd peek out through the small glass window in the swinging door to get a glimpse of the big shots of Memphis. None of these people were black.

The bartender, Randolph, reminded me of my uncle Jesse. His graying hair had receded, leaving a shiny brown forehead. He wore a bow tie and a short white jacket and grinningly called all the customers "Boss." I caught glimpses of him through the swinging kitchen door. He never stopped smiling, until he came into the back, when his face collapsed under the weight of all that joviality and he stomped around the kitchen, cursing like a sailor and rolling his sallow eyes.

I worked six evenings a week, eight or nine hours a stretch. During the day, I went to the library. That was the summer I discovered black literature, something that had been overlooked at Astor and before. It was a breadmaker who turned me on to it. The breadmakers were a strange and ghostly bunch. They began work at 2 A.M. and were nearly done by the time the first lunch cooks arrived at the restaurant, around eight. The rest of the staff considered them nuts—what kind of person went to work in the middle of the night? I rarely encountered any of the breadmakers, but one morning I stopped by early to pick up a book I had left in my locker the night before. Instead of the usual soft, twangy music on the stereo in the dining room, I heard a woman singing. Her voice cut through the silence of the shuttered restaurant, high and clear, as heartachingly beautiful as trees in autumn. Leaning against the bar, I held my breath and listened. She was singing, beautifully, about fruit. Strange fruit.

It took me a while to realize what was really dangling from those trees.

I heard someone enter the dining room from the kitchen and opened my eyes. Rufus, one of the breadmakers, leaned against the doorframe with his arms crossed, staring at me. He was a huge man, with arms as thick as boards and skin like motor oil. Some of the other workers called him the African, because his skin was so dark and because he wore a shirt made of kente cloth beneath his apron and because he spoke to no one and occasionally muttered something nobody understood. People said his bread came out light as air because he beat the dough so mercilessly during kneading.

"Oh, hi. I left something here last night. Stopped by to pick it up." I turned to leave through the front door, then remembered it was probably locked. I had come in through the kitchen. Rufus blocked the doorway.

"Uh, who's that on the stereo? She's really good."

In the gray light from the window, Rufus's eyes seemed huge and unblinking. After a long minute he drawled, "That there is Lady Day," then he cocked his head as if to see what my response to this news might be. It was the first time I had ever heard him speak; his southern accent was as thick as a summer night along the Mississippi.

"Lady Day."

It took a second, but then it clicked. Billie Holiday. I had heard of her but never really heard her. My mother listened mostly to gospel music now, but when I was growing up she had filled our house with Motown music like the Temptations and Smokey Robinson. My sister Faith listened to Earth, Wind and Fire and Sly and the Family Stone and had gotten into disco, which everyone knew sucked. I liked James Taylor, Elvis Costello, and Billy Joel.

"Don't tell me you ain't never heard of Lady Day, college girl." Everyone at the restaurant called me college girl, usually with no small amount of pride. But Rufus stretched the words out, low and mean and nasty. He pushed himself up from the door-jamb and walked toward me. "What they teach you up there? Lot of white-folk mess, right? Bet you listen to country music and read Uncle Tom."

I moved away, down the bar. Rufus followed. His speech sped up, his breath squeezing out now between words.

"Bet you never read any black books, huh? Ralph Ellison. You ever heard of him?"

"Of course! Ellison!" I cried, desperately trying to remember what Ellison had written. I knew it, knew it like I knew Billie Holiday—around the edges. I moved away from the bar, into the dining room, trying not to hurry, trying to look calm. Rufus came at me slowly, like a dog deciding to attack. He smelled my fear.

"You little bitch." His voice was low, tight. "You think you better than me, don't you? But really you all messed up. Them white folks have messed your mind so bad you don't know shit. You don't even know what color you are."

"Rufus, I—"

The door from the kitchen swung open, and Randolph stepped in, headed for the bar.

"Oh." He stopped and smiled when he saw us. "Hey, Rufus. Hey, Hope. What you doing here so early?"

"Hey, Randolph!" I forced myself to walk slowly toward him, a smile pasted on my face. At his side, I reached out and touched his forearm, as sweet and solid as the ground beneath a tree you've just climbed down. "Good to see you, Randolph."

He patted my hand and moved toward the bar; He was in early to check the stock. "Working the early shift?"

"No. I—I had to get a book I left here last night," I said. "Gotta go now. See you tonight."

I went out without looking back at Rufus. That afternoon I went to the library and checked out *Invisible Man*. I read it straight through in two nights, staying up past the darkness until the birds began to chirp. Then I read Langston Hughes, James Baldwin, Eldridge Cleaver's *Soul on Ice*. I chucked my Astor summer reading list, full of Hemingway and Flaubert and James, and read up on the civil rights movement, less than twenty years old but as talked about as yesterday's trash. I went to the Lorraine Motel, where Martin Luther King, Jr., had been shot, the first time I had ever been there, and it was like coming awake from a deep and peaceful sleep. King shot right there, on that grainy concrete balcony, not two miles from where I lived. I had been, what, five at the time? It might have been a hundred years ago, for all people spoke of it. Dr. King's sad, knowing eyes looked out from every cardboard fan in church when I was a child, but his name was rarely mentioned in church, in school, at home, on the news. All I ever heard about was Elvis.

chapter seven

To help smooth over any bad feelings in the newsroom, Rob threw a party for the Fourth of July, to be held at one of the boathouses along the Schuylkill. On Saturday night I drove to Boathouse Row alone, figuring to spend an hour or so eating the shrimp, drinking the gin, and working the room, and then leave. From outside, the ten or so boathouses look like gingerbread palaces, but inside, this one was spectacularly unimpressive. There was a large room paneled in some kind of dark oak, and a hardwood floor turning gray with overuse. Two blue-and-white oars crisscrossed over the fireplace, and all around the room hung old black-and-white photographs of men—or boys—in rowing shorts and crew cuts, posed grinning along a dock. The room was dark and smelled faintly of chlorine and must. All the balloons and silver tassels suspended from the ceiling couldn't liven the place up. But there was a deck, leading off the main room and overlooking the water. I spent the first twenty minutes at the party out on the deck, standing in a corner, trying to make out the river's ripples in the soft black night.

"Penny for your thoughts."

It was David. He stood behind me, holding two bottles of beer. He held one out. "How about a brew?"

I didn't particularly like beer, but I accepted the bottle and took a swig.

"You know, you have an uncanny ability to sneak up on people. What are you, a cat?"

"Hardly. I hate cats. I'm a dog man."

"How telling," I said. "Cats too smart for you, huh?"

People had discovered the deck now. They poured out of the main room and pressed up against the railing to look across the river at the art museum, lit up like some ancient Roman temple. David moved closer. Over the sour smell of beer came a scent of something sweet. His shampoo.

"Where's Stephanie?"

"She's out of town, visiting relatives. Family situation."

"Not bad, I hope."

He shrugged. "Nothing she hasn't been through before."

Ah. I smiled like the Sphinx. If he didn't want to talk about Stephanie I wasn't going to force the subject.

"So what do you do with yourself while she's away?"

"I manage to keep busy. I actually do have a life."

"Really? Does it involve eating?" My brazenness amazed me.

"Quite frequently."

"Well, in that case we should have dinner sometime. I'd like to pick your brain. Learn exactly how one becomes an editorial writer."

"Mostly through dumb luck," he said. "But sure. How about Tuesday or Wednesday?"

I lifted a shrimp from the tray of a circulating waitress and licked the sauce off its little tail before sucking the creature into my mouth. "Tuesday it is."

But I had to break the date. A court hearing Tuesday on shutting down a homeless shelter sparked a protest, and the protest dragged on until after the sun had set and it got too cold for everyone to keep sitting on the sidewalk outside the county court building. By the time I returned to the newsroom and got the story written, edited, and out of my hair, it was nearly 10 P.M.

"We'll have to do it again," I told David over the phone. I'd called him earlier, asking if he wanted to have a late dinner; but I was exhausted.

"I understand." He sounded disappointed.

My editor bounced across the room and stuck his face two inches from my computer, reading the screen.

"How's it going?"

"Fine." The man had more energy than an electrical circuit. He found it impossible to stand still this near deadline.

"Close?"

"I'll have it to you in three minutes. Maybe two if you leave me alone."

"Okay, okay!" He skipped backward, hands up in surrender, a stupid grin stretched across his face. He loved this shit, this down-to-the-wire write-it-up-and-send-it-in crap. I hated it. I never did my best work under deadline pressure. Tom thought we should all be like Rosalind Russell and Cary Grant in *His Girl Friday*, fast-talking, slick-thinking reporters with the killer hidden away inside the rolltop desk.

"Gotta go, David. Tom's about to explode. We'll find another time."

"You bet," David said. I envisioned him in his office, surrounded by books and yellowing stacks of newspaper, sitting and waiting like a good little dog, his photograph of Stephanie turned to face the wall. "Just don't think this lets you off the hook," he said.

I laughed. With anyone else, I would not have even considered what I was considering. My mother always told me that a woman who goes after another woman's man was the worst kind of low-down dirty dog. "Men are weak, you can't blame them for playing around. But women know better," she always said. There was something powerful, though, about the idea of taking away Stephanie's boyfriend. Or just messing with him. I probably couldn't actually take him away. Probably not.

I had pretty much sworn off whiteguys after Astor, after Travis and Phil, and of course, living in the South for most of that time meant it wasn't hard. Interracial dating, especially black woman—white guy dating, was still unusual. I had white-guy acquaintances at college and later in Greenville, but not one of them would have dared ask me out. Which was fine with me.

I'd met Phil during my second semester at Astor. My transition from Memphis to prep school had not been smooth. Instead of being the smartest kid in my classes, I was now one of the dumbest, desperately behind and falling fast. English and history were still comprehensible to me, but math was like a foreign language and Latin a diabolical plot to drive me mad. Latin wasn't even required anymore; I was taking it only because my mother wanted me to.

So with all that, the first semester was so miserable that at Christmas vacation I begged my mother to let me stay home and go to school in Memphis with Charity, who had already flatly refused to go to Astor when she was old enough. Charity threatened to run away from Astor if my mother sent her there, and although that time was still years away, they were already fighting about it. So my mother didn't want to hear any noise from me.

"I can't believe you're going to let those people run you away from the best opportunity you've ever had," she said angrily.

Angry at Charity, taking it out on me. "You better go up there and learn what those whitefolks have to teach."

"But I hate it!"

"So?"

"You don't understand. It's too hard."

"What are they doing? Are they hurting you? Anybody put their hands on you, you tell me."

"No, it's not like that. But I feel . . . wrong. They make me feel wrong, and I'm failing my classes, I can't do it. I can't!"

"You have to," she said simply, turning away from my tears. I realized she just didn't care how I felt.

"We're counting on you," she said.

That was it: she was counting on me. She'd said it to Charity and me a million times after Faith left, and a million times I'd cringed and thought: Well, don't. I don't want you to, damn it. But of course I couldn't say that. She was counting on me, and I had to make it work, so back I went in January, and looked around at the ice-white winter landscape, and began trying to chip out a space in which I could live.

I had already joined Astor's fledgling black students' association. Of the thirty or so black kids on campus, about half belonged to the group, mostly poor kids like me who'd been recruited to the school on full scholarship. The other half, the wealthy black students, avoided it—and us—with casual determination. Our little band of outsiders spent most of its time sitting around in our room in the student center and holding dances on Saturday night as an alternative to the regular school party, where they played only rock. Once a year we held a dinner (usually fried chicken—I don't know why we picked that) to raise money for some black charity, and occasionally we wrote a letter to the admissions office, demanding that they recruit more black students. Especially boys. Of the fifteen people in our little group, ten were girls. Four were older boys, juniors and seniors like Kevin, who had long been claimed by the older black girls. The only available guy in our group was a five-foot-tall freshman from Cleveland, with a squeaky voice and no visible signs of having entered puberty. No one was interested in him.

After I came back to school in January I still hung out at the black students' center, but I had decided to spread out a little bit. If I was there to learn what there was to learn, I had to open myself up. I got rid of the skirts my mother had thought appropriate and bought corduroy jeans and turtleneck sweaters. I stopped listening to the Commodores and learned to like the Police. I stopped saying "ya'll" for "you" and "cut out the light" for "turn off the light." I didn't want to fit in so much as I just didn't want to stand out anymore.

Still, association with the black students' group gave me a kind of shield against the indifference of the whitegirls in my dorm, especially my roommate. For the first few weeks of school, Amy and I had actually pretended to be more than just living partners. We walked to class together and looked for each other at lunch and then sat in awkward silence. By the end of the first semester we'd given up and gone our separate ways. We saw each other only in the room at night, but I heard about her everywhere. She was wildly popular, both a jock and a cool girl, not beautiful but pretty enough. We moved in circles poles apart.

"Oh, you're Amy's roommate," was the statement I got upon meeting certain kids.

"Yeah," I answered at first. Then later, when it started getting on my nerves, I said, "No, she's mine."

She was always pleasant to me and I was pleasant to her, and whenever she found me in the room crying she asked what was wrong. But what could I say? How could I explain to the golden girl how lonely and confused and angry I was? I tried once, after I'd had a fight with my mother on the telephone. It was a bad week; I'd failed a Latin quiz and gotten confused in history and said something stupid that made everyone laugh. I called my mother in tears, still half hoping for escape. But she told me to tough it out. "Whatever doesn't kill you makes you stronger."

Back in my room, I collapsed sobbing on the bed, unable to control myself. Amy was lying on her bed, doing homework.

"Hope! What's wrong?"

"My stupid mother! I hate her, I hate her! She doesn't care about me at all!"

"Sure she does!" Amy said.

"No, she doesn't! If she did she'd let me come home, not make me stay in this horrible place, where I feel like a big, fat, stupid fool! You don't understand—she's just making me pay for my sister's mistakes. She's punishing me because Faith screwed up!"

"Wow," Amy said, dumbstruck. For a moment there was only the sound of my sniffling as I tried to calm down. "It must be tough to have a mother like that."

There was something in the way she said "a mother like that" I didn't like. Was she comparing my mother to hers? Did she think her mother was better just because she'd gone to Bryn Mawr, because she lived on Park Avenue and flew from New York to Boston once a month to have lunch with Amy and take her shopping for clothes she didn't need?

"I'm really lucky," she said. "Me and my mom get along great. But I know a lot of girls who don't."

"Yeah, well," I said, getting up from the bed.

"What was it your sister did? You said she screwed up. What did she do?"

I wiped the tears from my eyes and looked at her; she was shining with eagerness to hear the sordid details. I imagined her passing them on to her friends: "You won't believe this stuff about my roommate, the ghetto girl!"

"Nothing." I looked around for my towel and headed for the bathroom to wash my face. "She didn't do anything. Never mind."

After that night I began to believe that if I could just get away from Amy, could just get my own room, then life at Astor wouldn't be so bad. Everything about her began grating on my nerves: the way she brushed her hair a hundred strokes every night before bed and said I should do the same. The way she referred to New York as "the city" and Cape Cod, where her family had a summer home, as "the cape."

"My mother's coming up and we're going to the cape for the long weekend. Want to come?"

"Which cape? The Cape of Good Hope? Cape Canaveral? Capetown?"

"Cape Cod, of course. Wanna come?"

"Oh. No, thanks."

What really drove me nuts was the way she played that song "Amy" over and over. It wasn't even the music itself that bothered me, so much as the fact that she considered it her own song, as though the band had written it just for her. And in a way, I thought so too. Here was a girl who had all the advantages and none of the pressures, and she even had a sprightly musical accompaniment to her life. What did I have? The best I could come up with was a song my mother used to sing about having hope, but I didn't own a record of it, and anyway, who'd want to blast that through the dorm on Saturday night?

Then I met Phil, and it seemed Astor might offer me something after all. Phil was a sloe-eyed, gawky junior from England who hated the school as much as I did. His father, some rich and powerful government official, had sent him to Astor after Phil deliberately flunked out of three of the top British boarding schools. Phil's one joy was acting; we met in a drama class. When I realized how many of his off hours Phil spent in the theater, I started hanging out there too. While Phil rehearsed I worked backstage, stringing lights or building sets. After rehearsals we would sit in the empty theater and talk. Phil told me he hated Astor, and I confessed that I hated it too.

"This place is full of hypocrites," Phil said. I loved his accent;

it was exotic and cultured and thrilling. It was like all those people at Astor were pretending to be aristocrats but here was the real thing—and he liked me! It didn't much matter what Phil actually said. He could read the back of a cereal box and still sound like the most intelligent man I'd ever known.

"Americans are so shallow, so materialistic," he said. "This entire nation is built on greed and corruption. I suppose you learned that from us, just like everything else."

Phil disdained the entire concept of private education for the rich and elite, although of course he was part of that group. His father wanted him to go to law school. Phil wanted to be an actor. When I told him I wanted to be a writer—which was just something that came to me one day while I was listening to him talk—he got excited.

"Yes! You should be a writer. You will be able to reveal the corruption of this world."

Phil was eager to hear about my childhood. I slowly opened up, telling him bits and pieces, wary at first at exposing my poverty to this rich white guy. But he loved it. My history elevated me in Phil's eyes, and that was exhilarating.

"Tell me about your father. What does he do?"

"My father left us when I was little."

"Oh. How does your mother handle the expenses?"

"Well, she works. Kind of as a private nurse. In people's homes. But sometimes we had to, you know, get help. Like go on welfare."

"Yes, of course, the system would force you to do that! And then not provide sufficiently, I'm sure, all in an attempt to keep you oppressed. And yet here you are! How brave your mother must be!"

I told him about Memphis, about Beale Street (where I'd been only once or twice but which excited Phil because he loved the blues), about food stamps and canned mackerel for dinner and heating water to take a bath, and he looked at me, his eyes limpid with compassion. He said it was real, my life. And he told me I was beautiful. He was the first white person, the first boy, the first stranger, ever to do that. My heart clanged in my chest.

"I'm not!"

"Yes, you are! You're beautiful because you're so real," he said earnestly. "You're the most beautiful person in this whole bloody place."

Phil confused me—telling me I was beautiful and pecking me on the cheek when we said good night but never going further. He told me he had a girlfriend back in London—in his photograph she was a thin and ghost-pale presence with black rings around her eyes. Then he told me they'd broken up. He made fun of the pretty girls on campus, the Amy types, winning my heart. "They remind me of that vile substance Americans call beer," he said. "Watery and unsatisfying. No substance and all foam."

One night, after a conversation like that, in a kind of fit of love and desperation, I closed my eyes and hurled myself forward, kissing Phil on the lips. I could feel the surprise in his lips, which went slack and impassive. I pulled away, wanting to take it back, wanting to disappear, wanting to die.

"I . . . I'm sorry! I didn't mean . . ."

"Hope, love . . ." he stumbled. "I don't know what to say. I value your friendship so much."

"Right, right. Me too. I have to go."

I ran all the way back to my dorm room and crawled into bed, pretending to be asleep when Amy came in so she wouldn't see the puffiness around my eyes. For two weeks I avoided Phil, until one day he showed up at my dorm, looking pale and serious. At first I thought he was sick, and when I realized he was just unhappy about not seeing me, the anger and humiliation in the pit of my stomach liquefied and seeped away.

"Hope, love. You are a true friend, one of the few I have in this country," he said, filling my heart and breaking it at the same time. "What we have is special, deeper than any boyfriend-girlfriend stuff. I'd hate to lose you."

"Me too." I meant it. It hurt to know he didn't want me like that, but it would hurt more to be on the same campus and never talk. And probably part of me hoped that if we got back to where we were, if we became friends again, one of these days Phil would change his mind.

"You're a beautiful girl," he said. "I just don't . . ."

"It's okay. You don't have to explain." As we hugged, Amy came bounding down the stairs.

"Hi, roomie!" she said, then turned to Phil. "Hi, I'm Amy."

They shook hands, and a small hole opened inside me. So I wasn't surprised a week later when Amy came in and said Phil had asked her out.

"He said you guys were just friends," she said. "If that's not true, tell me."

"It's true," I said, wanting to die. "I hope you guys have a nice time. He's a really nice guy."

After the date she came back to the room giddy with happiness. I was already in bed, the covers pulled up, faking sleep, but I heard her singing to herself as she moved about the room. She sang "Hit the Road, Jack," a song she could only have learned from Phil.

Phil and I still saw each other at the theater and we still talked a little, but never about Amy. And I avoided my roommate as much as possible, studying in the library or the student center until curfew, then downstairs in the dorm common room until it was time for bed. It was spring; people were pairing up all over the place. Just make it to summer, I told myself. Just make it to summer and you won't have to see them together for a while.

But a few weeks before school was out, something happened. I walked into the room one night, and found Amy curled on her bed in tears.

"What's wrong?" The sight of Amy crying was shocking. In the months I'd known her, I'd rarely even seen her frown. A spark of hope flared inside me: Maybe it was Phil; maybe they had broken up.

"Nothing," Amy said, sniffling. "Please! Leave me alone!"

I shrugged. The next day Amy's mother showed up, her pretty face drawn and set. They packed a bag and left without saying a word to me, even though I sat in the room.

"Is Amy coming back?" I asked our dorm adviser, Ms. Pough.

"Oh, yes," she said sympathetically. "Apparently they had a death in the family. A grandmother. She'll be back in a week."

Amy did return in a week, looking tired but happy. When I told her I was sorry about her grandmother, she just smiled. When I told Phil he let out a laugh.

"It wasn't her grandmother," he said. "She had an abortion."

"What?" I was stunned. "Amy's pregnant?"

"She was. She isn't now, thank God." He laughed again and did a fake wipe of his brow. "Quite a dodge!"

I couldn't believe what I was hearing. Amy had gotten pregnant, but her life hadn't ended. It had barely even skipped a beat. One week she was pregnant, the next she wasn't and she was back at Astor, smiling like the Cheshire cat and getting ready for soccer practice. The unfairness of it made me gasp.

"Do her parents know?"

"Of course. It was her mother who found the physician. She knew just where to go, fortunately. Handled it quite well."

Phil and Amy broke up after that. I didn't know who dumped whom or if the relationship just fell apart, from boredom or from blame. Amy tore up the photograph of Phil that stood on her nightstand and found another boyfriend before school was out.

The last words Phil said to me, right before he went home to England, were, "I should have listened to my own advice about American girls." I wrote four letters to him over the summer but got no response. Then I came back in the fall and Amy came back in the fall, but Phil didn't. It cost extra money and I had to get two work-study jobs, but I made sure I had my own room.

chapter
eight

Life was rocky on my new beat. I kept coming up with story ideas and Tom, my editor, kept shooting them down, saying they were impractical or not newsworthy or too complicated. By the same token, I considered his ideas trite and passé. Which left us with a little bit of a hitch.

For example: I wanted to write a story about poverty, about the inconvenience of being poor and the slack-jawed patience it took to live that way. My idea was to use lines. There were lines of people everywhere in North Philadelphia—lines snaking out of welfare offices and curled around the unemployment place, lines forming at check-cashing stores that charged ten percent per transaction. Poor people probably spent a third of their lives waiting in line, and my idea was to show that for the poor, patience wasn't a virtue, it was an economic necessity and a way of life. You get accustomed to moving slowly and you forget the value of efficiency, because hey, why rush? Even if you get there on time, somebody will make you wait. You wait for the bus, you wait to see the doctor at the free clinic, you wait in line with a thousand other people when a factory opens, only to be told they ran out of jobs.

The idea came to me one day on the way home from work as I stopped by a supermarket on Broad Street to pick up a few salad fixings for dinner. Inside the store, a sickly yellow light glowed down on the vegetable section, giving the anemic to-matoes an orange tint. There was no romaine lettuce, no mush-rooms, no sweet onions. The cucumbers sat shriveled in a pile. Still, I was tired and hungry, and I might have scraped together a few edible veggies had I not glanced over at the checkout counters. Two cashiers, moving at the speed of molasses, headed up lines that stretched across the front of the store, down the aisles and halfway back to the meat section. It was the first of the month, the welfare checks had been mailed, and yet some idiot of a manager decided to put only two cashiers on the af-ternoon shift. But what was more amazing was the way the peo-ple in line accepted the situation, their faces as blank as a chalkboard that's just been erased. Not one person tapped her foot or muttered angrily, as people would have at a suburban store. Instead the women—and they were mostly women—pushed their carts into line and settled down numbly to wait. The only thing that stirred them was a shriek from one of their kids.

But not me. There was no way I was cooling my heels in that line. I dumped my vegetables, left, and drove to a supermarket in an affluent neighborhood just over the city line. I picked up a few organically grown tomatoes and fresh basil for my salad and was through one of eight checkout lines and out the door in ten minutes. I had the car and the option.

I got very excited about my idea, but when I told Tom, he screwed up his face like a three-year-old.

"I don't know," he said. "Sounds pretty complicated. How would you frame it?"

"I'm not sure. I'd have to find the right person to hang the story on."

"Sounds too hard. Maybe you should do something else." He glanced across the newsroom. The metro editor and three reporters stood clustered together, laughing about something. Tom began shuffling his feet, eager to go play with the boys.

"I could probably figure it out, and I think it'd be worth it," I said. "But I'm going to need some time to do it."

"Sure, sure." He stood up. "Take some time. But while you're at it, go up to Strawberry Mansion and look into this murder they had last night. Might be gang-related. Try to find the mother. Good stuff. Could go A-one."

He scurried over to join the group.

That's the way it went. Tom wanted bang-'em-up stories, drugs and death in the Black Badlands, teenagers gone wrong, women selling their six-month-old babies for crack. Like any reporter in the business more than two years, I'd done my share of those stories. They were very dramatic. They'd seemed quite compelling to me at first, and my colleagues all clucked their tongues and patted me on the back, and once or twice I even won an award of some kind. But after a while those stories began to depress me, because while true, they distorted the larger picture. And because after I'd written them and spilled someone's wretched life onto the page for public consumption, nothing substantial would change. People's attention drifted away after a few days, and the only thing that happened was that white people were confirmed in their belief that the black part of town was a godless and dangerous place. Tom kept pushing, telling me this was reality, but I dug in my heels. Reality or not, I didn't want to write those stories anymore.

Every once in a while during my travels through North Philadelphia, I'd run into Malcolm, who seemed to get better and better looking as the summer progressed. The sun darkened his pinewood-colored skin and gave him a glow. I wondered if he tanned deliberately. When we met, Malcolm would smile slyly and ask what I was doing. If it was a "good" story, like one about a little girl from an amazingly dysfunctional home who was nevertheless an honor student at school, he'd shake my hand.

"Now, that's the way to write," Malcolm said. "We need to use our talents to build up our people. I don't know how you got that story past the man, but I'm impressed."

But if it was a "bad" story, a story that showed someone black in a less than flattering light, Malcolm would turn his thin lips down in disappointment and give me grief.

"Now, sister." He called me sister only when he wanted to prick me. "Why you want to write that trash? That's what they want you to do."

I was attracted to Malcolm, but he made me uncomfortable. I got flustered whenever I'd walk into a room and see him standing there, his microphone stuck in somebody's face, him talking as much as the person he was interviewing. If I'd written something he approved of, or not written anything at all lately, Malcolm would smile like he was happy to see me and turn on the charm and melt my uncomfortableness away. He asked me about growing up in the South. His mother was from Mississippi, but he had never been farther than Washington, D.C. We talked about how much we both liked old Bill Cosby albums and vintage TV shows like *The Mod Squad*. We both loved James Baldwin; Malcolm was always rereading him, and I liked that. Not many men I knew still read, let alone reread, great novels. It was like he was trying to get at the heart of what Baldwin was saying. If he just read it enough times, some greater truth would pop out.

Which just made it harder and harder to deal with his lecturing.

"Give me a break, X." I called him X when I got mad.

"I'm just trying to make you see that we can't afford to waste good people like you, working for *them*. We need your talents up here." He spread out his hands, indicating not the crowded little row home in which we sat but all North Philadelphia. The house was sweltering. Its sole occupant for the past fifty years had died the day before from heat exhaustion, because she was afraid to open her windows.

"Like this. This is a story not of one old woman afraid of her own sons and daughters, but of the failure of the system to provide for both her and them."

"That's a good point, Malcolm. I'll work it in."

"Working it in isn't enough, big eyes." He smiled, and I started to feel a little shaky. "You know that. You know it inside."

It was hard to figure out whether Malcolm liked me or not, and whether I cared.

The summer dragged on. Editors and reporters disappeared on vacation for two weeks, then reappeared, tanned and disgruntled. It was easier to get my stories in the paper because so few people were around.

Stephanie came back from her time off looking haggard, or as haggard as I had ever seen her look. She still dressed impeccably, and she still sauntered around the newsroom as if it were her backyard deck. But something was missing. Her hair seemed a shade darker, like someone had dimmed it with a switch.

She kept asking me to lunch, asking and asking as though we were somehow friends, which struck me as strange. I put her off, not being able to imagine anything I wanted less, until finally I ran out of excuses and decided to just go and get it over with. Maybe this was some kind of initiation rite among white people—take the black person out to lunch. I had gotten a flurry of invitations after the first few months at the paper, as if, once assured that I was not going to disappear, the natives decided to make friends. I accepted a few, rejected most, and eventually they dwindled off. Now here was Stephanie. We went to a little café off Callowhill Street and sat at a table in the window. The scorching sun lit Stephanie's milky skin like a lamp. She seemed never to tan. But she was perky. Perky, perky girl.

"So how are you settling in?" she asked.

"I'm as settled as a can of paint."

I didn't know why I said that. I was never one of those southerners who engaged in cute aphorisms. Stephanie laughed.

"Do you like it?"

"It's fine." Like I was going to share anything substantial with this chick.

"It can be a hard place," Stephanie said. "Sometimes you feel like everyone's watching. Waiting for you to fail."

The waitress brought us our food—Stephanie a chef salad, dressing on the side, me the grilled chicken salad with mango salsa. She ate the whole thing, eggs, ham strips, turkey, all of it, and three wheat rolls from the bread basket they brought. So, not one of those anorexic whitegirls. Nor did she go running to the bathroom after we finished. Apparently she maintained that figure on willpower alone, or else she exercised like hell.

"Everybody thinks you're very talented," she said. I smiled. My mother told me that when people start flattering you, check your wallet.

"Tom, Jason, all the editors. David says you're one of the best hires they've made in a long time."

"How nice."

"I think so too." Then, after an awkward pause: "I really admire your toughness. Your independence."

"Well, thanks."

"I could use a friend like that." Stephanie looked up from her salad, turning her face to me as if it were the sun. She wore diamond stud earrings as big as the pimple forming on my chin. What was this? I felt like I was back in third grade, choosing up friends for the week. "She's my friend!" "No, she's mine!" What kind of adult asked another adult to be her friend? What was I supposed to say: Honey, I wouldn't be your friend if we were the last two people on earth? We have nothing in common. You're a pretty little whitegirl who owns the world and I'm not.

"I'm sure you have plenty of friends, Stephanie," I said, deciding to be nice. "You seem quite popular."

She smiled.

"Yeah, usually I get along well with people." She tugged at the sleeve of her blouse. "But things aren't always what they seem. . . ."

We were done with our food. I signaled the waitress for a check. Whatever petty confession Stephanie had been about to make—some black girl in third grade didn't like her, she had once been kicked out of Kappa Kappa Mu, whatever—I didn't want to hear it.

"Well, my mother used to say, 'Whatever doesn't kill you makes you stronger.' She used to tell us that all the time as kids."

The waitress was taking forever. Stephanie frowned.

"Really? That seems like a harsh thing to tell a child."

I looked at her. "Nice earrings," I said.

"Oh, thanks," she said. "David gave them to me."

"How sweet."

We paid the check and stepped out into the blistering heat and went back to work. That afternoon I called David and invited him to dinner. He hesitated not.

D avid and I were scheduled to get together Monday night.
On Sunday I went in to the *Record* to work. George, one of
the guards, sat at the front desk in his gray uniform and a
sweater, hands clasped across his lap. The sweet thumping beat
of a gospel choir in full throttle poured from a radio at his side.
A biblical passage swam up inside my head from the forced Sunday mornings of my childhood: Train up a child in the way he
should go, and when he is old he shall not depart from it. I guess
that was true, in a way. I certainly remembered a lot of passages
from the Bible. On the other hand, when was the last time I had
been to church?

"Morning, George. How you doing today?"

He smiled at me beneath his graying mustache.

"I'm claiming blessed," he said. "How 'bout you, Hope?"

"Can't complain," I said. Then, because he seemed to expect it and it was beyond me to disappoint these old church black folks, "The Lord is good."

"Yes, He is."

"Good choir you're listening to there."

"That's my choir, the choir at my church, Bethel A.M.E. I'd be there right now if I didn't have to work. You ought to come on over next Sunday. We're having women's day."

"Thanks. I'll try."

The elevator door closed, shutting off George and his music. We both knew I was never coming to his church. Or maybe he didn't know. Maybe it was just me who walked through the world so insincere.

Working on weekends was hazing work for the new kid in the newsroom, something most people got away from as soon as they could, but I didn't mind it. I had Fridays free, a weekday to run errands when the entire rest of the world wasn't trying to do the same. Plus, working on Sundays meant only four days of dealing with newsroom craziness. On weekdays, the newsroom always felt slightly alien to me, the way you feel visiting your old college campus. The place is familiar, but it really isn't yours anymore. But on Sundays the newsroom was mine. It belonged to me, this reporter named Joe, the Sunday editor, and a copy editor or two.

As soon as I stepped off the elevator, the Sunday editor rushed toward me. Bad sign.

"Hope! Glad you're here! I've got a great story for you today!"

Lewis was this pudgy southern guy, as soft and puffy as biscuit dough. When he got excited, his face flushed red and his drawl sped up, like a 45 going 78, which is how you knew you were in trouble.

"Can I get to my desk before you tell me, Lewis?"

"Oh, sure," he said, backing away a few feet. "Let's go sit at your desk and talk."

I set down my purse and the Sunday paper I had picked up in the lobby and opened my coffee. Lewis plopped his big butt on my desk and leaned toward me.

"You ever heard about the Temple of Divine Love?"

I told him I had. It was a church in North Philadelphia founded by a man named Jeremiah Jones, whose followers thought he was God or a descendant of God or a disciple of God or something like that. They called him Father Jones, or sometimes Father Love. I had never paid much attention to the church. There were a lot of people preaching a lot of crazy stuff in the black community.

"Well, Jones died a year ago, and his followers have been in a period of mourning since then, waiting for him to be reincarnated or just return. But in the meantime his two sons, who aren't really his sons and who hate each other, have both been trying to take over the group. They call them princes: Prince Akbar and Prince Morias. And today the mourning period is over and they're having a church service to announce the new leader."

The elevator bell rang and Joe stepped out, carrying a white paper bag with a grease spot on the bottom. He nodded at Lewis, then retreated to the other side of the room. Crafty devil. He could tell something was afoot, and he didn't want to know about it, at least until he finished his sausage biscuit.

Anyway, I could see where this was going.

"We want you to go up there and sit in on the service," Lewis said.

"Who is we?" It was an irrelevant question, but I was stalling for time.

"Jack called. He's very interested in the story."

Jack, the metro editor, was Lewis's boss and my editor Tom's boss too. Clearly Lewis felt the need to roll out the big guns, editor-wise, which meant there was something he wasn't telling me.

"How do we know all this? And why do we care? This is a private church. Who they worship is their own business, isn't it?"

"We know this because Alex Webster has a source who told him," Lewis said, ignoring the second part of my question. "He's been working on the story."

"Then why doesn't he go cover the service?"

"He's afraid they won't let him in. They don't like reporters."

"I'm a reporter."

"But you don't have to tell them that," Lewis said. "You could just walk in and sit down."

There it was. They wanted me to sneak into this church, using my color as a cover. They wanted me to spy, to lie, and it would have to be an active lie too. Black churches, no matter how cultist and weird, are usually interactive. There's no sneaking in the back and sitting quietly in the last pew. Somebody's going to seek you out, to shake your hand or urge you up to the pulpit for prayer or rub your back or at least glance at you cockeyed and wonder why you aren't standing up and singing along with the rest of the crowd. It's hard to be a passive observer in a black church. So if I went I'd probably end up participating, out of habit and out of fear. That meant that every smile I returned, every amen I muttered would be a lie. In a church.

These people wanted me to sin against God, and I probably wouldn't even get a byline out of it.

"I don't know, Lewis," I said. "If it was a city council meeting or something that was supposed to be open and they were doing something sneaky, I wouldn't have a problem sneaking in. But this is a church."

Just then the elevator opened and the metro editor bounced out, followed by Alex Webster. The metro editor was wearing jeans, and the sleeves of his blue flannel shirt were splattered with white paint. Now I was really screwed. Lewis I could handle. But the metro editor coming in on a Sunday meant they were serious.

"Hope, Lewis," he said, coming over to my desk. "Just talking with Alex here about the church stuff. Great story! Everything all set?"

"Well—" I began. But Lewis cut me off.

"Actually, Jack, Hope is unconvinced about the worthiness of the story," he said, leaning toward Jack so hard I thought he was going to sniff the man.

I decided I'd better speak up. "What I'm concerned about is sneaking into a church and spying on people who have every right to privacy in their house of worship. I'm sure it's an interesting story. But do we have to lie to get it?"

Alex Webster spoke up. He was tall and stoop-shouldered, with tight curly black hair, a kind of whiteboy Afro.

"What makes this a compelling news story is that we have some indication that the leaders of this church demand huge sums of money from the congregation. These are poor people who can't afford to give that kind of money."

"All churches take up donations." My voice came out rushed and squeaky, and I paused to calm myself. "If people want to give their money to some nut, that's their business."

"These are more than regular donations, Hope," Alex said. "Some people give up to half of their income."

Alex sat on the desk across from mine, leaning toward me. The metro editor pulled up a chair and sat down, brushing my knees. They seemed to be pressing in all around me, pushing closer and closer with each sentence, each word. I tried to inch my chair back but found the wall.

Seeing me trapped, Lewis lumbered in. "I would think you'd want to help these people. You especially."

I looked at him. "Me especially?"

"Yeah—" Lewis began. But the metro editor cut him off with

a movement that rammed the metal leg of his chair into Lewis's foot. Lewis winced and stepped back.

"I understand your reservations, Hope, and I respect them," Jack said. "But this is not spying, this is investigating. If we didn't have a source in the church, someone who asked us to come in and take a look at what was going on, we wouldn't do it. I'm asking you to do this not just because you can get in but because you can be unbiased. You know what's reasonable and what's not. You can be fair to all sides and you are capable enough to take it all in without taking notes, which you will not be able to do. I'm asking you to do this because it's an important story for North Philadelphia, which I know you care about. But I won't make you go. It's your choice."

My choice. My choice to do what they wanted or cannonball my career right then and there. They couldn't fire me, but if I said no I'd probably find myself working nights at the cop shop. I'd never get a project, never get a national trip, never be considered for any of the big stories that can make a career. I pictured myself ten years down the road, covering the Dog Days parade or sleeping away on the obit desk.

The position seemed distressingly familiar. I was being asked to choose between my people, who weren't really my people except in some intangible way, and my would-be people—my professional, establishment people, to whom I owed some kind of allegiance, didn't I? Even if I hated them sometimes?

"Okay, Jack," I said. I didn't look at Lewis. "I'll see what I can do."

"Great! Alex will fill you in. Good luck."

The metro editor walked off, triumphant in victory, eager to return to his paint job and his beer.

The temple of Divine Love was, in the physical sense, a three-story brick building that had once been used in the making of lace. North Philadelphia was littered with these old factories—

abandoned, windowless hulking ghosts with boarded eyes and an irresistible attraction for graffiti artists and crack addicts and all the trash a neighborhood could produce.

But the Temple of Divine Love was clean. Whitewashed and graffiti-free, white curtains billowing in the double-wide windows on the second and third floors. Whatever else, you had to give it to these people. The church was like an island of order in the middle of a chaotic sea.

I arrived at the church twenty minutes late, having had to rush out first to buy new clothes. Alex had told me the women in the church wore white and suggested I go home and change, but the only white item in my wardrobe was a T-shirt.

"Then go buy something, quick," Alex said. "Charge it to the *Record*."

During a frantic dash through Wanamaker's, I found a white cotton skirt I'd probably never wear again and a gorgeous white blouse, some kind of silk blend, that I certainly would. The outfit, including shoes and stockings, cost more than two hundred dollars. Buying it made me feel both better and worse. Not only was I lying, but I was profiting from my lie. And for two hundred dollars the metro editor would expect results. On the other hand, the blouse was beautiful. I might not get a byline, but at least I'd have something to show.

At the entrance to the parking lot, young men in suits and dark glasses stopped cars and leaned into windows. My heart skittered at the sight of them. They were stone-cold serious; they'd sniff out my insincerity like a dog. I drove past, breathing hard, and searched for a spot on the street. But every block was lined with parked cars, and the sidewalks surged with women in white and men in dark suits, moving toward the church. Finally I found a spot nine blocks away, dragged myself from my car, and fell in behind a large woman who was headed for the church with four children. The woman was dressed in white from head to toe, including a hat and a veil. She looked like a bride. The hat made me panic. Was I supposed to cover my head? Would I be committing some kind of offense if I didn't? I pictured myself stepping inside the church and being seized by a group of outraged ushers. They would hurl me into the street, like Jesus throwing out the money changers. I would be cursed and called unclean.

Across the street, two men sat watching our little procession from the sagging porch of a row house. They passed a bottle in a brown paper bag between them, and every now and then they laughed. The oldest child, a boy of about twelve or thirteen, cringed at the noise, but the mother seemed not to notice. She floated along, humming to herself, as blissful and oblivious as a cloud.

The closer we got to the church, the faster my breath came, until I felt I was panting. At the corner of the building, the woman and her children turned toward the door, and I moved behind them, caught helplessly in their wake. We seemed to approach the door in slow motion. I took shallow breaths, trying to slow my racing heart. More of the somber young men stood guard at the front door, looking closely into the faces of the people streaming past. After a second, I saw the reason—a television truck from Channel 9 sat on the street half a block away. A perky blond reporter whose face I recognized stood beside it, tapping her foot in exasperation. Every now and then she walked toward the church with her hands thrown out in a pleading expression, but the men at the door shook their heads.

I wanted to bail out, but I felt trapped in the momentum, dragged toward the door like a nail toward a magnet. The woman reached the door first and glanced up at one of the men through her veil.

"Love, Brother Jones," she said, not pausing.

"Love, sister," he said, and looked behind her as she passed, sweeping the faces of her children and my own face. Because of the dark glasses he wore, I couldn't see his eyes, couldn't tell whether they lingered on my face or kept moving. The children followed their mother, snail-like, through the door, taking forever to get inside. I waited hours and days to reach the door. At last, walking past the man, I lowered my eyes and mumbled, "Love, Brother Jones."

"Love, sister," he said.

I was in.

The door opened into a long, dark hallway, lit along the way by clusters of women in their blinding white dresses, glowing like candle flames. At the end of the hallway, through an open door, I could see a slice of a large room with golden pews and a raised altar with red velvet chairs. I was surrounded by women—women talking, women humming, women embracing and touching hands and calling to one another with girlish joy. The men seemed to disappear; then I noticed two guys ducking into a room off to the right.

A voice, a man's voice, spoke up behind me.

"Well, well, Sister Robinson," he said. "What are you doing here?"

I turned around. Malcolm stood grinning at me. He wore a black suit, with his usual kente-cloth stole. A tape recorder hung from his shoulder, in plain display. Clearly they knew he was a reporter. Clearly they had allowed him in.

"Malcolm." It came out as a cross between a statement and a plea.

"Seeking a little spiritual enlightenment, sister?"

"I . . . I . . ." My mouth felt as dry as cotton. People rushed past us, whispering and laughing and heading for the large room, the sanctuary. I could feel the excitement mounting. Something was about to happen. Half an hour late, the service was about to start. Suddenly, from the room with the golden pews, came the ebullient cry of a piano and the roar of voices, singing, "Praise Him! Praise Him! Praise Him!"

"Are you a member?" I shouted at Malcolm. Now that the service had begun, I was hoping he would go inside, leave me alone, but he seemed to be in no hurry. Although he bent over to switch on his tape recorder, he made no move to leave. He stood there like the cat who had cornered the mouse; he wanted to play with me for a while.

"I'm here on assignment. And you?"

"I'm here on assignment too." Might as well admit it.

"So they knew you were a reporter when they let you in?"

From inside the sanctuary came "Praise Him! Praise Him! Praise Him!" faster and faster, louder and more frantic, somewhere between a song and a chant.

"Are you doing a story on the succession?"

"Inside politics," Malcolm said. "Prince Akbar and Prince Morias are both good brothers, and whichever one takes over will do the right thing and keep the church's work going strong in the community. Day care program, scholarships, all that. I'm doing a larger piece."

"Oh." My voice was so small I doubt if Malcolm heard me. Anyway, he went on talking.

"I'm on my way out," he said. "I came early, to interview Prince Morias. I'm not staying for the service, but I guess you are. Alex Webster and the rest of the whiteboys would be furious if you got this far and left."

The sound of Webster's name rang like a curse there in the hallway. I said nothing.

"Oh, I know all about Mr. Webster," Malcolm said. "He's been sniffing around, talking shit—sorry—stuff about the church, trying to dig up some dirt." He shrugged. "They know it too." He gestured toward the sanctuary, which had suddenly become quiet.

"Alex Webster wants to write another story about crazy black folks jumping around in a jungle frenzy and stealing from one another. Ain't nothing new in that. What surprises me is that you got dragged into this gig, Hope. I figured they'd ask, but I didn't think you'd do it."

"You talk as if you had some insight into my character. We barely know each other."

"I know a sister when I see one."

"Please. Don't give me that sister stuff."

I wondered if the tough act was going over. I hoped it was. I hoped Malcolm couldn't see the shame shimmering off my face in waves.

"My understanding is these folks take money from their followers—lots of money. That isn't right. Don't they get people to sell their houses and their cars and give money they can't afford?"

"I don't know," Malcolm said. "I don't have to agree with everything they do. I know they do a lot of good work in the community. I also know that none of this is Alex Webster's business. This is our stuff, and if it's dirty—and I don't know if it is—we shouldn't be airing our dirty laundry in public."

If he had attacked me head-on, if he had called me an Uncle Tom or an Oreo or something like that, it would have been better. It would have been easier to fight back. But Malcolm just stood there, looking at me with that expression your mother used after you'd broken the crystal candy dish she got on her honeymoon. Malcolm's big hazel eyes were nearly liquid with disappointment. Standing there, I felt like a real shit.

I turned away. "I have to go in now."

"Yeah. Guess you got to do what you got to do," he said. "Sister."

I didn't watch Malcolm leave. Instead I walked down the long hallway toward the open room, toward the singing and the praising and the noise. Stepping inside was like stepping into a waterfall; the noise crashed down on my head, and I almost staggered under its weight. A man in white gloves directed me to a pew on the left, where the women stood together, singing, a sea of white. I ducked into their midst and opened my mouth, but I didn't sing. I didn't know the words.

After ten minutes or so, the singing wound down and everyone sat. I looked around. The place looked like your average storefront black church, except that the chairs up on the altar were a little larger than normal, more thronelike, draped in purple and gold fabric, with high carved backs and golden wings sprouting on either side. And except that behind the pulpit, where most churches would have hung a cross, hung an oil painting of a man in a suit and a purple pillbox hat. He was very dark and his skin glowed, and there was an almost imperceptible halo of light around his face. He stared straight out at the congregation, his face as composed and severe as that of a father who has just scolded his child.

One of the three men on the pulpit stood and moved slowly to the microphone stand. He was young, no older than twenty, and very good looking. Every move he made was deliberate. He placed his hands on the lectern, raised his head, and stared out at the crowd. All rustling ceased. The room was dead silent; I held my breath, afraid to move. For a minute, two minutes, three minutes, the man gazed out over the congregation, holding them silent with his spell. Then he spoke.

"Brothers and sisters, I want you to know that the enemy is among us."

I felt a trickle of sweat form under my left arm and run down my side, soaking the white blouse and probably staining it. Good. I hoped it was ruined. My breath seemed to rattle from my chest; I tried to breathe more quietly. Everyone was so quiet. The minister stared right at me, or so it seemed. In a minute he would raise his hand and point me out, and the congregation would turn and rise as one and stomp me to death.

"The enemy is here, and he wants to destroy this church," he said, still speaking softly. "But we won't let him."

Next to me, a woman broke the spell. "Amen!" she cried.

"The enemy wants to break up this place of love, but we won't let him!"

"Amen!"

"The enemy wants to negate the teachings of our father, to ridicule us before men who know not what true happiness is. But we won't let him!"

"Amen! Amen!"

The man began pounding on the lectern, and the pounding seemed to energize the crowd. One by one they rose, rocking on their feet, fists clenched or hands held open to the skies, and the noise rose with them.

"You tell him, brother!"

"We plan to fight!"

"The enemy was once one of the chosen. But now he is lost! We're sad for the enemy! But we don't plan to be lost right along with him, because we know the truth, and the truth is Father Love!"

The crowd was roaring now. I looked around and realized I was the only person in the church not standing. I leapt up. Behind me I saw the woman I had followed inside and for a second I was convinced that she was staring at me, figuring it out, but then I realized she wasn't even looking my way. She stood with her head tilted back and her huge, white-draped arms thrust toward the pulpit. Fat tears streamed down her face into her open mouth, but she was smiling, smiling.

"Yes! Yes!" She began to moan, and the rest of the church took up the sound.

"Father Love is the power!"

"Yes! Yes!"

"Father Love is the power!"

"Oh, touch me, Father, touch me!"

"Father Love is the power!"

All around me women moaned and swayed. They ran their

hands frantically up and down the sides of their white-draped bodies, then thrust their hands forward, toward the pulpit, desperate for an embrace.

"Yes! Oh, yes! Heal me, Father! Heal me, touch me!"

The room felt like an oven, like someone had turned up the heat and people were beginning to fry. Sweat ran down my sides, but as people became more and more frantic, I realized that no one was the least bit interested in me, and I calmed down and looked around. Fascinating and strange. It was like a Twilight Zone version of the church of my childhood. All the singing and the moaning and the dancing, frantic and joyously uncontrolled—all this was familiar, but were these women crying out to God or to Father Love?

"Come on up, children!" The minister waved the dancing figures toward the altar, where two men in black held big baskets. "Come on up and give your material possessions to the father, and the father will give back great riches unto you!"

"Yes! Yes!"

People began dancing toward the altar, their feet driven by an accelerating drum beat. The woman standing next to me, a tall, skinny woman who reminded me of my aunt Grace, reached down into her bra and pulled out a damp roll of bills, then held it triumphantly in the air. She looked at me, and I was surprised by the calmness that pooled in her eyes. She didn't look frantic or crazed, despite the noise, despite the fact that she'd been participating in the chaos as much as anyone else. Sweat glistened on her dark face, but she smiled at me gently. Right then and there I decided to leave.

"Don't hold back, sister," the woman said, looking into my eyes. She leaned close to say it, as if whispering to me the secret of the universe. "Father Love is the power. Let him work. Let him work."

Then she gently pushed me aside so she could dance past me

and into the aisle. I followed, but instead of heading toward the pulpit, I lowered my head and hurried out of the sanctuary. One of the men guarding the church door frowned as I approached.

"Leaving early, sister?"

"I . . . have to get home to take care of my mother. She's sick."

He nodded somberly. "Love, sister. Watch out for the TV folks outside."

As soon as the door closed behind me, the blond television reporter rushed toward me, pushing her microphone into my face.

"Hi!" She beamed. "Can I talk to you a minute?"

"Get out of my face."

I drove to a parking lot near the river and sat in my car, trying to figure out what to do. The place had been strange, no question about it; I wouldn't want my aunt Grace going there. But I couldn't get that woman's face out of my mind. She hadn't seemed hypnotized or possessed or even vulnerable. She seemed to know what she was doing, and she seemed pretty damn happy about it. A lot happier than I'd been in a long time, in fact. Who was I to break that up, and for what reason?

Out on the river, a boat of whiteboys rowed slowly past. I had tried rowing at Astor once. During my second practice, when I lost my oar and almost tipped the boat, the girl behind me whispered to the one behind her, "Wish she'd just go back to basketball!" Since I'd never played basketball, I couldn't go back to it, but I didn't go back to rowing either.

The boys on the river rowed out of sight. I started up my car, drove back to the *Record*, and lied, lied, lied.

chapter ten

Lewis, of course, didn't believe me.

"You couldn't get in?"

I stood there feeling like Big Nurse in my white clothes, while he stared at me with skepticism all over his pudgy face.

"I got inside. But then in the hallway they stopped me and asked who I was and whether I was a member. And I said no. I told you I wasn't going to lie. So they threw me out."

"What took you so long, then?"

"I hung around for a while, trying to talk to people as they were walking in. No one would talk to me. I did what I could."

"I'll bet," he grumbled.

When Alex came back from lunch, Lewis told him what had happened.

"Forget it," Alex said. "I'll just have to go at it another way."

But the next morning all hell broke loose. I walked into the newsroom, picked up the *Daily Post*, and nearly dropped my cup of coffee. The *Post* had a front-page story about the ascension of Prince Akbar. Apparently he had been the one speaking at the church the day before, and the *Post* obviously had someone planted in the audience. Either that or a source who gave them the scoop. Sometime after I'd left, Prince Akbar had declared himself the reincarnation of Father Love and taken control of the church. A fistfight broke out between some of his supporters and those of his brother and ended with Prince Morias being thrown out of the church. He announced that he would file a lawsuit first thing Monday.

Jack was furious. He stomped into the newsroom and slammed the door to his office. Ten minutes later, Lewis and Alex were summoned in. I waited for my own call, but it didn't come.

Twenty minutes after they went into Jack's office, Lewis and Alex came out. Lewis looked like someone who'd been choking on a bone. His face was mottled red and twisted angrily. Alex just looked bemused. Screwing up my courage, I walked over to Alex's desk.

"Still standing?"

"Oh, he's just pissed. Rob is on his back, so he's on Lewis's back, and everybody's on mine. I have to rush my piece and get it ready to run tomorrow."

"I'm sorry about yesterday, Alex." I was, too—not about the lie but about the fact that my lie had caused Alex to get scooped. I didn't know him very well, but he seemed like a nice enough person. Or maybe it was just that next to Lewis, anyone would look decent.

"Not your fault," he said. "I've been in the business long enough to know that getting scooped is not the worst thing in the world. Tomorrow Rob and Jack will be bitching about something else. Don't worry about it."

But I *was* worried about it. I knew that Lewis wouldn't forget what had happened, and I knew damn well who he would blame. Not that he had that much power. But still. Having enemies was never a good thing.

I settled in at my desk and tried to get back to work on my own stories. The phone rang. It was Malcolm.

"What do you want? I'm having a bad enough day as it is. I don't need your grief."

"I didn't call to give you grief, girl." His voice was warm. "You didn't do it, did you?"

"No, I didn't," I said, lowering my voice. "I didn't, and you see what happened. The *Post* did it anyway. And now we look like fools, and my editors are trying to figure out whether I lied or I'm just incompetent."

"Who gives a damn what they think?"

"I have to."

"Let me take you out to dinner tonight. You did the right thing. You deserve a reward."

"I'm busy tonight." It was true; I was having dinner with David.

"Tomorrow night."

"My editor is glaring at me. I have to go. We'll talk next week."

"Okay. Keep the faith, baby. You did the right thing."

"Right," I said, and hung up. Guess I should have said "Right on."

I left the choice of restaurant up to David, figuring it would say something about how sneaky he planned to be with this thing. Maybe he and Stephanie had some kind of arrangement by which they could still date other people. But I doubted that. Even if David had somehow managed to talk golden girl into it for himself, he could never live with the thought of his princess being touched by other men. I had a friend once, a guy, who insisted that monogamy was invented and perpetuated by women; I told him he was nuts. Monogamy was a man's idea:

the idea was to keep women monogamous, but to do so, men had to pretend to be faithful themselves.

David and I met at the Garden Grill, in Chestnut Hill. It was a pretty place, a big, Colonial-style house turned into a restaurant, with white lace curtains hanging in the windows and antique watering cans lining the bookshelves. It was a neighborhood kind of place; I knew about it because I lived just down Germantown Avenue, in Mount Airy. But I wondered how David knew the restaurant, since he lived on the other side of town.

David was at the bar when I arrived, sipping a whiskey.

"A woman who arrives on time!" he said, standing up. "I'm aghast. And impressed."

"One can't always expect the world to wait."

I ordered a gin and tonic, my favorite drink when I was trying to be sophisticated. It came and I took a big sip; the liquor felt clean and tangy against my tongue. There was something about drinking tart cocktails that made me feel more like an adult. Plus, the air-conditioning was beginning to cool my skin. The air conditioner in my car was broken, and I'd gotten slightly sweaty. The hostess came over, smiling, and we moved to our table, out in the enclosed sunroom. Two huge hydrangeas pressed against the glass.

"So," David said. He gave me a nervous smile, but I didn't return it. I had decided to be sexy and mysterious and far, far away.

"So." I tilted my head.

"So why did you become a journalist? I always ask people that question. The answer usually falls into one of two categories: I wanted to be Woodward and Bernstein, or I wanted to be Ernest Hemingway and I just got stuck."

"I wanted to afflict the comfortable."

He laughed. "And comfort the afflicted?"

I smiled, slightly, and gave the barest perceptible shrug.

"That too. And you?"

"Oh, I wanted to be Hemingway. I thought I'd join a newspaper, get sent overseas in six months, and discover all sorts of exotic places. Then I'd quit and go write a novel. Instead I got sent to the suburbs of New York and nine years later, here I am."

"Why?"

"Why what?"

"Why are you still here?"

"Oh. Well. You know, things happen. I'm over thirty now. It's a little late to go running off to Africa."

"Yeah. You probably wouldn't have nearly as nice an office there as you do here."

"Ouch!" David said, laughing.

"Sorry. Did that hurt?" I laughed too.

Our food came. I ordered another drink. I was having fun. My pasta with broccoli and tomatoes sat before me like an impressionist painting, glowing with color, but I just dabbed at it. I felt that eating would make me heavy and dull, and I was feeling wonderfully light, light and sharp and beautiful. Outside the glass walls of the sun porch, the sky darkened, giving up the last few rays of day.

We talked a little about our childhoods. David grew up in some upper-middle-class New York suburb. His father was a doctor who worked in the city, his mother a socialite who ran fundraisers and otherwise stayed at home.

"Pretty basic. Pretty boring," David said.

"It sounds nice."

I told David about my childhood as though I were quoting the synopsis from the back of some book. Little black girl, abandoned by daddy, raised in the stony maw of poverty. I told him about my mother and my two sisters, about driving across town to go grocery shopping because we were embarrassed to be seen using food stamps. I told him about being whisked away to Astor and the ensuing culture shock. It was the way I always told my story to white people, and it dawned on me that I usually told it to make them either feel guilty or admire me and consider me brave.

David listened intently, staring at me as I spoke. He kept knitting his brow and nodding his head between sips of his drink, as if he were conducting an interview. And I was giving him exactly what he wanted.

"Sometimes the inequities in this society astound me," David said, looking down at his plate. His steak had gone cold and sat in a little pool of grease.

"Sometimes?"

"All the time. The way we allow this disparity between the haves and the have-nots to keep growing. The way we herd poor people into the cities and think we can just shut the gate and run away and not have to deal with them again."

"Yeah, well." Suddenly I was tired of the conversation. I didn't want to talk about disparities and inequality and despair. I felt myself sinking a little bit, like an old balloon. I took a long pull on my drink.

"Write an editorial about it, David. Maybe something will change. Let's talk about something else."

David looked up and smiled. "Okay. How about your face?"

"My face?"

"Yeah. I'd like to have a photograph of you to stare at, to study. There's something about your face. It's almost regal."

"You mean like a shiny African princess?"

"No! I mean, well, yeah. Is that bad?"

I laughed and felt myself ascending again. "I'm kidding. That's from Hemingway. *The Sun Also Rises.* Jake tells Robert Cohn to go read about the shiny African princesses and he'll want to go to Africa."

"I haven't read it in a long, long time."

"Me either. I don't know why I remember that passage. I used to like Hemingway, though I don't anymore. He was a real misogynist and probably a racist too. But I think he had a thing for black women."

"Yeah?" David sipped the wine he had switched to with dinner. Neither one of us had eaten much, but we had both had several drinks. David's face was flushed and his eyes were glazed from wine and heat and the desire he felt for me, which I could feel. It made me giddy and happy and cruel; I wanted to kiss him and bite his lip.

"Yeah. A lot of white guys do, you know."

"Yeah?" he said thickly.

"Oh, yeah," I said, smiling. "A lot."

The heat outside was surprising after the coolness of the restaurant, but it was a soft heat, cottony and caressing, not like during the day. I invited David for a nightcap, and he followed me back to my place.

My apartment seemed larger to me, more expansive, as if someone had come in while I was gone and pushed back the walls, and it was a good thing, because I felt larger too. But not big and dumb and awkward, the way I sometimes felt, the way I used to feel as a kid. This was different. We walked in, and I went over and put some Marvin Gaye on the CD player, and in a second his soulful voice came out and surrounded us. I opened a bottle of wine and poured us two glasses and we walked toward the sofa, not saying anything, just kind of looking at each other until David took the glass from my hand and set it down on the coffee table, next to his, untouched. He cupped his hands under my chin and pulled me toward him. Then he ran his hands over my neck and down to my breasts, gently. At first he wasn't talking, just breathing fast and licking my neck and kissing me, sucking away my breath. His mouth was constant movement. His lips opened and closed, approached and withdrew, teased and prodded; his tongue darted in and out of my mouth like a lizard through the underbrush. All the booze in my bloodstream evaporated, and I felt distinctly sober. And intoxicated.

I remembered that my grandmother used to say white people stank, that they smelled like wet dogs. David didn't stink. He smelled clean and green and slightly damp, like fresh cucumbers. I burrowed my face into his neck. The overhead light flickered and died and reappeared.

"Oh," I said. I wanted to say something else, but it wouldn't come. "Oh. Oh."

"Kissing you is like sunshine," he said, sucking at my mouth. "I've been thinking about you constantly since we met. You've invaded my dreams."

He bent to kiss my breasts; I giggled into his hair. Kissing me was like sunshine. Funny how sex brought out the poetry in men. I wondered if he *had* been thinking about me since we'd met, or whether that was just heat talking, and whether it mattered. Looking down at the pink flush of David's neck, I told myself to remember who was in charge here. If anyone was going to hand out lines, it was going to be me.

My mother liked to say that life was a seesaw; if one side went up, another side would have to come down. There was a balance to the universe that could be counted upon, depressing though it might be. Her point was that if at least one aspect of your life was going well, you should focus on that and be happy. You couldn't have everything. Or even most things.

So as the thing with David blossomed into whatever it was going to be, work went downhill. It became clear that both my editor, Tom, and the metro editor distrusted me over the Temple of Divine Love fiasco. When a group of parents staged an impromptu sit-in at a school in North Philadelphia to protest a principal they said was corrupt, Tom gave the story to Stephanie and another reporter. I didn't even find out about it until late that afternoon. When I saw it on the daily budget, I stormed up to Tom's desk. He was on the phone, dealing with a city councilman who was complaining about a story that said he often slept through important meetings. Tom signaled that he might be a while, but I took a chair and waited. He hung up, sighing in exasperation, but I had no time for sympathy. I asked why what should have been my story had been given to someone else.

"I looked for you when it broke," he said. "Couldn't find you."

"I was here all day. I even ate lunch upstairs, because I was expecting a phone call. I was gone maybe thirty minutes."

"That must have been when it broke."

I tried not to worry about it. There's an ebb and flow of newsroom life that can drive you mad if you let it. When you're new to a place, or when you're the flavor du jour, or when you're working an important breaking story that keeps unfolding, you might hit the paper three, four, five times a week with big flashy stories that show up on the front page and make people walk past your desk and clap you on the back and say, "Nice work" or "Good story" or "Great piece." It doesn't matter that half these people haven't even read the story—they just saw it was on the front page. That doesn't matter at all; it still feels wonderful. You walk through the day feeling like you really are accomplishing something with your life.

But then come the lulls—long dry spells where nothing you write seems to get in or you can't seem to finish a piece or your editor won't shake it loose because he has three other things on his plate and your story is not time-dependent. Those are the weeks that try your self-confidence. No matter how many interviews you've done or how much you've written or how hard you've worked, if it's not in the paper, it doesn't exist. Your friends say, "Haven't seen anything from you for a while." The assistant managing editor greets you in the elevator and asks if you've been on vacation. Byline deprivation—some reporters get really neurotic about it. You're only as good as your last story, and if your last story was a six-inch filler on the vitamin pages (B-6, B-12), what does that say about you?

So far at the *Record*, I had made the front page exactly twice— once with a weather story and once with a piece about a bad arson fire, which was so predictable it could have been written by a cow. I wanted to hit it again, with something big and important and well written. But now I was in the doghouse, and it looked like that might never go away.

To keep sane I focused on telling North Philadelphia's story, on finding bits and pieces that said something meaningful but that no one else (meaning reporters) would probably be interested in. Eventually almost everything got into the paper, although sometimes mangled beyond belief. There were slow news days and Saturdays and holidays, when the editors were desperate for stories; they would run pages of the dictionary if they could. I figured if I just kept busy writing stories that were forthright and meaningful and true, no one could fault me. Not honestly, anyway. And at least I'd have a few clips when it was time to look for another job. At least I was trying.

I usually showed up for work around 9 A.M., an hour earlier than most people, so I could be there if anything broke early and so I'd be sitting at my desk with my headphones strapped on when Tom came striding in. I hung around until lunchtime, making phone calls, setting up interviews, reading the wires to find out what was going on. I kept an eye on the desk; it was easy to tell when something was breaking, because all the editors started jumping around like popcorn. If nothing happened after lunch I'd get in my car and drive up Broad Street to North Philadelphia and wander around or go talk to some people I'd heard about.

Like Miss Liz, an older woman, sixtyish, with small black eyes and thick hair she wore brushed up to the top of her head like a hat. She lives in Strawberry Mansion, in a tight little row house she and her husband have owned for thirty-five years and which they refuse to abandon to crack and guns and crime. Across the way is a corner grocery, first run by Jewish immigrants, now run by Koreans, a dim hole-in-the-wall where a scared man and his family sell overpriced goods from behind a thick pane of plastic. Miss Liz sits in a lawn chair on the sidewalk in front of her house and greets the passersby.

"We moved here in 1963. We already had three kids, was on our way to six. There was nothing but families here then. Folks used to send their kids over here when they got tired, figuring I had so many I'd never notice a few more. I wasn't the partying type.

"It was a nice neighborhood until the gangs came in the seventies. The shootings would always happen at dinnertime. The kids would know enough to go hide under the bed. They could tell you the sound of every gun. They'd say, 'Mama, that's a Saturday-night special right there.'

"One day I was in the kitchen baking corn bread, and I heard this whizzing sound. And when I walked out to the living room to see what it was, there was my husband, lying on the floor in the doorway like a sack of potatoes. Doctor said the bullet just missed his heart. One more inch and he wouldn't have been getting up off that floor. They never found who did it. Just some fool shooting off a gun.

"John got mean after that. He wanted to move, but I said, 'Baby, where we gonna run that's gonna be any better than here? We got to do something.' So me and the other mothers started getting in the street when they was fighting. We'd say, 'You want to shoot somebody, shoot me.' They still had a little bit of respect back then. They'd leave, go somewhere else. Then we opened up the community center so the kids would have someplace to go. Then the gangs seemed to die down, and we thought we'd won, until this crack cocaine showed up. I ain't never seen nothing like this mess. People do horrible things

when they on it. Last summer we tried to run us a feeding program, so the kids who got free lunch when school was in would
still get at least one decent meal a day. But we had to shut it
down. It was just us women running the program, and these
crackheads kept coming up and messing with people and running
off with the food. You know you've seen everything you want
to see in this world when you see a grown man take food from
a child."

Like the minister trying to persuade his aging congregation to
open a youth center for gang members in the basement of their
church. He is young and energetic, just arrived from divinity
school and a one-year assignment in a small Mississippi town.
The old folks have lived in North Philadelphia all their lives.

"We can't just sit in here, praying for salvation and ignoring
what's going on in the streets. It's a shame to be afraid of our
own children."

"It's a shame these children have given us reason to be scared,"
says a seventy-four-year-old woman who lives behind bars in her
apartment and has twice been mugged. "It's a shame before God."

"The Lord's gonna ask what we've done."

"What *they* done. See this scar across my leg? That's where
they dragged me half a block."

"God knows you've suffered, sister."

"God knows I want to help. But do it have to be in the
church?"

"Jesus said suffer the little children."

"The ones what hit me in the head weren't no little children.
They was demons masquerading behind a child's eyes."

Like the old men in sweaters, reminiscing in barbershops. And
the grease-fat women in curlers and white shorts, sitting out in
the project courtyards to watch their children and catch a
breeze. And the earnest young fraternity brother from Lincoln
University who starts a mentoring program for young boys based

on some pseudo-African rites he dreamed up. And the couple—
she with skin the color of cocoa butter and dreadlocks cascading
down her head, he darker, leaner, more wary but soaked with
love—who buy a crumbling mansion in the heart of the neighborhood and declare their intentions to be the first of a new
wave of middle-class blacks returning home.

After work sometimes I wanted to see David but he was
"unavailable," meaning with Stephanie. He was straight up about
that. Near the beginning he told me he would probably keep
seeing her.

"Do you love her?" I asked.

"I don't know. I feel something, but I haven't figured it out.
I'm so attracted to you it makes me wonder what Stephanie and
I really have."

What garbage. But I just smiled.

"I'd like to keep seeing you, but I'll understand if you can't live
with that," he said.

I told myself I was in this thing mostly to see if I could do it,
if I could take this boy away from that whitegirl. So I could live
with it.

"Do you plan to tell her about us?" I asked, knowing the answer.

"No," he said. "Do you?"

"Hey, it's not my job."

So when David was unavailable I sometimes hung out with
Melvia. We went to Penn's Landing and sat in the breeze from
the river, listening to a jazz concert and gazing across the water
to Camden. One Saturday we walked the cobblestone streets of
the Old City, past Independence Hall and the Liberty Bell, both
surrounded by camera-clicking tourists, to a tiny seafood restaurant that served creamy oyster stew.

"So who is he?" Melvia asked after we'd ordered. We were at
one of only two occupied tables in the place. The restaurant was

well known to weekday regulars but mostly invisible to tourists, and Saturday afternoons were always slow. That's why Melvia chose it.

"Who's who?"

"The guy you've been seeing. Trying to keep him hidden from me?"

"What makes you think I've been seeing anyone?"

"Because when I called you on Wednesday to ask if you wanted to go see a movie you didn't, and you were in a big hurry to get off the phone. And that wasn't the first time."

She grinned at me, and I grinned back, caught. Despite the fact that she was on the far side of thirty, Melvia had a take-them-or-leave-them attitude toward guys that I admired. She enjoyed them when they came, and she didn't freak out when they left, unlike a lot of other women I knew. She once told me she'd like to get married and have children, but not at the expense of her dignity and self-respect. She couldn't be bothered to play all the games it seemed you had to play to catch an employed and half-intelligent black man in the scarce market out there. She would act like herself, she said, and what came would come.

"So?"

"Okay, okay. He's just some guy, nobody special. I started messing with him because I was bored."

"Oh, really? How liberated of you."

I laughed. "If you think that's liberated, wait till you hear this. He's white. And he has a girlfriend."

Melvia looked up sharply.

"Oh, I don't care," I said. "I told you I'm just messing with him because I'm bored. If anything, he's the one in trouble. I think he really likes me."

I lowered my head for a spoonful of stew. It was rich and creamy, with rubbery bits of oysters that gritted against my teeth.

Melvia snorted. "Don't worry," she said.

"No, I'm serious."

"Yeah, right."

"Well, it's been a couple of months. If all he wanted was sex, he would have taken it and run."

"Sex ain't like measles, you know. You can have it more than once."

"You're such a romantic."

Melvia shrugged. "Well, at least I'm not crazy enough to get involved with a white guy. A white guy who already has a white girlfriend, one he's not even trying to hide from you. And you don't know what is going on in that warped little mind."

"Oh, as opposed to any other man. Did you know what was going on in Stewart's warped little mind?" Stewart was an attorney she had dated for six months, until one night he called to say that six months was his limit on a relationship if he didn't plan to marry the woman. And he did not foresee marrying Melvia.

"That asshole didn't have a mind," she said. "Just a Rolodex where his brain should be. But at least I knew he wasn't with me because he was curious about sex with a black woman. At least I knew he didn't harbor some fantasy about screwing the savage beast."

"Melvia!"

"I mean, your boy is probably out somewhere right now, high-fiving it with his ofay friends!" She did a tight-lipped imitation of John Whiteboy jumping awkwardly into the air, which made me laugh.

The waitress stopped to check on us. She was blond and dressed in a tight black skirt and come-hither heels, all of which was wasted on us and the elderly white couple in the corner. She must have been dressed for the dinner shift. Deciding to be decadent, we ordered a bottle of wine.

"Listen," Melvia said when the waitress had gone. "Mama's gonna tell you a story. I dated a white guy once, in college. He was an engineer, and he seemed really sweet. I liked him. I was going to sleep with him, and we went to his room one night and he put on some music and we started making out. When the record ended I jumped up to change it, and I noticed another record, one he'd obviously been listening to recently, so I put it on.

"It was the Rolling Stones, the one with that song 'Some Girls' on it. Do you know that song, Hope?"

I nodded. During my freshman year at college some guy in my dorm had played it continuously throughout the day, as if he were advertising for companionship.

"Well, I'd never heard it before," Melvia said. "When the music started he went stiff. He sat up, embarrassed, and said, 'Let's play something else.' But I said no. I wanted to hear it. So we sat on his mattress on the floor and listened to the song and the part that says black girls just want to fuck all night, and when it was over I looked at him and asked him, 'Is that what you think?' He said, 'No. No. No,' and tried to grab my hand. But he couldn't meet my eyes. He had beautiful green eyes, but I couldn't see them."

We were quiet for a moment. What was left of my stew had gone cold, and my wineglass sat empty.

"That was my last white man," Melvia said. I looked across the table at her.

"Not that I care, because I'm just messing around. But this guy's not like that, Melvia. He likes me for me."

Melvia shrugged and dug into the ice bucket. "Maybe," she said. "Better have some more wine."

chapter eleven

When I was at Astor and the girls in my dorm found out I wasn't going to the senior dance, they panicked. It was as though if I didn't go they couldn't go. I was pretty used to this attitude from people at Astor; the deep and personal interest they seemed to take in my well-being pissed me off. People kept insisting that I look happier. "Come on, smile!" they'd say, as if my scowl were marring their view of the world. "Cheer up! Things aren't that bad." Although of course they had no way of knowing whether things were bad or not. In my teenage angst and anger, I figured they really didn't care; they just wanted me to look pleasant. But the more they insisted, the more I resisted, until I became this miserable, sullen piece of work.

So when these girls found out I had no plans to attend the senior dance, they pushed their way into my room.

"You have to go to the dance!" said one of them, a girl named Gail.

I sat on my bed, doing some homework. "Why? Is it a graduation requirement?"

"But we're all going," whined another one, Bonnie. She was a California girl, the large, cushiony type who looked good now but in ten years would spread like frosting left out in the sun. She was incredibly, amazingly stupid. Her private tutor wrote nearly all of her assignments. Only her father's gifts to the campus had gotten her into the school.

"My mother taught me not to jump off a bridge just because everyone else was doing it."

"What's that got to do with this?" Bonnie asked, stroking her hair. She couldn't help preening herself, like a cat.

"Hope," Gail said. "We can find you a date, if that's what this is about."

Gail happened to be good friends with my old roommate, Amy, whom I hadn't spoken to since freshman year. I couldn't figure out what she was doing among the chamber of commerce bunch.

"That is *not* what this is about," I said, pushing them toward the door. "I do not care to attend your little dance, so thanks but no thanks."

"But—"

"Out, please," I said.

Later that night I got a phone call from a boy named Rajiv. He was a beautiful, cocoa-colored Indian kid who had been educated in Britain and was at Astor for a postgraduate year to augment hopes of getting into Harvard or Yale. He was nineteen years old, reed slim and very sophisticated. He went to Boston every weekend, studied the rest of the time, and seemed bored with the whole prep school experience. I knew him from English class; once, I lent him my copy of *The Catcher in the Rye* because the library was out and he needed it for another class. He gave it back three weeks later, with a little laugh. "Americans," he said. We had barely spoken since.

But there he was, calling me and asking me to the senior dance.

"What?" I was astonished. Outside the wooden phone booth, three or four girls sat on the floor, chatting and waiting their turn. It was hard to hear him over their inane laughter. I thought I'd misheard.

"I should like to invite you to the ball," he said in that dry, clipped accent that everybody loved.

"You mean the dance? The senior dance?"

"Ah yes, the dance," he said, drawing the word out flat, with a laugh. "If one dances it must be a dance. Americans." Then. "Now then, will you come?"

It was all I could do to keep from squealing like one of the idiots outside the door. Rajiv was asking me to the dance, this gorgeous, black-haired Indian with doe eyes and skinny ties and a long black leather jacket he somehow managed to get away with wearing to class. Half the girls at school had wiggled their breasts in front of him, but he showed no interest. People decided he had a girlfriend in Boston. Perhaps a Harvard student or someone older, a woman. Someone tall and sure and grown. But he was asking *me* to the dance.

"I'd love to," I said, and even as he began speaking of plans, I imagined myself gliding over the library floor in his arms. In happiness, I rubbed my hand across my forehead and felt there the first splinter of doubt.

"Rajiv, wait a minute. Why are you asking me?"

"Why? What a strange question. Why not?"

His voice, usually so sure, seemed to waver.

"We barely know one another."

"I barely know anyone at this school."

"You could take someone who wasn't at school. A girlfriend from Boston maybe."

"You lent me your book."

"My book? So what? What if I'd lent you my Walkman? Would you ask me to marry you?"

I knew I should just shut up and go, just dance across the floor with my Prince Charming and for one night pretend. But I couldn't shake a suspicion that someone, someone who pitied me, had put him up to this. Some of the girls in my dorm.

"You Americans are so suspicious," Rajiv said. "Look, you're a nice girl. A pretty girl. I want to go to the dance. That's all."

"No one put you up to this?"

"What a bloody stupid question!" He mumbled something into the phone, his voice low and tight. All I heard was "bloody Americans." Then he paused and took a breath. When he spoke again, his voice sounded so angry I thought he would split the telephone.

"Would you care to attend or not? It's quite simple. Yes or no. Please give me an answer."

In the bathroom down the hall, water smashed against a sink and someone brushed her teeth. Everything else was quiet. I couldn't tell if the girls had given up and gone to bed or were waiting there outside the door, holding their breaths and listening to me.

"No, I don't think so, Rajiv," I said. "But thank you for asking."

"Right," he said. And hung up.

By the time I told David that story we'd been sleeping together for more than two months. It came up one night, in bed, my place, me complaining that I'd been in a bad mood at work lately and people kept telling me to smile. I hated it when people told me to smile.

"Even if they did put the guy up to it, they were just trying to be nice," David said. He lay on his back with his arms folded beneath his head. Brownish tufts of hair stuck out from his armpits, darker than the hair on his head, lighter than the patch at his crotch. It was weird with white people, the way their hair could be different colors on different parts of their bodies. My hair was black, black and black. No variations on that theme.

"You don't get it. They weren't trying to be nice. They wanted to make themselves feel better. It had nothing to do with me."

We lay in silence for a few minutes, listening to the murmur of Mrs. Scott's television next door.

"That's pretty harsh," David said.

"Life is harsh. Or rather, life is harsh for some people. For some folks life is one golden dream after another."

David grunted and turned over to check his watch. He was always anxious to get home before midnight. "I'd like to meet one of those people."

"You already have."

In general, we avoided talking about Stephanie, although I did ask him what he told her he was doing all those nights. He got a bit defensive, said they didn't live together and weren't engaged or anything and he didn't have to explain his whereabouts to anyone. He was a free man, no chains on him, all that bullshit. Except he never asked to spend the night and we never saw each other on weekends and we saw each other more than once a week only if Stephanie happened to be out of town. And in all the time we were screwing, we only once did it at his apartment. Stephanie, I knew, had a key.

I didn't want David to think I was jealous, so I stepped around Stephanie's name. But when I wanted to tease him, I called her Blondie. "Where's Blondie tonight? Sorority meeting? Out practicing her Pulitzer acceptance speech?" David always laughed it off.

Once, as he was leaving, I said, "Better run along home before Barbie gets mad."

"She doesn't get mad," David said. "That's part of her problem."

Another time, he looked at me and said, "You know, Stephanie's life has not been as carefree as it might seem."

How very valiant. Sticking up for his lover.

"I'm sure it hasn't," I said, trying to end the conversation. I didn't want to hear him defend her. "My mother always said, 'No one gets through this life unscathed.'"

But David flushed as he took another sip of the wine he'd brought me, a California Cabernet, quite expensive. He was teaching me a lot about wines.

"Everybody thinks that she's beautiful, smart, ambitious, well educated, well off. I could see how you might think her life was perfect. When we first met, that's what I thought."

"I didn't mean anything, David." His eyes glowed, and he leaned forward to splash more wine into his glass. He gulped a mouthful, something he never did. You gulped beer or water, he always said. Fine wine should be allowed to linger on the tongue.

"Have you ever noticed how she never shows her arms? She always wears long sleeves. Ever notice that?"

I tried to think back. Whenever I noticed Stephanie's clothes it was to note how nice they were, not the length of the sleeves. What was he hinting at?

"Not really. Why?"

But David's mind had changed direction again. He sipped his wine. "What I'm trying to say is, she has her problems just like anyone else. Her family . . . her father is very, very hard on her. You shouldn't be mean to her just because she looks the way she looks. Isn't that prejudice, judging people before you know them?" He looked up at me, his eyes as wide and as innocent as a calf's.

I chuckled and stroked his cheek. "Absolutely right," I said.

Sometimes I complained to David about the metro desk, about how I couldn't get the stories that I wanted to do into the paper.

Since he worked upstairs on the editorial board, he didn't really know how the desk worked. His only point of view came through Stephanie, and she obviously had no problems at all.

"I know they think you're a good writer," he said. "Maybe they just want you to be more of a team player."

"That's boy talk."

"Okay. I'm not going to give you advice."

"I want to hear what you think. Just don't give me platitudes."

"I don't think we should talk about work."

"What should we talk about, then?"

"Anything else," he said, bending down to unbutton my blouse and kiss my breast. "But especially this."

We never planned anything. I'd go for days without hearing from him, except maybe to pass him in the building's long, blue-gray hallway, where he'd be with colleagues and I'd be with Melvia or Georgia, and we'd studiously avoid each other's eyes. But sometimes, when I got back to my desk, the phone would ring.

"Hi, it's David." He always identified himself, like he was worried I might have forgotten who he was. I thought it was cute. "You wouldn't be free for a French lesson tonight, would you?"

That's what we had begun calling it. Once, when we were kissing, I had called out something like "C'est bon!" and David had laughed and asked if I spoke French, and I said no, not since studying it badly in high school. I had no idea where my outburst had come from. So he said he would have to help me recapture my French and then I could teach it to him.

I was almost always free, but he never assumed. He would ask with that prepared-to-be-disappointed tone darkening his voice, and because he did, I never felt the need to pretend I was busy or find other dates to keep him interested. All that would have been a waste of time anyway, I told myself. He *wasn't* interested, not in that way. And it was a relief not to have to play games.

Sometimes we went out, to dark Italian restaurants deep in South Philly or neon-bright Cuban storefront dives downtown.

But more often David volunteered to bring takeout food to my apartment, and we ate in my living room, talking office politics across the couch. At first I was so caught up in his new-grass smell and the cool, clean, lime-ice taste of him that I didn't think about what his reluctance to go out meant. And then when I noticed it I thought it was romantic for a while. And then I decided not to think about it at all. David would show up at my door bearing wine and ice cream and cartons of Thai food or a grease-stained brown paper bag fragrant with ribs. Usually we ate afterward. Sometimes not at all. I'd sit in my living room, listening to every set of footsteps in the hallway, until I heard what I was sure were his coming off the elevator. By the time he got to the door I was standing there. I'd pull him inside, pull him by his shirt or his tie or whatever piece of cloth my hand landed on, and he would put down the food and kick the door closed and we'd fall on one another, like two animals so intent on devouring each other that neither realizes his own arm is being chewed.

"How's your boy? Still sniffing around?"

"Melvia . . ."

"Just asking. I want to be prepared for the night you call me up in tears and I have to run over to your apartment and scrape you off the floor."

"I know what I'm doing."

"Glad to hear it." She stopped grinning and touched me on the arm. "But you know you can call me, anytime. I'm a good scraper. Lord knows I've done it enough times."

One night David brought Vietnamese food. I'd been looking forward to it, and when I opened the door I said, "I'm starving," but David kissed me and then we were in the bedroom and he

was whispering, "Oh, please. Take me in your mouth." He loved
oral sex, more than any black man I had ever known. I was
willing to comply. It made him happy, and he was eager to
reciprocate whenever I'd allow it. On that night David gasped
as I took his penis into my mouth. He began to moan so loud I
worried Mrs. Scott would bang on the wall, wondering if someone was hurt.

"Oh, that's so good!" David said. He was in a trance. "So good.
God! I love you!"

My heart contracted. I managed to keep doing what I was
doing, but my breathing sped up. Had he said what I thought
he said? And if he had, what the hell did that mean?

"Oh, yes! Yes!" he moaned. "I love you!"

We lay in bed for a while afterward, curled in each other's arms
the way I imagined people in love really did. Half asleep, listening
to the sounds of the nine-year-old next door playing minibasket-
ball against the wall, I leaned my head on David's chest.

"You know, you say some pretty interesting things at the
height of orgasm," I said, stroking his chest.

"Now you're going to embarrass me," he said. "Did I say something sick? It's your fault for getting me so excited."

"Actually, you said you loved me. You said it twice."

The thumping next door died, and in the silence that followed
I could hear very clearly the beating of David's heart. His hand,
which had been stroking my hair, slid to a stop. David eased
himself away from me.

"I'm sorry. I didn't mean it."

"Oh, that's okay," I said, playing easy. Hearing him say he
didn't mean it shouldn't have hurt as much as it did. After all, I
was in this thing only for kicks, wasn't I?

"I was just warning you." I tried to laugh. "So next affair, you'd
know. Some women don't like to mess around like that."

·   ·   ·

November came, cool and wet after the long, dry summer. Everyone cheered the rain the first few days, but after a week everyone was depressed. In the winter it seems that all you do is work, go home in the dark, eat, sleep, and get up to work again.

"Are you still messing with that whiteboy?" Melvia was cranky. Being from South Carolina, she hated northern winters. Her patience shortened with the days. "You better quit. This isn't funny any more."

"It's cool, Melvia."

"No, it's not. But you'll learn."

It was election day, which meant nothing to me because, unlike almost everyone else in the newsroom, I wasn't scheduled to work that night. Which could be viewed two ways. On the one hand, it was bad. I didn't get any of the big stories—the mayoral race, the council races, the state legislature—and I knew what that signified. But at least I didn't have to do the grunt work, go stand outside polling places and interview people on whom they had voted for and why, which I always hated. Some people considered it downright un-American to reveal how they'd voted, and they could get nasty about it. And the rewrite person would end up using one quote from you, so all the work was for nothing. I guessed the editors were still punishing me for the Temple of Divine Love story. It was as if I'd become a nonentity, a being invisible among the pillars and the staff.

Melvia was working on one of the council races. Georgia was covering the results of a bond referendum to finance school repairs. Stephanie was lead writer on one of the big state legislative races. She would probably work until 2 or 3 A.M., then go home and drop into bed and get up early for the second-day coverage.

Sitting in the deserted newsroom at noon, I felt lonely, but at least I'd get to see David that night. We had seen each other only once since the "I love you" incident, for a brief and awkward afternoon tryst one Saturday afternoon. I wanted to tell him it was okay, all I wanted was to be with him. I was hoping maybe he'd even be able to spend the night.

I left work at five. Everyone else was just arriving, starting the night by writing background material that they'd use to fill in their stories. By seven I had gone for a run, showered, changed, and opened a bottle of wine. I was watching the local news; people were already predicting who would win.

David showed up empty-handed.

"Hey, what about dinner!" I was happy to see him and felt like teasing a bit. I stood in the doorway with my hands on my hips. "You think you can just show up here and get sex and not even cough up the money to feed me? What kind of girl do you think I am?"

David stood in the doorway, not smiling. His hair was pushed back on the right side, as though he had been running his hand through it. I reached out to smooth it.

"I forgot. You want me to leave?"

"Don't be silly. I was just teasing."

He came in and plopped on the couch with his head back and his eyes closed. Slowly he rotated his neck.

"You look like shit. Long day?"

"Very long."

"How 'bout we order pizza?"

"Fine," he said flatly. He sat up and glanced around the apartment as if distracted. "Can I have a drink?"

I brought him a glass of wine and decided to wait on the pizza.

"I had a lousy day too. They didn't put me on any of the election coverage, and when I went to ask Tom about a story I wrote a week ago, he brushed me off and said I'd have to wait until things calmed down. I'm being punished. I can't stand this cold-shoulder treatment much longer."

David had finished his wine and was twirling the glass in his hand, trying to make it catch the light.

"Um hmm," he said.

"Um hmm? That's all I get?"

He looked up, but his eyes didn't seem to connect.

"Hello? Hello?" I waved my hands in front of his face.

David put down his glass and scooted across the couch to me, catching my lips against his in a hard kiss. For two seconds I resisted, out of instinct more than thought, and then I stopped resisting and we were pawing at each other, wrestling to the carpet below the couch, pulling at each other's clothes, and David was breathing so hard I couldn't hear anything else, not even the television, which was still on, trumpeting election returns. I pulled down David's jeans and he pulled down mine and pushed up my bra and slammed his mouth onto my breasts, first one, then the other, pulling with his teeth until I cried out, and he stopped and reached for the box to turn off the television and then reached up above me to turn off the lamp.

Which was funny. When we'd first begun, I had kept trying to turn off the light when we went to bed, but David stopped me. "I love to look at your skin," he said. "It's beautiful. So rich." That night when he snapped off the light the darkness fell over me like an affront, and he plunged into me, breathing hard, and pumped away, hard at first, but then more slowly and dutifully, like a man filling a tractor tire with a bicycle pump. After a while he asked, "Are you close?"

I lay there, hands resting lightly on his back. "I don't think I'm going to make it."

"Then I'll go ahead and come, if you don't mind."

"Be my guest."

I almost laughed at the formality of our words. With a few more pumps, David came and then rolled off me onto the carpet. From next door came the dull hum of Mrs. Scott's vacuum as she rolled it across her pristine floors.

"What was that?" I asked. "What we just did."

David didn't answer. In the light from outside I could just make out the back of his head. His face was turned toward the window. He must have been looking at the bare trees.

For some reason I thought about my uncle Jesse and the story he used to tell us, when my mother wasn't listening, about the fight that had sent him to jail. It was a Saturday-night fight, a juke joint rumpus. Both men were drunk and some woman was involved and the other man had a switchblade that he pulled from his pocket while they were circling each other. All Uncle Jesse had was a bottle he grabbed from the bar. He lost two fingers and went to jail, but the other man went to the hospital.

"Sometimes you just got to decide it's him or me," Uncle Jesse told us, shaking his three-fingered hand in front of our faces for dramatic effect. "And I always decided that it was going to be me."

"What's going on, David?"

"I don't have the energy for this."

"You better find it. What the hell are you doing?"

But before he could answer, a beeping noise cut through the darkness. David sighed and crawled toward his clothes. I switched on the light.

"I have to make a call," he said, looking up from his beeper.

"You know where the phone is."

But instead of using the phone in the kitchen, David walked into my bedroom, dragging his pants behind him. I sat back against the couch, my shirt and bra still twisted around my chest. What was it about half-dressed sex that always seemed so dirty? Naked sex could seem innocent and sweet. But half dressed, I always felt tawdry. Something sticky and cool rolled down my thigh and onto the carpet. I was dripping on the floor. Suddenly I needed to be dressed, dressed and cleaned. I got up and went to the bathroom; passing the bedroom, I heard David mumble, "Okay, okay. Calm down. I'll be right there."

When I got back to the living room, he sat on the couch, tying his shoelaces.

"I have to go," he said.

Then go, I thought. But I was afraid of what my voice would sound like if I spoke, so I pulled on my jeans and walked to the kitchen and poured myself another glass of wine.

"It's Stephanie," David said, coming into the kitchen.

"Serious?" It was work getting anything out of my mouth, which had gone dry. I sipped some wine.

"No. But I have to go."

"You know how to operate the door."

David looked at me. I tried to hide the tears forming in my eyes behind my glass.

"Maybe this was a mistake," he said.

The word came to me soft and velvety over the wine.

"A mistake. Okay."

"Things have gotten complicated. She suspects. Not you, but something, and it's made her . . . unhappy."

"Can't have that."

"When she gets unhappy she does things. To herself. It's very hard. I can't be responsible."

"Of course."

"She needs me."

"Yes."

"I have to go now."

"Yes."

"I'm sorry, Hope. I never meant to hurt you."

"Oh, no."

"I have to go."

After he left I dragged the blue comforter from my bed—my mother had given it to me at college graduation—and went into the living room, stopping off in the kitchen to open another bottle of wine.

She needed him and I didn't. And that was true, so what was my problem? I didn't need anybody. People always thought that, looking at me. Once, in college, I showed the first short story I had ever written to a good friend of mine. It was an assignment for an English class; I worked hard, and it seemed to flow out of my typewriter like it had been waiting, and I was excited. Maybe this was something I could do. But when I showed the story to my friend, he pulled it apart. He said it was immature and implausible and stilted and a whole lot of other things. And at the end of his tirade he got up from our table in the cafeteria and, smiling, said, "I hope I wasn't too harsh, Hope, but I know you're the kind of girl who doesn't need any silly stroking. You're tough. You can take it." I told him he was right; I could.

The couch seemed way too far from the television. I wrapped the comforter around my shoulders and crawled onto the floor, curling up like a baby beneath my fourteen inches of flickering reality. The returns were rolling in now. The whole city held its breath. I drank the wine. On the screen, the news announcer went away and somebody started singing a song about chocolate milk.

chapter twelve

I woke up on the floor next to two empty wine bottles, the chatter of some giggly morning-TV blonde bouncing above me. Dragging my head up from the floor, I saw that the blonde and a man in a big white hat were in a kitchen, laughing and talking and whipping egg whites. From my vantage point they looked like giants. I lay still for a few minutes, waiting for them to step off the screen and crush me to death.

When that didn't happen, I decided I'd better try to get up. It took several minutes for me to rise, and when I finally made it I was unsteady on my feet and my arm hurt. I'd slept on it. The blood rushing back to the nerves hurt like hell. I decided to focus on showering and getting dressed. But I'd forgotten to do laundry. I had to reach back into my closet for a brown corduroy skirt I never wore, for obvious reasons. While curling my hair, I seared the back of my ear and screamed, out of frustration more than pain. The sound brought Mrs. Scott pounding on my door.

"What's going on in there?" she barked.

"Sorry. Burned my ear."

"Well, keep it down. I'm trying to sleep."

It was raining, which didn't surprise me one bit. Cold rain, sooty and fat. I drove to work, trying to figure out why I wasn't at home in bed with a cup of tea. I had to cover a meeting of the city's redevelopment council that afternoon. A group of civic leaders from North Philadelphia planned to show up and demand that the city do something about the derelict train station on Broad Street, a beautiful old structure going slowly to the rats. One of the leaders had begged me to cover the meeting, to give them some exposure. They knew and I knew that the City Hall reporter wouldn't give them two lines at the bottom of page 36, but I felt it was my duty to at least try to get something in. That was the only reason I went to work.

My umbrella, which I usually left in my car, was nowhere to be found. I hit every overhanging roof between the parking lot and work but still got wet. While I was drying off in the bathroom, a woman I didn't know pointed to the back of my skirt.

"Your zipper's broken," she said.

At my desk, I found a message on my voice mail.

"Hope, this is Reverend Wilson. I wanted to let you know they canceled that meeting today. Probably canceled it because they knew we were coming. We had fifteen carloads ready to come on down and stand on the floor. Don't know how we're going to get all those people together again." He sighed onto the tape. "Well, the Lord will make a way. All we can do is wait." *Beeeep.*

The resignation in his voice grated against my already tender nerves. All they could do was wait. That's all we ever did. What they should have done was march down Broad Street, right up to the steps of City Hall. It wasn't that big a deal, that old boarded-up station, except that it symbolized the city's neglect of an entire neighborhood. And Reverend Wilson's quiet acceptance represented a neighborhood's defeat.

With my last bit of energy, I tried calling the church. But the sad, vanquished sound of the busy signal sapped my strength. What was I going to do anyway—incite a riot? It wasn't my problem. Let them figure it out themselves.

It was almost noon. The newsroom had filled up with people—chattering, laughing whitefolks who made my head hurt. The day was looking grimmer and grimmer. All I needed now was for David to come waltzing through the newsroom, looking for Stephanie. Maybe bearing an engagement ring. As these thoughts flitted through my mind, my phone rang and I picked it up without thinking it might not be a good thing to do.

"This is Mrs. Albert Cohane," a voice announced. As if I should recognize her.

"Yes?"

"You wrote an obituary on my husband today?"

"Oh. Yes." I'd been drafted to help the obit writer. I didn't want the desk to get into the habit, so I complained, but really it wasn't that bad. As the obit writer said to me, at least the subjects never complain.

This woman was probably calling to thank me.

"I want to tell you that you have ruined my husband's final legacy!" she said. "You've taken what is already a difficult time for me and made it even harder to bear. I hope you're happy."

It took me a second to register what she was saying.

"Excuse me?"

"You wrote that he won the Purple Heart!" She was yelling now. Not screaming like she was hysterical with grief or something; that I might have understood. But yelling, as if dealing with some thickheaded clerk who'd gotten her order wrong. "He never won the Purple Heart!"

"Oh. Well, I'm sorry. I used whatever I was given by the funeral home."

"You did not! I gave them the proper information. You deliberately wrote the wrong thing!"

I tried to stay calm, but her yelling was hurting my head.

"Why would I do that, ma'am? That doesn't make sense. It was a mistake."

"I want you to know you've ruined everything!" She was going for it now, the top of her lungs. It was insane. Had anyone in the newsroom been paying attention, he would have seen my mouth drop wide with disbelief. "How am I going to make copies of this? I can't even show it to his friends! I'll be a laughingstock!"

I told myself to stay calm. Get this nut off the phone and go home before something else happened. It was turning out to be the day from hell. "We'll run a correction," I said.

"A correction! A correction tomorrow won't help me today!"

"I'm sorry. There's nothing else I can do today."

"Of course! Destroy someone's life and then say there's nothing you can do about it. Reporters!"

"Destroyed your life? Isn't that a bit of an overstatement?"

"Oh! Now you're telling me you know more about my life than I do? I ought to call your editor!"

I hate it when people threaten to call my editor. Only jerks do it, and only when they know they have no legitimate gripe with whatever you're talking about. They expect you to quiver and give in. It always reminded me of my sister Charity, who used to get mad when I wouldn't let her play with my things and run through the house screaming, "I'm gonna tell Mommy!"

"That's what I'm going to do," the woman threatened. "I'm going to call your editor. I'm sure he'd like to know about this."

"Go right ahead," I said, and hung up the phone.

That was it. Now I must absolutely head home. But just as I was about to leave, Melvia messaged me.

"Did you see the announcements?"

"No," I wrote back. "What?"

"Go out in the hallway and look. You won't believe it!"

I pulled out my shirttail in an attempt to cover my broken zipper and walked to the hallway, praying no one would stop and talk to me. An announcement from Rob was posted on the wall next to the elevators. I don't know how I had missed it coming in.

I'm pleased to announce that Stephanie Woodbridge will be the new Washington bureau reporter, replacing John Stone, who departs shortly for Moscow. In the short time she has been with us, Stephanie has demonstrated remarkable drive and the willingness to pursue a story to the far corners of the earth to uncover the truth. That plus her fine writing should serve her in good stead in Washington.

I could barely get through the paragraph. Stephanie was taking the job Melvia had wanted, the one she had been asking for and been promised for years. I limped back to my desk, my head pounding.

"Girl, I'm sorry," I wrote to Melvia. "I can't even believe that shit. What are you going to do?"

"What can I do?" she wrote back. "Kick and scream. Kick and scream."

I didn't know what to write. "It sucks," was the best I could think of. "Want to take an early lunch?"

"No. I have a dentist appointment, and if I'm lucky, he'll give me some Valium. Either way I'm taking the rest of the day off."

"Do it! Take the week off. Go to the beach and find a stud and have wild sex!"

From across the newsroom came the ripple of Melvia's laughter.

"At least I don't have to deal with that asshole Richard," she wrote. "I feel sorry for you there, girlfriend. I'm out of here."

I messaged back to ask what she meant, but already I heard Melvia's pumps clicking across the newsroom floor. It could wait until tomorrow. I was out of there too. But while waiting for the elevator, I noticed a second posting from Rob, beneath the one about Stephanie.

I am pleased to announce that Richard Goldin will join the city desk as an assistant deputy editor. His areas of oversight will include education, social service, and the neighborhood beats. Richard brings to the desk nearly fifteen years of experience as a reporter in politics, police reporting, and investigative work. His contribution will be invaluable, as we seek to toughen the look and feel of the metro report.

Things had gone from bad to worse in split-second time. Richard, the guy I disliked most in the newsroom, was going to be my editor. Richard, the guy who thought I didn't even deserve to be at the paper. As I stood there absorbing the news, the man himself stepped off the elevator, trailed by two reporters, who had obviously seen the note and were starting their brown-nosing early.

"Oh, hello, Hope," Richard said, then, as he passed me, "Your skirt's not zipped."

Richard and his entourage marched into the newsroom. The elevator door closed before I could catch it. My head pounded, a sour taste rose in my mouth, and just when I thought things really couldn't get much worse, Stephanie appeared. She came whizzing around the corner and stopped, smiling at me. She was wearing a cobalt-blue suit, cut like custom made, which set off the blue of her eyes. For someone who'd had a crisis last night, she looked pretty good. I tugged at the back of my skirt and pushed the elevator button.

"Hi, Hope!" She was beaming so brightly I felt like squinting. I mumbled something back at her and turned away.

"Is something wrong? You don't look so great."

"Thanks." I mashed the elevator button again, but nothing happened.

"You look upset."

"I'm fine."

"Did something happen? Did somebody say something to you?"

"Other than to tell me I looked like shit, you mean?" Where in the hell was the elevator? I turned toward the stairs.

"Was it Richard? I was just upstairs, listening to him bitch about affirmative action again. And now he gets promoted. Can you believe that? It just isn't fair."

"Unlike the rest of life." I headed for the stairway, figuring Stephanie would get the point and leave me alone. But to my surprise, she followed me. I couldn't believe her nerve. She seemed oblivious to my go-away vibes, so at the stairwell door I turned and faced her.

"Go away, Stephanie." My head hurt so much I felt like crying. I was beginning to worry that if I didn't get home soon I'd collapse on the street like an old paper bag.

"But I can see you're upset!"

"Please leave me alone!"

"Oh, Hope, you're very talented, much more talented than Richard. You shouldn't let people like that get to you!"

Stephanie followed me into the dim stairwell, where dust balls the size of mice cowered in the corners and footsteps echoed above our heads. I couldn't stand it anymore; I started crying, more from pain and frustration and especially anger than from sadness. Crying when I got angry was a bad habit I'd had since childhood. My uncle used to call me "tenderhearted," because I'd sit there leaking tears when he teased me. It wasn't a compliment. Faith would laugh at his jeering words and poking hands. Charity would get mad and fight him back, but I'd just cry, all the while silently plotting his death. Growing up, I tried thinking mean thoughts when I got angry, tried pinching the bridge of my nose or holding my breath. Nothing helped. I still cried. It was infuriating. There I'd be, in the midst of some argument, pissed as hell, but then I'd feel that hot, stinging sensation behind my eyes, and out gushed the tears, and the next thing I knew, whoever I was arguing with was feeling sorry for me. Which just pissed me off more.

"Oh, Hope!" Stephanie's voice turned all sympathetic at the sight of my tears. "Don't cry. Don't let them get to you!"

She moved toward me, arms outstretched as if to hug me, and the thought of being comforted by this whitegirl sent me over the edge. I knocked her arms away, and then suddenly I wasn't crying anymore. My eyes cleared; my head cleared. The stairwell seemed to light up from my glow. I reached out and pushed Stephanie again.

"You stupid bitch! You're the one who gets to me! You're the one who makes me sick!"

Stephanie stumbled back against the wall, her eyes cloudy with confusion. "What did I do?"

"Oh, nothing! Just stood there looking smug."

"You looked so upset."

"So what's it to you? We aren't even friends!"

"I just wanted to help you," she said softly.

"What makes you think I need your help?"

"I was only trying to help." She was almost whimpering, which really infuriated me. On top of everything else, I was the bad guy now!

"Oh, shut up!" I screamed, and before I realized what I was doing, I reached out and struck her face.

It wasn't really a hard slap. I hadn't hit anyone since childhood, and striking a human being efficiently is something that takes practice. Plus at the moment of impact, Stephanie had her head turned to look down at something she'd nearly tripped on—which turned out to be my purse. When the blow struck, I caught her face with my fingertips instead of my palm.

Still. I had slapped her.

In the silent moment after the slap, Stephanie cringed and I held my breath, waiting for her to scream. She'd scream and people would come running through the door, piling into the stairwell to see what was going on. Stephanie would accuse me with her slender finger, and then what? I'd lose my job, I'd go to jail, I'd be strung kicking and screaming from the top of a tree. I stood there waiting, willing her to scream and get it started, but Stephanie just touched her hand gently to her cheek.

"I'm sorry," she whispered.

"What?" I was sure I'd misheard her.

"It was my fault. I should have left you alone."

"Are you nuts? Why don't you scream!?"

The door behind us opened. A man I recognized as a sportswriter stepped into the hallway and stopped short.

"Oops! Sorry!" He smiled, embarrassed. "Just got to get through." He tucked the papers he was carrying beneath his arm and took the stairs two at a time up to the next floor. I wondered what he imagined he had disturbed.

While I was watching the man, Stephanie slipped back through the closing door. I saw her turn left, toward the bathroom. I grabbed my purse and headed down the stairs, toward the light of the front lobby.

My headache, strangely, had disappeared.

part 2

chapter thirteen

Between my first and second visits to the shrink, I went to church—which says a lot about how bad things were. I hadn't been to church in years, except for the occasional guilty Easter visit. That I was considering it said I needed help, bad. Something was wrong, and I had to fix it. If I started slapping every whitegirl I felt like smacking in the course of a day, I'd wind up in jail.

In the yellow pages I found a surprising number of Churches of God in Christ—I had assumed that brand of Pentecostal churches was mostly a southern thing. But then most blacks in Philadelphia had come up from the South at some point. And also, downtrodden black folks lived everywhere.

What I loved about the church of my childhood, what I

missed most about not attending as an adult, was the music. The first time I ever attended a white church, at Astor, I had to bite the inside of my cheek to keep from laughing. Those hymns— they called that music? People around me kind of mumbled along, always slightly behind the organ and frequently off key, even though they had all the notes right there in front of their faces in a hymnal. The only time the congregation sang with passion was on the last two notes of every song, which everybody hit with force, as if relieved the ordeal was over. And even when the choir sang and got the notes right, it was boring. Nobody rocked or clapped along; I could have napped through the entire thing.

There were no hymnals in my church. Everybody knew all the words to every song, even the youngest children, and if by some chance you didn't know the words, it was easy enough to catch on, because the chorus was always sung again and again, with such joy and purpose and driving rhythm that only a dead man could resist joining in. Unhappiness was impossible when that music was swaying the church. So was disbelief. I'd always believed in God, of course, the way I believed that night followed day, but the only time I really felt His presence, the way the elders of the church said they did every day, was when I was singing. After twenty or thirty or forty minutes of singing to glory, I'd sink down in the pew, moist and happy, knowing that God knew who I was. If church had been just music, I'd have gone every day and gotten saved over and over again.

But eventually the music stopped, and the preacher stood up and ruined it all. The sweet, smiling God I had just met metamorphosed into a sullen old man pissed off at everything I did. He was going to send me straight to hell for wearing pants, not to mention talking back to my mother and thinking, late at night, about sex. This God was merciless. This God was guilt, and He sent the saints of the church, those old women in their white dresses and those old men with their slicked-back hair, to sniff out my sins: soul music and card games with my friends and dirty thoughts. I couldn't live up to the standards of this God, and so finally I quit trying.

I used to slouch in the pew and stare out the dusty windows, daydreaming my way through a sermon that dragged on and on. But there was nowhere to hide when the time came for saving souls. Everybody knew who was saved and who wasn't. The saints carried their salvation like banners and scanned the congregation; the rest of us prayed fervently to sink out of sight.

"Come, sinner! Come!" the preacher cried. The choir plunged into song: "I'm so glad, Jesus lifted me! I'm so glad that Jesus lifted me!" Old women fanned themselves with cardboard fans picturing Martin Luther King, Jr., and sang along.

People turned around in their seats, sniffing for sinners. My mother stood next to me, swaying to the music with her eyes closed. It would make her so happy to see me head for the altar. The Sunday my aunt Lisa got saved, my mother had grinned for the rest of the night.

"Anyone else? Anyone?" the preacher called. The music slowed, catching its breath, and transformed into a plaintive, two-word song. "Yes, Lord! Yess, Lord! Yesss, Looord! Yess, Lord! Yes, Lord!" The preacher stood over the three or four quivering bodies standing before him, his hands outstretched to the congregation, his eyes staring straight at me.

"Anyone else want to come? Anyone? Anyone? Better come to the Lord today, for we are not promised tomorrow. Anyone? Anyone? Oh, thank you, Jesus! No one knows the day nor the hour when the Lord shall appear. Anyone? Anyone? All right."

He never got me. I stood planted near my seat, head bowed, resisting the magnetic tug of the preacher's eyes, thinking, praying, "Lord, I love you and I believe in your son, Jesus, and I know that He died on the cross for me and I confess my sins. Really, I do. But no way on this earth am I going up there."

.   .   .

I got dressed and drove to an interracial Methodist church someone had told me about. It was huge, old, Gothic, its white stone facade painted gray by city grime. I snuck in late, sat way in the back, so far from the pulpit that the minister's face was a dancing white dot above black robes. No one paid me much attention. A tiny old white lady in a Jackie O suit sat at the opposite end of my pew and dozed. There were no calls to the altar to confess my sins. No two-hour sermons—the minister wrapped it up in twenty minutes. The music was flat and uninspiring, but you couldn't have everything. Just being in a church, sitting there in the somber coolness of that house of God, calmed me a little. I whispered a prayer, asked God to forgive me for slapping Stephanie. There was no immediate response.

Sunday night I drank a bottle of wine and prepared myself to be fired the next morning. But when I got to work Monday everything was pretty much the same. No staring, no finger-pointing like I'd expected. Richard handed me an assignment as soon as I walked in the door, sent me to interview a group of women living at the King projects, who complained that their heat didn't work and now their water had been shut off. One woman dragged me through her shabby apartment to show me a toilet she said had been backed up for nearly a month. A teenage girl, her hair wound brokenly around pink curlers, sat in the living room, holding a dull-eyed baby to her chest and staring at the TV. Sheets hung against the windows blocked any sliver of sun that might have brightened the dim apartment. Going to the projects always depressed me. I couldn't wait to get out.

I didn't see Stephanie that day, or the next, or the one after that; then I heard she was out sick. I imagined her prostrate on a four-poster bed, her back propped up with feather pillows, a cold towel pressed over her swollen cheek. As soon as she recovered, she'd report me to Rob, and that would be that—career down the drain. She could even press charges against me for assault. I imagined trying to explain that to my mother. "I didn't raise you for this," she'd say, as she used to whenever we did anything bad. She rarely said exactly what it was she had raised us for, but we knew. For something better.

I didn't see David either, but that might have been because I was avoiding him. I stayed out of the cafeteria, took the stairs between floors to avoid the elevator. There was little I could do about my exposure in the newsroom: if he came in, he'd see me. I kept expecting to look up from my computer screen and see him pointing an accusing finger in my face.

On the fourth day after "the incident," Stephanie reappeared, looking none the worse for wear. That afternoon, because I couldn't stand it anymore, I went to her desk.

"Could we talk for a few minutes?"

"Sure!" She smiled brightly at me, but I could tell she was nervous. I steered her toward the conference room, but with the click of the door behind us, my mind emptied. What the hell was there to say? I knew I should apologize, beg her forgiveness. Man, that was going to be hard. And mostly what I wanted to know was what she had said to whom.

"Look, Stephanie . . ."

"I didn't tell anyone," she said quietly.

"What?"

"You don't have to worry. I didn't tell anyone anything. Nothing at all."

I stared hard at her, trying to see if she was joking or just playing with me. Did the bitch have it in her to be that coy? I might almost respect her for that.

"Come on. If someone slapped me I'd sure as hell turn them in."

"I didn't say anything."

"Not even to David?"

I had no idea how much she knew about David. I tried to make my voice neutral when I said his name. Her expression did not change.

"No," she said. "As far as I'm concerned, it never happened. I don't know what was going on with you, why you did it, but I know you didn't mean it. I could see that."

"Unbelievable." I didn't know whether to laugh, kiss her, or slap her again. This chick was nuts.

"Things happen," she said, stepping toward me now. Her nervousness seemed to be easing. "Sometimes things just . . . get out of control. I know about that."

She knew about that. Mother Teresa turning the other cheek. I knew I should feel grateful, but I was starting to feel angry again. Calm down, I told myself. Just apologize and get out.

"I apologize for striking you. I haven't hit anyone in my adult life, and I don't plan to do so again. Thanks for not reporting me."

She shrugged. "Like I said, I understand. Why don't you come over for dinner tonight? We could talk. I could use someone to talk to."

"You want to have dinner with me?" I couldn't hide my scorn any longer, but Stephanie seemed not to notice.

"Sure. Why not?" She smiled. What was it with this girl? Did everyone have to love her?

"I'm afraid I'm busy."

"Well, next week, then. I'll be packing for Washington, but we could get together one evening, have a drink."

It was all I could do not to laugh in her face, but I resisted. She was letting me off the hook, for whatever crazy reason. I guess she could afford to be magnanimous. All I had to do was take the stick and run.

"Right," I said. "Tell you what—I'll give you a call."

.   .   .

At my second session with Cindy, I told her what had happened with Stephanie. "Isn't that strange? What do you think her problem is?"

"I couldn't begin to talk about Stephanie, and I wouldn't want to," Cindy said. "We're here to talk about you."

Cindy had been happy to see me. She'd opened the door wearing a smile.

"I wasn't sure you'd come back," she said. Not so stupid after all.

Cindy began the session by asking about Astor. She was fascinated by the thought of my going off to that lily-white prep school so young. I told her I didn't want to talk about it.

"Astor isn't the issue. My anger's the issue. The fact that I sometimes feel so mad I think I'm going insane."

"What triggers this anger?"

"People. People make me nuts. People like Stephanie."

"You mean white people."

There it was, out in the open. Well, hell, why not? Might as well make her earn her dough.

"Yeah, white people. Not all of them, but white people like Stephanie, people who have it all and never had to worry about anything. It just isn't fair."

"Who told you life was fair?" Cindy said this like it was some great revelation. Is that what she went to school six years for?

"Knowing life is unfair and seeing it sitting across the room from you every day are two different things."

"I see," Cindy said. More brilliant strategy.

"Let me tell you a story. One summer during college, I worked at a newspaper in a small town in Massachusetts, and I helped cover a mayoral campaign. One of the candidates was this woman. I hated her the first time I saw her. She wore corduroy pants and sweaters with her initials on the front and little shell earrings, and her face was like . . . pudding. Just that smooth and blank and pleased with the world. She was rich, grew up rich, went to college someplace like Smith, and married the first rich, ambitious guy she met. They had two kids—smart and good looking. She piddled around doing Junior League stuff, until one day she decided to run for mayor. All during the campaign her opponent called her a rich bitch and attacked her as a dilettante, but it never fazed her. Never. I'd pelt her with questions; she was thick as a brick and totally unprepared, and I'd make her look like a fool, but she'd just sit there and smile. She had this air about her that was amazing. It took me a long time to figure out what it was, but I finally did. It was that she didn't care. She was the only politician I've ever met who really didn't care if she won or lost. If she lost, she'd just go back to being rich—big loss! I don't even know why she bothered to run; some sense of noblesse oblige, I guess. But there was no doubt in her mind that life brought good things, because it had brought only good things to her. And of course she won. That woman drove me nuts. I couldn't stand her. I kept telling myself not to let her get me mad, but I couldn't help it. I can never help it."

"Why do you think that is?"

"You tell me. You're the expert."

"Okay. This is just a theory, but maybe it's because you want to make sure that the one thing these people who have it all don't get is your forgiveness. Or your friendship. You figure at least you can make them suffer that much."

"Doesn't seem to be working, does it?" I laughed; Cindy didn't even smile. She was starting to get on my nerves.

"I know you don't want to spend the next three years in psycho-analysis," she said. "That's not the kind of therapy I practice anyway. But to deal with a problem, it helps to understand its source."

"Does it? If I'm fat because I eat too much, can't I just stop eating too much? Do I need to understand that I eat too much because my mother never loved me or whatever?"

"You could try, but my guess is you already *have* tried. If you could make yourself stop being angry, would you be sitting here right now?"

To her credit, Cindy allowed not a flicker of smugness to cross her face as she said this.

"What I'm suggesting is this: maybe part of your anger toward white people comes from what happened to you at Astor. You were made to feel like you weren't smart enough or pretty enough, and that got translated into being white enough."

I snorted. "Listen, not being white enough was never my problem. Just the opposite, in fact."

Cindy cocked her head. "What do you mean?"

"I mean that if anything, I'm too white. I've spent too much of my life surrounded by white people; their essence has soaked into my skin. I can't get it off."

"Interesting. Let me ask you a question. Do you like being black?"

"That's a stupid question. Do you like being white?"

"Well . . ." She paused and tapped her pen against her pearly teeth. "I guess I don't think about it much."

"I bet you don't," I said. "Yeah, I like being black. I'm proud of being black, if you can be proud about something you had no control over. I love being black; I just don't want to be only black."

"So who's making you?"

"Who isn't?"

"I'm not."

"Yes. Well." I stopped. I did not want to get into this with her. "We're off track here. We were talking about anger. All the rest is beside the point."

"I don't think so. But okay, here's the point as I see it, and it's an important one: All this anger you're carrying around isn't hurting those white people you hate so much. They don't even know you're pissed off. The only person you're hurting is yourself. That's the point."

Cindy's words hung in the silence between us. Of course I knew that I was the one being hurt. But hearing it from Cindy put bite behind the words; the idea registered with a new force. She was right, damn it. I was the one who ended up crying in my car after work. I was the one on the verge of a breakdown, not sweet little Steffie or her kind.

I looked across the room at Cindy. Her hair shimmered in the waning light of the sun. This was what it was like to have a revelation. This was what they called an epiphany.

But then the sun slipped a notch and the room shifted into dimness, as though someone had turned off a light far away. Cindy's hair dulled. My epiphany dissolved.

"So you're saying my anger is irrational, that I really don't have any reason to be so pissed off?"

"I'm not saying that at all. I'm saying it's not your job to hate Stephanie, that doing so doesn't even the score."

"You don't understand a thing, not a damn thing."

Cindy leaned back in her chair and spread her hands out, smoothing the air.

"Okay, tell me. Make me understand."

"I can't."

"Can't or won't?"

"Can not," I said, emphasizing the words.

Cindy shrugged and scribbled something in the notebook she kept hidden in her lap.

"What about this guy you mentioned the first time. You said he might have had something to do with you losing your temper. What happened there?"

What *had* happened with David? What happened was that I'd gotten involved—deliberately, knowingly, stupidly—with a guy who was already involved with a girl he would never leave, especially not for me. Stephanie had him, she had him so casually she didn't even know it, and that was part of what made me dislike her so intensely. But I couldn't complain about what had happened with David, because I'd walked into the situation with my eyes open. I felt used, but whose fault was that?

"It doesn't matter," I told Cindy. "He doesn't have much to do with this."

Cindy sighed and glanced at her watch. I looked at mine. The time was up.

"You've got a lot of work to do, Hope," she said as I was leaving. "I hope you'll stick with it."

I rolled my eyes. "What does that mean—'a lot of work to do'?"

"It means you can't go on living like this, boiling away inside. If you can't let go of your anger, you've got to figure out some way of living with it."

"I thought that was why I'm paying you."

Cindy smiled. "You're paying me to help, and I can. But you have to do it."

"Right."

Outside Cindy's house the trees were nearly bare. Autumn had been beautiful but succinct; a month or so of brilliant color, and then, boom, the cold swept in. My first winter in Philadelphia, my first winter north of the Mason-Dixon line since high school. I wondered if it would snow.

The things Cindy said had made sense to me while I was sitting in her office. But her words were like a fire in a fireplace: you had to be standing right in front of them for them to have any effect. The moment you stepped away, the heat was lost. As I drove home from Cindy's office, the idea of my paying some blonde to fix my life seemed ridiculous. What did I have to complain about anyway? Therapy was self-indulgent. My grandmother would have called it 'whitefolks mess.' My mother would say the same thing, essentially, except she wouldn't actually use the word "whitefolks." She rarely referred to white people as such, preferring to use "they" or "them"—as if in naming the enemy you gave him power. "They've finally done it," she would say. "They've driven my daughter crazy. You don't need a psychologist. What you need is to come on home."

My mother and I had rarely talked, really talked, about race or identity or our place as black women in the world. Not that I didn't have a sense of how she felt. Every time some famous black man got in trouble and ended up in the newspaper—James Brown beating his wife or Clarence Thomas defending his honor—my mother would complain that it was a deliberate attempt by "them" to keep "us" from getting anything good. But that was about as far as it went between us. Before Astor, I hadn't been interested in probing deeper into my mother's feelings about race. And after Astor, well, I just never got around to it. Maybe I was afraid of what my mother would think of me.

When the time came for my third appointment with Cindy, my heart just wasn't in it. I called and canceled. I would not be going back.

chapter fourteen

On the night of Stephanie's going-away party, I sat on the couch in my living room, drinking wine and drawing tattoos on my body with a red felt-tip pen. I drew a heart on my arm and daisies on the back of my hand. On my stomach I drew a sun, using my navel as its fiery core.

I wasn't sure what to expect from David with Stephanie gone. He might come sniffing around as soon as her train pulled out of the city; then again, he might not. What was that thing my mother used to say about buying the cow and getting the milk?

A couple of days passed with no sign of David. I spent a lot of time thinking about him, trying not to think about him, wondering if he was thinking about me. It was so hard to know with men. But no, that wasn't true with David. With David things were crystal clear: he'd chosen Stephanie. He chose her over me, for whatever reason. I would do well to remember that fact.

My nerves were so raw I had to concentrate on keeping calm. The worst times were late mornings in the newsroom, when people didn't have enough to do yet to focus on their business and leave mine alone. Everybody would just mill around, waiting for lunch or for some story to pop, and in the meantime talk and talk, never saying a damn thing.

All that babble got on my nerves. When it reached the point where I couldn't stand it another minute, I'd grab my purse and a notebook and leave the building. That was one of the best things about being a journalist—not having to punch a time clock. Of course you could take it too far, and maybe I did sometimes, but I didn't care. When I had to either scream or leave, I'd leave, maybe walking over to the Reading Terminal Market and looking at vegetables. Or getting in my car and driving to the big outlet mall just outside town. I could kill whole afternoons that way.

The mall was like another world, an amusement park where the streets were clean and the air was fragrant with melting chocolate chips. It was always crowded, no matter the time of day, packed with chubby white women in polyester sweatsuits, pawing away at racks of half-priced clothes. I'd browse the aisles, picking up this or that item to try on, only half intending to buy.

One afternoon, as I stood in a store debating whether or not to try on a short black dress, three whitegirls galloped in. They came giggling over to the rack where I browsed. One had small brown ringlets that set off her eyes—a perm, no doubt, but an expensive perm. The other two were blondes. They descended on the rack, babbling like geese, oblivious to the small Asian woman who stood next to them, oblivious to me.

"Ashley found her dress in Macy's," said one.

One of the other girls made a face. "Ugh."

I watched them, marveling at the way they moved through

the store, through life. They seemed to gaze at the world as if it were their bedroom and they were trying to figure out what shade of rose it ought to be. One of the girls held up a dress just like the one I was holding.

"This is cute!" she squealed, holding the dress out for inspection. Her friends cooed in agreement. Then the girl looked at the tag and made a face.

"Oh! It's a size twelve!" She sounded disgusted. Twelve was my size.

Shoving the dress back, the girl riffled through the rack, searching for a smaller size. No luck. At the end of the rack she turned away empty-handed and stamped her foot.

"All they have left is these big old tents!"

Her friends gathered around, consoling her. "Don't worry!" "We'll find something!" "Let's try Saks." Together they traipsed from the store, leaving me and my big black tent behind. I put the dress on a rack that held miniskirts. Somebody would have to come through after the place closed and put the dress back where it belonged.

Thanksgiving came. I volunteered to work and spent the day following the mayor around town as he dished up stuffing at homeless shelters. After work I stopped off at Melvia's apartment and ate cold turkey left over from her annual orphans' Thanksgiving dinner.

"You're in a funky mood these days," she said. "Broke up with that whiteboy, didn't you?"

"You want to say 'I told you so'?"

"I do, but I won't. You all right?"

"I'm fine."

"Believe me, it's for the best."

I saw David the following Tuesday, when he came into the newsroom. He spent about ten minutes talking to a couple of people who were working on a series of articles about school tax, and then he headed toward my desk. I picked up the phone and dialed my home phone number and starting talking, trying hard to control what sounded like a dangerous trembling in my voice. I kept my eyes down, pretended I was taking notes, but out of the corner of my eye I could see David standing by my desk, waiting. I kept talking to myself and scribbling nonsense notes until he left.

An hour later he called from his office.

"Hi. I stopped by your desk earlier, but you were on the phone. Wanted to say hello."

"Just a second, my other line." I put him on hold, counted to thirty, came back laughing as though I had just heard the funniest joke in the world.

"You're in a good mood!"

"Yes, I am, and I plan to stay that way. What did you want?"

"Just saying hello. I was wondering if maybe we could have dinner sometime. Talk things over."

"You want to talk?"

"I miss talking to you. I liked talking to you, even before everything happened."

"In other words, why can't we be friends?"

"Why can't we?"

"My other line is ringing again. I have to go."

I was proud of myself for hanging up on him. But ten minutes later I was so tempted to call him back I could taste it. My dignity was slipping. I flipped through the papers on my desk, trying to resist the urge to pick up the phone, and just as the urge was winning, the phone rang.

"Miss Robinson? This is Ed Turner."

Not David. I was both relieved and disappointed. "Yes, Mr. Turner. What can I do for you?"

"I was calling to make sure you still planned to attend our demonstration today. At noon. We spoke about it last week."

I had planned to attend, although I didn't think the protest would turn into much of anything. But the excitement of talking to David had driven everything from my mind.

"I'll be right there."

I drove to the site, an empty lot on Germantown Avenue, sandwiched between a chicken joint and a store whose Asian owners sold synthetic hair. The demonstration had been called to protest a new ordinance making it illegal for vendors to sell their wares on the city's sidewalks. Instead they were supposed to wheel their aluminum-sided booths to lots designated by the city. The vendors were furious, especially in North Philly, where the law seemed to be enforced with particular zeal. Since the sidewalk vendors were mostly black and the store owners who had promoted the law were mostly white or Asian, the whole thing got turned into a racial argument.

The crowd was much smaller than I'd anticipated, no more than thirty people. I looked around for Ed Turner but couldn't find him. But I did see someone I knew. Malcolm stood in the middle of six or eight men, microphone in hand, while the men talked loudly and angrily about the new law. I slid into the group and started taking notes. Malcolm saw me and smiled, and I registered again how good looking he was.

After a few minutes a car pulled up, and Ed Turner stepped out. The crowd turned toward him and began to chant, "No justice, no peace!" But Turner held up his hand like a principal trying to quiet his pupils.

"I have news, my brothers and sisters. I have just come from a meeting with the city council president. He told me he spent all morning in meetings with his colleagues, and he now has enough votes to get the law repealed!"

The crowd clapped and cheered.

"The vote is this afternoon. We need each and every one of you to get down to City Hall as soon as possible. We'll reassemble inside the council chambers!"

Turner stepped back into his car and drove off before I could get to him. The story was pretty much out of my hands now: the City Hall reporter would cover it. I looked around for a telephone to call my editor, spotted one across the street.

"Flip you for it."

I turned around to see the voice's owner. It was Malcolm.

"For what?"

"The phone." He was still smiling. Although his deadline was sooner than mine—he did radio and would probably need to have something quick within the hour—he seemed unhurried.

"Take it. But make it fast."

"Nah, I was just kidding. You can have it. I'll wait until you're done."

"What a gentleman."

"I try. By the way, nice job on the housing authority last Sunday. You must be pretty tough if the man lets you write stuff like that."

"I try." I smiled at Malcolm, feeling ridiculous, unable to stop myself. Malcolm had begun wearing his hair in tiny dreadlocks, and on him it looked good. He seemed taller than I remembered.

"Keep trying, sister. But be warned: working for the man can wear you down."

"So can not being able to eat."

He laughed. "Why don't we get together sometime? I'll show you the real Philly. What are you doing Saturday night?"

"Nothing."

"You are now."

I said yes before I could think about it. Malcolm was fine, but he was too serious for me. Or maybe I wouldn't be serious enough for him. On the other hand, it was a good way to stop thinking about David. Purge the bad with the too-good-to-be-true. I gave Malcolm my address.

"Mount Airy? You live up there?"

"Yeah. Does that pass the black test?"

"It'll do," he said, still grinning. "For now."

On Saturday night Malcolm picked me up in an ancient blue Dodge.

"An American car? I'm surprised."

"My sister gave it to me when she bought a new one," he said. "I barely use it. Most of the time, I take the train. But cars are tough. The Japanese and the Germans are just as bad as the Americans."

"If you ever buy a new car, guess it'll have to be a Yugo."

We went to Ida's, a beautiful new restaurant just north of Germantown Avenue that specialized in what Malcolm called "nouveau Negro" cuisine: food like grilled catfish and sautéed collard greens and good old fried chicken, except dredged in ground peanuts and deboned so you could cut it with a fork. The place was packed with buppie lawyers in pin-striped suits and City Hall types trying to look important. Malcolm rolled his eyes.

"I don't usually come to joints like this," he said. "See how far I'm willing to go to impress you?"

I had a hard time believing he wanted to impress me, but it was nice to hear.

"Where do you usually eat?" I asked. "Vendor carts?"

He smiled. "Sometimes. Nothing wrong with supporting a brother trying to make it in this corrupt system without selling his soul."

"Of course," I said, then amended it, trying hard to sound black. "Bet."

During dinner Malcolm told me a little about his childhood. He was born and raised in North Philadelphia, the only son of a Georgia farmer who'd come up North hoping to make a better life for himself. His father worked at a textile factory while his oldest sister took care of him and the two younger girls.

"What about your mother?" I asked.

"She left when I was three, ran off with some trumpet player," Malcolm said.

"I'm sorry. That must have been hard."

"It was for my father. I don't think he ever got over it."

"I meant for you, Malcolm. It must have been hard for you too."

He shrugged, as if he were telling me how he'd lost a jacket he once had. "Easy come, easy go. That's life."

Malcolm said he was radicalized by the boyfriend of his older sister, a man named Isaiah, who was active in the black power movement. Malcolm kept up with Isaiah even after his sister broke up with him. After school each day, Malcolm ran to Isaiah's apartment, where men with billowy Afros and colorful shirts were always talking about the revolution. They let Malcolm sit in the corner and listen, saying it was good he learned the truth early on.

Malcolm did well enough in school to win a scholarship to Temple, where he tried organizing the black students into a group that would demand that the university do more for the neighborhood.

"It was pitiful," he said. "Those bougie blacks were more interested in partying than in fixing all the injustice they saw around them."

I looked at Malcolm. The black students at Temple hardly struck me as bourgeois—certainly not compared to the people with whom I'd gone to college. Temple was a private college, but it recruited urban black kids, kids from the neighborhood in which it sat.

"Maybe they just felt like it was too much for them to take on," I said. "Maybe they were just trying to make it through school, pull themselves up, get through the day. You can't expect everyone to take on the world the way you do."

"There's no room for getting by in our community, Hope," he said. "We need everybody to fight the power."

After dinner we drove to a nightclub and listened to a skinny woman dressed in a too-tight dress scratch out the blues between drags on her cigarette. Then Malcolm drove me home and walked me to the entrance of my apartment building and said good night.

"Don't you want to come in for a drink?"

"Not tonight, my queen."

"Queen?" I laughed.

"Yes, queen. Our women are queens and deserve respect. Don't you know that?"

He kissed me, lightly, then turned and walked back to his car. I was flattered. No man had ever called me a queen before, and who could resist a man who offered his respect? Still, there was something about the idea that made me nervous. People had high expectations of a queen. And if she failed them somehow, if she stepped off the throne, they were likely to cut off her head.

It took me a week to figure out what to give Malcolm for Christmas. The traditional guy stuff—ties, sweaters, cologne—wouldn't work, that much was obvious. He didn't wear ties much, didn't seem the sweater type, and cologne was the coward's way out. I knew he liked blues and jazz, but I hadn't been to his apartment and didn't know what he already had. Then one day when I was out on a story, I stumbled across an African arts boutique on Pine Street. I bought Malcolm a ceremonial mask from Nigeria, the smallest they had but still two hundred fifty dollars, way too much for a first gift, but it was cool. Malcolm loved it.

"I'm going to hang it over my bed," he said. Then he pulled out my gift. A copy of *The Autobiography of Malcolm X*. Paperback.

"Is this about you?" I joked. But Malcolm was serious.

"Ever read it?"

"Of course. I read it in school."

"Yeah, right. In school. With a white teacher, I'll bet."

"Yeah. So?"

"You need to read it again."

I must have looked surprised at the tone of his voice, because he smiled. "What I mean is, I think you'll enjoy it a lot more now that you're an adult," he said. Okay.

My mother called to ask if I was coming home for Christmas for the first time in five years.

"I have to work," I lied.

"Didn't you work Thanksgiving?"

"Yes."

"And they're still making you work Christmas?"

"Yeah."

"Are you the only reporter they have at that paper?"

"I'm still new there. They always make the new ones work the holidays."

There was no particular reason I didn't want to go to Memphis for the holidays. It just seemed like too much trouble, and avoiding home was a habit into which I'd fallen hard. Plus, I wasn't a big fan of Christmas. Christmas was greatly overrated and never as good as it was when you were a kid. People spent their entire adult lives trying to get over the disappointment, but it couldn't be done. The magic was gone. Maybe that's why people had kids—a last-ditch attempt to revive the enchantment. Otherwise, no matter how big a tree you bought or how much tinsel you spread around, it was just another day off. The next day you felt let down and the tree looked silly and the gifts were just things and everywhere you went there was a lot of mess to clean up.

Melvia and Georgia went home for the holidays. I told Malcolm I was going to Memphis, so he wouldn't invite me to his home. It seemed too soon. I spent Christmas Eve in my apartment, watching *It's a Wonderful Life* on TV. I'd always liked that movie, but for the first time I noticed how depressing it was, when you thought about it. The bottom line was that everybody got what they wanted except George. His wife got him; his brother got to go to college; but George never escaped that tiny, life-sucking town. All he got was a chance to see what life would have been like without him, and fortunately for him, the answer was that things would have been a lot worse. But that wasn't a gift you'd want to give everybody. I thought about myself. How different would the world be if I hadn't been born? Maybe a parade wouldn't have gotten covered or my landlord would have had to find somebody else to rent the place.

Christmas was on a Wednesday. On Saturday, after I "got back to town," Malcolm called and asked if I wanted to see Spike Lee's new film. He picked me up at six, and we drove to a theater downtown, instead of the one in Chestnut Hill, which was showing the same thing and was closer. I didn't say a word. We both voted for seats as far back as possible—me because the fewer people sitting behind me and yapping the better, and Malcolm because he said he always "liked to be near the door." We were munching popcorn when a young black guy walked down the aisle with his arm around a plump whitegirl with mounds of dirty-blond hair permed to death and teased high, the way New Jersey girls did. The rat's-nest style. Malcolm groaned.

"Man, I hate to see that shit."

I knew which shit he was talking about, but I played dumb. I wanted to see how deep it was.

"What?"

"That brother flapping around with that skank, parading her down the aisle like she's some prize, when in reality he ought to be ashamed of himself."

"Because she's—let's be gracious—unattractive?"

"Because she's white! And yeah, because she looks like something somebody scraped off the bottom of their shoe and you know the only reason he's with her is that pearly white skin. Brother's been so brainwashed he wouldn't know beauty if it walked up to him and slapped him in the face. Doesn't it make you mad?"

I shrugged but said nothing. What was I going to say?

"Most sisters I know can't stand it. I can't either. Every time I see something like that I want to go up to the brother and shake him by the neck."

"What if it's a sister?"

"That's worse. No self-respecting sister would be caught dead sleeping with a slavemaster."

Uh oh. I tried to sneak a peek at Malcolm's face in the half darkness of the theater, wondering if he had somehow heard about David. Maybe Melvia had told him—they knew each other. But no, Melvia wouldn't do something like that. Perhaps Malcolm had seen us together late one night in some Italian dive in South Philly. But that was silly. Malcolm didn't go to South Philly if he could help it. And he wouldn't have said what he said if he had known. He wouldn't be with me, he would never have asked me out.

The lights went down and the movie began.

"I should warn you," Malcolm whispered, taking my hand. "I'm one of those folks who prefer if people don't talk during movies."

Afterward we drove back to my apartment.

"Like to come in?" I asked, figuring he'd say no or repeat that message about me being a queen. But I guess he thought he'd made his point, because he said, "Yes. I would."

We rode up to my floor in fidgety silence. It was still early in the evening, but the whole building seemed to have gone to sleep. Inside my apartment I looked through my records and CDs for the John Coltrane record Charity had given me for my birthday three years before. I put it on, and Malcolm began bobbing his head up and down, like one of those dolls with their necks on springs.

"Trane! All right! Good choice."

I forced out a little air with my smile and realized I'd been holding my breath. I told myself to relax. It wasn't like I'd never danced this dance before.

"Like a beer? I think that's the only thing I have."

"That's cool."

We sat on the couch, sipping our beers and listening to Coltrane play "My Favorite Things."

"I love that movie."

"What movie?"

"*The Sound of Music*. That's where that song is from. I love old musicals."

"Really? That ofay stuff? Like 'Bess, you is my woman now'?"

"They're not all like that."

Malcolm smiled and put his beer on the coffee table. Then he leaned over, and his smile turned into a long kiss.

"My queen," he said when the kiss was over. He took my hand and pulled me to my feet. "Which way."

"That way." My voice sounded like a teenager's squeak.

I was relieved to see I'd made my bed that morning. In the soft light from the alley, my bedroom looked soft-focus and romantic, like something from a women's magazine, and for that reason, and others, I prayed Malcolm wouldn't turn on the light. He did.

"Do we need that?" I reached toward the switch, but Malcolm caught my hand and kissed it.

"I want to see you."

"Believe me, it's better if you don't."

"Please?"

"I'm fat."

"Compared to who? Some skinny-ass white chick on a magazine cover? Don't believe the hype, baby. You're beautiful. I want to see every inch of your beautiful African self."

He took off my blouse and bra and stopped for a moment, caressing and gazing at my breasts, which weren't as firm as they might have been. I squirmed a little. If only he'd let me lie down. But Malcolm laid his warm hands on my back and held me upright on the bed, pressing my chest toward his lips the way a man buries his face in the softness of a towel. My self-consciousness receded, pushed back into the ocean of my mind by something else, a warmness rising from my thighs. I sighed.

When Malcolm sat up again, I smiled and reached for his fly. "Wait," he said, removing my hand.

"What's wrong?"

"Why don't you lie back and let me take care of you."

He pushed me gently back onto the bed, leaning over me. Malcolm peeled off my clothes, kissing my body as he went. Then he undressed himself, still kissing me, and while Malcolm moved I lay still, smiling up at the ceiling the way I had as a child whenever I talked to God. We hadn't spoken in a while, me and God, but I sensed His humor in this thing. Just when you stopped looking for answers He sent one, next-day mail. This thing with Malcolm was going to be good. Here was the man who was going to erase my memories of David and help me figure out where I stood in this world. Here was a man who could teach me to love myself. Malcolm was crystal clear about himself, about who he was and why that mattered. Maybe some of that certainty would rub off on me.

Malcolm explored my body, down between my legs, up again to my mouth, and then he climbed on top of me as I waited and then he penetrated me in a sweet flash. He began moving, slowly, gently, not taking his eyes from my face. It embarrassed me. I closed my eyes.

"Open your eyes, baby," he said. "Look at me."

I did. Malcolm was staring down at me, intent and amazed and so serious I almost wanted to laugh. But then he whispered, "Oh, Hope. Oh, my queen," and began to move faster, and I stopped seeing his face, saw only his eyes, and I caught his rhythm. We drove and pressed, moving and thrashing until we came, and then we gasped, falling hard into each other's arms.

chapter fifteen

Malcolm liked to sleep over after we made love, and I liked having him there. I liked the way he wrapped his muscular arms around my waist and pulled me close to him in bed and gave off little sighs of contentment as he fell asleep. I liked that he wanted to stay with me, that he didn't want to jump up and run home as soon as his breath slowed down. Malcolm didn't come and go, so to speak. There was nobody waiting for him at home, nobody else.

But having someone in your space takes adjustments. For one thing, Malcolm was a wild sleeper. He twisted and turned, his left leg twitching so violently the first night I wondered if he was having an epileptic fit. He'd usually settle down after an hour or so, but then he'd sleep flat on his back, his arms and legs splayed across the bed, as if he were making a speech.

Also, with Malcolm sleeping over, I had to worry about my looks all the time. I couldn't roll my hair at night, which meant I had to wake up before he did, looking like Godzilla, and run to the bathroom and curl my hair, which added an extra twenty minutes to my morning routine and wasn't really good for my hair. Of course, neither was sleeping in curlers. Like most black women, I have a very complicated relationship with my hair. That's one thing I have to admit I envy about whitegirls—the ease with which they do their dos. There's a woman at work who often arrives with her hair still wet from the shower; she lets the air dry it, and in an hour or so she looks like she just stepped out of a beauty parlor. No black woman I know can manage that.

After a few weeks of sneaking out of bed for hair purposes, I decided to compromise. One night after Malcolm and I had made love, I went to the bathroom, and came back to bed with a blue silk scarf wrapped as jauntily as possible around my head. Malcolm was snoozing when I climbed into bed, but he rolled over to kiss me good night and his hand brushed my scarf. He opened his eyes and made a face.

"Do you have to wear that?"

"I have to do something so I don't wake up looking all rough in the morning." I'd noticed that when I was around Malcolm, my language changed. I sounded more black. It was one of the things I liked about him.

"Can't you do something else? I hate seeing women with rags on their heads. Makes me think of Aunt Jemima."

"This is a scarf, not a rag. A forty-dollar scarf."

"I don't know why you don't just stop putting all those chemicals in your hair anyway. Relaxers are all about trying to emulate white hair. You should go natural."

"I'm not trying to emulate anybody. I'm trying to make it so

I don't have to spend three hours a day combing out this nappy stuff."

"Don't say nappy."

"Kinky, then. My hair is very thick. I can't handle it unrelaxed."

"You could wear one of those cute little 'fros. I saw a sister the other day with one, and she was fine."

"My head's too big."

Malcolm grinned and reached for me.

"You do have a big old head, girl. But I like it. It goes with those big eyes and those big, beautiful lips. And those big, sexy breasts."

Malcolm also thought I should quit my job at the *Record* and go to work for the *Philadelphia Freedom*, the black-owned weekly with a circulation of about twelve. I learned not to complain about work or Richard to Malcolm, because he'd just look at me and say, "Well, what do you expect?"

"But, Malcolm, it's so frustrating. Richard is such an asshole. He's always on me to get my stories done, and then he lets them sit in the computer for two weeks. He drives me nuts."

"That's the way the man operates, baby."

"Richard ain't the man. He's just a wannabe."

"They're all the man. You need to get out."

"Why should I leave? I deserve to be there as much as anyone."

Malcolm took my face in his hands and kissed me lightly on the lips.

"Okay, baby, if you say so. But remember: the leopard doesn't change his spots."

We had fun, though, when we weren't arguing about hair status or work or politics or where to eat. I found myself biting my tongue a lot, which surprised me but in a good sort of way. Maybe I needed to just calm down and listen for a change. Malcolm took it as his job to school me in all things black, and I was willing to learn. I looked at it as kind of an anti-Astor education, counterbalancing all the crap I'd picked up from white-folks over the years. Malcolm agreed. "The thing I like about you, baby, is that you're retrievable," he said. "Not like all those other bougie blacks, trying so hard to please the man they've lost themselves. At least you know what you're missing. At least you trying to get it back."

We spent most of our time in North Philadelphia, scouring the neighborhood as though the rest of the city did not exist. We visited every fledgling revolutionary bookstore, dive bar, and pool house on North Broad Street. We went to meetings in grungy little storefront "revolution halls" and sat among skinny, pinched-face people who wanted to sue the United States government for slavery reparations or free some guy named Mumia, who was in jail for allegedly killing a cop. I kept my mouth shut, not wanting to draw attention to myself, but Malcolm was always one of the ones talking. He lit up during these debates—arguing, speechifying, quoting history and facts and figures like a walking encyclopedia of black oppression. People always crowded around him afterward to slap his back and shake his hand. "Preach, brother!" they'd say. "You go!"

A couple of times we went to Joe Frazier's gym to see sweaty young guys in silk trunks dance around the ring and pound one another. The first time Malcolm suggested it, I was game. I'd never seen a fight in the flesh. But when they weren't hitting each other I was bored, and when they were hitting each other I was disgusted. The hard, wet smack of leather hitting skin made me sick, but Malcolm loved it.

"How can you condone two black men beating the crap out of each other for entertainment?" I asked him after he'd dragged me to the gym a second time.

"They're fighting for themselves," he yelled. The gym was full of people, mostly men, screaming and crying for blood. "They're making their own destiny."

"Some destiny."

"This is a black gym. These guys have black promoters."

"Malcolm, I think you're kidding yourself."

"Watch the fight," he said.

No matter how much we disagreed, we always ended the night in bed. Usually I gave in, but sometimes Malcolm did, enough to make me believe he respected my opinion. "You're tough, girl. I'll give you that," he would say with a laugh, throwing up his hands in surrender. Or he'd just stop arguing and come over to where I sat, or maybe stood, cooking dinner, and start kissing the back of my neck soft and slow. "My beautiful, misguided queen," he'd whisper, his hands exploring my body, and it was the sweetest endearment I'd ever heard. Malcolm always liked to make love with the lights on, he liked to stare at me greedily as his hands roamed my body, and I flourished under his eyes. Malcolm made me feel dangerously sexy; I started acting so wanton that sometimes I surprised myself.

"Whoa, girl. You about to wear me out!" he said one night. His chest rose and fell in the light from the lamp. "Where did you learn all this stuff?"

Now, I knew this was dangerous territory with any man. I expected it would be doubly so with Malcolm, so I dodged the question.

"You make me so crazy I just get wild," I said, nuzzling his neck. It worked. Malcolm rolled onto his stomach and began rolling his shoulders, a signal that he wished I'd rub his back. I straddled his hips and began kneading.

"I don't mind if you've had men in the past, baby. That's natural. Just as long as you never mess around on me. That's one thing I won't take."

I leaned over and kissed the back of his neck. I knew he was thinking about his mother. I knew her abandonment must have hurt more than he liked to let on.

"I wouldn't do that, Malcolm. Any more than you would cheat on me."

Malcolm didn't seem to hear me. He was talking softly, almost as if to himself.

"That's a big part of our problem—too many sisters out there not backing their men up. Too busy tearing them down. It's bad enough to have to cop shit from the whitefolks in the world. To come home and get it from your woman—that's cold. Black folks have got to learn some loyalty. Loyalty is what makes a people great."

I rubbed until Malcolm began to snore softly, then I got out of bed and went into the kitchen for a glass of water, feeling warm and happy and content. For the second time in a row, I was sleeping with a guy who was big on loyalty. Except that this time the guy was going to be loyal to me.

"R.E.M.? Elvis Costello? Billy Joel?"

Malcolm couldn't believe my taste in music. He sat on the floor near my stereo, pulling albums out of the blue milk crate and looking incredulous. He held up my *Piano Man* album with the tips of his fingers, as though the jacket were coated with germs.

"That's mostly stuff I listened to in college," I lied. "Give me a break."

Malcolm said I needed to hear the people's music, and he dragged me to a concert by some rap group called Pit Bill and the Dangerous Dogs. Just walking into the Spectrum, where the concert was being held, made me nervous. All those rough-looking teenage boys swaggering around in their baggy jeans and oversize shirts, bandannas wrapped around their heads. Then I thought I should be ashamed of myself, thinking like a white woman, judging these kids by their clothes. Afraid of my own people. Thank goodness I hadn't said anything to Malcolm.

The Dangerous Dogs turned out to be three kids dressed like

most of the audience, except with bigger gold chains around their necks. For two hours they jumped and pranced across the stage, gesturing and rapping about guns and shooting the police, and about alternately screwing and beating "bitches and whores" who made them mad. The stuff about shooting people was bad enough, but I couldn't believe some of the things they said about women. At one point I turned to Malcolm to say I wanted to leave, but I stopped. His eyes were glazed and his face was shiny with sweat, and he was screaming the words along with the kids up on stage.

Afterward, driving back to my place, I asked Malcolm if he didn't think the songs were unnecessarily violent, not to mention misogynistic.

He shrugged. "They're just speaking the truth."

My heart leapt a little. "What truth? That women are bitches and whores?"

"They're not calling all women those things," Malcolm said. "They're talking about certain kinds of women. Whores are women who only want a man for the money he brings home. Bitches are women who nag and bitch and try to drag a black man down."

"You think women can be broken down like that? Are we that simple?"

"Some are."

"But if I say all men are dogs, I'm not being fair, right?"

Malcolm let out a halfhearted grunt. Then, after a minute: "I don't approve of all the language the brothers use, but I know where they're coming from."

"Those kids probably grew up in Bryn Mawr."

"They're expressing reality as they know it. If it makes the man uncomfortable to hear the truth about the society he's created, that's too damn bad."

"It makes me uncomfortable."

Malcolm didn't respond.

"I just don't understand why they have to be so . . . so vicious," I said.

Malcolm glanced at me with a little twist of his mouth, and we rode in silence for a while, the only sound that of the tires whirling on rainy streets.

Finally he said, "You hang around white folks too much. They've just about messed up your brain."

"My brain is fine."

"You need to stay real, Hope. Don't turn your back on the people in the hood just 'cause you got out."

I wanted to tell him that I'd never been in the hood, not in the way he meant. My mother had scraped and scratched and sacrificed so that we would grow up in a house—a modest house, but a house nonetheless. And anyway, even the projects in Memphis weren't that bad. People didn't live all packed in on top of one another like they did in North Philly. I was tempted to tell Malcolm we didn't have hoods where I grew up, but it seemed important to him and I didn't want to argue, and besides, he was right about the larger point. I had spent too much time around white people; I had come to see the world through their eyes. It felt warm inside the car. I turned off the heat and rolled down my window. The falling rain was cool against my face, but it smelled good. Like damp earth. Spring was coming. The streets of North Philadelphia moved past in a sloppy blur.

Weeks passed. At work, Richard and I reached an unspoken agreement wherein he pretty much left me alone and I did the same with him. For Richard this meant more time to work with his pet reporters, the ones who did what he said without bitching and consequently got the big assignments and garnered all the praise. Me, I got a kind of self-determined oblivion out of the agreement. Richard was off my back; I could search out and write my own stories. But all my stories ended up buried in the back of the paper.

That was probably just as well. My writing wasn't what it had been—I couldn't seem to find the energy to put into making a story sing. Everything I wrote about seemed insignificant and redundant. Man Fights System—done that. Neighborhood Deteriorates—done that. Neighborhood Fights Back—done that. I had to drag myself into the newsroom every day, and Malcolm's pushing me to quit the *Record* didn't help. He wanted me to work for the *Philadelphia Freedom*, talked about it as if just walking in there each day would be a cultural high. But I knew enough about those fledgling weeklies and their low pay and shaky security to know I didn't want to work there. I wasn't that noble. Plus, I wasn't quite ready to leave the *Record*. There was still something I wanted to accomplish. What, I wasn't sure.

Going into work every day was hard, though; everyone I met got on my nerves. The reporter who sat across from me, Lisa, drove me nuts. She was this aging bimbo, whose full-time occupation was landing a man before the next wrinkle cracked her face. Any hour that she wasn't on the phone cooing to a guy she was trying to reel in, she was on the phone seeking advice from one of her friends.

"He's been in Chicago three days and I haven't heard from him," she would whine. "Maybe I should give him a call?"

Her friends all talked so loud I could hear the squeal of their voices from the earpiece of Lisa's phone. The louder they talked, the louder Lisa responded, oblivious to the fact that the entire newsroom was monitoring her love life.

"But I can't call him! I don't want to scare him away!"

One day when I couldn't stand it anymore, I shushed her. My face must have twisted up more than I'd planned, because Lisa stopped midsentence, mouth gaping.

"What?" she said.

"I'm sure you don't realize it, but you're talking pretty loud."

"What?" It was like I was speaking Greek. She couldn't believe it.

"You're talking too loud. I can't hear myself think."

"Oh. Oh. Sorry." She whispered something—exaggeratedly—
into the phone and hung up. Then she sat at her desk for an
hour looking hurt and not talking to anyone, waiting for me to
apologize. And waiting and waiting and waiting. I went home.

Every now and then David would come into the newsroom,
and we'd both work very hard pretending not to see each other.
The sight of him still triggered a pang in my heart, I wasn't sure
why. Was it regret? Lingering love or just the spasmodic after-
effects of once again not being chosen? Having Malcolm eased
the pain, and I wished there was some way David could find out
about him. I wanted to shout, "Hey, I've got someone!" If David
was nearby, I'd pick up my phone and pretend to be having an
intimate conversation, my voice low and soft. I kept inviting
Malcolm to stop by the *Record*, but he refused. He wanted nothing to do with the place.

Richard hatched an idea for a big series on the explosive
growth of the suburbs. Next to the big disaster, the big series is
the mother's milk of journalism. That's where you win your
prizes, and that's how you make your rep. Richard's brainstorm
came out of his own experience. He and his wife, after many
years in the city, had finally given up and moved to the burbs,
and as they confessed to anyone who would listen, they felt a
little guilty about the whole thing. All those years of shooting
off their mouths about the city being the cultural heart of American life, etc., etc. So Richard decided to do a series that essentially justified his decision. That was the sole reason, as is so
often the case. I have to laugh when people say newspapers are
run according to some kind of organized political agenda, left
or right. The truth is that things are much more personal and
infinitely more chaotic than that. If an editor has a hard time
getting a driver's license, we do a story. If his son gets beat up

at school, we do a story. In Greenville, I knew a columnist who liked to say that news was what the editor's wife saw on her way home yesterday.

Richard's proposed series would focus on all the horrible things about the city that drove people to the burbs. We could do stories on the soaring crime rate and the lousy schools and all the overblown city services for poor people that pushed the tax rate up. It was an old story, as old as the Bible, but Rob embraced it.

My assignment—surprise!—was to do a sidebar for the welfare portion of the series. The main story would be full of facts and figures about the cost of social services in the city versus towns in the burbs, and the percent of the budget they consumed. I was to find a typical North Philadelphia resident and detail the quantity of city services she devoured. Of course she'd be on welfare, and either living in public housing or receiving a Section 8 housing stipend. When I pointed out to Richard that these were in fact federal, not city, dollars, he pursed his lips.

"But they still have to be administered by the city, and that costs money, right? They still have to flow through City Hall."

Richard envisioned that this woman would have several children, all of them receiving free lunch at school. They'd get free medical care and food stamps. They might have had a collision or two with child welfare officials or a run-in with the law. No thoughts about why in the world such a person would want to cooperate with me in spreading her life before the world.

"When you find the right person, be sure to take photo along," Richard said.

I knew I wasn't going to do it—though I didn't know how I was going to not do it. The first week, I stalled. The second week, I called a few of my sources in social service agencies and asked about the most unusual cases they had. One source came up with a twenty-eight-year-old white woman, the daughter of a car dealer, who grew up in the suburbs and went to Yale before being struck with schizophrenia in her sophomore year. Her family tried helping her for a while, but when she didn't get better they became embarrassed and cut their ties. They moved her from their lovely King of Prussia home into a studio apartment in the city and then cut her off financially, so that she'd be eligible for city services. That was six years and two kids ago.

I wrote up the story and handed it in. Richard wasn't pleased.

"You might have picked someone a tad more representative," he said.

"She's a typical welfare mother. She's got two kids. She's been on welfare for six years—that's almost exactly the average amount of time."

Richard peered at the photographs. "Does she live in public housing?"

"Kind of. She rents an apartment from an uncle, a slumlord. He gets Section Eight money to rent it below market cost. It's actually a better story."

Richard tossed the pictures down on his desk and began rubbing his temples. "It's not exactly what we had in mind."

I shrugged. "I did my best."

"I'm sure you did." His voice was acid. "Perhaps we'd better let someone else have a try. No offense. Just get a fresh start."

I shrugged again.

"Maybe Jeffrey." Jeffrey was one of his pets.

"Fine. I've got other stories to write."

"Don't worry, Hope," Richard said as I turned away. "I'll speak to Rob so he doesn't get the wrong impression about this."

He'd speak to Rob all right. His little forked tongue would be wagging as soon as he could get in the door. He'd tell Rob how I'd nearly ruined his precious series. He'd suggest that, much to his surprise, I was an affirmative action mistake. He'd say I hadn't been very productive lately, hadn't been on the front page in months, didn't seem to care whether I got in the paper at all.

Richard finally had his ammunition for blasting holes in my career, and I had delivered it to him, gift-wrapped.

Besides Malcolm, the only thing that seemed even vaguely interesting to me was the upcoming convention of the National Association of Black Journalists. NABJ did a lot of admirable things, like giving scholarships to college students and monitoring newspapers for racial bias, but I paid little attention to all that. The main reason I belonged to NABJ was to attend the convention every year, and the main reason I attended the convention—or at least the main reason I started attending it in the first place—was because while working in Greenville I had learned, too late, that not attending the convention could be counted against you in the constant game among black professionals of deciding who was a sellout and who was not. I went to the convention the first time out of obligation and duty. But to my surprise I liked being surrounded by smart, funny professional black people, liked the feeling of power and purpose that surged through the hotel. I liked not wondering if I'd be the only black person at the party when I entered the room. And I liked sitting in the bar and drinking with friends and watching people go past.

Malcolm called NABJ a "bougie organization for bougie blacks," which is why I assumed he would not want to attend the convention.

"Most of these house niggers would sell their black souls for a corporate donation from RJR," he'd said once. But the closer the convention got, the more he moderated his tone. Until one day he announced that he planned to go.

"But you said—"

"I know, I know," he interrupted me, irritated at being quoted to himself. "Still, it's the best we got."

In fact, Malcolm was very excited about the convention. A friend of his, a cameraman from Chicago named Kwame Gray, was running for president on a platform that promised to take the association back to its radical roots. Malcolm loved it, loved all his tough, nationalistic talk. He went so far as to volunteer for the campaign, and he wanted me to do the same.

"I don't even know this guy," I said. Besides which, I lacked the inclination to be a volunteer.

"I know him, baby." Malcolm pushed his chair back from the table and stretched out his legs. We were in my apartment, finishing dinner. We rarely hung out in Malcolm's apartment, a tiny, one-bedroom basement place in a North Philadelphia brownstone. It was a typical bachelor pad: dozens of jazz albums stacked in milk crates, dirty dishes in the sink, and a single bed. He had no plants, no photographs, nothing on the walls except a poster of a seated Huey Newton brandishing guns. Malcolm said he preferred hanging out at my place. He said it was dangerous for me to leave his apartment in the middle of the night and tacky for me to leave early in the morning. "Can't have my queen dragging around the city like some tramp," he said. "I'm the man. I should come to you."

Now he said, "Kwame's solid. Trust me."

"I need a little more than that."

"Okay." Malcolm got up and walked over to the green canvas bag he always carried around. He dug around inside, then pulled out several pamphlets and gave them to me. It was campaign literature. Apparently Kwame's motto was "Vote Black, Vote Gray." I thought it was pretty dumb.

"Somebody told me this guy's real name was Harold," I said, flipping through the literature.

"So?"

"I can understand changing your name, but why change Harold to Kwame and then leave Gray? Gray's the slave name, if that's the way you look at it."

Malcolm looked at me and sucked his teeth. I went back to reading the campaign literature. It was full of quotes from Malcolm X and Huey Newton, and between these were wedged calls for things like "returning the organization to the people" and using NABJ to "fight the white slavemasters." Among his more solid suggestions was banning white people from membership in NABJ. I had no idea how many whites were official members and whether any of them had joined on their own, outside the bounds of a corporate membership. But the idea of banning made me uneasy, though I couldn't say why.

"Why?" Malcolm asked. "They don't need to be in there. Can't we have one thing without white folks? Just one thing they ain't trying to run?"

"I don't think white people are trying to run NABJ."

"Then you're more naive than you look," he said, sounding incredulous. "It's supposed to be an organization for black journalists."

"It's supposed to be an organization that supports black journalists and advocates black issues in the media."

"And you think any white people want to do that?"

I rubbed my temples; my head was starting to pound. Maybe he was right: maybe I was being naive.

"I don't know. You may be right. But that's not the only reason I wouldn't vote for this guy."

Malcolm came around behind me. He took my hands, put them on my lap, and began massaging my temples.

"Just do this for me, baby, okay? What's it going to look like if I can't even control my own woman?"

He chuckled, as if it were a joke. Beneath the soft pressure of his hands, I tried to smile.

The closer we got to the convention, the more Malcolm pressed the issue. I was willing to call it a draw: I didn't care whom Malcolm voted for; I didn't really care who was president. But Malcolm seemed determined to make sure I did what he said, and he wouldn't let it alone. He kept pestering me, asking me repeatedly, bringing the topic up even once when we were in bed. It was like the vote had become some kind of test, and I recognized that but couldn't do anything about it. How could you pass a test when you didn't know what subject it was in?

"So you're going to vote for that house nigger? That Oreo?" Malcolm asked one day. He had taken to phoning me at work just to check if I'd changed my mind. He was referring to a talk show host from Los Angeles, a pretty boy and a flyweight, harmless enough. I hadn't decided to vote for him. Maybe I wouldn't vote at all. It was, after all, just one unimportant little organization. We weren't talking about the future of the free world.

"Why does it matter so much to you?"

"Because you need to decide which side you're on," he said. "If you're going to be with me, you got to be on my side."

His voice was hard, as it had been lately. He hadn't called me his queen in weeks.

"I don't like the sound of that, Malcolm."

"Like it or not, that's the way it is," he said. "You need to think about who you are. You need to decide who means more to you, baby—them ofays or me."

"That's ridiculous."

"Is it?"

"Those people don't mean squat to me, and you know it. I don't even understand what it is you're asking me to choose."

"Yeah," he said angrily. "And that's your problem right there."

He hung up. I sat there cradling the phone between my shoulder and my neck, against all ergonomic advice, and with Malcolm's words ringing in my ears, I felt something firm take shape against my back. It was a terrible habit of mine, to resist fiercely whenever someone tried to force something on me. It didn't matter if the thing was worthwhile or not; my back went up. "You're hardheaded," my mother used to say. "If somebody handed you a glass of water on a hot day and told you to drink it, you'd probably pour it in the dust just for spite." As I got older, I recognized her point.

I sat at my desk, working myself into a fury, and then I picked up the phone and called Malcolm's apartment. I knew he wasn't home; he'd called me from the radio station. I left a message saying I wouldn't be voting for his friend because I wouldn't be attending the convention. I told him I didn't appreciate his little test and that if I hadn't already proved how much I cared about him in the months we'd been dating, casting a vote wouldn't do it. When I hung up, my hand was shaking, but I told myself I'd done the right thing. Every time I ran into David in the building I still flushed with anger, though that was diminishing. It was too soon to let another man step all over my pride.

I waited four days for Malcolm's call, filling in the empty nights with television and wine. My anger softened as the days passed. What a stupid thing to fight about! If he would only call, I'd apologize myself. I'd tell him how much I missed him and say that this silly argument wasn't worth messing us up. We hadn't got to the L-word stage yet, we hadn't talked about love, but I thought, I felt, that Malcolm cared about me. I was his queen. Wasn't I?

We were supposed to fly to Houston Tuesday night. Two hours before the plane was scheduled to leave, I called Malcolm's apartment. The phone rang and rang. I called the radio station.

"He's out of town," the secretary said. "He won't be back for a week."

I sat in my apartment, staring at my packed bags, the phone screeching at me to hang it up. He'd left without me. Just like that—*bam!*. No apologies, no begging me to come along, not even a phone call to say he was going. Was he really that stubborn, or did I just mean so little to him? I looked at my watch. I had an hour to make the airport. If I drove like a madwoman,

I could probably make it, but then I'd have to sit next to Malcolm on the plane. I picked up my bag and tossed it into my bedroom and shut the door.

The next Monday, I took Melvia out to lunch so she could fill me in on all the convention gossip I had missed. Kwame lost, big time, and was so pissed he went around disrupting workshops, calling people Uncle Toms and vowing to return next year. Most folks ignored him. Melvia said she'd had a blast.

"I'm sorry I missed it." And I was, too. Sorry and pissed.

"It sounds like it was fun. Did you see Malcolm around?"

Something swept across Melvia's face and quickly disappeared. "Not much. I was so busy."

"What?"

Melvia tried to look innocent.

"What is it?"

"Nothing."

"You lie like a rug. You did see him. Was he with someone else?"

Melvia shifted in her seat and glanced around the restaurant, searching for escape.

"Tell me, Melvia."

"Nothing to tell, really."

"Look, it's not like we're married. I'm not even sure if we're still together, so you might as well pour gas onto the flames."

"Oh, great." She rolled her eyes. "Okay. It was probably nothing. One night I saw him hanging off this woman. No big deal."

"Hanging off?"

Melvia squirmed. "You know, dancing with, laughing with, sitting a little too close to. It could have been nothing. It could have been her coming on to Malcolm—he's a good-looking brother, and you know how these young girls can be."

"Do you know who she was?"

"No." Melvia dug into her soup, some kind of pumpkin con-coction that swirled thick and orange in a wide-lipped bowl. "Mmm, this is delicious! Want some?"

I shook my head. "What'd she look like?"

"Oh, I don't know. You know."

"Was she pretty?"

"I don't know; I didn't get a good look at her."

"How was she dressed?"

"Look, Hope. Why don't you call him and sit down and talk about what happened before the convention. Don't obsess on this silly girl and don't let some stupid vote tear you two apart. Good brothers are too hard to find."

The waitress brought our entrées.

"He left me, Melvia. I was waiting for him to call, and he just got on the plane and left, because I wouldn't vote the way he told me. If he'd leave me over something that silly, what kind of future could we have?"

I looked down at my plate: turkey sandwich made with Brie and sun-dried tomatoes. Nine bucks because it was "gourmet," and it tasted like ashes in my mouth.

chapter
sixteen

Beware of guilty boyfriends bearing gifts. Coming home from work a few days after the convention, I found a velvety red box outside my apartment door, along with a note: "I'm sorry, baby. I need to see you. Call."

My first impulse was to send it back unopened. Maybe with a note that read, "Save it for your other queen," or just, "Screw you." But then curiosity got the better of me and I opened it. Inside was a belt, black leather with a delicate gold buckle. Very nice, except who the hell wore belts anymore? I didn't. Emphasizing my waist made my hips look that much larger. In all the time he had known me, Malcolm had never seen me bring a belt anywhere near my body, which showed me how much thought he had put into the gift. I threw the box under my bed.

And what, exactly, was he sorry about anyway? The argument we'd had before he left? The woman in Houston? Did he know I knew about that—if there was even something to know about? I probably should have made the effort to find out before I wrote Malcolm out of my life, but it seemed like too much trouble. I didn't have the energy to do it. It took everything I had just to get up and go in to work in the morning.

Malcolm called the day after the belt appeared outside my door. He left messages at my apartment and on my machine at work, where I let my voice mail screen my calls. Then I'd play back the tape, listening to Malcolm's honeyed voice with a dispassion that surprised me.

"Come on, baby, pick up the phone. I said I was sorry. Talk to me, please?"

In a way it was a relief to be angry at Malcolm. I didn't have to worry about not living up to his standards, about listening to the wrong music or giving aid to the enemy or slipping and saying something "white." A lot of times Malcolm made me feel like I was back in junior high school, a geek trying desperately to fit in and doing everything wrong. It was hard to feel that way, and I wouldn't miss it. I *would* miss the times he made me feel beautiful, made me feel special and wanted and desired. And not alone.

I received a call from the metro editor's secretary.

"Jack would like to talk to you this afternoon. Can you meet him in his office after the five o'clock meeting? Around five-thirty?"

"Sure. What's it about?"

"Oh, I don't know," she said, sounding bored. "I never know these things."

It was noon when she called, which gave me five and a half hours to worry about why Jack wanted to see me. Maybe Stephanie had changed her mind, down there in Washington, and had blown the whistle after all. Maybe she'd gotten pissed because

I'd blown off dinner with her, hadn't made even the slightest attempt to carry out that bizarre request. Or maybe it was something else entirely. Maybe Richard had turned me in to his boss, had told Jack that my productivity was way off. Maybe Jack was getting ready to fire me or to put me on probation. That was all I needed. One more blow and I'd crumble into dust.

At five-thirty I stood outside Jack's office and knocked, thinking that whatever it was, it was better to get it over with. Jack was on the phone with somebody out in one of the bureaus, but he waved me in. I took a seat on the couch. His office was smaller than Rob's, but at least it wasn't a cubicle like the one they gave Betty. The walls were decorated with the awards and prizes he had won and that the staff had won under his direction, about six in all, none of them major. The desk was bare; Jack really used the office only for private chats. Most of the time he sat outside, at his other desk in the newsroom.

Jack hung up the phone and rubbed his hand over his eyes. He looked more tired than usual.

"A piece of advice," he said. "If you're going to interview someone who's sued three different newspapers, get it on tape."

I laughed. "I'll make sure I write that down."

"Anyway. I didn't call you in here to listen to my problems. How are things going? Everything okay?"

You knew you were in trouble when they opened with questions like that. I didn't know whether to jump in and start slashing Richard as a preventive measure or just sit there and take the beating.

"Things are fine," I said cautiously. "A little slow, but that's because I'm really digging into my beat. I'm trying to make sure I understand the kinds of stories the desk wants, because sometimes the ones I offer don't seem to go over very well."

I waited for Jack to begin the dismantling, but he just nodded, a distracted smile still on his face.

"Good. Well, the reason I wanted to see you was to ask if you were up for an adventure. We have something in mind, and we thought you'd be the perfect person for it."

I smiled. "Adventure" was one of those code words they used before banishing you to night cops or Sunday obits or some other desolate beat. This was going to be worse than I thought.

"How would you like to go to Africa?" Jack asked. It took a moment for me to understand what he was saying; I was still waiting for the words "night police beat" to emerge from his mouth. But no, he'd said Africa. This man was asking me if I wanted to go to Africa. My first thought was of camps full of starving children, their bellies swollen, flies buzzing around their lifeless eyes. But that wasn't all of Africa; that was just the slice of it we saw in this country. Africa was verdant jungles and vibrant cities and golden plains and lots and lots of black folks.

Malcolm would chew out his heart.

"Absolutely!" I said.

Jack chuckled at my enthusiasm. "Wouldn't you like to know where, exactly? Africa's a very big place."

Jack had spent three years based in Johannesburg, traversing the African continent. Living in Africa had made him an expert on all things African. He knew countries, conflicts, ethnic groups, and he never tired of telling you about it. Like a lot of whiteboys who go to Africa, he came back thinking he knew more about being black than most black folks. And like most journalists who spent more than a year on the continent, he'd written a book about the place to explain why the whole thing was such a big and bloody mess. People in the newsroom raved about how good the book was. I hadn't read it.

"Okay," I said. "Where?"

"Liberia. That's in West Africa, near Sierre Leone and Côte d'Ivoire. By the way, do you speak French?"

"*Un peu*," I said. Those and about six other words were all that I retained from my high school French classes, but Jack didn't need to know that.

"Bon. You won't need it in Liberia, but it'll come in handy when you travel through Côte d'Ivoire."

Jack started talking about the war in Liberia, but I wasn't listening. I was flying over the homeland, looking down on endless plains so green they shimmered. Hills like white elephants. A village beneath the trees. People standing in the shade, glancing up with mysterious smiles.

After college I had considered, briefly, a stint in the Peace Corps. My mother thought I was nuts. "Why go over there and get depressed?" she asked, but everyone my age knew exactly why I'd wanted to go. We'd all sat transfixed in front of the television, watching *Roots* in the darkness, then gone to school the next day and glared at white people. We all remembered that footage of Alex Haley himself, stepping off the boat and being welcomed by a crowd of giddy villagers, people clapping and singing and rejoicing that the long-lost son had returned home. Not that I believed it would really be like that, Africa. I wasn't stupid. That was television; this was reality. For all I knew, those people had been paid.

chapter seventeen

With less than a week to prepare, I ran around frantically, trying to get everything done. I had to check my passport, get shots, read everything I could on Liberia. My ignorance of the country was pretty appalling. How was it that I didn't know about a nation in Africa that had been founded by freed American slaves? Did they forget to mention that back in my junior high history class, or was I out sick that day?

I had lunch with Walter Steeple, one of the few black photographers on staff, who'd been assigned to go with me. As it turned out, the assignment was very much against Walter's will. He said he'd had his Africa stint, back in the 1970s, when he covered East Africa for another newspaper.

"That was back in the day when folks thought we were all going to pack our bags and just boogie back to the homeland," he said. "I couldn't wait to get over there. And let me tell you, three and half years later I couldn't wait to get back home. Couldn't wait."

Walter was big, way over six feet tall, with broad, curved shoulders and the belly of an aging football star. He seemed like the kind of guy who loved his creature comforts—television, cold beer, air-conditioning. He devoured his hamburger, then lingered over his french fries as if they were the last he'd ever have.

"What was the problem?" I asked.

"Africa is rough," he said. "It can be cool, but it can also be rough like you've never seen."

"Well, of course they don't have all our material goods, all our conveniences. That's no reason to condemn them."

"I'm not talking about inconveniences," Walter said, reaching for a stack of paper napkins to wipe his hands. "Let me school you, young'un. I was there in 1972, in Nairobi, and I had to go on over to Burundi and photograph what was left of the Hutu after the Tutsi, this other tribe—"

"Ethnic group," I corrected. "You shouldn't call them tribes."

Walter looked at me a moment, then went on.

"—after this other tribe, the Tutsis, got through trying to wipe them out. The Tutsis weren't even slick about it, not at first. Told them Hutus to report to the police stations, and those fools walked right on in, one after another, and got their butts shot or their heads hacked off. Africa is full of that shit, black folks slaughtering each other, hacking each other to bits just because they belong to the wrong tribe. We were back here screaming about black power and black pride, and they were over there wiping each other out!"

"But that conflict was created by the British. They set it up!"

"And who's carrying it on?"

"Yeah, but—"

"But nothing," Walter said, rolling his eyes. "All you young folk think Africa is the promised land. I'm just telling you that it's not."

I decided not to argue with him. If Walter wanted to believe all the myths about Africa, all the negative pictures painted by Tarzan movies and Conrad novels, he could. There was no point in our antagonizing each other from the start: it was going to be a long trip.

Walter told me what to bring for the cities—a money belt, small bank notes for bribing officials, and a swimsuit for the pool at the luxury hotel we'd be treating ourselves to on the way out. For the refugee camps and Monrovia, I was to bring water purification tablets, as much jerky as I could carry, and mosquito repellent. And a hat with a brim and sunscreen.

"Sunscreen?" Now I knew he was nuts. Black people did not use sunscreen. That was the white man's burden. "I don't think so."

"Suit yourself," Walter said.

We flew to New York, then changed planes for Paris and a connection to Abidjan, the capital of the Ivory Coast. It took an eternity just to get to Paris; then, because the plane was late, we had to rush through the airport to catch our next plane; and then we spent another hundred years flying south to the western coast of Africa. By the time we landed, I was exhausted and achy from being cooped up so long in economy class. But my fatigue disappeared as soon as we stepped outside. The Abidjan airport was alive with activity—businessmen running to catch planes, families greeting their loved ones. And all—or mostly all—of the flight attendants and pilots and customs agents were black. I felt absurdly proud.

"*Je suis American et cette est mon première fois entre dans Côte d'Ivoire, dans Afrique,*" I said to the customs agent. I knew my French was terrible, but I smiled at him. His face was like stone while he searched my luggage. When he was done he barked something in French and waved us through.

"Probably wanted a bribe," Walter muttered.

"Walter . . ."

"Well, it's probably true! You haven't seen corruption until you've seen it African style. Go to Lagos sometime."

"Yeah, yeah." I shut him out, determined not to let Walter ruin my first glimpse of Africa. I was happy to be there, even if he wasn't. How could you be unhappy in a place where you belonged?

Outside the airport, we were hit by a pocket of air so dense and moist it seemed easier to drink than to breathe. The heat was palpable; Walter muttered more and began peeling off clothes. And there was noise, noise everywhere—the honking of horns, the roar of cars without mufflers, the lilting, lyrical cries of black people greeting each other in French. There was something so cool about black folks speaking French. I was giddy and excited, and I wanted to laugh out loud.

A crowd of men descended upon us, talking loudly and pushing one another and trying to grab our bags. Walter pointed to one man, who smiled and waved the other men away. We walked toward his taxi, Walter wiping his forehead of sweat, me gawking at the palm trees like a tourist. Africa. I was in Africa!

Our plan was to spend a day resting in Abidjan, then hook up with a group of officials from the United Nations touring Liberian refugee camps. We were going to tag along for part of their journey, then break off and fly alone to Monrovia.

But it turned out that the UN officials had left Abidjan a day early. A message at our hotel told us we would be taken to meet them in the town of Danané. We barely had time to take a shower and change clothes before a driver arrived in a jeep.

"*Bonjour, madame, monsieur.*" He was one of the most beautiful black men I had ever seen—not good looking, not handsome; beautiful. He was about my height, thin, with ebony skin that shone like satin and cheekbones sharp enough to prick my heart. It took me a while to realize that the symmetrical scars on both cheeks were ritual markings. I sat in the back seat, staring at his profile, thinking those markings were the sexiest things I'd ever laid eyes on.

Unfortunately, he spoke nothing but French and, after telling us his name was Philippe, seemed uninterested in saying much more. He loaded our bags in silence and ushered us into our seats, all business, and I was too ashamed of my pathetic French to press the issue. We headed north, into the lush countryside, Philippe driving at some death-defying speed I couldn't register because the speedometer was in kilometers. Every now and then he'd blow his horn, and people trudging along the side of the road would stand back to let us pass. Most of the women wore African fabrics wrapped around them as dresses or skirts. The men were dressed in T-shirts and pants. Once, when Philippe slowed down for a pothole, I caught a glimpse of an old man standing in the grass. He stared blankly at us as we passed. His T-shirt said: "Eric Clapton Is God."

We reached the town of Danané after dark and were driven to the house of a white American UN worker named Charles. He told us the two officials from New York were staying somewhere else. The plan was to rendezvous with them the next morning, then drive to a nearby village whose residents had taken in dozens of Liberian refugees. The UN officials wanted to check on their food supply. Walter and I wanted to interview them.

The next morning we climbed back into our jeep and drove closer to the Liberian border. I stared out the window, drinking in the colors of the countryside—the red-clay dirt, the burnt-orange anthills rising to the sky, the bleached bones of dead trees drying in the sun. It was a kaleidoscope of colors, so much more vibrant than the greens and browns of home.

About a mile from the refugee camp, we stopped at a small village, where we met up with the two UN folks: a thin white woman named Nan and a dark-haired French guy named Jean-Pierre.

"Glad you could make it!" Nan said. She wore a wide straw hat against the sun and smiled a lot. "Why don't we all climb into one jeep, if that's okay, and then on the way Charles can begin briefing us about the problems and difficulties they face in the camps."

"Take your pick," Charles said. "Trying to get food through the system without losing half of it to the black market. Diarrhea, malaria, cholera, though mostly that's under control. Three hundred and thirty-six orphaned children. Oh, and fighting. Fighting is getting to be a big problem."

"Fighting over food?" asked Jean-Pierre. He seemed disdainful.

"No. There's enough food, enough for people not to starve anyway. The fighting is a continuation of the war. We've got people from all different ethnic groups—Krahn, Gio, Mano, even some of the Americo-Liberians. They hate each other, and believe me, it doesn't stop at the gates."

Our arrival at the camp attracted a crush of children, who spilled out of the tents and came running as we stepped from the jeep. They swarmed around Charles, calling his name, pulling at his pockets and the small brown bag he carried.

"Hey, guys, cool it!" Charles said, grinning. "Calm down. I brought you some treats, but I can't hand them out now. You'll get them later."

A couple of children broke away from Charles and closed in on Walter. It was the camera that drew them. Even in Africa, everybody wants to be on TV.

"What village are you from?" one boy asked Walter. He was about ten, very thin, with dusty feet and torn clothes. He held himself back from the other children and stared at us with suspicion.

"A village called Philadelphia," Walter said dryly. "It's in America."

"Yes, I know America," the boy said. He spat in the dirt and turned and walked away.

Charles told us that most of the children were orphans. Their parents had been killed by Doe's soldiers for being Gio or Mano, or killed by Taylor's soldiers for being Krahn or Mandingo, or killed for looking too prosperous, or just caught in the cross fires of war.

Walter lifted his camera and tried to ease out of the crowd, inching backward so he could get a few shots. None of the children appeared to be starving, but they were all thin and dirty, caked from head to toe in reddish dust. Still, they struck me as beautiful, beautiful in a sad, painful way, like the first golden leaves of autumn. Nearly all of them were boys. Where were the girls? Back with their mothers? Or maybe the girls had to work even here in the camps, had to search for water and firewood while their brothers played. I'd have to ask Charles. As I stood there thinking, a boy of about five or six or maybe ten—it was hard to tell—rushed up and without a word wrapped his arms around my leg.

"Hi. What's your name?"

He didn't answer. I tilted his chin to see his eyes; they were vast and empty, the desert at noon. I reached into my bag for a jerky bar and held it out to him. He took it, bit it in two, and put both pieces in his mouth. Then he grabbed my leg again with his rough little hands. Bruising my leg. Bruising my heart.

An older boy, fifteen or so, pushed his way through the crowd and stopped before me. He wore ragged black pants and a T-shirt with a Boston Celtics emblem on the front, but he wore them with the bearing of a prince.

"Miss. My name is Thomas. The soldiers killed my parents. I would like to go with you to America."

He said it simply and with precision, as if it were a speech he had prepared for school, and he stood there waiting for my response. There was a remarkable stillness about him, a calmness unlike the dead-eyed silence of the other, younger boy.

"Now, Thomas. You know we're doing everything we can to

find your aunt," Charles said. Then he whispered to me, "She isn't his real aunt. Charles was adopted by an Americo-Liberian couple."

"But if I could go to America I could find her myself," he said disdainfully, as if Charles were too stupid to understand what he said. "Please, miss. I want to go to America. Everyone says America is better than this place."

"This lady can't help you, Thomas," Charles said. "She's a journalist. Right now she has to go talk with the adults."

The boy ignored Charles. "Let me ask you something, miss. Why does America not come and stop this war?"

It was a question I'd be asked a lot once we reached Monrovia, but this was before, and I was unprepared to answer it. I mumbled something about Americans being reluctant to involve troops in foreign civil wars. Thomas waited politely until I was done.

"I want to go to America," he said again. "You must take me."

Before I could answer, Charles cut in again. "We'll talk later, but right now we have to go." He turned to the little boy still clinging to my leg. "You'll have to let go, Amos." When the boy didn't move, Charles reached down and peeled his hands from my leg, then he led me away.

The camp stretched south for nearly a mile and backed up against the bush. It was easy to tell who had been at the camp for a while and who had just arrived. The more recent refugees lived close to the road, in tents donated by the UN. During the day, driven outside by the climbing temperatures in their oven-like homes, they eyed the road, as if waiting for the all-clear signal, the okay to go home. But the older refugees lived farther back from the road, in mud-brick huts with thatched roofs carefully constructed to block out the sun and maybe any hope of returning home.

I left the others to their work and wandered around the camp, interviewing people as I went. Most people were eager to talk once they found out I was American. A woman named Emma invited me inside her cone-shaped hut and made me tea while telling me her story.

"I was a secretary. I had a husband, a house with running water. A television set. My husband was driving from work on the day the soldiers came. They pulled him from his car and cut off his ears before killing him to death. Someone who saw it ran to tell me. I grabbed the television and headed for the border. But the rebels had set up a checkpoint just outside town. They took the TV and danced around me, laughing, poking their guns into my breasts."

Emma paused to sip her tea. A chill washed over me, although I was still sweating. I wiped my forehead. My skin felt hot.

"After a while two of the soldiers took me behind a tree and raped me. Then they left and two more came and then two more. I lost count of the number who came, but in the end, the last one put his gun to my head and said, 'Now let the Mano whore die.'

"I closed my eyes and heard a sound like thunder in my head, and I thought that I was dead. But I woke up in the darkness with my head on fire and feeling something heavy and wet on my legs. I managed to sit up and reach down; it was a man, also shot. But he was dead. There were bodies all around me, but the soldiers were gone and I was still alive. Somehow the bullet had just gone in and out without touching anything. There was blood all over me, but I could walk. I stumbled along the road all night and all the next day. Every time a tree branch moved, I feared it was the soldiers, coming back to kill me again. But finally I reached here."

It seemed indecent to be taking notes, but this was why I was in Africa, wasn't it? To report this stuff. I kept writing.

"There are Krahn here," Emma said, spitting the words. "That's why I keep my distance from the others. Can't you see how evil they are? You can tell just by looking at them."

Emma stopped talking, and we sat in silence. I looked around the hut at her furnishings—clothes folded neatly on a rough wooden bench, a cot, two plastic jugs for carrying water.

"I'm sorry," I said. It sounded idiotic and inadequate, but I couldn't think of what else to say. "It's terrible."

"Yes, it is."

We heard shouts from outside. We ran out, to see a group of people—boys, mostly, but a few men and women—gathered together, all facing inward, all screaming and yelling words I couldn't understand. A red-faced and frightened-looking Charles was trying to fight his way into the crowd's center, while Nan stood there shrieking, her mouth a red hole in her tiny white face.

"*Mon Dieu! Mon Dieu!*" cried Jean-Pierre over and over. He stood far away from the crowd, pointing toward it, as if directing the police to the problem, only there were no police. Walter was circling, snapping photographs, the whir of his camera lost in the noise.

"What's going on?!" I shouted at him.

"Fight!" he shouted back, still snapping away.

I heard it then, above the screams and cheers of the crowd, a howling high and frightened, a cry like the wrenching of metal. It keened higher and higher and mixed with Nan's shriek in a piercing duet until, suddenly, it stopped, leaving only Nan to scream.

The crowd quieted like a radio snapped off, and people began slipping away. Within a few moments the only people left were Walter and I and the aid workers. Nan stood shaking, silent now, her face contorted. Charles walked over and enfolded her in his arms.

It took a moment for my brain to register the broken mass on the ground as a body; it looked more like a pile of old clothes, tangled and filthy, mashed into the red-clay dirt. But when the aid workers rolled the body over on its back, I recognized the Boston Celtics shirt.

"My God!"

I must have been shaking, because when Walter walked over and wrapped his arm around my shoulder, the world stilled. I pressed my face into Walter's chest and felt the skin on my cheeks begin to sting.

"You've got sunburn," Walter said, pushing me away from him so he could peer down at my face. "We need to get you back to the house, where you can lie down."

"But why? Why?" My head whirled. I felt like I was going to faint, or maybe throw up. I tried stepping back from Walter and raising my eyes to steady myself. I was searching for the horizon; weren't you supposed to look to the horizon when you were sick? But all I could see was the smashed remains of Thomas's face. Walter thought I was asking why I had burned and started to chastise me for not wearing a hat. But Emma, who had come up to look at the body, understood what I meant.

"Because he was Krahn," she said, folding her arms with satisfaction. "Because he was a dog."

People told Charles that Thomas had been killed because he stole a bowl of rice from one of the younger children. He didn't think it was true, but really, in the end, what difference did it make? I asked if the UN officials planned to arrest the killers.

"We don't have that authority," Charles said. "It's not our job. Besides, we don't know who did it. You saw the mob."

At any rate, Thomas's beating resolved the problem of fighting at the camp. We learned that all the remaining Krahn and Americo-Liberian refugees packed up and fled in the night.

In Abidjan, Walter and I said goodbye to a shaken Nan and Jean-Pierre and flew to Freetown, Sierra Leone. At the airport in Freetown we were each required to change one hundred dollars into the local currency, despite the fact that we were only spending the night in the country. We caught a cab to the airport hotel, five hundred yards away. During check-in the clerk asked how we intended to pay for our rooms. When I told him we had local currency, he shook his head and pointed to a sign on the desk that read: "We take only dollars or American Express cards." Walter sighed and pulled out his wallet.

My room was airy and bright, with white curtains at the window and a ceiling fan stirring the warm air overhead. After settling in, I paced around. There was nothing to do—no television, no books, still hours before dinner. Walter knocked on my door to say he was going for a swim.

"You should come," he said. "It'll do you good. Cool you down."

"Maybe later."

Walter strolled off down the hallway, a small towel draped over his shoulders like a cape. Superman, or maybe Superfly. It sounded good, a dip in the pool. Wash off the sweat and the dirt from the road and the red grit from the camp, which had worked itself deep into my skin. But I couldn't go. It was too incongruous—to one minute watch a boy being beaten into the African dust and the next minute frolic in a pool, gin and tonic in hand. They'd bury Thomas in a makeshift cemetery just outside the camp, with the other victims of war and hate. Outside my window, Walter floated lazily in the pool, his baseball cap pulled low over his eyes. He looked like he was dozing, but I knew he was just making himself comfortable. And as if to make up for him, I felt even worse.

We hitched a ride to Liberia aboard a plane chartered by a French aid organization. Seeing Monrovia for the first time was like discovering an unknown little sister, except by the time you discovered her she was already dead. There were pieces of America scattered everywhere, from the bombed-out Baptist church to the posters of Sylvester Stallone at the video store to the tattered red, white, and blue flag above Capitol Hill. We bumped along cratered streets, past buildings pockmarked with bullet holes, their windows shattered, their roofs caved in. A jackknifed truck blocked two of the four lanes; our cabdriver wheeled around it as if it were a bottle in the road. Every store along Broad Street had been looted.

But the fighting had stopped and people were out, reclaiming their lives. Walter and I dropped our things at the only operating hotel and headed for the marketplace to do interviews.

"At least now there is peace," one man said. His name was Franklin, and he was selling toilet seats from a makeshift stall. As we stood talking, all around us the market hummed with people pushing, calling to one another, hawking their goods. Doughnuts, dresses, fabric, soap—it seemed everybody was selling something. Nobody had much money, but a lot of people had looted goods, and there was much bartering going on.

"You would not have wanted to be here before," Franklin said. "Thank God for ECOMOG. You like this seat?"

ECOMOG was a peacekeeping force from five of the surrounding West African nations. The troops were everywhere around the city, at roadblocks and food distribution sites. They were the only reason the civil war had stopped, or at least been pushed out of Monrovia, into the countryside.

Most of the people I met in Monrovia asked one of two questions, sometimes both, until the words became a song I sang in my dreams: Could I sponsor them in the United States? And why hadn't America come to stop the war?

Walter warned me about the sponsorship questions. "Just say no," he said, and did, without hesitation. But I was a coward. I usually tried to dodge the question, or I lied my way out of it.

"I'm a journalist. I can't. It's against the rules."

But if those requests were hard, the questions about why America had not intervened in the war were harder. People asked it with such bewilderment, such broken innocence, and I never came up with a satisfactory answer. All these years they had thought they held a special place in most American hearts.

Probably the worst of these confrontations occurred on our last day in Monrovia, when I interviewed a professor at the university. He was about fifty, a dun-colored, delicate, almost foppish man who used his education as a platform. We sat in his bullet-riddled office, cooled by a breeze through the shattered window, but he might have been sitting in England's House of Lords. His metal bookshelves were empty; all his books had been stolen and burned for fuel.

"You must understand. We Liberians have long considered America to be our father," he said. He sat bolt upright and spoke with exaggerated preciseness. "Liberia, of course, is home, our beloved home. But America is the homeland."

I didn't know what to say to that. America the homeland? It felt like somebody somewhere was playing a cruel joke—on me and on him. What could I tell this man: That most Americans had never heard of Liberia? That those who had probably couldn't find it on a map? Liberia looking for a father and America denying paternity.

"So you see why we were surprised when you did not help." He said it as if I personally had turned my back on him. His voice trembled, and I shifted in my seat. "We do not understand. Why did those marines sit on their ships right off the coast, waiting and waiting while we were being slaughtered like animals?"

Walter moved behind me, snapping pictures, saying nothing, and it was as if his silence and his camera made him invisible. The professor ignored Walter, although he was black, was an American. He ignored Walter and hurled all his anger straight at me, and I sat there and took it, unable to defend myself, because what was the defense? We were busy? We didn't know?

"I am asking you a question! Please do me the courtesy of responding to it."

"Americans don't like to get involved in foreign wars," I stammered. "In civil wars, I mean." Walter's camera whirred behind me.

"Nonsense! America is involved all the time when the wars are elsewhere!"

"I . . ."

"I do not understand! The Jewish people in America would never have sat by and watched Israel be destroyed, even from within. They would have demanded that their government do something! Why did black Americans, at least, not send us help?"

"I don't know." I looked around, desperate to catch Walter's eye. But Walter was busy.

"You *should* know!" the professor yelled. His eyes were red with exhaustion and strain, and he began to cry. "You are a black American—you should know! They killed my wife. My son was shot in the street like a dog! Like a dog, and do you know why? Because he wore glasses! For no other reason than that."

With a moan, the professor collapsed against his desk and sobbed. I backed toward the doorway, desperate to get out. It was horrible to hear the noise he made, to know that he was humiliated by the messiness of his grief. Walter lowered his camera.

"Look, Professor—" Walter began.

But the man cut him off. "You have abandoned us! You black Americans love to cry about brotherhood and the diaspora, but when the crucible came, you abandoned your brothers to death!"

"We're sorry," I stammered. "We're so sorry for your loss." It was feeble, but it was all I could think of to say.

"Sorry is nothing," the professor said, raising his tear-streaked face to stare as we backed from the room. "Being sorry is easy. But you are not forgiven."

On our last night in Africa, back in Abidjan, Walter and I went to dinner with a group of foreign correspondents. By coincidence, I sat next to the only other black guy in the group, a reporter for the *Chicago Herald* named Terence. He told me a story.

"I was with some of these guys once at a restaurant in Free-town. We had just come out from Monrovia, when things were getting really bad there last year. Everybody going crazy, bodies piling up on the beach. I dream about it some nights. But we got out and went to Freetown and went to this restaurant to eat, and we ordered and I noticed that the waiter served all the white reporters first. First with the drinks, then with the food. He went all around the table to the white reporters and always ended with me. None of the other guys noticed it, but I did. Finally I confronted the waiter. I said something like, 'My brother, why are you doing this? Why are you treating the white men better than you treat me?' The man got very flustered and apologized. He said, 'I thought you were Temne. I thought you were African and would want me to serve our foreign guests first.'"

Terence laughed and sipped his beer.

"Is there supposed to be some lesson in that for me?" I asked.

He shrugged. "I was hoping you'd tell me."

Back at the hotel, I changed into my swimsuit and went out-side to the pool. It was a velvety night, the sky brilliant with cool white stars. I thought about the scene from *Roots* in which the father holds his newborn son up to the night sky and says something like, "Behold the only thing greater than yourself." Alex Haley really ruined a generation of black Americans with that stuff; somebody should have made him pay. The truth was, one way or the other, Africa was just another fantasy you had to give up.

chapter eighteen

Walter got drunk on the plane home, and somewhere over the Atlantic he started singing "Change Gonna Come," this old Sam Cooke song my mother used to sing. I could tell from his voice how tired he was. When I looked into his eyes, I saw tears.

"I know the food is bad, but it's not worth crying about," I joked. It scared me a little to see him weepy. He had been a rock during the entire trip, and although it annoyed me at first, after Thomas was killed I came to rely on Walter's steadiness. He bathed my sunburn with ice water, made me take my malaria tablets, helped me figure out whom to interview and whom to leave alone. Despite myself I liked him. I liked him a lot.

"That poor kid," he muttered drunkenly. "That poor damn kid.

That poor, stupid kid. Guess he thought the change had already come." He giggled and took another sip of his drink. "Like we used to say back in the day: My people, my people." He began singing again. A flight attendant, a young and pretty sister, hurried down the aisle.

"Sir, could you please quiet down? You're disturbing the other passengers." She gave me a pleading look, and I felt bad for her. She was the only black attendant on the plane; they'd probably figured she would have more pull with us.

"I think he'd like some coffee," I said. She scurried to get it as I eased Walter's drink out of his hand.

"Sometimes I hate this job," he said. His voice was thick and his eyes were half closed. "It depresses me so."

I knew Walter was thinking about Thomas, about the way he'd died and the reason he'd died—because he belonged to a different ethnic group. An image of Thomas's mangled body flashed into my brain, accompanied by Nan's shrill and useless screams. For the rest of my life, whenever I thought of that day, I'd hear that woman screaming.

"Walter, can I ask you something?"

"Mm hmm."

"How could you stand there taking pictures when Thomas was being stomped? How could you do that?"

Walter sat up straight in his seat, staring at me. I lowered my eyes.

"Are you judging me?"

"No. No, of course not. I . . . I just mean . . ."

"You think I could have done something?" His eyes blazed at me for a second, then he collapsed back against the cushions with a sigh. "You're so young."

We were quiet a moment. Behind us, a baby who had been crying intermittently throughout the flight began to wail.

"I tried to pull him out when I first got there," Walter said softly. "They pushed me back; one guy shook his fist in my face.

They were so angry, so frenzied, they would have killed me too. So I did my job. I put my emotions on hold and did what I had to do. What would you prefer—that I fall apart? That I stand around screeching like that silly Nan twit? I did what I had to do, because that's what it's all about, Hope. That's what life's about."

Walter began singing again, softly now. By the time the flight attendant got back with the coffee, he'd passed out.

It took me nearly forty minutes to make my way through the insanity of JFK—waiting in the passport line, getting my bags, fighting my way through the Tower of Babel crowds. But I was so happy to be home, happy—although I didn't admit it to Walter—to be back in America. A hungover Walter said he was going into New York to stay with friends for the weekend, then staggered off to find a taxi. I called a van service to take me from the airport all the way to Philadelphia—the *Record* was paying. Three hours later, so tired my legs were trembling, I climbed from the van and dragged myself to the elevator, then down the hall to my apartment door.

Every plant in my apartment was withered and brown and sitting in its own desolate puddle. I had asked my neighbor's teenage daughter, Makinya, to keep them watered; obviously she forgot until the last minute, then tried to drown them back to life. At least she'd remembered to bring in my mail. It sat piled on the kitchen table, staring at me in reproach. I'd fled to Africa without paying any of my bills; a few creditors had sent nasty notes. But the lights still worked and my car was still parked in the lot downstairs, so nothing was irretrievable.

It was late afternoon in Philadelphia, almost midnight across the ocean. My stomach rumbled. I stood in the kitchen, staring at the moldy food in my refrigerator, debating whether to clean, shop, or just forget everything and fall into bed. In the living room, the light on my answering machine stared me down. Not one message after three weeks; how pathetic. I'd told my mother I was leaving the country, and Melvia knew, but what about Malcolm? I hadn't told him anything. I searched the dining room table for messages, thinking maybe he'd called while Makinya was there, but found none. I pulled down the shades and turned off the lights and crawled into bed.

I was in the middle of a dream about Thomas when the telephone rang, jarring me awake. For a moment I didn't know where I was.

"Hello?"

"Hey! She lives! I was just beginning to think you'd decided to stay in Africa."

"Georgia!" If it was Georgia, I must be home. Relief flooded over me. "Hey, girl. I just woke up. What time is it?"

"Nearly seven."

I yawned. "That's like . . . one in the morning Africa time."

"Well, it's the shank of the evening America time, and you need to wake up or you'll never get rid of that jet lag. You're back just in time for the party. Get dressed and let's go."

Georgia said the *Record* was throwing a retirement party for Bernard somebody, some wizened assistant editor whom no one had seen for more than fifteen minutes a day for years. The newspaper was rife with this kind of deadwood, former go-getters who sat at their desks looking up their old stories in the computer library or writing memos nobody read. They had big titles and big salaries and arrived promptly at ten and left promptly at six and never accomplished a thing. Nobody spoke to them until they announced their retirement, at which time they got a party on the company's dime. I didn't know Bernard from Adam, but everything in my refrigerator had hair on it and I didn't feel like sitting at home.

"I'll swing by in an hour. We'll go together," Georgia said.

The party was being held at somebody's house on the Main

Line, in one of those neighborhoods where the houses sat so far back from the road you could plant crops on the front lawn. The living room was packed with people. The hostess, a taut, tanned woman with a rounded forehead, flitted about the room opening windows, her face suggesting that all these people were just stinking up her house.

I whispered to Georgia as we made our way through the crowd toward the bar: "She doesn't look happy to have us here. Does she work at the paper?"

"No, she's married to Jeff, the head of the copy desk. She hates newsroom parties. Last time they had a party here, she stayed in her room all night and refused to come down. Nobody cared. We danced until four."

At the bar I ordered a gin and tonic, sucked it up, ordered another. The liquor slid down my throat, warming me, loosening the awkwardness I suddenly felt. It was strange to be back among all these shiny white Americans with their opalescent teeth and braying laughs. Someone hailed me; I turned toward the voice and found Richard.

"Welcome home, Hope. How did you find Africa?"

"Went to Europe and turned right." I was too tired to joust with him.

Richard smiled. "But seriously. I'm curious to know what you thought. Was Africa what you expected?"

"It was great, Richard," I lied. "Never had a better time in my life."

"Really? That's wonderful, but I must say I'm surprised. I have a very dear black friend who went to Africa and came home quite disappointed. He tells me he knows several other blacks who felt the same."

"It's quite possible, Richard, that your black friends are not representative of the entire race."

"Oh, of course not. But still . . ."

I pretended to wave at someone behind Richard, then gave

him my most insincere smile. "Excuse me, Richard. I see someone I know. We'll talk on Monday." I walked away, not wanting to deal with him any more than was necessary. Monday would be soon enough.

I stopped at the bar for another drink, then made my way into the dining room. There, under a crystal chandelier, stood a table laden with food. Piles of smoked turkey and ham, platters of raw vegetables, three kinds of pâté. I popped a tiny quiche into my mouth and realized I hadn't eaten since breakfast on the plane.

A hand appeared and lifted a piece of meat onto my plate. I looked up at David and waited for my heart to speed up. It didn't.

"Welcome home," David said.

"Thanks." I checked my breathing—steady as a metronome. No palpitations.

"How was it?" David asked.

"Great. How are you? How's Stephanie? She like it in D.C.?"

"I think so. She's in town this weekend. She's here, in fact, upstairs on the phone with the copy desk. She's been there for ten minutes already."

"Must be a big story." People behind us were sending dirty looks, so I moved on down the line, piling food on my plate. David followed me out to the sun porch, then stood awkwardly over me as I began devouring my food. The fact that I was still hungry, the fact that seeing him hadn't affected my appetite, made me feel good. I slurped the rest of my drink, then held up my glass. "Get me another drink."

David took the glass and scurried off. I laughed and plowed into my ham, feeling strangely powerful.

Returning, David set the drink near the foot of my chair, then pulled up a chair for himself.

"What do you want, David?" I was still eating.

"I just wanted to make sure we were okay. I mean, I hope we are."

"I'm fine. Want a quiche?" When David shook his head, I shrugged and popped it into my mouth.

"I care about you a lot," he said. "As a friend. I'd still like to be friends."

Something in his words made me think about Phil, all those years ago at Astor. Wanted to be friends. Everybody wanted to be my friend. Always a friend, never a bride. I giggled, amused at myself. "You going to eat that?" I picked a hunk of Brie from David's plate. It was soft and smooth, faintly warm, and it melted in my mouth.

"David," I said calmly, "go to hell."

I stood and strode from the room, or at least I tried. Someone had moved the door. Finally I found it and pranced into the living room, searching for Georgia. She stood in a corner talking to some white guy I didn't know.

"You're drunk," she said when I approached her. She was laughing at me.

I pulled myself up. "Am not! I just wanted to tell you I was leaving. You don't have to come."

"You plan to walk? We came together. Or don't you remember?"

In the car, Georgia turned on the radio to a soul station.

"One request," she said. "Don't get sick in my car."

"I won't. I'm sorry, Georgia. I don't know how I got so tipsy." She chuckled. "I do. I saw you chugging those drinks."

I closed my eyes and leaned back against my seat, feigning sleep. In the darkness, the music from the radio surrounded me, those old, sexy-sad songs by popular groups from my childhood. Cameo, Earth, Wind and Fire, Gladys Knight and her Pips. Bubba had always reminded me of my uncle Willie, who got drunk one night and lay down on the railroad tracks to get warm.

His was the first funeral I had ever attended, held in the sweltering heat of my grandmother's storefront church. My grandmother sat in the front row, rocking and moaning, crying louder because the casket was closed; she was propped up by fat black ladies with shiny faces and eyes so wet and deep you feared to look into them. I didn't know these ladies, but I knew what they were: mothers of the church. They sat with my grandmother and moved with her when she stood and faced the casket and helped her back to her chair when her knees gave out. They wiped my grandmother's face with white lace handkerchiefs and cooled her sweat with the wind from their Martin Luther King fans. They also cried, but quietly, in deference to her loud grief.

The car had stopped, and we sat idling in the driveway of my building.

"Want me to help you upstairs?" Georgia asked.

"No, I'm fine."

"Are you sure? Maybe I should stay here with you tonight. You look pretty wasted."

"I'm fine, Georgia. Thanks for worrying about me. I'll call you tomorrow."

I felt her watch me walk into the building. I waved from the door and she drove off, smiling still. That girl probably woke up smiling, had probably come into the world smiling, the only baby ever born who laughed when the doctor slapped her on the ass. She was sweet, though. Very thoughtful. I waved again, although Georgia's car was long gone.

It took forever for the elevator to arrive. I closed my eyes and almost fell asleep waiting for it. When the doors finally opened, I saw Malcolm standing there under the light. He had a cigarette in his hand and had just blown a trail of smoke toward the No Smoking sign.

"Malcolm."

"Hey, baby," he said quietly.

I was too tired to ask what he was doing there, too tired to do anything but stumble inside and push my floor button. The door slid closed, locking us in.

"Sorry about this," he said, dropping the cigarette to the floor. He crushed it with his shoe, then reached down to pick up the butt and stick it in his pocket. "Bad habit. I quit for five years, but for some reason lately, I've had the urge to get back into it."

He followed me off the elevator. The hideous brown carpet rose and dipped before me like a country road, tricky to negotiate in the yellow hallway light. I slid my hand along the wall to steady myself. It was late. Silence held the building in its grasp.

"I heard you were back from Africa." Malcolm spoke barely above a whisper. "I can't believe you left the country, left the continent, without telling me. You didn't even call."

"Malcolm . . ."

"But I'm glad you're home, baby. I was worried about you. I brought you those flowers, see?"

A huge bouquet sat on the carpet before my door—daisies and jonquils and yellow roses, in a tall woven basket shaped like a water jar. The bouquet was stunning, so large it nearly reached the doorknob. I stared at it, astonished. Malcolm had once told me he was opposed to buying flowers on principle. He said most flowers were grown by oppressed people in Mexico or Central America, who earned ten cents an hour. He said they took up valuable land that should be used to grow food for the world's starving poor. He said they cost too much and died too soon and were a commercialized society's crafty image of what a man should do. The only thing worse than flowers, according to Malcolm, were diamonds. But there they were.

"They're beautiful."

"Not as beautiful as you, baby." Malcolm stepped toward me, reaching out with one hand to stroke my cheek. "I miss you."

We stood like that a minute, then Malcolm asked, "Can we go inside?"

Malcolm carried the bouquet into the living room and set it on the coffee table. Then he pulled me to him and took my face in his hands.

"What happened, baby? I mean, is all this about the NABJ thing? That wasn't important."

"It was important to you then."

"Nah, baby. Not as important as you."

"Not as important as whoever it was you were screwing at the convention." For a moment Malcolm was quiet. But he must have been expecting it, because he didn't seem surprised.

"I'm sorry about that, baby. I was angry because you wouldn't vote for Kwame. No, wait—I know that's a stupid reason, but that's the way I felt. You know I didn't care about that girl."

I laughed. "That's just it. I don't know anything. Nothing at all."

I was so tired. Malcolm began nuzzling my neck and stroking my back, heating my brain. I was fuzzy; I couldn't think.

"Your shirt stinks," I said.

"I'll take it off."

"Your breath stinks."

"I'll brush my teeth." He kept touching me, stroking my body. "You still got my old toothbrush here?"

"I threw it away."

"That's okay. I'll work it out." He kissed me on the forehead. "Baby, baby, why are you crying?"

"You stink."

"I'll take a shower. Don't cry, Hope. It's okay."

"You stink," I said, as Malcolm led me toward the couch. He set me down and stroked my forehead and then kissed me, mingling his smoky, honey tongue with my own.

chapter
nineteen

I dreamed I was back home in Memphis, in our house on Wall-stone Street, waiting in the kitchen for my mother to come home and celebrate my birthday. She had promised a cake from the bakery, a pink cake shaped like a flower, with my name written in fluffy white frosting. I was so excited I couldn't sit still; I kept standing on a chair to peek out the window in the front door.

But my mother came home empty-handed and mad. She said the bakery had given my cake to someone else and it was my fault. I hadn't called to make sure they would hold it, like I was supposed to do, so they gave it away before my mother could arrive. Now my birthday was ruined, and I had only myself to blame. I sat in my chair on the dirt from my shoes and cried a torrent of tears.

I awoke sweating. I wanted to get up and turn on the fan, but I couldn't because my head had grown overnight to the size of a watermelon. I tried my eyes. The lids creaked a bit but opened normally, and the world lightened from black to gray. The bottom of the bed, near my feet, felt damp, and as the heavy smell of wet bricks rose to my nostrils, I realized it was raining. Fat drops of rain spilled through the open window, soaking everything in reach. My books on the windowsill, the sheets, the bed—all wet.

My books! In a rush to save them I sat up too quickly and got punched in the head for my effort. A hangover, and a bad one too. A wave of sickness passed over me, rose high, receded. I decided the better part of valor was to lie back down for a few minutes, but when I did I found myself facing a muscular wall of flesh.

Malcolm. It all came flooding back to me: the wine, the second bottle we'd opened, Malcolm in the living room, kissing my neck. Now he lay next to me, heavy and warm, his legs sprawled wide, his hands curled over his penis and balls. His chest rose and fell slowly. He was in a deep, deep sleep. I had to kick him twice before he stirred.

"Malcolm! Close the window! It's raining all over my books."

Obediently he rose and staggered to the window, still half asleep until his hands brushed the puddle on the windowsill.

"Oh, shit!" He held up my copy of *All the King's Men* and let it drip water onto the floor. "I'm sorry, baby. I'll buy you a new one."

"Forget it." I buried my throbbing head under the pillow. "Just be quiet."

He flopped down on the bed and began nuzzling my neck, but the stubble on his chin felt like bits of brick against my skin. I pushed him away.

"Stop it!"

"Well! Somebody's a hurting dog this morning," he said. "You need aspirin. Got any in the house?"

I shook my head, too hard. The room fragmented.

"I'll zip down to the drugstore."

"I just need sleep."

"It'll only take a second."

"That's okay."

"Then how about some food?" He was bouncing the bed, making me seasick.

"No."

"Sure? Eggs, bacon? Best thing. You'll feel a lot better. Then you can tell me about Africa, about the homeland. Man, I can't wait to go, to get away from this country and see something real. I bet it was great."

For some reason I thought about Walter, and thinking about Walter made Malcolm seem silly to me. Before, I thought he was so smart, so perceptive, but now I saw that he was just naive. He didn't know anything.

"I really want to sleep, Malcolm. I want you to go."

"What?" He stopped bouncing, looked at me with surprise.

"I want you to leave, and I'm not sure I want you to come back."

Malcolm stood and began silently kicking through the tangle of clothes on the floor, searching for his underwear. Standing there, naked and vulnerable, he looked like a little boy whose mother had scolded him. Remorse seeped in below my hangover.

"Malcolm . . ."

"Nah, nah, baby, that's cool." He found his shorts and his pants and pulled them on like armor, getting tougher as he dressed.

"You don't want me here, I'm gone. Later!" He stamped from the room, slamming the door behind him.

"I'm sorry!" I called, but he was gone. I fell back onto the bed.

The rain beat a tune against the window, matching the pounding in my head. Malcolm. He thought it was the girl at the convention that bothered me, but she was the least of it. I'd thought Malcolm was going to show me something, teach me how to be at ease with myself in the world, but he couldn't. It was probably too much to ask.

Heading for the bathroom, I had a moment of panic. I sat on the toilet and held my breath and reached inside myself, praying. When my finger hit the rubbery rim, I sighed a little prayer of thanks. At least I hadn't been a total idiot.

I felt bad about Malcolm all day Sunday, except when I was feeling bad about myself. The hangover resisted two doses of aspirin, a gallon of water, and enough coffee to float my kidneys up to my nose. The only way not to feel nauseous was to sleep, so I slept most of the afternoon and much of the evening, and by 9 P.M. it seemed that I'd probably live.

I still had to write the Liberia stories. The foreign editor gave me two weeks to get three fairly long stories done—not a lot of time. The metro desk took me off weekends, which was nice. I got to work early, when the newsroom was empty, because I concentrated better in the silence. I wanted the stories to be good, not for my sake but for Thomas and Emma and the rest of the Liberians waiting patiently for America to intervene. Not that it would do any good.

Before I knew it, the week was up and I hadn't called Malcolm and he hadn't called me. I missed him a little, or maybe not him but just somebody or something. It was hard to tell. Until I figured it out, there was no sense dragging him back in.

A few days later I began looking for my period. My system was as reliable as a Swiss watch: blood every twenty-nine days, come stress or high water or hell. I loved that about myself.

My periods were fairly easy affairs—a little bloating, a few cramps, and I was done. But even if my body had bucked and contracted, even if each ruby drop had cost me pain, I would still have loved my period. Menstruation was salvation. A gift. A reprieve. Each cramp was a sweet voice whispering the words "not pregnant" to my thankful psyche. Not pregnant, not pregnant, still whole.

I grew up in a house full of women, in an estrogen palace as musky and rich as Georgia clay after a summer rain. Among my two sisters, my mother, and myself, we practically floated the place on feminine hormones. It's a wonder men visiting our house weren't driven mad by the richness of it all. Or maybe they were.

My mother suffered horrible, gut-twisting periods. For a week or so each month she'd stop eating and take to her bed after work with a hot-water bottle, a few dozen Midols, and the brave resignation of a woman marching toward war. My sisters and I would make soup or milk shakes, depending on the season, then tiptoe into the darkened bedroom to beg our mother to eat. Her moans were terrifying, all the more so because she tried to muffle them when we were around. But the truth couldn't be hidden. This terrible thing was going to happen to us too, and there was nothing, nothing we could do about it.

At church, Sister Simpson sat before the young ladies' class and read soberly from Leviticus:

"When a woman has a discharge of blood which is a regular discharge from her body, she shall be in her impurity for seven days, and who ever touches her shall be unclean until the evening." Plus more like that, about the disgusting thing that would happen to us, how unclean it was and unclean we'd be and how our impurity could be spread like the plague.

"The whole thing is disgusting," Charity whispered to me, making a face. "I'm gonna stuff a stone up myself. That way, nothing will be able to get out."

I scoffed at her. She was so young and stupid. A stone wouldn't do it; I planned to use a bottle cap.

One by one we went toward adolescence like women toward execution. My sister Faith was the first to fall. One day she came home from school crying and locked herself in the bathroom, while my mother knocked on the door, pleading with her to come out, and I pleaded too, because I had to pee. Finally Faith emerged, her face reddened and puffy, and ran into the bedroom. My mother took a Kotex package from the closet and went in after her and closed the door.

After that I checked myself every day before school. No way was I going to be caught bleeding in my math class. On the fateful day that I found a streak of red on my panties, I cried and begged my mother to let me stay home from school. The thought of stuffing a pad between my thighs and waddling down the hallways made me sick. I imagined that everyone would be able to see through my jeans to my horrible secret. My mother, fortunately, understood.

"The first time is the hardest," she said that afternoon, after making me a cup of tea. We were all alone in the house, us two women, facing our womanly pain. My mother looked at me somberly.

"Now you understand," she said.

This was the price of being a woman, this horrifying leakage every month for, I thought, the rest of your life. Lying in bed that afternoon, I braced myself for the pain, vowing to suffer in silence as long as I could. I was a woman now, an adult. But except for a tingling in my breasts, no pain materialized. The bleeding streamed, then slowed, then stopped, and the next day I went back to school, telling everyone that I'd had the flu. People nodded and went on talking about the upcoming football game. My life had been transformed, but nobody could even tell.

After that, my period was just a minor nuisance. It meant for three or four days a month I couldn't stand without worrying whether the back of my skirt held a telltale smudge, a red Rorschach blot. It meant I had to begin carrying a purse, which I hated; had to be careful whenever I opened it not to expose those fat white pads to—gasp!—a boy. I longed for the tiny pink tampon boxes shown in the pages of my girl-teen magazines, but my mother refused to allow us to use tampons. She considered them dirty, or maybe vaguely sexual; she wouldn't allow them in the house.

Senior year at Astor I met Travis, a lanky whiteboy from New York City, who sounded black, walked black, listened to black music, and hung around with the small group of black kids on campus. He told me his mother had married a black man when he was six, and so he had been raised mostly around black people, in a section of the city called Washington Heights. Travis kissed me hard and fast, like he was stealing something valuable from me and had to be quick. I felt consumed, and I loved it. I loved him. Early evenings before curfew, we'd wander out beyond the football fields to mesh our bodies together against the sweet, rough bark of a tree. I wanted to spend the rest of my life breathing his smell, feeling his chest pressed against mine. But Travis wanted more.

"Please? Pretty please?" he begged. I'd laugh it off, pretending he didn't really want to have sex, he was just kidding. Then one weekend Travis got caught smoking pot in his dorm room. He was given a week to pack his things and leave school. Just like that, he was ripped from my life. He promised to stay in touch, but I knew he wouldn't. I would probably never see him again.

I wanted to give Travis something to remember me by. Part of me hoped that if I slept with him, somehow we wouldn't end.

I got a weekend pass to stay at the house of a day-student friend; Travis promised to meet me there Saturday night. My friend, Liz, showed us to her bedroom and left us alone. Her parents were out at a concert and would be home late. We had until midnight, she said, but it didn't take that long. I was scared, Travis was scared and, I realized, a little drunk. Thirty minutes later he zipped up his pants and left. I remember more about the shower afterward than about the sex. I remember standing in the blue-tiled stall, the hot water beating my skin and the roar drowning out the television that Liz had turned up loud so as not to hear whatever she might hear. I stood under the water, and the only thing that was clear was that I'd just had sex. I'd had sex, and despite the condom we'd used, I might now be pregnant. My first time out of the box, and I'd get nailed, sure as shit, end up just like my sister Faith.

I crawled through the next three weeks, praying every day for blood. I made deals with God. I'd go to church every Sunday. I'd call my mother, be nicer to her. I would never, ever have sex again, not even after I got married.

My terror at the prospect of being pregnant had one advantage: it kept me from mourning Travis. When I thought of him it was mostly with anger at leaving me knocked up and stranded, at ruining my life while he went traipsing back to New York. The campus never looked so beautiful, my little room never seemed so special, as they did now that I was about to lose it all. All day long I daydreamed about going home in shame to face my mother. All night long I prayed for blood: Please, God, please let me bleed.

Just as I was about to crack, my period arrived. I was sitting in Latin class, translating Virgil, when I felt something warm tickle me down there. I was so excited I nearly laughed out loud. Old Mr. Harris, the teacher, must have noticed the smile on my face, because he slithered up to me with a snarl. He hated girls. Rumor had it he'd cried all night when the school admitted them, and believed that if he drove enough girls to tears they'd stop coming.

"Is there something you would like to share with the class, Miss Robinson?" he sneered. "Some brilliant insight into Virgil you have divined?"

The class fell silent. Everybody dreaded a Harris attack.

"No, sir." I grinned at him. "In fact, I failed to understand the passage altogether. Could you explain it to me?"

"Well! How refreshing to see someone who recognizes her own incalculable incompetence and admits it before the world! Hats off to you, Miss Robinson. You will of course remain after class."

Normally this directive would have frightened me; a minute alone with Harris was like an eternity in Dante's hell. But as soon as the room cleared I stood up, glanced down at the back of my skirt, and announced that I was having feminine problems.

"I need to go to the ladies' room," I said. "I need to go now."

Harris turned pale and began coughing so violently I wondered if he was having a stroke. I imagined myself the slayer of old Harris, a destroyer of dragons. People would cheer me as I walked the campus! But Harris recovered enough to yell at me to get out of his room, get out of his sight. I left him muttering about the foulness of women and ran to the bathroom, praying all the while. And I got to the bathroom and closed my eyes for a moment, afraid to look, but when I did I saw there, on my panties, in the blurred, stained shape of a tiny hand, the sweet red elixir of life.

chapter twenty

Panic set in two days after my period was scheduled to arrive. Please, God, I couldn't be pregnant. I thought back to that morning after Malcolm, remembered pulling out the diaphragm and being relieved. But I didn't remember putting it in the night before, and that was a problem. I could have put it in wrong, or forgotten to use spermicide. Maybe in my drunkenness I'd squeezed on antibiotic gel instead. Or toothpaste; pregnant but cavity-free.

Day six, no period, I awoke from a nightmare I couldn't remember. Something about the beach and water, but as I opened my eyes the dream slipped away, just beyond my grasp. Light the color of apricots slanted through the window. Sunrise. Without moving, without even turning my head, I started to pray.

Please. Please, Lord, don't let me be pregnant. My hand slid down into my panties but came back dry.

At work, I forced myself to concentrate on the last Liberian story, told myself it was probably just stress from having this albatross around my neck that was holding up my period. I wrote hard for four days, stopping only to eat and to make hopeful, desperate visits to the bathroom, after which I staggered back to my desk, heavy and depressed, and could barely stand to look at the green words glowing on my computer screen. Finally I just stopped writing and sent the piece over to the foreign editor. It wasn't a complete story, but it was long enough, and anyway, who really cared? He E-mailed me back: "Okay, thanks. We're a little backed up now, so it may be a while before we get to it."

Georgia stopped by my desk to ask me to lunch. The thought of gossiping with her, of talking about beats and promotions and whose story made the front page, while waiting for the little bomb inside to detonate, was unbearable.

"I'm kind of busy. Maybe next week."

"Okay." She leaned close to me, whispering conspiratorially. "You don't look so good. Is your favorite aunt visiting? I've got Midol in my bag."

She scampered to get the pills, and I took them, hoping that maybe taking period medicine would bring on my period.

By day ten I couldn't stand it anymore. I got out of bed in a panic at 5 A.M. and drove to a twenty-four-hour drugstore. When I arrived at the counter with the white box, the woman working the register took one look and grinned.

"Take it from me: if you think you might be, you probably are." She laughed. "No sense wasting money on this."

She rang up the sale, babbling on about how angry her boyfriend had been when she got pregnant the first time, how he'd smacked her in the stomach to make her lose the child, how it didn't work and the kid had come anyway and now her boyfriend loved his son but didn't want to give her any money for support. She moved slowly, pausing during sentences as though she couldn't speak and move her hands at the same time. Her voice was like a car alarm going off somewhere in the distance, distracting me so much I couldn't think.

"Could you hurry it up?"

She started as if I'd smacked her, then dropped my change onto the counter beside my hand.

"Bitch," she mumbled as I turned away. "I hope you are."

At home I pissed into the little plastic cup with fury, then dropped the urine sample into the slide window and got down on my knees on the cold, hard tile to pray. But either God was busy or he'd heard it all before, because two little blue lines appeared in the window. Two clear blue lines. I reread the directions, checked the stick, stared at it a while. The lines stared back at me, growing darker by the minute, until I wrapped the evil thing in toilet paper and took it out to the trash.

It was a Sunday, fortunately. I didn't have to go to work, so I wandered around my apartment, picking up objects and putting them back down in the same place. Something told me to call Malcolm, to tell him. He'd rush over and wrap his arms around me and kiss my forehead and tell me what to do. And that was what stopped me—Malcolm would know right away what he wanted me to do; he'd be as certain as thunder, and I wasn't, not yet. Not yet.

I was too ashamed to see my regular gynecologist, so the next day I looked up women's clinics in the phone book and chose the one in West Philadelphia, way out on Market Street, in a neighborhood no one I knew was likely to be hanging around. The clinic was tucked inside an office building, plain, brownbrick, two stories high, with a parking lot out back. In the lobby were signs for a dentist's office, a collection agency, and a guy promising to get you car insurance even if your driving record sucked. The clinic was on the second floor.

A dozen tired faces turned toward me when I opened the door, then turned away, uninterested. In a corner of the room, a group of kids played with a couple of dingy stuffed animals. Two boys were fighting over one of the animals—a zebra— hitting each other as hard as they could. None of the adults paid them any attention. The woman closest to them sat with her head tilted back against the wall, hands clasped over her purse, eyes closed.

The room had been painted a bright yellow, probably in an attempt to make it seem cheery. It didn't work. There were posters on the walls, posters of women doing exciting and purposeful things like operating on a patient and climbing into the cockpit of a fighter plane. Probably the same person who painted the walls thought the posters were a good idea, thought they'd help the women who came limping into the clinic believe they could actually take control of their lives.

I checked in at the desk and sat down to wait. My appointment was scheduled for 11 A.M. At eleven-thirty I asked the receptionist how much longer.

"Until they can see you," she said, not bothering to look up from her book.

Which was pretty much what I figured. Clinics were for poor people, and if there was one thing a poor person had better know how to do, it was wait. I remembered sitting with my mother in the free clinic in Memphis, waiting and waiting for some four-eyed doctor to give me a shot I didn't want. Anytime we had to go to the clinic we'd get up before the sun rose, and my mother would cook breakfast and pack a bag full of bologna sandwiches for lunch. We'd arrive at the clinic just as the sun began to spill over the horizon, to find five or six people already in line, standing patiently and silent as the dawn.

At noon, my head aching from the screaming of the children,

I asked again and got the same response from the receptionist. At twelve-thirty, a nurse called my name and showed me into a room with pale-blue walls. At one, another nurse walked in. She handed me a blue paper gown and told me to take off my clothes.

"Here for an annual?"

"What? Oh, no."

She waited a moment, then said, exasperated, "What, then?"

"I . . . I think I'm pregnant." It was the first time I'd actually said the word out loud, and it sounded dirty. The nurse didn't blink. She turned away to take a cup out of the cabinet beneath the sink, then she turned back, and I realized I'd been worried what she would think.

"Urine sample," she said. "Bathroom across the hall. Hand it to me when you come out."

Afterward I sat in the exam room and waited some more. The biggest thing in the room was one of those reclining tables with stirrups. After twenty minutes or so, another woman came in. She was dark-skinned, beautiful, and she wore a white coat and bright-red lipstick.

"Sorry to keep you waiting so long," she said, speaking with a lilt. She must have been from some island, Haiti maybe. "This place is always hectic on Monday. I'm Patricia. And you are—" she looked down at the chart—"Hope?"

"Are you a doctor?" Doctors never introduced themselves by their first names.

"I'm a nurse practitioner. We handle most of the cases around here, depending upon what the client wants. Well, Hope, you were correct. You are pregnant. Tell me, is this good news or not good news for you?"

My stomach heaved, and the last thin splinter of hope that this wasn't happening flared and burned. I was tired, too tired to raise my hands and wipe away the tears slipping down my face.

Patricia handed me a tissue. "Have you thought about what you're going to do?"

Had I thought about it? I'd been trying not to think about it, hoping it wouldn't be necessary. My stomach tightened again, twisting in on itself, and my head spun dizzily about the room. All I wanted was to be home in my bed, blankets pulled up against the truth.

I stood, and I must have been swaying, because Patricia put her hand on my shoulder to steady me.

"I don't know what to do."

She nodded, like I'd asked her something, then released my shoulder, and I sank back into the chair as though her hand had been the only thing holding me up.

"I'll do an exam, take some blood, and we'll get a better idea of how far along you might be. Then we can talk about options."

"Options," I repeated, too tired to think.

"You'll have to decide whether you want to continue the pregnancy or terminate," she said, handing me a gown. "You can talk to a counselor if you'd like. We have good people here."

But I didn't want to talk to anyone else, not for a while. Patricia told me to get undressed, then started to leave. She opened the door, and there were two women standing in the hallway, talking. I was already pulling off my shirt, and Patricia hurried to close the door to give me some privacy, but I just kept undressing. It didn't matter who saw me now.

The first thing I thought about when I came out of shock was my mother. I wanted to pick up the phone and call her: "Mommy, help." But how could I tell her what I'd done? It'd break her heart to see me pregnant, pregnant and alone after having come so far. I could hear her voice saying, "You almost made it. You almost had it, but you messed everything up." I pushed her out of my mind.

Then I thought about Malcolm, and I decided not to tell him until I knew what I was going to do. And depending upon what that was, I might not tell him at all. Somehow abortion was the one controversial topic about which Malcolm and I had never talked, but I knew just about what he would say. Not a conspiracy, exactly, but certainly convenient. A handy means for keeping the black population in check.

It was funny in a way, ironic really, because unlike most of the guys I knew, unlike my father, who'd disappeared, and unlike the series of worthless pigs who'd abandoned Faith, Malcolm would want to be involved. He'd probably want the kid; at least he'd want me to have it and raise it, so he could tell everyone about his son, his little African prince. But no matter how involved Malcolm was, I'd still be the main one, the one on call twenty-four hours a day, the mother, the parent. I'd be the one whose job would have to take a back seat, whose social life would dwindle to zero. Good-bye parties, good-bye vacations, good-bye even sitting down uninterrupted to read a book. I'd be the one who ceased to exist, my identity sucked away by a seven-pound tyrant just as I was starting to figure out who I was.

On Monday I called the clinic and made an appointment. The voice on the other end asked if I'd been there before and whom I had seen. After a few minutes, Patricia came on the line.

"I want an abortion," I said. "I don't want counseling. I know what I want. Please, just let me come in."

"Okay," she said soothingly. "Saturday at nine."

Patricia explained the procedure: how they detached the fetal tissue from the wall of the uterus, using vacuum suction; how long it would take. I was grateful for her flat tone, her clinical words: tissue, aspirate, vacuum. She made it seem that I could walk into the clinic and with just a little vacuuming clean up the huge mess I'd made.

She told me to bring someone with me to drive me home afterward. I thought about asking Georgia but dismissed that idea—she'd probably spend the entire time in tears. Malcolm was out. So I asked Melvia to lunch. We went to a nouveau diner not far from the paper, a chrome-filled trailer staffed by skinny young white kids in black, where the menu featured entrées such as millet meat loaf with mushroom sauce.

We found a booth in the back, as far from the kitchen as possible. The waitress who brought us menus wore a small gold cross around her neck.

"Oh, man!" I said to Melvia. "I just remembered. You're Catholic, aren't you? I forgot."

"Hey, I forget sometimes too. I haven't been to Mass in a year and a day." She was digging around in her purse for gum. That meant she wanted a cigarette, but she knew I didn't like smoke. She came up with a piece, stuck it in her mouth, and turned back to me with an appraising look.

"And what, pray tell, does my religious affiliation have to do with anything? Are you working on a story that will bring down the one true church?"

A wave of fatigue swept over me. What I needed was a cup of coffee. Except that I really shouldn't have any caffeine.

"Hey, what's the matter?" Melvia asked. "You look like something the cat dragged in."

"Gee, thanks." Why shouldn't I have caffeine? What the hell was I thinking? Here I was trying to protect something I was going to kill in a week; the situation was so ludicrous I began to cry.

"Whoa!" Melvia said. "Must be serious."

"It is. I've screwed up big time, and I was going to ask you to help me, except I can't now. I can't because you're Catholic, and I forgot. What an idiot I am!" I felt faintly hysterical; for the first time in my life I could see why people gave in to hysteria. What a relief it would have been, such sweet relief, to just toss back my head in the middle of that diner and scream.

Melvia reached across the table and grabbed my shoulder.

"Calm down," she said. Her voice was low and gentle. "Take a deep breath. In and out. Calm down and tell me what's happened. I'm sure it can't be that bad."

After a moment I looked up from the table. The waitresses were leaning against the kitchen door, deliberately not staring our way.

"I'm sorry. Everybody's looking at us."

Melvia didn't even glance around. "Please, girl. I don't care about these people. I'm worried about you. If it's what I think it is, it's rough."

The waitress came to take our order. After she left, Melvia took a breath and leaned toward me, lowering her voice.

"Are you pregnant?"

I nodded. Melvia sat back hard against the red leather backing of her booth. "Shit. Who is he?"

"What? That doesn't matter."

"The hell it doesn't!" Melvia was livid. I could see the muscles working behind the taut, beautiful skin of her face. "Oh, no! It's not that whiteboy, is it?"

I almost laughed when I realized who Melvia meant. I hadn't thought about David in a long, long time.

"No!"

"Well, that's something anyway," Melvia muttered. "I guess."

"Look, it doesn't matter who the father is. I mean, it does but it doesn't. I don't know what the hell I mean!"

She reached across the table and took my hand.

"What are you going to do?"

"I can't keep it, Melvia. I can't have it, I just can't."

"Oh, Hope." Her voice was low, bereft. Then: "Is it financial? If it's money, I can help you out. I have lots saved up and nothing to spend it on. And we can get you a raise. You deserve a raise, and those bastards should damn well give you one!"

The hopefulness in her voice made me ashamed. "It's not just money, Melvia."

"Look, you didn't plan this. It's not a perfect time, but sometimes things happen on a schedule of their own. And anyway that doesn't matter. It's here now, Hope. It's in there. You can't just wish it away."

The waitress brought our Greek salads and a basket of rolls still warm from the oven. Melvia ordered a gin and tonic, while I sat there crying. Neither one of us touched the food.

"Please don't hate me."

"I don't, of course, I don't. I don't want you to end up hating yourself."

The smell of olives rose from my salad, making me queasy. I pushed my bowl away.

"I'm sorry I dragged you into this."

"You're going to do it? Have the abortion?"

"I don't know. I think I have to. I don't want to suffocate, like my sister, like my mother. I don't want my life to end."

Melvia sighed. "Oh, Hope," she said wearily. Then she said, "I'll go with you to the clinic. You'll need someone."

"Are you sure?"

"I'll go with you." Melvia pushed her salad away and signaled the waitress to bring a drink for me. "I hope you change your mind, Hope. I pray you do, but if you have to go through with this, you won't have to go through it alone."

chapter twenty-one

After lunch I skipped out of work and went home, thinking about my sister Faith. My sister and I weren't much alike. She was skinny and cute and bubbly; I took after my father. People always told me I'd be pretty too, later in life, when I grew into my features. Wait, they said until I was tired of hearing it. But my mother must have seen enough of a resemblance to be worried, and she sent me to Astor, praying disappointment wouldn't claim another child.

The day we found out about Faith's pregnancy, I got home from school late. When I walked up the driveway, Charity sat on the front porch, reading. Through the open door I heard my mother screaming and Faith crying and apologizing over and over again. I wasn't particularly worried, they'd been fighting a lot lately. But something in Faith's voice was off.

"What's going on?" I asked Charity.

"Mom and Faith are having a fight," she said, not looking up from her book. "I wouldn't go in."

"Obviously they're having a fight, stupid. I can hear that. The whole neighborhood can hear that. What are they fighting about?"

Charity closed her book on her finger and looked up at me. Faith was the prettiest, and I, supposedly, was the smartest. But Charity had the self-confidence of a movie star, and nothing bothered her. She had us both beat.

"They're fighting because Faith is pregnant," she said. Then she reopened her book. I noticed the title: *To Kill a Mockingbird*.

"You lie!" Faith pregnant? It was too horrible to believe.

Charity shrugged. "Believe it or not. Just leave me alone. I'm trying to read."

I sat down, too scared to go into the house. This was crazy. Getting pregnant was the worst thing that could happen to you. It was like some disease that floated around the city, infecting girls haphazardly; we prayed we wouldn't catch it, but somehow Faith had.

My mother's voice spilled out to us from inside the house— loud, then fainter, then loud again, as she hounded Faith from room to room.

"Slut! You no-good dirty slut! You had to do it, didn't you?"

"I'm sorry, Mommy!" Faith's voice was tiny with fear.

If there were two things my mother was absolutely clear about, it was school and pregnancy. School was the way out of the poverty in which we lived; pregnancy was the way to ruin your life. Babies had ruined our mother's life. She'd been headed to college when she met my father, but she put it off to marry him. Still, she might have gone back if she hadn't gotten pregnant. Once that happened, there was no returning.

Sometimes, when Charity and I were bickering or tearing apart the house with one of our fights, my mother would load us into the car and drive us downtown to St. Peter's Home for Children. She'd park the car outside the gate and walk us to the fence.

"That's what will happen to ya'll if you drive me crazy," she'd say. "I could just walk out tomorrow. I could leave you the way my mother left me, and you'd have to go live up there with all those other children."

"It doesn't look so bad," Charity said once. She was looking at the slides and the swings. I punched her in the arm, hard enough to raise a bruise. Most days I knew my mother would never leave us, but sometimes I wondered why she didn't. Without us, she could do anything. She could work without fear of leaving us home alone at nights. She could have a house where the heat worked, a bathroom without cracks for the slugs to crawl through, a car she didn't have to coax down a hill to get started. My mother never had a boyfriend, because she worried that a strange man might find the temptation to molest one of her daughters far too strong. She rarely went out, never bought new clothes for herself or had her hair done at the beauty parlor; what little money came in went toward the house or for shoes or clothes for us. She had no girlfriends to laugh and cry with, only her sisters, and she came to believe that friends were useless at best, treacherous at worst, that family was all. She could have abandoned us, but instead she abandoned herself.

All she wanted was for us to become something.

My mother screamed at Faith for what seemed like hours, but finally the house fell silent. Charity and I crept through the front door and found my mother sitting in the kitchen, bent double as if recovering from a blow, her head in her hands.

"Mom?" She looked up at us, tears running down her face. It was only the second or third time I'd ever seen my mother cry, and it scared me.

"Your sister is pregnant," she said flatly.

Charity sighed and left the room, but I stayed.

"Mommy, maybe we can do something. Maybe we can fix it." I didn't know what I meant, I was just talking, trying to say something to beat back the anguish in my mother's face.

Her head jerked up so fast it startled me. I staggered back a step.

"Don't ever say that," my mother said, wiping her face. Her eyes were fierce. "That child is here now, and it's coming. There is nothing else to be done."

Charity and I made spaghetti for dinner, while my mother closed herself away in the front bedroom. We could hear her fervid mumbles through the door; she was praying.

Faith was in the back bedroom, in the dark. I was scared to go in and look at her, scared she'd somehow look different, diseased. She called to me.

"Hope? Hope, could you bring me something to drink?"

Her voice was so small, not that of the smart-aleck older sister I knew.

I poured a glass of milk and went in. Faith lay curled up on the bed, holding her stomach. The sight of her swollen, puffy face made me angry.

"Here's your milk," I said, slamming it down on the floor so hard it spilled. She didn't answer or even look up. I left the room.

That night Charity slept on the couch and I made a pallet on the floor in the living room; we were too scared to go into either one of the bedrooms to sleep. As I was drifting off, I heard my mother in the kitchen. A few minutes later, she went into the back bedroom and turned on the light.

"Faith, wake up," she said. Her voice was ragged. I held my breath, wondering if Charity was awake.

"Wake up," she said again. Then, after a pause, "Eat this."

"What is it?"

"A sandwich. Eat it. You have to eat. Only thing worse than

a baby is a sick baby. You ain't bringing no sick babies into this house."

Food became one of the few topics of conversation between Faith and my mother over the next few months—food, and medical care, and school. My mother was determined that Faith would get her high school diploma—a real diploma, not a GED. Faith had enough credits so that if she finished out her junior year and then doubled up on classes at both sessions of summer school, she'd be able to graduate. It was ironic that Faith had the credits only because of my mother. She was always pushing us to take advanced classes and extra courses, to prepare for college.

"I knew it was for something," she said to Faith. "I didn't know it would be this."

Faith moved through the months like a robot, my mother at the controls. She drank the glasses of milk my mother placed before her, went to the doctor when my mother said it was time, worked on her homework when my mother told her to do so. But when my mother wasn't around, she sat on the couch staring blankly at television. Her stomach grew huge, her face got puffy, her skin shone as if someone greased it every morning before she got up. The cute, vivacious Faith I knew was gone, and I'd sometimes stare in dismay at her dull replacement. The bigger Faith got, the more lethargic she became, as if the baby were sucking away not only nutrients but brain cells, willpower, life.

I hated being at home; I couldn't breathe through the tension that grew thick and muggy as the hot Memphis air. I found a summer job, one of those make-work programs for poor teenagers, and spent the mornings sorting mail at a government office downtown, grateful to be away. In the afternoons I went to the library and stayed as long as I could, holed up in the calm, cool building. It seemed like sanity compared to the madness at home, and that's what I came to associate with books—sanity and control and peace. When I had to go home, I avoided Faith. We barely spoke. My feelings toward her changed like the wind: One minute I was angry at her for screwing up, for making our mother so miserable. Then she'd pass me in the kitchen, her eyes lowered to avoid mine, and I'd just want my sister back. When my girlfriends came over they did not ask to come inside and I didn't invite them; we sat outside and avoided conversation about Faith's contagious disease.

My mother kept pointing out the disturbing parts of pregnancy, to make sure Charity and I didn't miss them:

"Ah, sick again, huh?" she'd announce as Faith went reeling into the bathroom. "They say it only last the first three months, but I was sick as a dog the whole time with Charity."

"Boy, you're getting big as a house, girl! Don't think you're going to lose all that weight after the baby comes. Once it's there, it's there for good."

"Oh, those are stretch marks. Ugly, huh? No more bikinis for Faith!"

My sister took it all in silence, even when my mother got off the phone one day and said, "You're going to California. Your aunt Ruth has agreed to take you in."

I was stunned. We'd never even met Aunt Ruth; she'd left the South years before we were born and never looked back. I couldn't believe my mother would ship Faith off to someone she didn't know, would send her away. In that moment I caught a glimpse of the old Faith, of my funny, popular, beautiful older sister, the one I'd lost.

"Please don't make her go," I begged.

"It's better this way," my mother said. "Better for her. Better for you."

Faith didn't fight. Probably she was glad to get away from my mother, from Memphis, from whoever the father was—she never told us. Probably she was relieved to get away from the whole ruined scene of her life. She finished summer school seven months pregnant but refused to go to the citywide summer graduation.

"Are you crazy? How would I look, waddling down the aisle? I'd look like a cow."

Charity looked up from the couch, where she sat reading. "It's not like you'd be the only pregnant girl at graduation," she pointed out. "Probably half the girls there will be knocked up. That's why they're there."

"Watch your mouth," my mother said to Charity, then turned to Faith. "You might as well go. This may be the only graduation you'll ever have."

But Faith refused. She spent graduation day packing for California. The next day we loaded her trunk into the car and drove to the bus station. Faith walked to the three empty seats that stretched across the back of the steamy bus, and we followed with her things. My mother leaned over her to open a window, then handed Faith a pillow, a flashlight, a plastic bag with a washcloth and soap, a basket with a chicken dinner and some oranges.

"You got your ticket?" she asked.

"Yes." Her voice was blank.

"And your money?" my mother whispered.

"Yes."

Other passengers began filing onto the bus and searching for seats. An old woman in a faded print dress. A tired-looking woman with three suitcases and two small boys. A young man in uniform. They all seemed exhausted, though the trip had not yet begun.

"I wish we could fly you," my mother said.

"I don't mind."

"You sure you want to sit back here?" Charity asked, glancing at the bathroom. "What if it starts to smell?"

Faith shrugged. "I'll move. You guys should go."

I handed Faith three issues of *Teen Beat*, her favorite magazine. In another lifetime we used to sit together, giggling over pictures of the Jackson Five. Faith looked down at the magazines, then back up at me. She held out her arms and pulled me against the hardness of her stomach.

"I don't want to go, Hope," she whispered. Her face was wet. "I'm scared."

Up front, the driver climbed aboard and started the bus engine, sending a blast of hot air from the vent over Faith's head. "Departure in five minutes."

The fear in Faith's voice pierced my heart, but I didn't know what to say. I started to cry, and my mother put her hand on my shoulder and gently pulled me away.

"Don't make her go, Mom! Please!"

"Call us when you get there," my mother said to Faith. "And along the way if you want. Call collect."

Faith nodded, tears falling quietly down her face. My mother reached into her purse and pulled out a small vial of yellow oil. She poured a drop onto her fingertips, then placed the hand on Faith's forehead and raised her other hand as if to wave. She closed her eyes, and we did the same.

"Lord, watch over this child as she travels to California and thereafter. Send your angels to protect her, Lord. Turn back Satan when he steps into her path. Rebuke the devil, Lord. Guide and protect this child. In the name of Jesus we pray. Amen."

"Amen," we mumbled.

Then my mother opened her eyes and gave Faith's shoulder a pat.

"I'll be praying for you."

"I know," Faith said. "You always do."

After Faith left, my mother turned her magnifying glass on me, examining me for signs of the same disease that had claimed her oldest daughter. The pressure of her gaze was like a weight on my back. I did everything I could think of to reassure her that I was still a "good girl," but nothing helped.

School began and, as usual, I was placed in advanced classes. When I brought my schedule home to show my mother, I found her in the bedroom, counting the pads in my Kotex box. She asked if I had a boyfriend. I told her truthfully that no one in school seemed to be interested in the position, but she didn't believe me. If I lingered in the bathroom, she'd bang on the door and ask what was wrong. I learned to leap out of bed every morning, feigning peppiness, and to eat well but not too well. She monitored my phone calls, sometimes snatching the phone away mid-conversation and demanding, "Who's this?" Then I'd have to get back on the phone and apologize to whichever girlfriend it was, my voice thick with shame.

My mother insisted on picking up Charity and me after school. "There's your mom," someone would say, and the crowd would snicker as Charity and I slunk across the street to the car. We begged and pleaded with her not to embarrass us, but my mother was unmoved.

"Ten years from now you won't remember these people's names," she said, sweeping a dismissive hand over the crowd. "But you can bet you'll remember any babies you make. You can bet Faith won't be forgetting anytime soon."

Faith had a boy, eight pounds, three ounces, healthy and kicking, and she named him Luke, after my mother's father, whom none of us knew. My mother cried silently while telling Faith to be careful of the kid's soft spot and to feed him cereal after the second week to help him sleep and to put him to bed stomach down. When Charity asked to speak to Faith, my mother refused and hung up the phone.

"That's it for her," she said, tears slipping down her face. "You two still have a chance to make something of your lives. Don't mess it up."

chapter
twenty-two

The week lasted for two centuries. I spent the days nauseous and fearful or asleep. Everything exhausted me—climbing stairs, walking to lunch, sitting in traffic. After ten minutes on the treadmill at the gym, I had to go home to bed. At work I kept dragging my body into the women's lounge for a nap, so I wouldn't fall asleep at my desk. One day I closed my eyes to rest for ten minutes and didn't wake for nearly an hour; the cushion on the couch was wet with drool.

Crazy thoughts kept pushing themselves into my mind. I knew it wasn't even the size of my little finger, but already it had a heartbeat. I wondered if it might have Malcolm's eyes. He had beautiful eyes. I knew it had already decided what sex it wanted to be while swimming around in there. A girl probably. Almost certainly a girl. My body would have rejected a male fetus, and then I wouldn't have been in this mess.

One morning I even caught my traitorous brain calculating the due date, thinking that the kid would be born sometime in late April or early May. Spring. My favorite season, all the flowers and trees bursting into bloom. Right outside my apartment building was a group of trees that produced tiny white flowers as delicate as angel wings. What were they? I should have known the name.

Sitting at my desk the day before the procedure, looking around the newsroom in a daze, I was filled with the need to talk to my mother. She'd be at work, at the home of the white couple she took care of, and if I called her there she'd come to the phone frightened, expecting the worst. I dialed anyway, not able to stop myself.

"Hello? Hello?" An old man's voice shouted into the phone. "Hello?"

"Mr. Price, this is Hope Robinson. Is my mother there?"

"Who?"

"My mother, Mary. May I speak to her, please."

"Mary? She's not here. She's out with my wife."

"Oh." The disappointment was hard. But it was for the best, really. "Oh. Well . . ."

"Good-bye," he said, and hung up. Maybe I should have told him not to tell her I called; she'd just worry. But then I realized he'd never remember.

That night I stayed up late, trying to read Toni Morrison—a woman in complete and utter control of her life. When that didn't work, I turned on the television, but the commercials seemed especially annoying. Sex, sex, sex, that's all it was. Drink this soda, have some sex. Drive this car, have some sex. I turned the TV off, and the hours until dawn sat mute before me. When I couldn't stand it in the living room anymore, I went to bed.

I knew I wouldn't sleep, but maybe I could at least rest. I

closed my eyes. In the darkness I flashed on a photograph of a botched back-alley abortion I had seen once in a book. The woman lay curled on the floor, naked, covered with blood, dead. I saw myself sneaking through an alley into some grimy top-floor room where a man with yellow teeth pushed me onto a table and pried apart my legs. Smoke from his cigarette curled into his eyes, making him squint. Trying to remember if he had washed his hands, I looked around for a sink, but I couldn't see one. While I was looking, the man leaned over me. It was Mr. Nelson, my junior high school principal. He smiled, and his wavy, processed black hair slipped down over his eyes. All the girls had thought him unbearably cute.

"Just relax," he said, and reached between my legs with a giant ice cream scoop. I woke up thrashing, the sheets twisted around my thighs. The clock showed 5:32 A.M.

At seven I took a shower and wondered, crazily, if I should shave my pubic hair. No, that's what they did to women who were having children. Get control, Hope, pull it together. I stuck my head under the shower, hoping the force of the water would beat away my thoughts.

What to wear, what to wear? I pulled jeans and a T-shirt from the dresser, threw them on. Back into the bathroom, humid and wet, where I plugged in the curling iron. My face stared back at me from the mirror: dark circles under my eyes, a turgid white pimple on my chin, a shiny forehead. I thought about Sunday afternoons when we were growing up. My sisters and I used to walk around the house with our foreheads glowing from the blessing with holy oil at church.

Heat pinched my ear: caught up in my daydream, I'd singed myself with the curling iron. Served me right. I unplugged the iron and put it away, my hair half done. What was I doing? Getting all dolled up to go kill my kid!

Outside, the air was like sap, liquid and sticky and warm; the curls in my hair sagged like old women. I'd told Melvia to meet me at the clinic; I didn't want to have to face her beforehand. I got in my car and drove, leaving the air conditioner off, trying to salvage virtue where I could. The parking lot at the clinic was full, and I had to circle and circle, waiting for someone to leave, and when no one did I finally gave up and drove back onto the street to search for a spot, thinking that maybe it was some kind of sign. But that was ridiculous. I didn't need a sign to figure out what God would have wanted me to do, and anyway, He'd have come up with something more potent than a lot full of cars.

I found a spot, parked, stepped outside. The thick air was hard to breathe, the buildings and trees shimmied before my eyes. I felt nauseous. My stomach bucked, trying to force something up, but there was nothing there. On doctor's orders, I hadn't eaten since the night before. I staggered down the sidewalk, nearly plowing into an old woman, who cursed at me, probably thinking I was drunk. I was aiming for a bus stop bench about forty yards from the front of the clinic. When I reached it I collapsed, sat hunched over, dry heaving onto the street, with the sweat rolling down my face. I started to laugh. It seemed such a comical thing for an endangered fetus to do, make me sick. If the kid was trying to get me to change my mind, this was not the way to go. Hey, kid, you'd better make nice-nice with Mommy, or Mommy will be mad.

The word sliced into my heart like a scalpel, deep and clean. Mommy. It was as if my subconscious had gone over to the other side and was working against me. The kid had made an ally. Pretty smart, calling me Mommy. But it didn't make a difference, this was just nerves speaking, not a change of heart. Couldn't I expect to be nervous, doing something this hard? Nausea pressed up against my throat; I swallowed hard to force it back and rubbed my forehead, trying to think. Why hadn't I asked Melvia to bring me. Maybe I should call her. But why? No, I just needed to think. I shook my head, but it was like shaking a rattle. The thoughts bounced around inside, making an awful noise.

Sit still I told myself. Wait for your brain to settle. Calm down. While I waited I watched two women get out of a Mercedes and walk toward me. The older one had a cheap perm and a double chin and was dressed in black stretch pants, white T-shirt, and a black jacket. The other, a younger woman, about my age, had that money look: tawny skin and blond hair and simple gold jewelry that clearly cost a lot. Glancing at her from the corner of my eye, I was reminded of my roommate, Amy. She wore a black skirt and a beautiful gray blouse, as fresh and starched as though she were inside some air-conditioned office instead of standing in the blazing August sun.

Her face was soft, smiling.

"Miss? May I talk to you a minute? Before you go in?"

I stood and waited, thinking she was going to ask directions since she didn't look like she belonged in the neighborhood. But the older woman pushed forward, got in my face.

"Are you about to have an abortion?" The harshness in her voice jarred me more than her words. I saw the younger one give her an angry look.

"What?" I tried to take it in. "What did you say?"

"Please don't do it," the younger one said. "Please, there are alternatives. You don't have to just because they say you do."

Then it clicked: the women were protesters, anti-abortion types. I looked around for the rest of them. They usually ran in packs, pushing and singing and praying and getting in the way. I had covered a protest once, long ago, in Greenville, one that had gotten ugly. Funny how I hadn't even considered they might show up here.

But the two women seemed to be alone.

"Mind your own business," I said, trying to push past them. They moved ahead to block my path.

"This *is* our business," the younger woman said.

"This is everyone's business!" the older one barked. Her fat, jowly face was red. "You have no right to kill this baby!"

"Margaret! Please." The younger one stared at the older one, then turned back to me. "Miss, we just want to talk with you for a minute, show you some pictures. We want to make sure you understand what you're about to do. It's not like they told you in there. This is a decision that will haunt you the rest of your life."

She spoke slowly and gently, patronizing me. She made me angrier than the other woman with her barking and her hostile glares. There was something about the milky mildness of the young woman's voice, about the way she tilted her head while her flat blue eyes sought mine. It was like she was talking to a child, or an idiot, a mental defective. Someone incapable of making a decision for herself.

"That's a baby you're carrying, not a fetus."

"Just leave me alone."

"Its heart is beating," she said. "It's alive."

"What do you think I am—stupid?"

"I think you're misguided," she said patiently. "I think we can help. We've helped dozens of girls like you."

"Girls?" I looked at her closely; young as she was, she was calling me girl.

"There are programs that will help you raise your child."

She stood on one side of me, the older woman on the other. They were crowding me much too close.

"Something called Aid to Families—"

"You want me to go on welfare? What the hell do you know about living on welfare?"

"It's better than murder."

I found her eyes and said as viciously as I could, "Yeah? How would you know?"

She seemed shocked, but she kept talking.

"I understand what you're going through," she said. Her smug attitude was as thick as the air, suffocating me.

"You understand?"

"I've been there. I made a terrible mistake, and I've regretted it ever since."

"That has nothing to do with me." I couldn't believe it. Here was this whitegirl, all golden and rich, telling me not to have an abortion because she'd had one once and it ruined her life. "Get away!" I tried to push past her, but the older woman grabbed my arm and attempted to pull me back, away from the sidewalk, away from the clinic doors.

"Well, then, think about your people!" the young one cried, and grabbed my other arm. "Think about the hundreds of years that white people have tried to kill you off and now you're helping them do it!"

I snatched my arm from her so hard she stumbled back a few steps, and the other woman dropped her hands. I couldn't believe this whitegirl was using that racial genocide crap on me.

"Them? Them! Who is *them*, whitegirl? What the hell are you talking about? Who do you think you are—Malcolm X?"

From the clinic door came a woman's angry voice, yelling, "Leave her alone! We're calling the police!" But instead of backing off, the young woman rushed in again, grabbing my hand, standing so close I could smell her shampoo, the faint juniper sweetness of her breath. The older woman came close too, her mouth stinking of onions, and began screaming out a hymn, "Jesus Loves the Little Children," a song my mother used to sing. The sound of her ragged voice on the familiar words scraped my skin.

"Please," the young woman begged. "You could put the child up for adoption!" She was panting now, her eyes wild.

"Yeah? You want to adopt it? Take a little black baby home to Skippy? Get out of my face!" I was screaming now, trying to regain my hand. "Let me go!"

"Don't do it! Don't kill your baby!"

"Who the hell are you to tell me what to do?"

"Please!" She began pulling me back down the sidewalk, and

to save myself I reached over and, grabbing the underside of her upper arm, pinched as hard as I could, just as a white woman and a black woman from the clinic ran down the steps, trailing a cop.

The blonde dropped my hand and grabbed her arm, screaming. "She pinched me! That black bitch!"

"You white whore!"

The cop pushed himself between us. "Get her inside if she's going!" he yelled to the two women from the clinic. "Now!"

The black one turned to me and took my arm. "Let's go," she said. But I couldn't move. The two protesters were still screaming and fighting with the cop, trying to get to me.

"It's murder! It's murder! Don't do it!"

"Screw you!" I screamed at them.

"It's okay," said the woman from the clinic. "We'll protect you. Let's go." She tugged at my arm.

"Get her inside!" the cop yelled.

My head ached and my heart was pounding and something hung on the back of my subconscious, obscured by flame. My feet wouldn't move.

"Come on, honey. It's okay. You want to go?"

"I'm not going to warn you again!" the cop yelled.

The two protesters began singing "We Shall Overcome." And then the older one ran to their car and came back with a poster and handed it to the blonde, who held it high over her head, still pushing against the cop, and she looked me in the eyes and screamed, "Look! This is how they kill your baby! Don't do it! I'm telling you for your own good, don't do it! Listen to me!"

The black woman from the clinic tugged again on my arm.

"Honey? Are you ready?"

"Damn straight," I said. "Let's go."

chapter twenty-three

W hen I walked out into the waiting room, Melvia sat cradling an unread magazine in her lap. Her face was closed.

"Is it over?"

I nodded, unable to meet her eyes. "Let's go out the back."

We drove in silence, Melvia concentrating on the streets, me focusing on the cramps that seized my gut. They were like menstrual cramps, only worse, tighter and more intense, which was appropriate. I had a prescription for something to ease the pain, but I threw it away, wanting to suffer. Enduring pain isn't the worst thing that can happen in life.

Melvia took me upstairs to my apartment and sat me on the couch.

"You don't have to stay," I said.

"Of course I'm staying."

"I'm fine. Really. You go on."

"*You* go on. You're going to bed."

She bent over to take my arm, but I pulled back so hard her hand jerked away. She looked at me in surprise.

"I'm sorry. I didn't mean that. I just . . . I just need to be alone. Thanks for everything, girl."

She sighed. "Okay, I'll go. But you have to promise to call me if you need anything."

I nodded my head, managing what felt like it might be a smile.

"Look, try not to be too hard on yourself," Melvia said. "You did what you thought was right."

Did I? I wasn't sure. My brain wasn't functioning. I kept feeling things that weren't there anymore—the cold bite of the table, the soft whir of the machine, the pressure of the nurse's hand squeezing mine. Instead of Melvia's face I saw the white stucco of the clinic ceiling. As soon as Melvia left I closed my eyes to push it back, and then I fell asleep.

I woke at dusk, so hollow and lonely I had to get up and turn on every light in the place. I switched on the television and muted the sound, then put on a tape of Ella Fitzgerald. My stomach growled. I went into the kitchen and opened one of the cans of chicken soup Melvia had left, and I ate it straight from the can, without warming it up.

The counter around my dish drain was brown with water stains, so I cleaned it. I noticed that the rest of the kitchen was filthy too; I was living in a pigsty. Everything needed to be scrubbed. All the food in the refrigerator went into the garbage, and I hauled the whole mess down to the basement, taking the stairs both ways. I scrubbed the toaster oven and the regular oven and the floor, and then I moved on to the bathroom. I scoured the tub and the sink and the cracked floor around the base of the toilet, with its hair and bits of tissue and ugly grime. I stripped my bed and flipped the mattress, and then got down on my knees to check what dusty horrors lay underneath. I found a black bra that had long gone missing, a comb, my overnight bag. And a condom wrapper, ripped across the top. I flushed it down the toilet.

I kept waiting for relief, the kind of relief I always felt when my period appeared, but instead I was filled with an aching emptiness. Everything seemed off kilter, out of whack, as if some prankster had snuck into my life when I was away and shuffled things around. Back in the living room, I got down on my knees to pick lint out of the carpet. The specks of dirt swam before my eyes, and I started to cry.

By dawn there was nothing left to clean. I went out to the convenience store for a newspaper and coffee, came back and read the paper cover to cover before nine o'clock. I began feeling desperate. The rest of the day stood before me like a rebuke. I paged through the entertainment section, looking for something to eat up the time so I wouldn't have to think, wouldn't have to remember the sound of that whirring machine. I didn't want a movie. Nobody ever shut up in movies anymore, and I wasn't in the mood to hear insipid chitchat. Not a museum. Certainly not the mall.

What did people do on Sunday anyway? They went to church. That's what I should do. Go to church, and not that polite, structured, integrated Methodist one either. If I was going to church that day, I was going to a real church, a gospel-singing, hell-preaching, dancing-in-the-aisles black church, a church to which I'd have to wear stockings and a dress. A heavy-duty church for heavy-duty sin.

I had a lot of skirts but only one dress, the one my mother had bought me to wear to my grandmother's funeral. It was black with tiny white flowers, cut narrow in the waist and wide in the hips, and it made me look like a blackened rotten pear. I pulled on black stockings and a pair of pumps and glanced at myself in the mirror. But only for a second.

I looked up Bethel A.M.E. in the phone book. It was George the security guard's church, the one he had invited me to once. It turned out to be a beautiful old building, with a gray stone steeple and tons of stained glass. I arrived twenty minutes before the 11 A.M. service, which gave me plenty of time to grab a seat in the back. George was standing up front, his white gloves flashing as he ushered people to their seats. But I didn't want to talk to him. I wanted to sit and get what I needed and not draw attention to myself.

The ceremony began ten minutes late, with music and singing and then announcements, and then it was time for people to stand and testify. Nobody bothered me until the preacher told the congregation to turn around and find a visitor in the crowd and take his hand. I glanced around like everyone else, trying to look like a regular, but my deception was thin. The woman next to me turned and looked me dead in the eye, then took my hand. She was about fifty years old, her skin the color of butterscotch, and she smiled with every inch of her sweaty, shining face. One of those women who live in the church, live there all week. She wore a hat as purple as my life.

"Welcome, daughter," she said. She said it quietly and sincerely. "God is here if you want Him."

Her hand was rough but warm, and it felt good, like a blanket. She squeezed my hand for a second and then let go. She didn't ask if I was saved, like everyone else around me was doing at the pastor's orders. I reached over and took her hand again, and she let me, not turning back to look at me but grasping my hand tight, tight, and when the singing started we sang together and the tears swarmed up behind my eyes and pushed themselves out, fat and warm, right down my face. I cried all through the singing, which was a long time. And as I stood there, crying and swaying and holding this woman's hand, I realized that the sad thing about black churches, the sad, wonderful, sweetly heart-wrenching thing, was that a person could go through a whole service, could sing and pray and listen and shout and dance, all with tears streaming down her face, and no one would think she was crazy. No one stared or even looked at me, and if people's eyes fell on my face as they were looking somewhere else, they just smiled. The woman next to me sang like she meant it, and once she eased her hand from mine so she could clap along with the music, but when that song melded into the next one, she reached over and rubbed my back.

"That's all right, daughter," she murmured, still not looking at me. "That's all right."

I wanted to cry, "But it's not all right, Mom. If there's one thing in the world it's not, it's all right." I wanted to crawl into her arms and never leave. I wanted to go home.

I fell asleep right after church, a deep, dreamless sleep like the day before, only this time I didn't wake up until after nine. It wasn't so bad, waking up in the darkness; it was the fading of the light that made everything seem so empty. I was up for a few hours, and then when it was time to go to sleep I couldn't, so I ended up staying awake all night again. I was too exhausted to go to work the next morning. It was all I could do to stay awake until the first clerk arrived in the newsroom so that I could call in sick.

I noticed that I didn't tend to dream during the day, as if day sleeping was a different creature than night sleeping. And night thinking was a different kind than day thinking too. At 4 A.M., my brain played out extended "what if" scenarios against the silver twitching of the television screen. What if those women hadn't been at the clinic that day? What if they had tried to stop someone else? What if Melvia had been with me? What if I hadn't gotten so mad? In the darkness it seemed important to remember what it was exactly I'd been thinking before the women showed up, and I tried but my brain was slippery. My thoughts kept wriggling away from me. I remembered nausea, the green bench, the feeling of wanting to laugh at the absurdity of it all. I remembered panic, and fear, and surprise, and then a wave of forlornness would wash over me, and I couldn't remember anything else.

I told myself to settle down, the crisis was over, get back into things, go back to work. But the thought of walking into the newsroom, sitting down at that desk, pretending nothing had happened . . . it was too much. I called in sick the rest of that week.

"Wait a second," the clerk said when I called the following Monday. "Richard wants to speak to you."

It was too late to hang up; I was stuck. Richard's voice came on the line, dripping with fake concern.

"Are you all right? Need anything?"

I made my voice low and thick.

"I'm fine. Went to the doctor. He said it was some kind of bacterial infection. I just have to stay in bed a couple more days."

"Well, take care of yourself," he said. "By the way, they're going to run your Africa stories sometime this week. The foreign desk says they're quite good." He sounded surprised. "This could be the one that does it for you."

"Yeah. Great."

"The copy desk did have a few questions. They'll be giving you a call." Richard hung up. I should have been happy they were going to run the stories, but it seemed unimportant. Words on a piece of paper. Tomorrow's fish wrap, something left on the train. I turned the ringer on the phone off. The rest of the week I didn't bother to call in.

Life arranged itself into a pattern: sleep all day, awake all night, crying minutes at a stretch. I gave up being steadfast. When the tears backed up behind my eyes, I let them out. They gushed, then trickled, then stopped, and a few hours later the process began again.

At some point Melvia showed up and banged on my door. "I know you're in here!" she called. I let her bang, hoping she'd give up and go away. But of course she didn't.

"If you don't open up in one minute, I'm calling the cops. They'll break it down."

I cracked the door.

"Hey, girl!" She pushed past me and inside.

"You look like shit," she said. "And it stinks in here. When was the last time you took your garbage out?"

"I'll take it out now. I'm only letting you in so you can see I'm fine."

"Yeah, you look great." She was already bustling around the apartment, opening windows, picking stuff up from the floor. "Stunning, even. I don't think I've ever seen you look so well."

"I'm fine."

"People at work are worried about you. Richard said you haven't been heard from in days."

I shrugged. "I got tired of calling every day. Tell him I'm fine."

"Well, if you're fine you better get your ass back into the newsroom, or you won't have a job."

"I'm going tomorrow," I lied.

Melvia stopped fussing and turned around. She walked toward me, toward where I stood in the open doorway.

"Look, Hope. It was a hard thing, but it's over now. You have to move on. You can't let this break you."

"I know."

"You're stronger than that."

I hung my head. "I'm going to get it together, I promise."

"You have to get back to work," she said.

"I will, Melvia. Please, could you . . . could you give me a hug?"

She folded me in her arms. "It's over," she said, patting my back. "Move on."

We stood there, swaying together, until Melvia was close

enough to the doorway for me to shove her into the hall and slam the door shut.

"Hey!" she screamed, furious. "You've lost your mind!"

"And you're gullible as hell!" I yelled back. She sounded so mad I had to laugh.

"You act like you're the only person who's ever been hurt," she called through the door. "We all have. Join the club."

But she was wrong. Being hurt wasn't the problem. It was the guilt that was killing me.

"Fine!" Melvia yelled when I was silent. "Be that way. I was only trying to help. I'll just tell the folks at work you've lost your frigging mind!"

I heard her turn and stomp off down the hall, leaving me, and I felt frightened. But by the time I opened the door she was gone.

The next day I woke up in time to catch the last few minutes of *All My Children*. Erica Kane was giving an interview at the fake television studio, looking good and flying high. When the show ended I pulled a pair of sweatpants on under my nightgown and wandered down to the mailbox. There was a ton of mail, since I hadn't checked in a while, and I just grabbed it all, plus a newspaper someone had left on the hall table, and trundled back upstairs.

One of Georgia's stories was on the front page, something about some foster care agency director caught embezzling funds; I skipped it, flipping through the paper, not really reading anything, noticing how easily the ink, the ink that made all those words we worked so hard to put down on paper, rubbed off onto my hands. On a page inside the foreign section was a photograph of Stephanie, next to one of a dark-haired guy I recognized as a reporter in the Russian bureau. The story read:

James W. Whitehead was named foreign editor of the *Philadelphia Record* in a series of management changes announced yesterday. Whitehead, 45, has worked for the *Record* since 1976 in a series of positions, including deputy metro editor and London bureau chief. He is currently a reporter in the *Record*'s Moscow bureau. Whitehead will be replaced in the Moscow bureau by Stephanie Woodbridge, a Washington correspondent.

The story went on about some other people, but I didn't read the rest; I was busy getting angry. This was perfect, this was just great: Stephanie going to the most important, most prestigious bureau the paper had. A job most people worked years to get. Clearly the last guy had; he was forty-five. Stephanie was twenty-nine. Twenty-nine and way ahead on the fast track, while my life, my stupid life, was twisting in knots. With an energy I hadn't felt in days, I picked up the telephone and dialed Georgia's number at work.

"Hope! Hi! I'm so glad to hear your voice. I've been trying to call you, but your machine always picks up. Melvia says you've been sick?"

"Yeah. But I'm fine. Listen, Georgia, I saw this thing about Stephanie Woodbridge in the paper today. How did that happen?"

"You mean about her going to Russia? I don't know. They just announced it yesterday."

"But she's only been at the paper a couple of years!"

"Yeah, I know," Georgia said mildly. "I guess they must like her."

"I guess so!" Georgia's affability just made me angrier. Couldn't she see that Stephanie's advancement came at her expense, just like it came at mine?

"Yeah, and she's getting married to that guy in editorial. He's going with her."

"David?"

"Yeah, that's it."

It was unbelievable. Somehow the announcement about Stephanie, coming as it did in the middle of my stuff about the abortion, my guilt and confusion and not-knowing, was like a sign from the Fates, like one good rub of salt into the wound, like someone whispering maliciously into my ear, "People like her have it and people like you don't. You might as well accept it." I wanted to scream.

"I can't believe it! It's just not fair!"

"Well," Georgia said, "I don't know. What's interesting, though, is that they gave it to her despite what happened. Some people are saying it's because of what happened. Like they wanted to show her they still had confidence in her, so they gave her this."

It took a moment for me to focus on what Georgia was saying.

"What are you talking about? What happened?"

"Didn't you hear about that?" She lowered her voice. "Stephanie has a problem. She cuts herself when she gets upset. They found her in the bathroom one day down in Washington. She'd messed up on some story, and some senator called the office and cursed her out, and she got so upset she went into the bathroom and cut her arms with a razor blade."

"You mean she tried to commit suicide? I don't believe it." Why would someone who had everything try to kill herself? It didn't make sense.

"I don't think she tried to kill herself," Georgia said. "They said the cuts weren't deep. Just enough to draw blood. It's like some weird psychological thing, some self-destructive habit. When she gets upset, she cuts herself. Then she has to go to the emergency room and get fixed up and then go see her therapist. Apparently she's been in therapy for years. She's pretty messed up."

Suddenly it all made sense: the long sleeves Stephanie wore even in summer; the sudden vacation that time; the way David kept saying how fragile she was. Georgia was saying something else, but she stopped midsentence. I heard myself laughing, a high, frenzied giggle I couldn't control.

"It's not really funny, Hope," Georgia said. "You shouldn't laugh."

I fought to calm down, but the giggles kept coming, pushing themselves out from some space deep inside. "I know. . . . I'm sorry. I'm not laughing at Stephanie. . . . It's just . . ."

"Hope?"

"Sorry!"

"Are you all right?"

"Fine . . . better go! Call you again!"

I hung up the phone and collapsed onto the floor, giggling wildly, until the rough feel of the woolen carpet against my cheek killed my laughter, and my head cleared. Here I had envisioned Stephanie as the perfect girl with the perfect life, perky and pretty and smart and, most of all, loved; and all that time, she was sneaking around slicing into her arms. And why? There must have been some reason; people didn't do things like that for fun. Maybe her daddy didn't love her—hadn't David said something about that? Maybe somebody messed with her as a child. It was something, but it didn't really matter. I didn't feel bad for Stephanie—she was, after all, going to Russia, but I didn't hate her anymore. When I realized that, I gasped, because it was frightening, all that energy I'd expended being angry. And now my anger collapsed, and I fell.

I slept all day, and this time images invaded my sleep. In one dream Amy showed up at my desk in the newsroom and refused to leave. She stood there laughing at me, laughing at the clothes I wore, which were dusty and tattered. She made me so mad I chased her, and she ran into a strange neighborhood full of looming dark buildings and long sweeping driveways, and although I was running full out, she pulled away from me and turned a corner and disappeared, and I was the one who wound up getting lost.

In another dream I was back in the kitchen of our house in Memphis, braiding somebody's hair. She had thick, beautiful hair; it felt soft against my hands as I braided it. I couldn't see her face, for she was turned away from me, but she had one arm draped over my thigh and her cheek was warm against my knee and her head was heavy. She was asleep.

That was it for that dream: nothing happened, nothing bad. But I had it for two days straight, and then I fell asleep one night and had it again and woke up screaming, the monster staring me in the face. I'd killed my daughter. Worse, I'd killed her out of anger and out of spite, and if those women hadn't shown up I might have changed my mind. I was even granted the peace of having done what I thought was right. I cried so hard I breathed mucus and began to gag. Blind with tears and alone in my bed, I was going to die, and I deserved it.

I stumbled to the phone, ripped through the phone book, found the number for Cindy.

"Dr. Shepherd's service. May I help you?"

I glanced out the window. Not even dawn.

"I need to speak to Cindy, Dr. Shepherd. I know it's late, or early, but I need to speak to her, please, right away."

The voice was gentle, composed. It came to me that its owner was used to dealing with lunatics in the middle of the night, that every hour of every day, someone somewhere was desperate.

"I'm sorry, Dr. Shepherd is on vacation. Dr. Zinn is covering for her. If you give me your number, I'll page him and have him call you right back."

How could I tell what I'd done to some guy named Dr. Zinn? He sounded like a hack, somebody who advertised for patients on the side of a bus. Probably what I deserved.

"That's okay." I tried to match the calmness in the voice. "Never mind."

chapter twenty-four

At dawn I lay on the couch, listening to the footfalls of the paperman as he thumped his way up the hall. After a few minutes I got up and looked outside; the paper lay unfurled on my neighbor's mat. My story about Liberia had made the front page—my first really significant front page. Next to the story was a huge picture of the crowd stoning Thomas to death. I left the paper in the hallway and went back inside.

When the phone rang, I ignored it. The answering machine picked up, and out came my mother's voice, filling me with an ache so fierce I almost couldn't breathe.

"Hi! It's me! Boy, you're up and out early. Call me—"

I snatched up the receiver.

"Mom."

"Morning! Too busy to pick up the phone?"

"Mom . . . Mommy." And before I could stop myself I was crying, probably scaring my poor mother to death. I gulped air, tried to calm down. "I'm sorry. I'm okay. Why are you calling so early?"

"Baby, you okay? I got up to pray, and something told me to call you. What's wrong?"

"Nothing, nothing really. But I think I'm going to come for a visit. Is that all right?"

"Of course."

I told her I'd call when I knew my flight information, then I hung up. It was going to cost an arm and a leg to get a last-minute ticket, but I had to get out of that apartment, I had to go home. Sometimes you had to go crying to Mom.

I called work and told them I was taking my vacation time. Then I packed and moved all my plants into the bathtub and ran water in the tub. They'd have to take their chances; I didn't know how long I'd be gone.

After I'd packed and cleaned, I sat in the living room, waiting for the time when I could leave for the airport. The phone rang. I stood over the answering machine and listened, figuring it was someone calling from work to find out what was going on. But it wasn't Richard's voice that came sneaking out of the speaker. It was Malcolm's.

"Hope? You there?"

My heart thudded guiltily against my chest.

"Hope, I've been calling you at work. You missed the redevelopment meeting yesterday. The guy covering for your paper said you were sick. I wanted to make sure you're okay."

I picked up the phone. The answering machine squealed until I turned it off.

"Hey," I said.

"You all right?"

"Yeah. Fine. I'm on my way out of town for a few days. Going home to see my mom. I'll call you when I get back."

"Is she sick? Is there anything I can do?"

"No, she's fine. I just need to go see her for a while."

"What's going on, Hope?" he pleaded. "How many times do I have to say I'm sorry? Don't push me away."

The longing and pain in his voice filled me with confused emotions. I didn't know what to say, so I said the first thing that came to mind, "You walked out on me, Malcolm. You left me."

"Baby, I'm sorry, but I was angry. And I came back. I came back again, and again, because I realized what I was throwing away. I've grown up a lot. You're the one walking out now, Hope. You're rejecting me because you're afraid I might reject you."

"Oh, great. Now you're Dr. Ruth."

"Hope, I love you."

It was the first time he'd said it, but instead of sailing, my heart sank, threatening to suffocate me. I could barely talk.

"No, you don't. You might love who you think I am, who you think I should be."

"I love *you*, baby. I'd like to try and prove it to you."

"My cab's here," I lied.

"Hope, please . . ."

I hung up the phone.

My mother was the first person I saw when I stepped off the plane. She stood off to the side, close to the gate, wearing a blue skirt I had given her five or six years before. Apparently she wore it only when I came home, which explained why it still looked like new.

"Hi," I said, smiling. I was determined not to burst into tears at the sight of her.

"Hello," she said, patting me briefly on the back. She was not one for public affection, and it wasn't until we had climbed into the car in the parking lot that she turned to me and asked, "What's wrong?"

Looking at my mother's face, I realized what a terrible mistake I'd made. I could never tell her about the abortion. She wouldn't understand, wouldn't forgive.

"It's nothing, really. Just work, stuff—I needed a break. From those people. You know."

My mother gave me what my sister Faith used to call the Look.

"I remember when you came back home the summer after graduating from Astor," my mother said. "I met you at that gate right over there and said, 'Welcome home.' You said, 'This ain't my home anymore. It's just a way station.'"

I winced. "I was such a smart-ass back then. Thought I knew everything."

"Yeah," she said, starting the car. "Well."

On the way home we detoured off the highway for a drive through downtown Memphis to see what was new, the way we always did, sort of my mother's way of reminding me how much time had passed since I'd last been back. Goldsmith's department store stood empty, and there was a hotel where the old Plath mansion used to stand. We passed the new Pyramid Arena, part of the city's pitiful attempt to keep people in town longer than the time it took to tour Graceland. The pyramid towered over the river like a cheap, gigantic glass figurine.

"Fifty million dollars to build a pyramid." My mother shook her head. "White folks is crazy."

It was strange being home; it felt like ten years had passed instead of nearly two. The house looked the same, fresh paint on the porch, but the neighborhood had gone down. Tony's, the corner store, had closed and sat boarded up. Clumps of young men wearing oversize jackets and baggy pants stood outside it, listening to loud music and calling to one another.

"Dope dealers," my mother said, disgusted.

My mother kept the back bedroom just the way it had been when we were growing up—two beds, one full, one twin, shoved into opposite corners, three small dressers wedged into the spaces between. There was a stretch of pretty blue fabric and a pattern spread out over the larger bed.

"My sewing table," my mother said. "Course, that will have to change when Faith and the kids get here."

"They're coming for a visit?"

"No," she said. "That's what I called to tell you this morning. Faith has left Harold. She got accepted at the university here, and she's going back to school to become a teacher. They're going to live here with me, so I can help with the kids."

My mother stood there beaming, clearly proud of Faith and thrilled at the chance to help raise her grandchildren. She loved those kids, was always saying how much she missed them. And oddly enough, the one she loved most of all—her favorite, although she tried not to show it—was Luke.

"Did you see their latest school pictures?" My mother held up one of those three-sided frames, and the faces of my nephew and two nieces grinned out at me, heartbreakingly sweet. Faith had sent me copies of those same pictures, but I'd stuck them in a photo album without really looking at them. They were beautiful children, their big brown eyes bright, their faces aglow with an inner excitement. Faith must have gotten up every morning and looked at them and known that at least something was right with the world. And now she was going back to school, and she'd have those children and a degree, and she'd be only what? thirty-five or so when she graduated? That was still young. Her life wasn't over, it was just beginning.

"That's great," I said. It was ironic, Faith getting her life together just as mine was falling apart. "I'm happy for her."

"And look here." She handed me a magazine.

"What's this?"

"It's the *Howard Law Review*. Charity's in it. She had some article, isn't that wonderful? She's coming home in a few weeks for a visit. Too bad you'll miss her."

It *was* too bad; suddenly I wanted to see my baby sister. My family, climbing the ladder of success.

At dinner my mother talked about the wealthy couple she took care of, who had been old when she began working for them twenty years ago and were now nearing ancient. They were surly and peevish in their aging dementia. Mrs. Price, one of those Daughters of the Confederacy types, had gotten into her head that fruits and vegetables were poisonous. My mother had to come up with ways to disguise any vegetables she served, like pureeing carrots into a soup and adding red food color.

"What's that?" the old woman would ask suspiciously as my mother served her. "Looks like vegetables. You trying to poison me, gal?"

My mother would tell her something ridiculous, like, "It's liver soup." The old bat couldn't taste anything anyway. If you told her it was liver soup and she believed it was liver soup, she'd eat it happily.

"It's just like taking care of two spoiled babies," my mother said. She paused to carve the turkey she had cooked for the two of us. She always cooked big when one of us came home.

"I wouldn't want to change their diapers," I said.

My mother shrugged. "Thank goodness it's not to that point, not yet anyway. So how long are you here?"

"Oh, I don't know. A week or so."

She wrinkled her eyebrows, and I could tell the vagueness of my answer worried her. But all she said was, "Want to come with me tomorrow?"

I was surprised. When we were small, my mother had never taken us to the Prices' or to the home of any of the other white people she'd worked for. She said we didn't need to see how they lived, and when I was young I imagined those homes were too grand and too fine for us to be allowed inside. Now that I'd been in nice homes, I was no longer curious.

"To the Prices'? No, thanks."

"You got other plans?"

"Yeah."

My mother went to bed at nine; I flipped through the channels on TV until three, then dug out one of my mother's old *Reader's Digest* condensed books and took it to bed. By dawn I'd read the condensed versions of *My Friend Flicka*, *The Red Pony*, and four other horse books. When I heard my mother stirring in the other bedroom, I turned out the light and closed my eyes.

I was still asleep when she came home that afternoon.

"Taking a nap?" she asked, eyeing my nightgown.

"Yeah. Didn't want to wrinkle my clothes."

"You ought to be up, go downtown or something. Plenty of time to sleep when you're dead." It was one of her sayings.

The next day my mother took the bus to work, leaving me her car in case I wanted to "get out and get some air." I dragged myself out of bed at noon and drove aimlessly around Memphis, trying to figure out my future. I drove past my old elementary school and then the junior high; both looked the shabbier for wear. The mobile homes behind my junior high, the temporary classrooms where I'd taken English and French, were still there. I drove past the convenience store we used to stop at on the way home, to see if the sign was still there: "Only Two Students Allowed in Store at Once."

The next few days I slept until my mother returned from work. I'd get up after she left, get dressed, turn the TV on, and curl up on the couch. Made it look better when my mother came home, and sometimes I even woke up enough to watch *All My Children* for an hour. Erica Kane was always pouting about something. That woman had more trials than Job, but you had to hand it to her: she never let herself look bad while suffering.

Finally, at the end of the week, my mother came home and shook me awake.

"What's wrong with you?" She leaned over me, still dressed in the white uniform she always wore to work. "Are you sick? You don't have some . . . disease, do you?"

"No."

"Thank God for that. What is it, then? Are you pregnant? Is that it?"

My heart lurched and staggered inside me, threatening to fall. I couldn't look her in the face, but I had to say it. The time had come, and I had to tell her, had to know what she would do before I could go on.

"I'm not pregnant, Mommy. I'm sorry. I wish I were."

"You wish?" It took her a moment to understand what I was saying, then horror washed over her face.

"Oh my God, Hope! Don't tell me!"

"I had an abortion."

Her hands were pressed against her stomach. "Why?" she whispered. "Why?"

The words rushed out. "I was pregnant and I was scared. I didn't know what to do. I went to the clinic but I still wasn't sure and then these women showed up, these white women, these protesters. They started pushing me around and yelling at me not to do it and I don't know what happened but I went inside. God help me, I went inside, and I don't even know why. I'm sorry, Mom."

Her silence was like an anvil, pressing down on me. It took all the strength I had to raise my head.

"Mom?"

When I looked at my mother her face was unreadable, closed. Closed to me forever. That was my answer. She stood smoothing her uniform. Then she went into her bedroom and closed the door.

I don't know if my mother ate dinner that night. I hung out in my bedroom, afraid to face her, and because I had no TV and nothing to read, I fell asleep. The next morning, at dawn, she came into the room and shook my shoulder.

"Get up," she said. "You're coming to work with me."

It was cool out, and we got into the car without speaking. We drove down through the heart of the sleeping city and out again, to a wealthy old suburb on the western side of town. The streets were lined by magnolia trees with fat, glossy leaves, and little black jockey statues stood guard on more than one lawn.

The Prices lived at the end of their street, in a miniature plantation with tall white columns and verandas that skirted the house on two floors. We climbed the steps to the front door and stepped inside, to a dark entranceway with marble floors. My mother led me through a shuttered living room and a musty parlor and into the kitchen, where an older black woman sat reading the newspaper at the table.

"Good morning, Sister James," my mother said. "This is my daughter Hope."

"Nice to meet you," I said.

The old woman smiled wearily at me. "Going to help your mother today? She'll need it. Those two were up half the night, fussing about something that happened thirty years ago. They're asleep now, but when they wake up they'll be hungry. And cranky."

"What else is new?" my mother asked.

Sister James patted me on the arm as she left. My mother went upstairs to check on the old couple and returned carrying a bundle of sheets and towels, which she shoved into my arms, still not meeting my eyes.

"Washing machine's down in the basement. Detergent and bleach on the table. Don't use too much bleach. Mrs. Price complains if she even gets a whiff of the stuff."

I spent the morning doing laundry, cleaning the bathrooms, mopping the kitchen floor and laughing at myself. All that education—Astor, college—all that time and effort, and here I was cleaning up after white people as if I'd been destined to do so. All that education shot because I didn't learn what was important in life, how to control my anger, how to live in a world that isn't just but just is. It seemed a fitting punishment.

At noon I helped my mother carry lunch upstairs. Mr. Price sat in a recliner, in the sitting room, watching an old movie on television. Mrs. Price lounged in her bed in the room next door.

"This is Hope, my second girl," my mother said to Mrs. Price. The old woman just stared blankly at me. I put her tray on the cart and rolled it toward her, while my mother took a tray into the room next door.

"Where's my grits, gal?" the old woman croaked. "I'm supposed to have grits, so don't try to trick me, ya hear? I know how you people are."

She'd probably been an attractive woman in her time, one of those pale southern flowers, deliberately delicate. She kept a wig of tight yellow curls on her dresser for visitors, but her own hair had thinned and whitened and now barely covered her wrinkly head, and the rest of her body had shrunk back into itself, like fruit collapsing as it rots.

"Your grits are right there." I pointed to the bowl.

"That's not grits! That's applesauce! You're trying to poison me, you shiftless nigger!" I couldn't believe she called me nigger, but just as I was about to call her a name, the old woman picked up the bowl and hurled it against the wall. Then my mother came into the room.

"Now, Mrs. Price. Stop acting ugly." My mother turned to me

and said, "Scrape as much as you can back into the bowl and give it to her. Then clean up the rest of it."

"What?"

"Clean up the rest of it. What you want to do, leave it there to rot?"

"Make her clean it up—she threw it!"

"Hope," my mother said, "grow up."

She left to see about Mr. Price, who was as docile and sweet as his wife was mean. I scraped the grits into the bowl and handed it to Mrs. Price, who seemed to recognize them this time; she dug in greedily.

"That's better," she said. I went for a bucket and a sponge.

My mother and I ate downstairs in the kitchen, or at least we tried. Every few minutes one of the Prices interrupted our meal, calling my mother's name.

"Mary! Mary! Where's my juice?"

"Mary! I dropped my spoon!"

"I need to go to the bathroom, Mary!"

"You just went, Mrs. Price." My mother looked at me and rolled her eyes, but her voice was calm.

"I need to go again."

My mother looked at me. "Better go up and help her."

"She doesn't need to go. She can wait." I dug into my sandwich. My mother shrugged. "Okay."

When I'd finished my lunch I climbed the stairs and entered Mrs. Price's room. She sat on the bed, smiling, a big wet stain spreading out on the mattress beneath her.

"You stupid old cow!" I yelled. "Why didn't you wait? I wasn't five minutes."

"I want to go to sleep," she said, snuggling down onto the wet sheets.

"Don't let her do that," my mother said from the doorway. "She'll get a rash. I'll clean her up. You'd better strip the mattress and drag it downstairs and out back to dry. Then you'd better wash those blankets and sheets."

It'd take me half an hour to drag that big mattress two flights down a twisty staircase and outside, if I could do it without breaking my back. I stared at my mother in frustration.

"Is this just my luck, or is she always like this?"

My mother laughed. "Always like this. Mrs. Price likes to wait until she knows I'm right in the middle of something, like making dinner or down in the basement doing laundry, and then call me to come upstairs to help her go to the bathroom. If she's done it once she's done it a thousand times. When I first came here I'd get so mad I'd pretend not to hear her. But after a couple times of this, I realized that ignoring Mrs. Price didn't hurt her. She doesn't care if she's wet. She doesn't care if she stinks. Just more work for me."

"You could let her stay wet; maybe she'd stop doing it." I stripped the sheets.

"She wouldn't," my mother said, helping Mrs. Price toward the bathroom. "And her son wouldn't like it when he came to visit, and then I'd be out of a job. And she won't sleep on plastic, either."

I shook my head. "I don't know how you put up with them all these years. I would have gone crazy. Or wrung their scrawny little necks. Don't you ever get angry?"

I expected her to say something saintly, something forgiving like, "Anger doesn't do anyone any good." But she surprised me.

"Honey, I stay angry," my mother said. "But what's that got to do with anything?"

That afternoon, right in the middle of a Shirley Temple movie, Mr. Price went into a coughing fit. After ten minutes of hacking and wheezing, he brought up a clot of blood, and his face turned a funny shade of gray. Calmly, my mother lifted him from his chair and half carried him to her car.

"Better stay here with her while I drive him to the hospital," she said. "If today's the day he's going, I want witnesses around."

The old woman was taking a nap when they left. I hoped she'd stay asleep until my mother returned; I didn't want to mess with her. But no sooner had I gone into the basement to run another load of laundry than I heard a loud thump. I ran upstairs, praying the old bat hadn't killed herself. Mrs. Price sat sprawled on the bathroom floor in her pink nightgown, looking stunned.

"Are you okay? Did you hurt yourself?"

I imagined her fragile bones snapping like twigs and turned around, heading out to the bedroom to search for a phone. But Mrs. Price called me back.

"Help me up, you! Don't leave me!" she ordered. "I'm fine."

As I bent to lift her I noticed the reason she had slipped. There was toothpaste everywhere, smeared on the sink, the toilet, the walls. The mirror was so coated I couldn't see into it. The shower stall was covered with toothpaste handprints. I looked around the room in surprise and yelled before I could stop myself.

"What were you doing?"

Mrs. Price had recovered herself. She looked up from the floor, a mischievous smile on her sunken old face.

"You're not mad, are you, Mary?"

I stared at her. The mean, crazy old fart. She thought I was my mother, and she was giving me grief like this. She probably pulled crap like this all the time.

"You think it's funny to make messes for other people to clean up?"

She peered through her lashes, like a young girl trying to be coy.

"I'm sorry, Mary. Don't be mad. Sing the song."

"What song?"

"You know. That song you always sing when you get angry

with me." She sat back against the tub and began singing in a thin, ruined voice:

Have Faith, Hope, and Charity.
That's the way to live successfully.
How do I know? The Bible tells me so.
Don't worry about tomorrow.
Just be real good today.
The Lord will stand beside you.
He'll guide you all the way. . . .

She butchered the tune, and her singing was painful, but I recognized the song immediately. It was a song from my childhood, one my mother sang to us many nights before bed. She said it was our special song, about us, and we believed her until we heard the choir singing it in church. But by then it really was our special song. And now my mother sang it to this old bag.

"When do I sing that song?" I asked Mrs. Price.

She peered up at me, surprise mixing with suspicion.

"Why, Mary! You sing it every time I'm bad. You know you do."

Looking at Mrs. Price in that moment, I realized why my mother had never brought my sisters and me to this house. She didn't want us to see her serving these old white folks and taking their crap, but not because she was embarrassed. She didn't want us to get caught up in it, to get tangled in the net of anger and hatred and fear; she wanted to keep us as separated as possible from all that. She did what she had to do. She did her job and then she came home and raised us and prayed for better, because that was what life was all about.

I understood, for the first time in any meaningful way, why my mother pushed so hard for us to succeed and why she'd been willing to send me away. If she didn't comprehend, when she sent me to Astor, what I would lose by going to that place, I couldn't blame her for that. And she certainly knew what it was I had to gain.

"Mary?" Mrs. Price held her arms aloft like a baby waiting to be picked up. But when I didn't move she lowered them, understanding dawning in her eyes.

"Why, you're not Mary!" She looked scared. "Where is she? Where's my Mary? Who are you? Oh dear, oh dear!"

I knelt to help her up, the poor old bigot. She was crying now, so pitifully I searched for something to say that would comfort her.

"Don't worry, Mrs. Price." I helped her to her bed. "If you're good and eat your vegetables, the South will rise again."

A few days later my mother drove me to the airport, and instead of just dropping me off, she insisted on coming inside. It was one of the things we did in my family: we stayed and stood by the big plate-glass window in the waiting area while the plane was boarded and sealed and wheeled out onto the runway and took off, as if by being there, serving as witness to the event, we were somehow helping it to happen. As if the plane would rise or fall on the weight of our presence and prayers.

We checked my luggage and walked to the gate. There were a few minutes left before boarding began. I turned to my mother. Her face was still as smooth as melted caramel, but the smile put a few wrinkles at the corners of her eyes. I noticed too, for the first time, some lines in her plump neck.

"Mom, I'm sorry for what I did." I was able to say it without crying, which seemed a good thing. "I hope you can forgive me."

"Baby, ask God's forgiveness. You don't have to ask mine."

"But I need to, Mom. I need to know you forgive me. I need to know that I can come home."

"Why don't you stay, live with us? Faith would be glad to have you."

"No, I have to go back to Philadelphia. I have to go back to work, if I still have a job. I want to. But I just need to know that if things get bad again I can come home."

She reached over and took my hand, squeezing it gently. With her other hand she stroked my cheek.

"Baby, you can always come home. Don't you know that? I love you and I forgive you, if that's what you want, although it's not really mine to forgive. Things happen. Believe me I know. You just have to pray for forgiveness and go on."

The ticket agent announced the boarding of first-class passengers. I clung to my mother's hand.

My mother opened her purse and pulled out a compact. She stuck the mirror in my face.

"What do you see?"

"I see a mess."

"I see my daughter. My beautiful and intelligent and strong black child. You can do it."

I peered at my face. It looked all right; a little dry around the edges but okay. "You have better eyes than me."

My mother laughed. "Come on now. I didn't send my baby into the world to get her head all messed up. You'll be fine."

"Think so?"

My mother reached out and stroked my cheek. I was so surprised all my resolve melted and I began to cry. But these were good tears.

"You know how to make it in this world. Even if you don't believe it, I know it's true. Just remember what I always told you when something bad happened. Whatever doesn't kill you makes you stronger."

"I remember," I said. "I actually said that once, to this white woman at work. We were talking about our parents, and I told her you used to tell us that all the time as kids. She said it sounded like a cruel thing to tell a child."

My mother and I looked at each other and started to laugh,

and over our laughter I heard my row being called. My mother pulled me into her arms, hugged me hard, then pushed me toward the open gate. We were both still laughing.

"Oh yeah?" she called as I walked away. "Well, what does she know?"

As the plane rose toward the clouds, I thought about Malcolm. I'd have to call him when I got back, tell him the truth, figure out where we stood. He would be angry about the abortion, hurt and angry. Whether we could get past that I didn't know.

The woman in the seat next to me took out a brush and began brushing her hair, swinging it back over her shoulder like a movie star. When one of her golden strands wafted into my cup, I picked it out and handed it back.

"I believe this is yours."

Her face reddened. "Oh, I'm sorry! How terrible of me! What am I thinking of?" She took the hair, wrapped it around her brush, and stuffed the brush back into her creamy leather bag. "It's just that this has been a crazy morning. My husband forgot I was leaving today, so he got up early and went to play golf, and then the nanny didn't show, so I had to take the boys to my mother's house, and everything was so crazy I didn't even have time to put on my makeup." She was wearing pearls and she fingered them as she spoke, tilting her head a little. She was probably quite charming. "But you don't want to hear this," she said.

"No, I don't, actually." And it was true, I didn't. But I smiled at her, smiled and broke the tension gathered between us because I realized as I said it that I could. I could sit on an airplane for a few hours and make idle conversation with a blonde in expensive jewelry and even listen to her imagined tribulations and not get nuts. I could do that.

"Rough morning, huh?" I said.

"Oh, yes! Plus I'm nervous about going to Philadelphia. Big cities frighten me. Perhaps you can give me some tips on what to do." She stuck out a manicured hand. "I'm Stephanie."

I couldn't help laughing. The woman grinned, willing to join in the joke. "What's so funny?"

"Oh, nothing, nothing. That's just one of my favorite names, Stephanie. Always has been."

"How sweet of you to say so! What's your name?"

"Me?" I took her hand and shook it. "My name is Hope."